LIQuID 5

Patricia Ruth

LIQuID 5

ISBN: 978-1-916954-16-8

Dedication

This book is dedicated to my family – Weslie, Miriam, Michael + Jessica, Alex + Melanie, Evan and Jordan. Your love and care mean everything to me.

LIQuID 5 is the product of many human hours spent writing, re-writing, and editing. The entire story is a work of fiction. All characters, dialogue, and incidents are drawn from the author's imagination and are not to be construed as real. Any references to real people, events, establishments, organizations, or locales are intended only to provide a sense of authenticity and are used fictitiously.

Acknowledgments

I'd like to acknowledge the support of my friends Lynn, Beverly, Cora, Terri, Joan, Valerie, Lynore, Gert, Fran, Beth, and Robin, who read early versions of LIQuID 5 and provided much-appreciated guidance.

Special appreciation goes to Noah Packard and Lindsey Dannenberg for their consultation and suggestions concerning the book cover design.

Table of Contents

Part 7
Intensification

Part 8
Obstruction

Part 9
Combination

Part 10
Implications

Part 11
Culmination

About the Author

Patricia always wondered what it would be like to have superpowers, such as predicting the future, altering time, or perceiving the inner thoughts of others. Exploring this fantasy led to the creation of LIQuID 5. As a fan of adventure and Science Fiction, Patricia enjoyed letting her imagination take hold when she created this character-driven story filled with action and intrigue.

Check out Patricia Ruth's first novel, *Holly Heights,* which chronicles the escapades of three couples. Set in a fictional community where sexual perversion, infidelity, drug use, and deception play out amid the luxury of fabulous wealth, these *Holly Heights* friends end up learning the hard way that self-indulgence is not without consequences.

18 Lines

Did life today get away from me?

My words were short, my actions thoughtless,

Was my conduct all it could be?

Those small, quiet moments were too few.

The rush, the hustle, the frantic pace,

Conspired to keep me from seeing things true.

Life can be profound and profoundly contrary,

A prism of shifting images

So difficult to discern the real from imaginary.

Love lost and gained, moments to treasure and forget,

The fleeting glimpse of insight

Illume those actions I now regret.

It's elusive; this quest for a 'happy' life,

Ironically seeking that spiritual spark

While facing each day's earthly strife.

Thankfully, faith sees me through.

As wisdom's slippery nugget is revealed,

Life's a wonder when I recognize You.

By Patricia Ruth

Prologue

Jolted awake by the blaring alarm, Kevin jumped out of his seat. The drool was still warm on his chin. Rubbing his eyes, it took a minute to shake his groggy brain awake as he scanned the dozen or so gauges arrayed before him. Every light on his control panel flashed red.

Of course, he thought, quickly spotting the problem. *The biohazard detector in Lab 8 tripped . . . again*. Kevin was familiar with Lab 8 and their frequent mishaps. A quick press on the exhaust button and the powerful fan sucked contaminated air out of Lab 8 before he could say, "May the force be with you."

The LIQuID policy required him to vent first and ask questions later, a protocol Kevin had never been comfortable following. If it was dangerous enough to cause a problem inside the lab, maybe it could be unsafe outside as well. Just what the hell am I releasing this time? He wondered. Until now, it had been an uneventful night. The overnight shift was quiet, as a rule, and Kevin often nodded off in between security checks, typically during the darkest hours before the new day made its arrival.

Kevin toggled the intercom switch. "Is everything okay down there?" he asked, leaning toward the metallic microphone built into the control console, mentally crossing his fingers. So far, he never had to call for a medical emergency, but there was always a first time.

"Yes, everything's all right," an anonymous voice replied. "We had factored in a slower reaction time. The 'R's' were way out of whack and metabolized quicker than we anticipated. The mylozene couldn't convert fast enough. Now we need to recalibrate the spectrometer and start all over again."

Kevin was relieved, although he had no idea what the scientist was talking about. After almost two years as part of LIQuID security, he had a fairly good idea about the projects and experiments being conducted on-site. With a name like Long Island Quality Intellectual Development, you didn't need to be a Grade Four scientist to deduce sophisticated scientific research was being conducted. Some of the projects were straightforward, such as obesity experiments on mice or computer simulations showing complex weather patterns. However, the experiments in Lab 8 were different. Word around the building speculated the Lab 8 team was experimenting on the brain, researching a cure for Alzheimer's or some other mind-destroying disease. LIQuID's newest team seemed to work around the clock, and they rarely socialized with the other researchers, which made them a ripe target for gossip and conjecture. The scientists in Lab 8 were a weird group, even by LIQuID standards.

After tonight's mishap, Kevin would submit a report to his supervisor detailing the incident. *What a waste of time*, he thought. *Well, time is something I have plenty of.* Would there even be an investigation? He doubted it. As long as the place didn't blow up or catch fire, it was unlikely anyone would even read his report or look too closely into the doings in Lab 8. Kevin settled in, scrolling through YouTube videos for the remainder of his shift.

Part 1
Introduction

Chapter 1

Glynn stirred, not ready to open her eyes. Cozy and comfortable, she was in no rush to leave the warmth of her bed for the cold of the bathroom. Stretching, she buried her head a little deeper into the pillows, breathing in the smell. She loved the aroma, and after another deep intake, she felt a subtle bump from the warm body lying next to her.

The response was predictable. An arm reached over and landed on her shoulder. *He awakes*, Glynn thought and smiled. She loved waking to her husband's semiconscious movements. It was far superior to the daily drone of a digital alarm. Not one for body spray, Glynn loved his natural scent—it reinforced her conclusion that he was Mr. Right.

Smart, sensitive, and handsome, Gil Patrick was Glynn's dream come true. Even after three months of marriage, waking next to him was still a thrill, like needing a pinch to be certain of her good fortune. As if reading her mind, Gil grabbed her butt and gave it a firm, loving squeeze as he stretched, leaned over, depositing a kiss before bounding out of bed. It had taken Glynn a couple of months to get used to her new husband's morning routine; no lounging in bed for him. Not wanting to waste a minute, he could shave, shower, and perform his daily hygiene in less time than it took Glynn to brush her teeth. From start to finish, Gil would be dressed and out the front door in under 20 minutes–the exact opposite of her routine.

Glynn loved to lie in bed and wait for him to emerge from the bathroom, smelling all freshly soaped and clean. Six feet tall with a wrestler's muscular physique gone slightly soft, Gil was the personification of her male fantasy. She had never considered him handsome, not in the romance novel way—Gil had a manly look. He moved with a distinct purpose, not wasting any time as he laid out his clothing. Glynn sat up in bed to watch him dress. *It must be love*, she thought, enthralled by this mundane task.

"I have that LIMBO luncheon today. What do you think of this tie and shirt?" Gil asked, checking himself out in the mirror. He was up for board membership at the region's most powerful and important business association—Long Island Metro Business Organization (LIMBO). During today's meeting, Gil expected the LIMBO executive committee to recommend he be admitted to the governing board. It was a big coup, not only personally but for his firm as well.

"So, what do they do after they announce you've been voted in— release white smoke or something?" Glynn teased. "Do I become Mrs. Lim; I mean LIM-BO?" She couldn't help making a joke. He could be so intense when serious.

A smile crossed Gil's lips. "Come on. Honestly, does this combo go? Maybe the blue-striped tie would be better?"

"You look fine," she assured him with a slight mocking tone. "Appropriate, serious, distinguished, and ready to deliver LIMBO's important message to the rest of the world."

Attaining entrée to the governing board was Gil's equivalent of winning the Super Bowl; it meant he had arrived, he was "worthy," and the business community recognized his value. She knew it was a real feather in Gil's cap to be asked to become one of LIMBO's leaders at such a young age, but Glynn couldn't take the whole LIMBO thing too seriously. She considered LIMBO an example of "men playing at being men," another group of self-important guys convinced only they knew how to promote and attract businesses to Long Island. It is one big excuse to meet for lunch and play golf. Who knows what they accomplish? she thought. Women are much more sensible when it comes to joining organizations identified by an acronym.

"So, what's on your schedule today?" he asked.

"Oh, nothing too exciting," she replied, expecting another uneventful day in the law library. Lately, her days seemed to blend into each other, and Tuesday would end up being more or less like Monday.

"I almost forgot; I'll be meeting with my book group this evening. We're discussing my pick," Glynn added, her mood immediately perking up.

"What's the name of that book again?" he asked while straightening his tie.

"Shondra Knightly's *Exit Strategy*," she replied. "It was my choice, which means I'll be leading tonight's discussion."

"Hmmmm," he replied, making a final adjustment. "I'll phone you later," he called over his shoulder on the way to the door.

Glynn was looking forward to her book club meeting, a welcome change from her daily routine. Additionally, the group would be trying out a new restaurant, The Good Grill. It was getting respectable word-of-mouth reviews: "Good was good," she had heard. Anyway, she couldn't wait to learn what the others thought about Exit Strategy, a complicated tale of sex and intrigue.

Glynn loved stories about single, sexy go-getters. Even though Exit Strategy wasn't fine literature, it was smart and spicy and had enough twists and turns to keep her interest. One of the main characters, a foxy lawyer, was charged with tracking and prosecuting corruption in the city government. The girl was fearless, bedding key suspects as a means to uncover inside information, actively putting her life on the line in order to put the bad guys away for good.

Glynn knew it was a leap to identify with Bernice Bailey, the undercover investigator. Bernice relied on her beauty and sex appeal to get the job done, while Glynn prided herself on using logic and reason. Yet, it was fun to fantasize that maybe one day she could help solve an important crime or uncover an evil plot hatched by corrupt officials. *Now that's farfetched*, she snorted to herself, likening her current law library responsibilities to all the excitement of watching golf on TV.

Sadly, her job at the law firm had become painfully routine. Some days, it felt as if her career had crashed head-on into a dead-end. She didn't want to complain, but the excitement of handling her own cases, conferencing with clients and opposing attorneys, and even making court appearances had been severely curtailed. Reassigned was the polite office-speak.

Glynn fought to shove aside feelings of frustration. She had always looked forward to going to work, especially her first days at Shuster, Yleskin, and Matlock when she was a wide-eyed rookie. Back then, she had high expectations of making a solid legal career for herself, leaning toward protecting the underdog against corruption and greed. That was before she fell in love.

Rolling over to Gil's side of the bed, Glynn buried her head in his pillow and took in a deep lungful of his scent. It brought back memories of their first encounter three years ago. As a member of that year's crop of new associates, she was being escorted by Office Manager Rose Mantle on an introductory tour. Stopping outside Gil's office, six pairs of eyes peered in at the opportunity for the rookies to see a "live" attorney at work.

At first, Gil seemed annoyed by the interruption. But when Rose announced Gil Patrick was one of Shuster, Yleskin, and Matlock's rising stars, the pinched severity surrounding his mouth relaxed. And when Gil looked up from his papers, Glynn found herself staring directly into his café-latte brown eyes. She barely heard Rose make the introductions over her pounding heart. It was more than his penetrating stare that left her breathless when their eyes connected.

Unable to look away, she felt like they were the only two people in the room.

Commonly known as "Shylock" by those in Long Island's close-knit legal community, Shuster, Yleskin, and Matlock was THE powerhouse law firm everyone was watching. Their roster of clients included the biggest and best companies. The firm was also known for its pro bono work. *Being hired as a legal associate more than launched her legal career*, she remembered wistfully. *It was an opportunity to make a positive difference.*

As a new associate, Glynn worked under the supervision of various senior attorneys and partners, rotating to provide assistance where necessary. It didn't take long before she was assigned to work with Gil. As one of the firm's rising rainmakers, he had a reputation for being exacting and pushing new associates hard. Many had burned out trying to keep up with his work schedule. Glynn vowed that wasn't going to happen to her, and she wasn't going to be intimidated by the workload. Over time, she was able to anticipate his requests, and he appreciated her alternative ways of looking at legal issues. No one was surprised that she was assigned to work with Gil most of the time.

Working late was common—there were always teams of attorneys and associates hunched over computers well into the evening. Glynn drew the line at 9 p.m. But one night, she made an exception. Gil asked her to finish an important brief needed for court the next day. Hunched over her notepad, eyes shifting between the books spread out on the table and the computer screen on her right, so absorbed in her research that she barely detected the masculine presence standing behind her. His personal aroma was unmistakable. Suddenly, she felt him lean over her left shoulder to get a better look at her notes. She could feel the warmth of his body, the hair on her arms tingled, and the air felt heavy. She couldn't recall how he came to be standing so close. Turning her head slightly to the left, she merely glanced into his eyes; the room, the books, the computer all disappeared. And then her breathing stopped.

Talk about getting the vapors, she giggled, remembering the beginning of their courtship. *Those were the days: passionate, intense, innocent.* She sighed. They couldn't keep their affair secret for long.

Learning about the firm's personnel policies from Rose Mantle had been a blow. There was talk of an Employee Handbook, management guidelines about office etiquette, and too many trite phrases about what "shouldn't" be done with coworkers. Supposedly, there were rules about spouses working together, too. At least, that was what Rose warned. But no one said she would have to forfeit her career if she married Gil. That bit of news came after the wedding.

Initially, she toyed with the idea of leaving the firm. But that meant giving up. She loved working there and had developed close relationships with her coworkers. It seemed a shame to throw it away. *All those long hours . . .* She could still feel the sting of disappointment in her eyes. *I put my heart and soul into the work, only to be forced out to start from the beginning somewhere else?!* It seemed cruel and unfair. When the partners came to her with an offer to stay, she realized it wasn't a tough decision.

Glancing at the clock, Glynn decided she couldn't procrastinate any longer—time to get going. *Sigh!*

Chapter 2

Arnold Holtzmann hung up the phone. Slammed might be more accurate. *McCleary*. He'd be damned if he let that nitpicker get to him. Reaching into the top drawer, he located the bottle of antacids. Standing up, he stretched and popped a couple into his mouth. Arnie had been sitting at his desk with the phone pasted to his ear for the better part of two hours, making one call after another and getting a couple in between. He could feel the knots tighten in the small of his back as he twisted first right, then left to ease the tension.

Arnie was a thin, compact man, built more for speed than power. At 58, he was a fanatic about working out, successfully battling a nonexistent waistline bulge. There were two things Arnie could not tolerate: one of them was excess weight, hence his double-time exercise regimen. He would power through a 40-minute workout in half the time. He also walked quickly, rushed through his meals, and was known to talk fast and jump to conclusions.

His other pet peeve was suffering through the pedantic speeches of ideologues. He had little patience for those one-issue wonders; people who were so passionate, so focused, so narrow in their perspective, it was as if they saw the world through a microscope with their singular point of view magnified out of all proportion.

After more than 35 years in politics, he had seen the political pendulum swing to the left and then over to the right. From the Vietnam War to the war on drugs, allies becoming enemies and enemies turned into our new best friends; there had been civil rights, women's rights, gay rights, and now religious rights. Arnie witnessed the rise of pop culture, the decline of family values, and the gradual erosion of privacy. Nothing surprised him anymore. Pragmatic and cynical, he saw the world through a wide-angle lens and was very good at spotting the trends that poked through to his peripheral vision.

Arnie walked over to the floor-to-ceiling windows framing his corner office. He had an expansive view and never tired of surveying his territory. As President and Executive Director of Long Island's only business organization, Arnie enjoyed a degree of personal power rarely found outside of elected office. LIMBO, <u>L</u>ong <u>I</u>sland <u>M</u>etro <u>B</u>usiness <u>O</u>rganization, was formed almost 30 years ago on the very golf course spread out below. Its goal was to promote the interests of Long Island-based businesses, whether by influencing the decisions of town and county legislatures, lobbying Albany, or seeking to shape national policy. Over the years, LIMBO had developed into a bastion of rational thinking in a world increasingly populated by small-minded contrarians, so espoused its leader, Arnold Holtzmann.

Arnie's break was cut short by the expected call from one of his board members. Stan Piper was the founder and majority stockholder of Piper Rock, a vast real-estate conglomerate and one of the largest landowners on Long Island. Stan sat on the boards of over a half-dozen multinational corporations and nonprofits. Known locally for his generous philanthropy, it was no secret Stan had enormous political influence. And as a founding member of the exclusive Gold Coast Golf Club, he enjoyed special social status as well. Of course, it didn't hurt that he was a major contributor to both political parties.

"Did you hear the news?" Arnie asked, rushing past the pleasantries. "The SCAB tests were a huge success. I don't have to tell you the wine growers on the East End are clamoring for it. This could be big, Stan."

After almost two years, ChemoCo was finally completing field tests for their new crop fertilizer/weed suppressor, SCAB (<u>S</u>elective <u>C</u>hemical <u>A</u>gricultural <u>B</u>ioproducts.) The tests were being watched very closely by the vintners on the East End of the island. By almost every measure, SCAB had been responsible for making real improvements in crop production while simultaneously controlling the spread of weeds. This was a real achievement, especially because it was touted as being environmentally friendly.

"Yes, I heard," Stan replied, trying to overlook Arnie's brusque telephone manner. "How are you?" he asked in return. A gentleman from a bygone time, Stan pretended to care about the guy on the other end of the phone and carefully observed proper social protocols.

"If it wasn't for that jerk McCleary, I'd be great," complained the LIMBO director. Arnie had never mastered the skill of separating one's personal passions from the professional. "Did you talk to Kingsley? What did he say about their new facility?"

Bennett Kingsley, ChemoCo's CEO, happened to be an old-school chum of one of LIMBO's board members. Arnie couldn't believe his luck when he learned Stan Piper and Bennett Kingsley were friends from way back, a connection which could be described as an uncanny coincidence—and one Arnie was exploiting to the hilt.

"Yes, we spoke," Stan replied calmly, as if to an excited child. "Bennett says that because SCAB is performing beyond expectations, the board is moving forward with the expansion. ChemoCo plans to roll SCAB out across the country sooner than expected, including building a new factory. He says they're narrowing site evaluations to a couple of locations on the Eastern seaboard, Long Island being one of them.

"Goddamnit! I was right!" Arnie spat, quick to point out his superior thinking. He had been keeping his eye on the tests and knew SCAB would be a winner. Getting a new ChemoCo facility on Long Island would be a real feather in his cap. He could see the headlines: ARNIE HOLTZMANN AND LIMBO BRING HIGH-PAYING JOBS TO LONG ISLAND. Or even better, THE LOCAL ECONOMY IS ON THE UPSWING. THANKS TO ARNIE HOLTZMANN'S LIMBO.

"McCleary's the problem," Stan reiterated. Stating the obvious was one of Stan's habits that always annoyed Arnie.

"Tell me something I don't know," Arnie countered, his blood pressure rising at the mere mention of McCleary's name. "The latest news out of LICE is they need more time—a stall tactic if I ever saw one. If McCleary had an ounce of sense, he'd be the one spearheading this thing. Who wouldn't want environmentally friendly fertilizer?"

It was old news that Bill McCleary, head of Long Island's ecological watchdog agency LICE—Long Island Conservation and Environment—had tried (unsuccessfully) to block the SCAB trials from the very beginning. Now, everyone was waiting for their final approval. A thumbs-up from a tough-minded environmental group like McCleary's LICE would give ChemoCo the environmental green light to roll out SCAB like a blanket across the country, maybe even the world.

"Kingsley's concerned about McCleary and LICE. They are standing in our way," Stan reminded Arnie, trying to reel him back into discussing their next priority. "McCleary is still dragging his feet and could derail everything. Without approval from LICE, I hear any plans for a move to Long Island are dead on arrival." Even Stan was getting frustrated by McCleary's delays.

"Now's the time to act," Arnie roared, pacing around his desk. "I'll be damned if they build that new plant somewhere else." Not one to rest on his laurels, Arnie was prepared to launch an aggressive campaign. "We have to keep up the pressure. I'll make some calls locally, maybe suggest a story on McCleary's obstructionist stance for the news," Arnie suggested.

"You know Crystal Clam was one of the test sites, and my nephew Ted Landis is the owner and also president of the Wine Growers League (GRowLers). They've been clamoring for an environmentally sensitive fertilizer for years. Everyone seems to be drinking wine these days, and who would be against supporting the local wine industry? I'm sure Ted would be more than happy to explain the GRowLers' side of the story," Stan suggested.

Thinking ten steps ahead, Arnie's brain went into overdrive. "We need to bring Kingsley here for a tour of our LIQuID facility. LIMBO is already supporting scientific research locally. Once he sees what our people are capable of, well, I don't have to tell you," Arnie announced, letting Stan finish the thought.

Stan figured they could go on like this for hours, bouncing from one idea to another. "If only there was a way we could move McCleary aside. You know, find someone who could sign off on the favorable data. It would make everyone's life a whole lot easier," he ruminated. An industrialist from an earlier era, Stan was not used to relying on the approval of others when it came to making business decisions. If he wanted to take one of his companies in a particular direction, he just did it. All this "waiting for LICE's approval" was simply not the way things were done, not in his world at any rate.

"What was that?" Arnie asked, slowly coming to attention.

"Oh, you know, when there's a problem, we simply move it aside—that's how we get things done at Piper Rock. I guess we'll have to wait and see what McCleary does, eh? There's time, anyway. Kingsley says ChemoCo won't be making any decisions for a couple of months. Look, Arnie, take it easy. I'll let you know if I hear anything," Stan counseled.

Hanging up the phone, Arnie Holtzmann was having an epiphany. Stan's words rang in his ear: *Move McCleary aside*. Brilliant!

18

Chapter 3

"Hello, Unc . . . err, Mr. Kingsley. You wanted to see me?" Carl caught himself just in time. He was instructed to keep to strict conventions in the office. Carl poked his head in the half-opened door like a turtle leaving its shell to check on the safety of the surrounding area. Carl never felt comfortable coming to the executive suite. The air felt wrong, and he found it difficult to breathe. It was as if the supremacy and power of all the higher-ups absorbed all the oxygen. He was self-conscious about his appearance, too. A stained lab coat covered his navy pants and crinkled blue shirt. And while comfortable, even he knew enough to admit this was not executive suite attire. He should have left the lab coat behind.

Bennett Kingsley, CEO of ChemoCo, looked up at the intrusion as he finished his call. "Yes, sounds great. I'd love to come up for some golf. And you're suggesting a reception with local business leaders? I've heard of LIMBO. Yeah, the timing seems right to have a tour of possible factory locations. There's nothing to lose being seen in the area. Let me check my calendar and we'll come up with a date. Now, Stan, don't forget to make that purchase. The stock price is hovering about $33 or so. Start buying now. Yes, looking forward to it." He replaced the headset, a 20th-century artifact he couldn't quite leave behind. Glancing up, he saw his nephew loitering at the door and experienced an involuntary shrug. *It's amazing how smart he can be in some areas and how clueless in others*, Kingsley thought for what is the umpteenth time.

Always fastidious, Bennett Kingsley looked and dressed the part of a corporate titan right out of central casting. He was tall but not overly so. He had wide shoulders, a broad back, and a thick neck. His custom-made shirts fit comfortably, even over his barrel chest. Dark hair, with a hint of gray at the temples, was perfectly groomed. His thick hair wasn't just confined to his head. One look at his hands, and you could see the bushy clumps on each digit sprouting above his perfectly buffed nails. His fingers were thick, too, like sausages, powerful enough to easily pry open a melon. A large gold and diamond pinky ring, which would have weighed down a normal finger, flashed excitedly as Kingsley waved Carl into the office.

"Close the door behind you," Bennett barked, then thought better of his tone and offered a smile.

Carl Hammerling, ChemoCo's R&D guru and son of Bennett's sister, shut the door as instructed and hurried into the room. All knees and elbows, Carl never felt comfortable in Uncle Bennett's office. There were too many big pieces of furniture and too much space in between the pieces. Everything was positioned just so. The windows were tall, and looked onto the rolling corporate campus. It was an expansive view, almost overwhelming Bennett's huge desk, a sprawling slab of black granite supported by delicate-looking curved metal legs. Carl couldn't look away from the postcard view of the landscape and mountains in the distance, a panorama he didn't enjoy from his subterranean lab.

"Sit." Bennett pointed to one of the chairs facing the sofa. The smile was gone, and his beady black eyes absorbed Carl's person as a predator might evaluate dinner. "I need an update. The latest information you have. Don't sugarcoat it for me, either. Time's upon us and decisions need to be made."

"Right," responded Carl, clearing his throat. "We're ready. SCAB has passed all the tests with flying colors. The folks on Long Island's East End can't wait for their first shipment. They're practically begging for it. I recommend the following shipping schedule," he concluded, handing an iPad to Bennett for his review.

"The board will be voting on which location to build the new SCAB plant. Any thoughts?" It was a rhetorical question, as Bennett had already decided on his preference.

"If, or should I say when, we get the LICE approval, then Long Island would make a perfect location. Hiring would be easy with an educated and motivated workforce. We'd develop our own distribution channels, and the business community would welcome us with open arms. After years of the aerospace industry shrinking, they're looking to revive their sagging industrial base." Carl summarized, and Bennett agreed. They had discussed the situation many times.

"Well, that's it. I'll make the proposal to the board this week. We'll have to overcome some pushback from Dickson and his group. They're angling to put the plant in Oklahoma." Bennett rolled his eyes at the thought. "Do what you can to get the approvals from their environmental oversight agency. Let's see if we can push this along and present the plant going to Long Island as a fait accompli."

Bennett stood, signaling it was time for Carl to leave. "Thanks, Carl. In the meantime, keep things in production on track. No foul-ups—we can't afford it. I'll be in touch with the next steps."

Not bothering to watch Carl leave, Bennett took a quick glance at the stock price. ChemoCo had been languishing between $30–35 per share for what seemed like forever. A sleepy giant is what the analysts call the company, and it was consistently lumped in with other industrials, packaged as a safe bet, an investment going nowhere fast. *SCAB is going to be a real game changer*, he thought with barely suppressed satisfaction. The estimates suggested a doubling, maybe even tripling, of the share price. *Take it easy*, he had to remind himself. They had nurtured and planned SCAB and its rollout to the hour, and he wasn't going to get ahead of things, not at this stage.

Chapter 4

The safe opened with a click. Bill took a moment to consider the stack of documents inside. For the past 30 years, he has worked on an untold number of projects. In the beginning, his job was simply to identify and investigate environmental issues. He was so green in those early days, so open and trusting. The fact that prominent business leaders and politicians would use him and the agency to further their own agenda wasn't any less shocking than the lengths they would go. But once burned, he learned quickly. Detailing his work became the best solution to keep track of all the various projects, but even more importantly, it served as cover-your-ass insurance when dealing with fickle politicians.

The history of New York's environmental policy was written in those files and included pages recording exactly what went down. It was a complete detail of all the various underhanded, immoral, and illegal activities he had observed. There were reams of documented evidence, too, and a few tidbits that would more than embarrass today's officeholders, at the very least.

If those papers could talk, he ruminated, thinking back on all he had witnessed. Having these files see the light of day outside the safe would create an avalanche of legal and personal problems for those public figures, not to mention distract away from the good works LICE had accomplished under his leadership. *Exposure would be an environmental disaster of an altogether different nature.* It was too calamitous to imagine. Protecting decades of significant achievements was more important than the media circus that would surely result if the press got their hands on those files. *They served their purpose back then. One of these days, I'll take the stack out back and burn 'em all.*

Returning to his present purpose, Bill reached in to grab the manila envelope sitting shyly on top of the pile. This was his latest project and might be his last. The envelope had heft as if its physical weight corresponded to the weightiness of the material inside. *Yes*, he thought, *there is a lot of information in here, but not enough.* Bill had grown an overdeveloped sixth sense when it came to bullshit, and this SCAB information seemed to fit nicely into that category.

The head of LICE shut the safe and pressed the hidden button to slide the wall-sized photograph back down. When first appointed to the job, Bill arranged for a local safe company to come in unseen on the weekend to build and install this safe to his particular specifications. He wanted it hidden from view, but it was hiding in plain sight behind a huge aerial photograph of Long Island. One might be able to locate the button at the bottom right and figure out how to reveal the safe. That part was tricky but not impossible. But in order to open the safe, you needed an eight-digit code AND a special key, and Bill was the only person on the planet in possession of both.

Tall and trim, Bill McCleary maintained the same weight he had as a Marine. His craggy good looks could resemble etched stone when he was in one of his unforgiving moods. There was a grayness about him, blue-gray eyes, steel-gray buzz-cut hair, and a weathered complexion resembling the mountains he frequently hiked. People thought him hard, difficult to warm up to, and intimidating, maybe because he didn't suffer fools lightly. But underneath that tough exterior beat the heart of an idealist. His warmth and genuine compassion could transform that hardened shell, softening his rocky visage into malleable clay.

After a stint in the Marines toward the end of the Vietnam War, he became disgusted with the environmental damage he saw overseas. Conservation of the natural world became his calling. An environmentalist before anyone knew that was a field, Bill cut his teeth working with the Sierra Club out West. When New York decided to create their own environmental department, Bill McCleary was on the shortlist of candidates. About 30 years ago, he founded LICE—

<u>L</u>ong <u>I</u>sland <u>C</u>onservation and <u>E</u>nvironment—which he built into an environmental powerhouse emulated and admired across the country. As head of LICE, he wrote clean air and clean water policies, along with advising multiple governors on how best to protect New York's unspoiled regions.

Walking back to his desk, Bill held the envelope gingerly for a minute before squeezing the metal clasp between his calloused fingers. The report was neatly typed and easy to read, as if written for an undergrad. To the uninitiated, it seemed complete– the operative word being "seemed." Key elements of the formula and chemical analysis were missing; he was sure of it. *Who writes a scientific report without including the science?* Bill thought.

Sliding the report out of the envelope, Bill scanned the first page. This wasn't his first read-through.

"Carl from ChemoCo is on the phone," Amber announced from outside his door. There was a tinge of annoyance in her voice. She knew when she took the job, she'd have to answer the director's phone, but Carl from ChemoCo seemed to call every 20 minutes.

"Amber, can you ring Andy in the lab and let him know I'll be on my way?" Bill asked. His voice was gravelly, always calm, and carefully modulated. It might appear to be just above a whisper, but it carried.

"Yeah, Carl, what is it?" Bill said in his soft-spoken, clipped tone into the phone. Getting this call was an odd coincidence, as he was about to reread the SCAB report.

"Thanks for taking my call, Bill," Carl replied with a touch of relief in his voice. "We did a second test of the numbers and there's good news. It's looking even better than the original report. Much better, in fact. I was hoping I could come in and go over the new report this week. How are you fixed for tomorrow?" It was Carl's single-minded mission to get SCAB approved, and Bill felt that intensity emanating through the phone.

Silence met the question. Carl was becoming a royal pain. What wouldn't he do to have LICE give their Seal of Approval? Bill considered. *Anything* was the answer. Carl would do anything to get SCAB approved.

Bill took no pleasure in making the guy squirm. "Let's set something up for next week. My LICE researchers still need to complete some tests. There's no point in talking until we know what we're dealing with—eh?"

"I'm checking to see if there might be some questions, some details I could address. I realize it's a complicated formula. It took a while to develop, a long while. We'd welcome your feedback."

Of course, you would, Bill whispered to himself. "Look, I hope to have our results next week. How does Thursday sound?" He wanted to be reasonable, even as he knew nothing short of full approval would make Carl and his overseers happy.

"Thursday it is. Thanks, Bill. Thank you. Appreciate it."

That was easy, Bill thought. Of course, he could always cancel and reschedule, should that be necessary. ChemoCo wasn't the problem. Pressure was building locally, mostly from that nutjob A Holtz at LIMBO. He could hear Arnie freaking out all the way across the island. It's a miracle the guy doesn't get a heart attack.

Slipping the report back into the envelope, Bill left his office. He walked over to Amber to see if she had completed her assignments. A hard worker, Amber had grown into the job nicely. Soon, she'd be leaving for a less demanding boss, looking to capitalize on her experience, and then Bill would have to find another willing recruit to train—a diamond in the rough. With a keen eye for talent, he'd lost track of how many assistants he'd gone through. A year working for Bill McCleary felt like a year of basic training. Most kept in touch when they left, and his former staffers now populated the environmental field across the country.

Bill marched to the lab, leaving behind a soft squish from his rubber-soled boots on the linoleum floor as he walked by the LICE staffers' desks–eyes straight but registering everything. The office décor was a government issue, with lots of metal. Occasionally, you might spot a Sierra Club poster or scenic vista from one of the national parks. But the drab furnishings couldn't dampen the staff's commitment to their mission. He loved feeling the positive energy radiating from those who knew they were making a practical difference for the planet.

Down two flights to the lab, he found Andy in the back, surrounded by candy wrappers and staring at his computer screen.

"Hey, boss, what's up?" Andy inquired, barely bothering to look up. It was likely he felt Bill's arrival, as his boss's vibe was hard to miss.

"So, tell me what you found out about SCAB. I know you'll be sending a report, but I want to hear it from you."

Andy looked into those granite blue-gray eyes, hard as the rock they resembled. "We've worked that formula six ways to Sunday. I must have followed their instructions to the letter at least as many times. The results are inconclusive. It's almost like they left something out, maybe a key step or missing pages. We tried mixing things up, too, using various substitutions. Nothing we did yielded the results they described.

"But we did find something interesting. It seems when heated and then cooled, the chemicals morphed into a kind of paste. We tried using it on some everyday weeds and on a tomato plant. The results were perplexing. The tomato plant almost doubled in size in a week while the weeds started to shrivel. So, at first glance, we assumed the formula must work. But after a couple of days, the tomato plant started dying, too. We noticed rapid degeneration in both plants.

"Without the complete formula, it's hard to know what is causing these uncertain results. Honestly, I'm not sure SCAB is bad, but I can't say it's good either. If I had to make a guess, I'd say SCAB could turn out to be an unfriendly agricultural ground cover. That's about as conclusive as I can get."

Unfriendly ground cover – that's a new one, Bill thought, rubbing his face in frustration. He wouldn't be surprised if ChemoCo tried to pull a fast one. Over the years, he'd seen a number of powerful companies try to muscle their products into commercial use. And while technically, the SCAB results were inconclusive, he had a deep feeling it might contribute to an ecological disaster. LICE's efforts at evaluating and picking apart SCAB seemed to create its own disaster as well.

Chapter 5

"Brett on line 2."

Iris glanced at her watch; the call was right on time. She said a little thank you prayer for Mrs. Bambino. Of course, that wasn't her real name—it was Bambarino or some such thing. Bambino was so much easier. Iris didn't care what she had to call the woman; Mrs. B. was a godsend, a lifesaver, a saint, the real-life female Clarence from *It's a Wonderful Life*. What Iris had put up with before her arrival was too painful to recall. Wireless headset in place, Iris quickly pressed the button on her phone labeled line 2.

"Hi, honey. So, you're ready for lunch? Tell Mommy what you did this morning," Iris cooed into the phone.

The conversation was one-sided, with Iris nodding and making approving noises as she listened to her three-year-old "speak" about his day. Everyone agreed Brett was bright and advanced for his age. Iris didn't care if the world thought she was over the top; she was going to check in with her precious boy as many times as necessary. When Iris was serious about something and what could be more important than her little boy, nothing—NO THING—would stand in her way. It had become a long-standing office joke, the one about the man-eater being transformed into the tiger mom. When her office mates took time off for an appointment, like a doctor's visit or family emergency, they would call it a "Brett break." There was no denying the company put up with a lot from Iris, but then she was their top broker.

Who would have thought this high-powered, no-nonsense bitch-on-heels could turn into a soft, slobbering, baby-talking mommy? But strange things do happen, and for Iris Carmichael, motherhood was more than strange. It was humanizing.

"Okay. Honey, let me speak with Mrs. Bambino," Iris interjected. "Mommy loves you. Mommy will be home soon. Be a good listener. Love you (kiss, kiss, kiss)." Iris could not get enough of him.

"Hi, Mrs. B. It sounds like Brett had a great morning. After lunch, I guess you'll take that walk. What about the Learning Tree? Did you call to arrange for a scheduled session? Try to nap him before three—I'll be out late today and going out to dinner with my book club tonight. Oh, before I forget, can you call Steven's mom? Her number is in the book and arrange a play date for tomorrow morning? I think Brett has some free time between ten and twelve. That's all for now. I'll call again before I leave. You know how to reach me. Enjoy lunch. Thanks."

It was always hard for her to get off the phone. Iris's style, commonly known as "micromanagement on steroids," was the major reason she had gone through so many nannies. Of course, this behavior came as no surprise to her coworkers. They knew Iris's idiosyncrasies all too well. After the first few caregivers got the boot, her male colleagues started a pool, happy to take bets on how long a particular nanny would last. The guys would tease and joke about her inflexibility and demands, but Iris didn't care. She was no stranger to office gossip. She could imagine what they said behind her back when she got pregnant—and without a husband, no less.

Right from their first meeting, Iris had known Mrs. B. was different from the multitude of other nannies. The woman was unshakeable, able to withstand Iris's occasional outbursts and withering stares. Mrs. B.'s calm, pleasant manner and, more importantly, her strict adherence to Iris's guidelines, more than reassured her high-strung employer. But it was Mrs. B.'s punctuality that set her apart from the other caregivers. Iris believed being punctual was an undervalued quality in today's fast-paced world.

As a child, Iris was not like most young girls. She rarely played with dolls and preferred to climb trees or play ball with the boys instead. As she got older, math and science were the subjects where she excelled. It was obvious Iris was one of those "nontraditional" women who forsaken boyfriends for books. After graduating magnum cum laude from a prestigious East Coast university, she immediately went into a high-powered MBA program. Snatched up by recruiters before graduation, Iris was on a fast track for upper management at one of the big financial brokerage houses. She had it all: the personality, the smarts, the drive, and the single-minded commitment to make it in a man's world.

That lasted about 12 years. Somewhere along the way, Iris got bored. The boardroom battles started to seem childish and petty. She had already made plenty of money and had spent a fair amount, too. There were closets filled with designer clothes and expensive shoes. She lunched at the finest restaurants, had theater tickets for all the top shows, and was manicured and coiffed at the best salons. Vacations were spent skiing out West, touring Europe, or cruising the Caribbean. But the rat race was getting to her. The long hours didn't leave much time for a social life, and after a while, her biological clock started ticking louder and louder.

Iris's disinterest in her job was growing in direct proportion to her increasing preoccupation with motherhood. After years of being single, thinking like a man, and beating them at their own game, Iris had never considered herself marriage material. Now nearing 40, she was faced with a hard choice. Should she stay married to her job, a tough broad who was "one of the guys," or should she answer the inner voice calling from deep inside? As fate would have it, the dilemma solved itself. Iris was given a chance to head up one of the company's suburban offices. Most guys would have considered the move an insult, knowing the real power and play was in Manhattan. But Iris saw the move as the answer to the biggest imperative weighing on her mind. A move to the suburbs would be the perfect place to start a family, and the new job would be less demanding. It was a chance at a new beginning, and Iris jumped at the opportunity. Her male colleagues were shocked, but they weren't privy to her ulterior motives.

The move to Long Island was a big transition. She bought a fancy house in a well-to-do neighborhood and spent the first six months redecorating it from top to bottom. Gradually, the high-powered lunches, social events, and theater tickets stopped, leaving her with large amounts of free time. After joining a couple of local business associations, Iris started meeting other women. That was step one of her plan to change the focus of her life. No more "one of the guys," Iris wanted to reconnect with her feminine side as she began the search for a possible mate. But finding one proved to be even more elusive than being a successful woman in a man's world. She went to singles events, tried online dating, and even spent hours hanging out at bars. It was easier making her first million than finding a suitable husband/future father.

Meanwhile, time was passing, and her clock was counting down. The tick tock, tick tock was getting louder and louder. Not one to be deterred in the face of defeat, Iris needed to rethink her strategy. After a week at Canyon Ranch in Arizona, she was ready to implement Plan B. It took her a solid two months of intensive research before choosing the right sperm bank. Then, it was months of injections and multiple tries at artificial insemination before the test came back positive. At 41, a confirmed bachelor and one of the Big Boys, Ms. Iris Carmichael, became pregnant. Needless to say, the office was shocked. All her NYC friends—men, mostly—couldn't believe the news, as she never struck them as being the maternal type. In fact, they considered Iris to be the antithesis of their own stay-at-home, mother-of-their-children wives.

Pregnancy was the best thing that ever happened to her body. She felt great and positively glowed. Her harsh, bony angles filled in and softened. As the baby grew, so did Iris's wonder and anticipation. The gradual change from being a high-powered bitch-on-heels to a high-powered pregnant witch was as natural as her growing maternity wardrobe. Her priorities shifted. She was still smart, secure, and significant, only now she carried the weight of impending motherhood, a condition which finally gave her something in common with other women. For the first time, she befriended the secretaries and support staff at work, actively feeding on their maternal knowledge like a hungry child. Between reading the "What to Expect" books, attending pregnancy workshops, and holding endless discussions with the other ladies in the office, Iris threw herself into motherhood with a zeal few could top.

When the BIG day finally arrived, she was whisked off to a private hospital room in a limo. Cathy, one of the secretaries the pregnant executive had relied on for advice, offered to be her coach. Iris might have been the equal of any man at the office, but when it came to the baby's delivery, there was no denying her body was made for childbirth. The birth couldn't have been easier. Brett was born during lunch hour on a beautiful fall Friday. Iris hired round-the-clock baby nurses and a housekeeper. By Monday afternoon, she was fielding phone calls and making deals as if motherhood had happened to someone else. But her life forever changed as she fell head-over-heels in love with her new baby boy.

Now, more than three years later, Iris took a minute to think back on life before Brett. It was as if she had lived in a barren wasteland, a desert devoid of delight, a dreary and dark twilight where it was somber all the time. Brett's arrival added a whole new dimension to her once-solitary life. She laughed to herself about all those naysayers who were shocked at her bold decision. Who said you had to be married to have kids? Yes, she was busier managing the life of a small child, but there was not one moment she didn't cherish. Iris still set aside time for herself: there were the weekly nail appointments, her early morning workouts, and the monthly book club meetings.

Iris joined the book club on a lark. She had learned about the group from her realtor, Sollie Gold. At first, it was simply another vehicle for meeting local women. But it quickly turned into her favorite social gathering. The other four women could not be more different from her and from each other. They took turns selecting a book each month, which was discussed at the next meeting. Over time, she developed a close kinship with these women. It was her book club friends who offered support and advice when she got in a bind. They were kind and nonjudgmental and enjoyed listening to stories about Brett.

Tonight's selection, *Exit Strategy*, was a fun read. While Iris never sold her body the way the lead character, Bernice Bailey did, she could relate very closely with the rest of the story. The intrigue, the backbiting, the "take no prisoner" mentality, these were things she had dealt with every day when she was a big shot in the city. *Exit Strategy* had conjured many memories from her years dealing with men and their games.

A phone call interrupted her thoughts. Her client arrived, and it was time to get back to business. There were portfolios to evaluate, stocks to be traded, and money to be made.

Chapter 6

"I'm coming," Sollie screeched from the second floor. "Now, where the hell is that other shoe?" She cursed under her breath. A quick glance at the clock confirmed she was late. *So, what else is new? It's not like this is the first time. I'm a pro at being late.* Sollie tried to convince herself it was no big deal.

"Mom, I needed to be at school ten minutes ago," grumbled Raychie. "Mr. Powell is going to be mad—I'll be penalized. That's what he does, ya know—he takes points off your grade for lateness. He said there were no more excuses. Why do you have to do this to me?"

Sollie heard the pleading in her daughter's voice. It was always the same whiney tone. Yesterday, she complained about being picked up late; the day before, it was something about not having her favorite pants washed, and the day before that . . . Sollie could spend the next two hours recounting her failings as a mother. It was a common complaint among mothers of teenage daughters. Who didn't have difficulties with these hormonal girls? But Raychie was particularly unforgiving when it came to her mother. Not that Sollie could blame her. Between keeping her messy house one step away from being condemned by the Board of Health, making sure her kids and husband were clothed and fed, and working her butt off at the agency, Sollie considered herself ahead of the game. Unfortunately, she was the only one who thought so.

"Okay, okay, I found it. Here I come. What's ten minutes? I'll talk to the teacher. Didn't Richie have him? I think it's the same guy. Don't worry, I take care of things."

"Come on, MOM. LET'S GO! Mr. Powell usually stops the lesson so everyone can watch me fumble for my notebook and pen. Why can't you be on time for once?!" Sollie was clomping down the stairs just in time to hear Raychie's final scream reverberate in her ear, along with "It's so unfair!" This last line was delivered in a whisper as the teen slammed the door on the way to the car.

"I heard you. Here I am, now let's go. Get into the car. I have to find my bag, and I'll be right there."

It would be another ten minutes before Sollie could locate all the bits and pieces of her life that were scattered around the kitchen: the cell phone, her wallet, keys, and the piece of paper that contained her to-do list.

"I've got everything! Let's go," called Sollie, trying to sound positive as she locked the garage door. Huffing and puffing, she squeezed herself into the car. She was sweating already, and it wasn't yet eight o'clock.

"Why can't you be more like Melissa's mom? Or Dana's? They're never late, their clothes are always pressed. They live in clean, neat homes, and eat dinner every night at 6 p.m."

Sollie was determined not to get drawn into a conversation about what was wrong in her daughter's life. "Okay, we're on our way. What time were you supposed to be there?" Sollie asked, ignoring the rebuke in her daughter's voice. She is trying to sound reasonable, trying her best to be positive and not make a mountain out of this minor misstep. After all, what could the teacher do? It was only ten minutes, after all.

"Seven forty. I was supposed to be in extra help at 7:40. As it is, I'll just make it to homeroom. Geez, Mom, why do I have to be late all the time? Why can't you get out on time? This always happens. I hate you." Raychie spoke the last words under her breath.

Sollie drove right to the main school entrance—the exact place parents were <u>not</u> supposed to use for school drop-offs. The approved location was around to the side. But Sollie Gold could never quite remember what the rules were.

"We're here," Sollie announced cheerfully. "Look, honey, I know you get frustrated because you're a couple minutes late. The good news is—lateness is not a crime. Just remember that. I'll see you later, have a good day, I love you, bye!" she added as her daughter hurriedly evacuated the car.

Watching Raychie run into the building, Sollie let out a sigh. Everyone complained about their teenage girls: they were difficult, moody, demanding, bitchy . . . She had heard it all and lived it, too. She wished they had a better relationship. Another sigh. Sollie tried; she really did. But the chance she'd wake one morning and find herself being a punctual clean freak was as remote as her losing those 20 (all right, maybe 30) pounds she always talked about.

"This is me. It's who I am. It's the way things are," she muttered to herself. "Count your blessings. I have two great kids (difficult, but that's what it is with teens), a nice house (a bit messy, nothing a couple of hours of cleaning wouldn't solve), and a loving husband (more lazy than loving, if I am being honest)—not perfect, but okay. Who wants perfect anyway? I wouldn't know what to do with myself if everything was perfect." The running monologue continued all the way to the office.

"If only there were more time," she lamented. "A free moment when I could simply catch my breath. Rush, rush, rush. If I could find a way to grab a minute or two for myself, I know I'd finally be able to get it all together."

That was the key—*time for myself*. It's a simple concept, just three little words. If only it were simple. She had jettisoned that superwoman crap years ago. "Bring home the bacon; fry it up in the pan." What bullshit. It was the 21st-century version of "barefoot, pregnant, and in the kitchen," and probably thought up by some male propaganda machine to keep women juggling an impossible number of jobs. Work, the kids, cleaning, cooking—and don't forget time for hubby. *What about time for me?* Being so harried and hassled, it was impossible to realize how out of control things really were. Sollie glanced at her watch. *She would be late for the sales meeting. So what?* Nothing new. She was glad she remembered her watch. *Be thankful for the little things,* she reminded herself.

Driving into the <u>L</u>ong <u>I</u>sland <u>S</u>uperior <u>P</u>roperty parking lot, Sollie quickly found a space and turned off the car. She grabbed for her LISP folder only to realize the materials she needed for the meeting must still be on the counter at home. *Oh well. Maybe there's an extra copy inside.* Shrugging out of the car, she looked at her feet and noticed her shoes didn't match. She was wearing one blue and one black. Buying two colors of the same shoe was supposed to simplify her life. Unfortunately, because the closet light bulb was out, she couldn't see their true color, and with Raychie rushing her so . . . *Well, it's no surprise this happened.* Another deep sigh. *Maybe no one will notice,* she hoped.

Sollie picked up her pace, feeling the sweat starting to bead (and bleed) under her arms. Ugh. The meeting had already started when she entered the conference room, and no one even looked up to see her walk in late. These weekly pep talks were intended to be a big motivator for the sales force. Discussions included new policies, added rules, administrative housekeeping, and upcoming house ads. Recent deals and closings were announced. Unfortunately, Sollie was having another dry week, and she didn't feel motivated when others were singled out for a job well done. Once the obligatory clapping and congratulations were done, everyone filed out. Myra, her manager, motioned Sollie over.

"Honestly, Sollie, everyone else can make it here on time," Myra reprimanded her. "You noticed we didn't wait. My new policy is to start the 8 o'clock meeting at 8 o'clock." Myra gave Sollie one of those once-over looks, her gaze stopping at Sollie's feet. Her expression changed from one of mild rebuke to undisguised distaste, not surprising from someone who put a premium on her appearance—hair, nails, pocketbook, shoes. Everything was always just so.

"I grabbed the wrong shoes this morning," Sollie explained, feeling sheepish after Myra's withering look. "Silly, I know, but in my rush to get here, I didn't look closely."

What more could she say? She was already feeling Myra's disapproval regarding her sales production. Sollie knew she was a bit of an odd duck in the LISP office. Most of the agents were like meticulous, Myra. Where these women found the time to get their nails done each week was a modern mystery.

"All right," Myra replied without missing a beat. "Just wanted to remind you you're taking out Huwang and Mita Li at 1 p.m. They're looking in the $750–800,000 range, and make sure you show them the Dyson place."

Sollie almost rolled her eyes. Of course, she remembered her appointment—they were her customers! Sollie knew what needed to be done—she'd been a realtor for years. In her heyday, they used to call her *Solid Gold*, a cute takeoff on Soledad, her formal name. But with the kids demanding more and more of her time and Stewie contributing less and less, everything fell on Sollie's slumped shoulders. Another deep breath.

"Don't worry, I know the drill. I have a good feeling about the Lis. I plan on doing more research and will have a couple of other places to visit as well," Sollie replied, trying to mollify Myra's concerns.

Myra gave a wan smile and another quick look over before she turned, heels clacking, and walked back to her office. Glad to have that over with, Sollie stopped by the coffee maker for a cup. Someone had left the empty pot on the burner, scorching the bottom. It fell to Sollie to scrub the burned coffee and make a fresh pot. It was a full hour after her arrival before she was finally able to prepare for her customers. With her desk a mess, papers piled helter-skelter, it took another ten minutes to sort through everything and get organized.

A quick look at the calendar caused a smile. She had almost forgotten the book club meeting tonight. She wasn't going to miss that for the world. It was the one purely Sollie thing she did. Meeting the girls meant her family was on their own for dinner. So, what if she didn't have time to finish the book? *Exit Strategy* was a convoluted tale, one which required her to constantly reread sections in order to keep up with the plot. She thought the whole premise was fanciful. Do people really have sex with strangers at the drop of a hat? And all that mystery and intrigue, honestly, who has time for such nonsense? But none of that mattered. The important thing was she'd be out to dinner, talking about things other than homework and laundry.

Sollie reviewed her notes, scrolled through some computer listings, and mapped out a proposed route, all in preparation for her appointments. Before she knew it, Huwang and Mita Li had arrived. *There's never enough time!*

Chapter 7

Leaving his car with the porter, Ted walked into the lobby of the Gold Coast Golf Club. A relic from a bygone time, the place never failed to impress. An enormous arrangement of fresh flowers dominated the entry foyer directly under the chandelier. Designed by Tiffany himself, he recalled. Handmade Persian rugs covered the gleaming dark wood floors. The greeters' desk was to the right and resembled a hotel reservation counter remembered from old movies. A grid of teak letter boxes sporting the names of each member framed the space behind the counter, which stood gleaming of forest green marble. There was even one of those desk-sized round silver metal bells standing ready to summon a clerk.

Ted always got a kick at coming to the GCGC. It felt like a step back in time. *This must be what it was like early in the century... the 20th century*, he thought.

"Can I help you, sir?" asked one of the clerks behind the counter, dressed in the club uniform that hadn't changed in over 100 years. Ted figured the green and purple striped bowtie would be considered part of a Halloween costume anywhere else.

"I'm here to meet Stan Piper," Ted replied, noticing the slight change in demeanor when Stan's name was mentioned.

The clerk gave Ted a quick look over to make sure this guest met the prescribed club attire before motioning to follow as he led Ted into the dining room and to Stan's favorite table.

The large dining room sported a 20-foot ceiling with a half-dozen or so lighting fixtures resembling upside-down mushrooms hanging from the ceiling. Tall windows lined one entire side of the room, allowing the bright sunlight to polish the gleaming furnishings. If it hadn't been for some of the club's duffers lining up for their tee shots, the view could have been a painting, so picture-perfect was the outside grounds. A soft hum engulfed Ted upon entering the dining room. Everything was hushed at the GCGC—a loud sneeze could create a commotion. He looked around at the members enjoying lunch, everyone wearing the prescribed dress code: long slacks, collared shirts, and loafers (no sneakers allowed). And, of course, there were no women.

Stan rose upon Ted's arrival. He thanked the steward, shook Ted's hand, and motioned for him to take the seat opposite, already set for today's luncheon.

"Glad you could make it," said Stan as he stroked his gray-and-white mustache. Known as the Gray Fox, Stan enjoyed a full head of hair, unusual at his age and only recently turning white at the temples. His sapphire-blue eyes stood out against a tanned complexion and missed nothing. One could almost see the mental wheels turning behind the bushy brows. There was something silky about Stan, from his soft hands to his smooth voice, which hid a steely resolve that frequently fooled the uninitiated. At the GCGC, he was the iron hand in the velvet glove, and everyone knew it.

Giving Ted a quick once-over, Stan was pleased his nephew was correctly dressed and cut such a dashing figure. He was sure if there had been any women present, they would be coveting Stan's view.

"Thanks for having me," Ted replied with an easy smile. Trips to the GCGC were always about more than the food. "How could I say no to all of this?" He nodded, looking around the opulent setting. It was a statement that could be taken two ways. Ted preferred Stan think he loved lunching at the GCGC, but in reality, he preferred the simpler, more relaxed atmosphere on the East End. Doing the whole dress-up thing was worth it, considering what he received in return.

The waiter came over to take their food and drink orders. Nothing of importance happened until after that ritual was completed.

"So, how are things at Crystal Clam?" Stan asked. As the majority owner of the winery, Stan liked to get his updates in person.

"Things are great—couldn't be better. We've exceeded our sales numbers for this month, and it's looking like we'll have a banner year. Of course, being part of the SCAB test didn't hurt. We're ahead by a week or two with production. The best part is we used half of the weed killer compared to last year." Looking at the menu, Ted was glad to see they offered a couple of Crystal Clam vintages on the menu.

"I'm glad you brought up SCAB. I've been getting an ever-increasing number of phone calls from Arnie Holtzmann at LIMBO," Stan explained with barely concealed sarcasm. "SCAB is a huge success, I'm told. Arnie says your wine growers are clamoring for it."

Ted smiled. Having lunch with Uncle Stan was an exercise in confirming yesterday's news. "Yes, the GRowLers love SCAB. If I were a betting man, I'd put my money on SCAB being a huge success."

Ted immediately regretted letting the B-word slip and noticed his uncle's brief eye roll. Gambling was his weakness, and if it wasn't for Uncle Stan's financial rescue, he'd likely be lunching at a very different location.

"I've been in touch with Bennett Kingsley," the older man revealed, moving the conversation along. "I'm arranging for him to come out for golf and to finalize his company's plans for expansion on Long Island."

Ted knew all about Stan and Bennett's long relationship. They met at prep school and have been besties ever since—this was ancient news. Ted even started a friendship with Bennett's nephew Carl, creator of SCAB. Over the past couple of years, the four of them became thick as thieves, actively scheming about SCAB production and rollout during rounds of golf. That Bennett (and Carl) was coming to Long Island was no news flash either. Carl confided as much in an email earlier.

"Arnie is looking to introduce Bennett and the ChemoCo team to the Long Island business community. What better way to get them to confirm opening a new office locally than to make the announcement during the festivities? I can remember when all major announcements were made face-to-face; no InstaChat, no Facetimes, no social media reveals," Stan remarked wistfully.

Ted had heard all about Uncle Stan's pining for the good old days. Ever the corporate titan, it was Stan who announced all the major decisions and made sure his employees knew who was responsible for the good news too.

"Look, I've been thinking of ways to discredit that Head Louse at LICE. Bill McCleary's made more than a few enemies these last years—his time is about up."

Ted nodded. He knew all about McCleary, LICE, A Holtz (that asshole) and LIMBO. Yesterday's headlines.

"Arnie's just realizing that our best chance of getting SCAB approved by LICE is to get McCleary out of the way. Finally, A Holtz is waking up. These things can't be left to chance. We can't afford to hope and pray the governor replaces McCleary on our timetable."

Ted looked up from his salad upon hearing the steel in his voice. It was unusual for his uncle to be so fervent. "Do you have something in mind? What are you suggesting?"

"What would you say to being part of a little mischief?" Stan asked as if he were considering covering McCleary's front yard in toilet paper.

Ted knew Uncle Stan didn't make idle threats or minor suggestions. "Look," Stan continued, "we need to discredit McCleary, turn him into a pariah. Make sure everyone dismisses his opinions and questions why they ever listened to him in the first place."

"How do you plan on doing that?" Ted asked, wondering what Stan was suggesting.

"I'm assuming you still have those bookie contacts. Maybe something good can come from all that gambling after all. If I recall, you were connected with a number of felonious types. Pretty unsavory, but always up for earning a couple of dollars, no questions asked. They'd understand the value of keeping their mouths shut—yes? I might have a job for them."

Ted was intrigued. This was breaking news, hot off the press.

46

Chapter 8

"Uncle Dominic, I'm leaving now," shouted Penna, hoping her uncle would hear her. Their cramped office space seemed to absorb all the sound. She decided to give it a minute before walking back. Her uncle's office was down a dark, and the narrow hallway made even more constricted due to piles of assorted papers and office supplies. File cabinets lined the dirty beige walls. A single ceiling fixture shed feeble light, giving everything a kind of faded-brown sepia tone. The one picture, which featured a rock and shrub landscape, hung a bit askew.

Before going back to her uncle's office, Penna made a sharp right into the bathroom—their only bathroom. Checking to make sure everything was clean, she stole a glance in the mirror. Her straight bangs ended right above her eyebrows, her brown hair fell neatly to her shoulders, and the simple gold hoop earrings poking through were just enough. Penna didn't waste much time with makeup. Her Mediterranean complexion gave her all the color she needed, and the naturally thick, dark lashes accented her light-brown eyes.

Penna had already stayed later than usual, timing her departure with a prearranged pickup. This was her book club night, and she was driving the carpool. Usually, Uncle Dominic would have easily heard her if his door were open, but tonight, he was ensconced in his office with that lowlife Pauly.

Pauly was one of Uncle Dominic's cronies. He belonged to a motley crew of assorted mafia types—mafia-type wannabes and ne'er-do-wells. There was something unsavory about Pauly and the others, even though they always smiled at her and were exceedingly polite. No curse words, no rough talk, but she had the sense they were hiding something. That things were not as they seemed.

Even so, one thing you had to give the guy: Pauly knew everything happening in a 20-block radius. Who got stiffed, who got robbed, who had their property roughed up, who was late on the rent, and had lost their lease; he was a wealth of local information and not the kind you'd read about in the paper. Pauly was connected.

Squaring her shoulders, she wasn't going to leave without bidding her uncle a good night. A quick knock on the office door, a count—one, two—and she pushed the door open. She looked in on the typical scene: Pauly slumped in the chair across from the left side of her uncle's massive wooden desk, feet resting on the stacks of papers living on top of the coffee table. Her uncle, behind his wooden desk, stopped midsentence as he turned toward her, all the while continuing to reach for his bottle of bourbon. Both men stared at her as if she had landed from outer space. They looked like two kids caught doing something they shouldn't. Uncle Dominic knew she didn't like Pauly. Even Pauly knew.

"I'm leaving, everything's cleaned up," Penna announced.

"Okay, have a good evening," her uncle replied with a smile and a wink. Penna knew what that wink meant as she closed the door behind her. The office and bathroom wouldn't be found in the same neat and tidy condition come the next morning; you could bet on that!

When Penna started working for her uncle, she had no idea what the job would entail. For all his big business talk and experience, Uncle Dominic's office was scattered and disorganized. She remembered being shocked that first day, finding his desk groaning under stacks of insurance manuals, client files, newspapers, racing sheets, and who knew what else. Papers were everywhere, except in the file cabinets, which stood unoccupied . . . if you didn't count the empty bottles of bourbon hiding inside the drawers. The filing system was nonexistent. Penna couldn't understand how he ran a business.

The phone would ring, people would stop by, and calls were made, but it didn't look as if anything was ever finalized or completed. It took months before Penna was able to figure out all the mess. From the get-go, it was abundantly clear Uncle Dominic was in desperate need of a back-office gal, and Penna was just the person for the job. It was one of those wonderful symbiotic relationships—she needed the extra money to make ends meet, and he needed someone to look out for his interests and, even more importantly, to look the other way.

At first, Penna had a hard time reconciling the Uncle Dominic she saw in the office with the one she knew as a child. If Aunt Lita only knew! Thankfully, Penna's mother, Sophia, was under no illusions. Growing up together, Sophia and Dominic were as close as brother and sister could be. It was Sophia who suggested Penna for the job, but only after her daughter had become a mother herself and was familiar with the ways of the male world. Sophia counseled Penna to keep her eyes open, to look out for Uncle Dominic, and then to leave it in the office. No one needs to know what happened there all day. Even though her extended family was close, some information kept better tightly sealed, her mother said.

It was the two of them in that office four hours a day/five days a week, and every other Saturday. She had been working there for almost five years, and in that time, they had developed an easy routine. Every day, he bought her lunch on top of paying her an outrageous salary. In at 10 a.m. and gone by 2 p.m.—where else could she get a job like that? Penna would be forever grateful to her uncle, a big man with a big personality and a heart of gold. There was nothing Uncle Dominic wouldn't do for his friends and family. He was a legend in the neighborhood.

But Uncle Dominic got the better of the deal. Penna was honest, friendly, reliable, and efficient. His clients loved her; he was more organized now than at any time in his life, and she was pretty good company, too. At first, Dominic worried his occasional peccadilloes and side businesses would pose a problem. But Penna was respectful and discreet. They agreed to the unspoken code of "What happens at the office, stays at the office." It was a business match made in heaven.

In fact, Penna knew more about Uncle Dominic's affairs, business, and otherwise than his wife. She had a record of all his bank accounts and their balances, kept track of his stock accounts and other investments, as well as his tab with some half-dozen bookies. As far as running the insurance business, Penna took care of the money, wrote the checks, and managed the books, the bookies, the debits, and the deadbeats. They worked out a system of communicating that would challenge an experienced cryptographer. It was Penna who ran The DiPalma Agency, and everyone knew it.

Possessing a natural intuition and sensitivity, Penna was good at reading people. That was the part of her job she liked the best. All different types would come into the office. They would sit with Uncle Dominic and talk about their needs, whether it was life insurance or some sort of annuity. He wrote auto and home policies as well.

Folks would open up, and Dominic learned about these people— their financial condition, their politics, their personal situation. The whole shebang. Once the customer was gone, Penna would go into Dominic's office and try to guess their story. She'd quiz him, make guesses at their personal circumstances, and her uncle would either confirm or correct. Penna had a kind of sixth sense, and more times than not, she was right on the money. It was a game she enjoyed.

Of course, when it came to Uncle Dominic's friends, her abilities were severely tested. Those guys made a profession out of concealment and secrecy. She always had a difficult time figuring out what they were up to. But with them, she reasoned, sometimes it was better not to know.

Looking at her watch, Penna figured she'd be right on time to pick up Onawhim for the book club meeting. Luckily, she had finished the book yesterday. *Exit Strategy* was a page-turner all right, with plenty of graft, gambling, payoffs, and all-around mischief. It sounded like a month in the life of Uncle Dominic's associates. She enjoyed the writing but couldn't believe the author was making money on a story Penna could as easily have written. After years with Uncle Dominic, she knew enough good tales to fill at least ten books. So far, Penna had read nothing half as interesting or unusual as what she witnessed at work each week. In fact, the *Exit Strategy* seemed pretty tame. She couldn't wait to hear what the other girls had to say.

52

Chapter 9

The front porch was the perfect place to wait for her ride. A shy smile escaped Onawhim's lips as Penna's silver SUV stopped at the curb. She had been looking forward to tonight's book club meeting, most especially the opportunity to catch up with her friend on the way. It was difficult for them to find time to socialize, as their lives were so different. Penna was busy with her husband, two kids, and an exuberant extended family while she had recently reentered the dating world.

"Right on time," Onawhim said, opening the passenger door. Of all her book club friends, Onawhim was closest to Penna.

They met during an outside field day program, one of those after-school activities, a couple of years ago. Onawhim was a new teacher at the elementary school, and Penna's oldest was starting kindergarten. Their friendship was cemented when they both realized they shared a love of reading and enjoyed the same types of books. If it wasn't for Penna, Onawhim wouldn't even be in the book club.

Small in stature, with an unassuming manner, Onawhim had a way of disappearing into her surroundings. Even after years of teaching, now in front of sixth graders, she still had trouble commanding attention. Being only slightly taller than many of her students didn't help. The slightest noise or distraction would drown out her reed-thin voice. Many in the back of the room simply couldn't hear what she was saying and would often lose interest in her lessons. The school fielded constant complaints from parents saying little Meaghan or Jordan never heard the assignment.

Whether it was having lunch in the teachers' staff room or attending an after-school event, Onawhim spent most of her day gliding from room to room, as inconspicuous as a ghost. Over the years, she had come to accept her fate. Being overlooked was frustrating at times, but it did have an upside. It forced her to notice small details about her surroundings—things other people often missed. Onawhim was a keen observer of human nature, too.

"You look nice," Penna commented, appreciating the way Onawhim's outfits always looked so well-considered. Today, she had on a smart navy dress and matching shoes, accented with a silk patterned scarf which tied in with her gray bag.

"Thanks." Onawhim blushed. She was fastidious about her appearance, especially her clothes, and superstitious about color. Perhaps because she was small and slight, everything had to be just so. She never purchased anything that wasn't some shade of blue, green, or gray. She couldn't understand the compulsion others had to call attention to themselves by wearing loud or provocative outfits. And there were many things other people couldn't understand about Onawhim.

"So, did you finish the book?" Penna asked.

"Yes, but I'm sure you'll not be surprised by my comments," Onawhim replied, figuring Penna could easily guess *Exit Strategy* was not to her taste. The characters were too hard-edged, the plot too farfetched, and she had guessed the ending after the first 100 pages. Onawhim liked period novels, stories from another time or faraway place. She believed books should be savored, read leisurely, and appreciated. *Exit Strategy* felt like someone took a sledgehammer to her head; it jarred her sensibilities. Her unflattering opinion of the book aside, she always enjoyed dinner with the group.

"I hope you'll not hold back tonight," Penna commented. "Everyone should speak their mind. Your opinions are as valued as mine or anyone's." Penna was always trying to encourage her friend to speak up, to come out of her quiet shell.

"I will," Onawhim replied, suppressing a smile. During book discussions, she especially liked when they would lean in, eager to catch her every word. Being soft-spoken and shy, Onawhim could remember only one time when she had purposely acted out and called attention to herself when a roomful of people turned their full attention to focus on her. It was a unique experience, one she remembered with pride, and it was the source of her nickname.

As a young child, Onawhim had difficulty being noticed. Naturally shy and quiet, it was normal for her to see rather than be seen. That changed during a schoolmate's birthday party. Onawhim became the scapegoat for a group of girls she barely knew, suffering under a barrage of teasing and even being excluded from the party games. She tried to tough it out, speaking up when it was her turn, ignoring their taunts, and effectively letting the bullies have their fun until it all became too much. They pushed her too far. Then, as if a switch was flicked, Onawhim did the opposite of what those mean girls expected. She jumped on top of the party table and proceeded to stomp on the plates of uneaten food, kicking over cups half-filled with soda, and even placed a perfectly aimed foot through the once beautifully decorated birthday cake.

When her parents learned about the outburst, she was forced to apologize to the girl and her family. She couldn't remember exactly what she had said but heard plenty about it afterward. "What were you thinking?" her mother asked, mortified by Onawhim's behavior. "It's as if you were acting on a whim in such a disrespectful manner."

The nickname stuck. *How ironic*—she smiled to herself—*that I was once considered so impetuous.*

"So, what's happening with you and Tru?" Penna asked, bringing Onawhim out of her reverie.

"Oh, we broke up. It was never going to work out," Onawhim replied with regret.

"You were so happy the last time we spoke. I thought Tru was a keeper."

"He smelled. I couldn't get past the odor."

"Really, it was his smell? Did he not shower? Was it his cologne?" Penna couldn't quite understand the problem.

"I know it sounds strange. It was bizarre, but it's better this way. Better for both of us."

Onawhim had confided to Penna about meeting Tru after her meditation class a couple of months ago. She was so happy, she couldn't hold it inside.

She had been meditating at one of those Karate/Tae Kwon Do storefronts in a strip mall near her house. The class had ended, but Onawhim was slow to return to the present moment. Taking a deep breath, she raised her head and opened her eyes. Her gaze landed on the most beautiful man she had ever seen walking into the now-empty room. Tru radiated confidence and a powerful sexual dynamic beyond anything she had encountered before. Their eyes met, her scalp tingled, and it felt as if he looked right into her soul.

Tru was exceptionally handsome, tall—by her standards—with straight black hair and black eyes. He possessed a dancer's body, lithe and powerful, and his movements carried the suggestion of control and strength. It seemed as if the laws of nature didn't apply. He walked without disturbing the air—his physical nature seemed to not occupy any space. An aura of tranquility surrounded his body like a dampening field. It kept him relaxed yet ready, prepared while poised. Onawhim was mesmerized by his presence.

They were drawn to each other. She was captivated by his strength and quiet certainty while he admired her flawless complexion and perfect proportions. They started dating right away: the usual routine of lunches, dinners, movies, weekend outings, etc. She loved being around him. They laughed, talked, and spent many happy silences together. Dating Tru was peaceful—he was so different from anyone she had known. They would talk for hours about everything under the sun, and they shared a deep thirst for history and culture. Once, they spent a whole day reading without talking at all. The more time they spent together, the more obvious their need for more than mental intercourse. Unfortunately, intimacy intruded.

"Sex with Tru was disgusting," Onawhim revealed. "That two people so compatible in so many areas could be so out of touch in the touching department was more than a shame, it was an outright tragedy," she recalled.

"At first, I thought our initial sexual encounter was a fluke. A freak event, an off night, the result of too much anticipation, too much pressure to make sure everything was perfect. But things didn't improve. I found myself actively scrubbing away all traces of him in the shower the next day. It was gross."

"Not a good sign for a budding romance," Penna agreed.

"I didn't want to believe there was something wrong with him," Onawhim continued. "I thought it might be me. Maybe too much to drink? Possibly it was the excitement, the anticipation, or the overwhelming desire for everything to be perfect?"

"Sure, with all that expectation, who can tell what was real and what imagined!" Penna sympathized.

"That first night was a total disaster. Words are useless in describing the experience. Imagine a putrid vapor invading your nostrils, blocking out everything else. I jumped out of bed and ran into the shower. I had to get clean. Obviously, nothing happened that night. *This must be a fluke*, I thought."

Penna drove, staring straight ahead, not trusting to take her eyes off the road. "How did Tru take it?"

"Tru was as ardent as ever. And I wanted him too. I wasn't going to let some indiscriminate smell ruin a budding relationship. We tried everything—perfumes, incense, body wash. Nothing worked! Things were getting worse. The smell would build through foreplay and intensify as our sexual activity increased. It would become so strong I could barely be close to him.

"It was more than B.O., more than unwashed sweat, and more than I could bear. We tried to figure out where it came from, and why it was present only when we were sexually active."

Penna was speechless. She had never heard of a situation such as this.

"We even went for a consultation with a smell specialist, hoping for an easy medical diagnosis, something cured by a pill, an injection, or a salve. Anything to take away the smell. He even tried a new diet, thinking different foods would change his body chemistry.

"Unfortunately, nothing worked. Ironically, the closer we grew emotionally, the more distant I grew physically. It was becoming too much to manage. It was repulsive.

"It took me a long time to accept the obvious, even as things were getting worse. I was left with no choice and had to make the break. Tru understood. He wanted me to be happy, and he deserved a woman who could love him, odor and all.

"We went to our favorite restaurant, and after dinner, I looked into his deep, fathomless eyes and uttered the words he was expecting. I brushed his cheek with a kiss, made a quick pirouette, and marched to my car, not looking back. I cried all the way home. It's such a shame."

"What a cruel twist of fate!" was the only thing Penna could say. "Can you imagine if you had met as pen pals, or email partners, corresponding to each other from across the miles? This would never have been an issue." She was trying to find something positive to say. "Better to end things now and move on. There are plenty of other guys out there. You'll see, you'll meet someone who'll be right for you in every way."

Penna made a right turn into the parking lot and looked over at Onawhim. Stoic, that's what Penna thought. It was a tough bit of luck, but Penna could see her friend was trying not to let her disappointment show.

"Enough about my sad tale," Onawhim offered, with a smile brightening her face. "Tonight's about *Exit Strategy*, and I'm ready to give it a piece of my mind."

Part 2

Inhalation

Chapter 10

"I think we're the first to arrive," Iris stated as she received welcome hugs from Penna and Onawhim. They spent the next couple of minutes on small talk and looking at the menu as they waited to be seated. Glynn arrived next, full of energy and ready to lead a lively discussion. All four found their seats and placed their drink orders. After years of book club meetings, everyone knew the routine: red for Penna and Iris, white for Glynn and Onawhim, and a white wine spritzer for Sollie. As if on cue, as the drinks arrived, Sollie rushed her way through the restaurant, making a beeline for the table.

"Sorry I'm late," Sollie sputtered out of habit. "Is that mine?" she asked, pointing to the glass with the bubbly liquid. "How did you know?" She smiled, falling into her chair.

All five women lifted their glasses for a toast.

"Here's to us," they spoke together, clinking glasses all around. The first sip induced an almost audible sigh as the day's stress and worries melted away.

All five knew how remarkable their association had become. Sure, there were hundreds of book clubs around the country, thousands even. But theirs was different. What started as a tentative meeting among strangers who shared a love of reading turned into a bond of sisterhood, not unlike the way a book's spine holds its pages together. Each came from a different cultural background, each at a different place along life's journey. They relished a good book and the opportunity to slip outside their busy lives once a month. The book club offered acceptance and appreciation. Complaints, criticisms, grievances, and grumbling were simply not allowed, and this unspoken canon served as the cornerstone of their meetings.

"Now that that's done," Glynn announced after they finished ordering the food, "I have some good news." As the evening's unofficial leader, it was her meeting to run and the first to share her own personal story with the group.

"Gil's up for a seat on the LIMBO board," she said, bubbling with the pride of a newlywed. Everyone knew Glynn's career had taken a backseat to Gil's, but that didn't stop them from offering congratulations as if it were her coup. "We hope to get the official word this week, and then we'll go out for a night on the town," she concluded, not hiding the crossed fingers on the table.

"Going out?" Sollie suggested with a knowing look. "I'd have thought the congratulations would happen under the sheets."

"Of course, that too," Glynn agreed, with her cheeks blushing a light pink.

"What about you?" Iris asked, knowing Glynn was adjusting to some changes of her own. "What's happening at Shylock?"

"Things are okay," Glynn replied with a note of disappointment. "It's a bit slow right now in the law library, but that could change at any moment," she added hopefully. "I'm ready to sink my teeth into a new assignment."

"I give you a lot of credit. Don't know if I could have made the same sacrifice. It must be love," Iris concluded, giving voice to the thoughts the others shared.

"Enough about me," Glynn concluded, looking at Onawhim, happy to move the conversation along around the table.

"Tru and I broke up," Onawhim replied in her quiet voice, causing the girls to lean forward to hear. "It's not much of a story, but it's better we ended it before things got too far along."

A series of knowing and sympathetic glances returned Onawhim's stare. They murmured caring remarks like, "It's better you found out early," "The right one will come along," "I hope you're doing okay," and "It'll get easier with time." They would never pry, even as they would enjoy hearing all the sordid details. But that was not their way. By not pushing in with trite remarks or inappropriate questions it allowed Onawhim to save face, and their quiet support made her feel special.

"Well, it's good riddance to Tru-blue. Time to move on. What you need now is an affair. We need to find you a nice guy," Sollie suggested, ready to put her matchmaking skills to the test.

"Yes, I suppose. Maybe I'll try one of those online dating sites, but I'm not ready yet."

"Something will happen. You wait and see," Penna said. "I have a feeling things will work out sooner than you think. You'll meet the right guy when you least expect it." A consensus around the table agreed with that last remark.

Penna's turn came next, and she continued by describing a day in the life of Uncle Dominic's office. Over the years, she shared tales about the many shady characters who sought her uncle's advice. Most of the time, Penna's observations provided a fun diversion for the group, but not tonight.

"I'm worried about my mother. I think there's something wrong with her," Penna confessed, outing her worst fear. "She's been secretive in a way only I would notice. It's like she is hiding something from me, and I sense it's not something good."

"Have you spoken to her about this?" Glynn asked.

"I've tried, but she's been avoiding me, like she knows I'm going to press her, and she doesn't want to be confronted."

"Maybe she's not prepared to talk yet. I'm sure she'll open up when ready. That's what I would do," Onawhim offered.

"You know how I've relied on my mother's guidance. Now when I need it the most, she's the one I can't ask," Penna replied.

"You have plenty of common sense, more than enough to go around. I don't think there's anyone I've known who is more down-to-earth. As someone once told me, 'Give it some time, and you'll come up with the right answer,'" Glynn suggested gently, using the very same words Penna had offered when Glynn was looking for direction.

Glancing around the table, Glynn's eyes rested on Sollie.

"You mean it's my turn? Well, I was late to work, got the evil eye from Myra, and I've been wearing two different colored shoes all day. You think you have problems?" Sollie joked, giving a touch of levity to the somber mood. "What can I say? Today was as typical as it gets." She gave her shoulders a shrug. Over the years, the book club had heard all about her slovenly housekeeping, her nebbishy husband, and her spoiled-rotten kids.

"Wouldn't it be something if I had three minutes to spare during the day? I don't think I'd know what to do," Sollie confessed.

"Three minutes can be a long time if you're twiddling your thumbs in the law library," Glynn answered.

"Three minutes can be a lifetime if you're watching the market nosedive," Iris added.

"If you're trying to get 20 sixth graders to be quiet and sit still, three minutes can be an eternity," Onawhim stated, reminding the group of the tough times she'd had getting through to her students.

"Okay, okay, I give," Sollie conceded. "I can't understand how the women in my office do it—their nails are done, their desks are organized, and they're never late. Just once, I'd like to get the nod of approval from Myra and not be considered the weakest link in her management-by-the-book chain."

As the last syllable left Sollie's lips, Iris jumped in, almost unable to wait. "I have to tell you what Brett did today," she interjected, as puffed up as a sage grouse. "Mrs. B. took him to a reading group for five-year-olds at the library, and he read better than most of the group," Iris cooed proudly. Expanding on her story, she was quick to credit Mrs. B. with how happy and well-adjusted Brett was and how smoothly her household had been running.

"Thank God for Mrs. B.," announced Glynn, Onawhim, Penna, and Sollie in unison. It was a chant that had become an instant book club hit. Over the years, they all sympathized with and laughed at Iris's nanny-gate stories. Finally, when Mrs. B. was hired, there was a collective sigh of relief, happy she finally found someone to trust.

"I have to say, life for me—right now, at this instant—is good," Iris summarized, thinking this might be the first time she was so content.

The food arrived as Iris was concluding her story.

"Part of me would like to experience what it would be like to be dating again," Sollie mentioned to Onawhim in between bites of her grilled chicken breast. "Wouldn't it be something if we could go back in time?"

Onawhim shook her head. "I'm sure things are not all that different from when you were single," Onawhim answered, trying to picture a young and flirty Sollie. "The challenge is to find someone that can stop talking about themselves and take a quiet moment to listen.

"I remember when I was dating Stewie. We were so young and clueless. We didn't know what to do or even if we were right for each other. Who knows where things would have ended up if we were dating today?"

"I've given up on the whole dating thing altogether," added Iris as she stabbed at another bite of her Cobb salad. "Whatever free time I have is spent with Brett or doing reading for the book club. In fact, I was thinking of starting a Mommy and Me stock investment club. You can't start saving for college soon enough."

"College saving is why I'm working for Uncle Dominic," Penna offered while twirling her spaghetti. "Even though he's pretty generous, it'll take forever to save all the money necessary to send two kids to college."

"Haven't you heard of loans?" Sollie chimed in. "That's what Stewie and I did, and it's what we'll do for Richie and Raychie. What about you, Glynn?"

Glynn put down her club sandwich before she answered. "I'm still paying those things off. Law school was a fortune. In any case, I'm in no hurry to start planning for my nonexistent kid's college education. Gil and I haven't even started talking about kids yet," she concluded, blushing.

"Ahh, to be young, in love, and child-free," mused Sollie, causing the rest of the table to smile.

Conversation and good-natured kidding ping-ponged across the table throughout dinner. As the busboy came to clear the plates, it signaled time to get down to business. Protocol required the person who picked the book to lead the discussion, and *Exit Strategy* was Glynn's pick. Relishing the opportunity to delve into the details, Glynn directed the meeting with skill. The discussion ranged from a review of the plot and characters to the author's voice and hidden meanings.

Glynn possessed an almost photographic memory and loved to interject little snippets from the story to keep things moving along.

The group was divided in opinion. Glynn had guessed *Exit Strategy* wouldn't be a favorite with Onawhim, who had more of a delicate sensibility. The book left Sollie confused most of the time, causing her to go back and reread portions of the fast-moving plot. Penna didn't have a problem with the story per se, but the backroom deals and shady characters didn't seem half as interesting as life in her uncle's office. Iris shared Glynn's appreciation of the *Exit Strategy*. They seemed to have the same taste in books, except when Iris was in one of her sci-fi moods. Despite the mixed reviews, Glynn was able to lead them through a lively discussion.

Once coffee and tea were finished, the meeting started to wind down.

"Great discussion," Iris offered. "One of the best."

Penna nodded in approval.

"I still don't get why the detective had to leave the department," Sollie complained. "I mean, she didn't do anything wrong. Why can't she keep her job?"

"That's the whole point of the book—it's called *Exit Strategy* for a reason," Glynn explained with a grin. She knew Sollie was being difficult in her own Sollie way. "In any case, it's Onawhim's turn next." Glynn gestured to the Asian woman across the table.

"This is a book I've been wanting us to read for some time," Onawhim began. "*The Generous Geisha* is a story set in rural Japan in the 1700s. It was written about 20 years ago by Hiro Ming, before he became famous. How about meeting in a month from today, say, May 12th?"

Everyone pulled out their phones or pocket calendars and made a note of the next date. Once done, they settled the check, rose from the table, and collected their coats and other belongings. As was customary, they left together, walking to their respective cars.

Chapter 11

It was a cool night with a slight breeze blowing from the east. The five women huddled in the parking lot, not ready to separate, only too happy to continue their conversations. Like many strip malls, The Good Grill parking lot was bordered on perpendicular sides by a row of stores, while the neighborhood streets formed the rest of the rectangle. It was a typical suburban setting and would have been unremarkable if it wasn't for the massive 19th-century building located behind the restaurant a short block away.

The old Wallace Fabric Mill loomed over The Good Grill as it had over the surrounding area for the past 150 years, a silent observer of the various changes to the landscape. It was an enormous, grim-looking building with a dirty red-brick exterior broken up by small murky windows evenly spaced across its four stories. It called to mind something you'd associate with those forbidding factories found in Charles Dickens's England.

"What's that place?" Sollie asked as she looked up. Her real-estate nose was always on the lookout for property. She didn't notice it on the way in—maybe because she was in too much of a rush.

"The Wallace Fabric Factory. It was the biggest employer around here more than 100 years ago. Sometime in the 1970s, it went out of business and became abandoned. It's been vacant, until recently when it was taken over by LIMBO," Glynn replied.

"Oh, yes," Iris chimed in. "I remember reading about this. I have a couple of clients who are investors. The purpose is to generate scientific discoveries, to spur economic development, and hopefully create good-paying jobs. It's for startups. Not the right investment for everybody," she concluded.

"That's right," Glynn continued. "It came out of a suggestion from a LIMBO committee Gil was on. It's a research incubator, attracting top scientists by giving them inexpensive lab and office space—Long Island Quality Intellectual Development, LIQuID. The idea is to provide all the back-office support and even financial investments, that could yield scientific breakthroughs. Like Alzheimer's research, or a cure for cancer."

Just then, Glynn became distracted by a powerful aroma—the air was suddenly infused with the smell of freshly cut grass. It was so strong she wondered why she hadn't noticed it earlier.

"Look. What's coming out of the side of the building?" asked Onawhim as she pointed skyward at a light-colored cloud billowing out.

"It's probably exhaust from an old boiler," Sollie offered. "Those contraptions are not very efficient; sometimes they end up venting as much heat as they retain."

Everyone seemed to be satisfied with her explanation as they stood quietly in the parking lot, watching the gas escape in what felt like slow motion. The cloud coalesced, resembling an amoeba floating in water. It was able to keep its shape as a gentle breeze blew it toward the parking lot.

"Do you smell that?" Onawhim whispered, mesmerized by a powerful memory. "It reminds me of my grandmother's herb tea: a mix of clove, ginger and lemon grass. I haven't smelled anything like that in years."

Penna was amazed by its light color, which was contrasted against the dark sky. Like a mushroom growing on the forest floor, Penna breathed in its earthy, musty scent. "This smells like something my family brought back from Italy. You know, a type of truffle . . . earthy, woodsy." Not believing her first impression, Penna gulped in multiple breaths as she watched the cloud move overhead.

"Wait a minute!" Sollie exclaimed. "I know this is crazy and it wouldn't be the first time people thought I was nuts, but I could swear I'm smelling chocolate. Not the candy bar kind, but the real stuff—you know, the expensive $100 a-box deep, dark, sexy kind. I can't believe it, but it's making me hungry all over again."

Iris was too focused on the cloud to hear what the others were saying. With undivided attention, she watched it slowly pass overhead. Gradually, she became aware of a subtle fragrance. It reminded her of her favorite perfume, Odyssey, which had notes of lavender, jasmine, and musk. Iris couldn't believe it, but it smelled as if Odyssey was surrounding her, permeating her coat, her hair, and her skin. She took a deep breath, delighting in its unique essence, and noticed the result: goose bumps popped up and down her arms, and she felt sexually aroused.

The five of them stood rooted to the ground, looking up at the sky. Each drew in deep lungfuls of the fresh, spicy, sweet, sexy, earthy aroma, captivated by the cloud's unearthly beauty. Slowly, it moved on, passing overhead and sliding through the night sky, continuing on its silent journey. A clean, cool breeze blew by, causing a shiver and breaking the spell as the cloud's wispy tendrils started to dissolve.

"Did you see that?" exclaimed Sollie, the first to speak. "I can almost taste the chocolate. It smelled so real!"

"It wasn't chocolate," Glynn corrected. "It was the most intense aroma of freshly cut grass after a summer shower. It reminded me of the camp I went to every summer. They had a big field, and this smelled exactly as newly mowed hay. So fresh . . . it was just so pure and fresh," she repeated, unable to get the memory or the smell of it out of her mind.

Onawhim spoke about her grandmother's tea, a unique blend no one else could know. Penna described in fine detail the woodsy fragrance she remembered as a small child watching her mother in the kitchen. The aroma conjured deep, powerful memories, some long dormant that had spontaneously come to life. Each one described in fine detail what they smelled, remembered, and experienced. When Iris spoke about her physical arousal, they all shared a good-natured laugh, a signal the moment had passed. Peeling off to find their respective cars, everyone dissipated home as the cloud vanished into the night sky.

Chapter 12

"Lois, I'm going into the sales meeting with Baxter now. It shouldn't be long. I'm still hoping to get out a bit early today," Iris said to her assistant. "If Dan Glassman calls, tell him I executed his trade for 5,000 shares of ChemoCo yesterday. He was giving me a hard time and didn't think the stock was going anywhere. But I told him I had a good feeling and that he had to trust me. He went along reluctantly, and now it's trading at 36 and a half, up three points. That should make him happy. See ya in a bit," Iris called over her shoulder on her way to the conference room with a spring in her step.

Things can't be going any better. So many odd coincidences have happened over the last couple of weeks, and all in my favor! Like the lucky break getting Brett into the gifted reading program at the library—a class notoriously hard to get into.

She simply suggested Mrs. B. take Brett to the library at one in the afternoon. It turned out to be just the right time, and he was the first to be enrolled. Then she happened to remember Mrs. B.'s birthday a full day before the actual date! There were other oddities, too—trades at work closing on the plus side, billing disputes being settled in her favor.

Maybe I should buy a lottery ticket!

Iris found Baxter Wright, the regional manager for the entire New York metropolitan area, calmly waiting in the conference room. As the head of her small suburban office, Iris sat directly across from her boss at the 20-foot-long conference table for the monthly meeting with the troops. Baxter generally took the opportunity to rally and motivate the staff on the front lines of the investment wars. Not that he was much of a speaker. He'd review new rules and policies, read the latest sales numbers, reference where they stood in relation to the other offices under his supervision, and then he'd congratulate the big sales winners and make the losers squirm. Not very inspiring.

Forty-ish, Baxter was rounding in the middle with thinning brown hair. He dressed in a preppy Brooks Brother uniform—like so many Wall Street types—but had taken off his jacket to give the impression this was an informal meeting. Everyone knew he'd risen through the ranks because he went to the right schools, knew the right people, and likely kissed the right asses. It also didn't hurt that he was related to one of the company's board members—a nephew or something was the rumor.

Iris didn't have any problem with Baxter. She knew what he wanted from his office managers: a steady increase in revenue. It was as simple as that. And being hard-working and smart, Iris always managed to deliver. Some quarters were stronger than others. After all, she had no control over the market. By and large, she ran a pretty well-oiled machine, and her team consistently produced results. That's what the big boys in corporate liked.

"All right, Iris?" Baxter began, checking it was okay to start.

"First thing first. You're all to be commended. This office ended the first quarter five percent ahead of projections. And the numbers for April look strong . . . Very strong." Baxter emphasized the last two words, making sure everyone knew he was happy with their performance.

Iris already knew the numbers, and the rest of the meeting followed the predictable pattern. Her boss droned on as she scanned the latest market report from the folks in technical analysis. She made some notes identifying stocks to mention to her clients—a couple of good ones to buy and some to sell. Her picks did not necessarily follow the analysts' recommendations, but she didn't care.

No one knows what a particular stock is going to do; it's an exercise in guesswork with a little intuition thrown in.

Before long, Baxter was wrapping things up. Iris stood to return to her office. There were a couple of things she needed to finish before she could cut out for the weekend.

"Iris, could you wait a minute? There's something I want to go over with you," Baxter asked as everyone was filing out. Speaking with her after the meeting was fairly routine. It was important to keep the office managers in the loop and give them a little more information than the troops.

"So, how are things in New York?" she asked, letting him think he was her main source of information. In reality, she had plenty of friends at corporate headquarters and knew well enough what was going on at the company's higher levels.

"Fine, just fine. A couple of the M&A guys always ask about you. It seems they're still talking about that Sturgis deal."

Iris let herself enjoy the moment. *Those were the days.*

"But I have some interesting data for you to look at," Baxter continued in his deadpan way. He laid out a couple of pages showing daily transactions for the past two weeks. There were a couple of hundred transactions, displaying the hard work of a busy office. The pages outlined the name of the stock, the number of shares, and whether it was a buy or sell, short or long. But when the stock positions got matched up with the transaction price, that's when things got interesting. It appeared that 64 percent of the time, the client benefited from the transaction.

As Iris scanned the pages, many of the positive transactions were the ones she executed.

"Looks like I'm doing okay," Iris remarked, waiting to hear what was on Baxter's mind. "Is there a problem? Don't tell me the company is concerned because my clients are making money."

Iris tossed this last statement out as part-joke, part-truth. Her radar was starting to ping. *What's up his sleeve?* She wondered how making money in an altogether legal and morally ethical way could be a problem.

"The company loves when it makes money," Baxter replied, ignoring her sarcasm. "But when the probability threshold hits 60 percent or more, it triggers an automatic review." He stopped talking and gave her an intense look.

The probability threshold described a basic trading theory that held, all things being equal, the financial success of all trades, all buys, sells, longs, and shorts, when added together, should not exceed 60 percent, given the unpredictable nature of a free market system. The operative word here was should. And as any statistician will tell you, 60 percent is a benchmark, a number that is reasonable, not something to be carved in stone. Occasionally, the probability threshold would hit 62 percent or even 64 percent, but that was all part of the science of probability. Things did sometimes happen, but they were rare and inconsistent. Iris knew all about the Probability Threshold. It was frequently the indicator that pointed to insider trading or other improprieties.

Baxter let the words Probability Threshold sink in before continuing. "The probability threshold in your office for the last three weeks has been high but not unusual. It's when we look at individual activity, specifically YOUR activity, that it starts to look inappropriate." Baxter was choosing his words very carefully now. He didn't want to accuse Iris of anything—not yet, anyway. The fact that the company's compliance boys were shocked at her PT was unusual enough.

"I've highlighted your trades," Baxter continued, watching as she scanned and flipped through the pages.

The pinging was getting louder now. *What is this windbag talking about?* Her PT was always in the normal range—it HAD to be. She knew she wasn't doing anything illegal. But the more she studied the papers in front of her, the more she realized the overwhelming majority of her transactions yielded a favorable financial outcome for her clients. The last page revealed the truth.

"Is this right?" Iris whispered incredulously. "Eighty-four percent?! My probability threshold is over 80 percent." She was stunned. In all her years in the business, in all the varied departments she had worked, with all her education and experience, she had never seen or even heard of a PT over 72 percent. Not one that wasn't tainted with dishonesty.

Baxter had focused his attention on Iris's face. He was studying her expression for any hint of duplicity. "As you can imagine, the compliance group went into overdrive. It seems when they reviewed your accounts, your PT was in the normal range until about three weeks ago. Then, for reasons they were unable to explain, it shot up to over 80. In fact, now it could be even higher."

"Wow! I knew I was good but didn't think that good," she muttered to herself. It was an inside joke that didn't seem so funny now. Of course, who wouldn't want to be right about their stock trades over 80 percent of the time? But the laws of probability didn't work that way. In the stock market, where the reward is always balanced by risk, the chances one broker would be guessing correctly more than 75 percent of the time was more than unlikely. It was damn near impossible, with illegal activity being often cited as the cause. "I'm here to look into this. You know how skittish those compliance guys can be. My guess is you're having a good run, a string of good fortune. Let's make sure it's nothing more than that," Baxter concluded sternly. He made it abundantly clear her documents and backup paperwork had better be transparent. Following company policy, each transaction was going to be scrutinized, and if there was one dark blemish, one smudge found inside her shiny glass house, there would be big problems in River City.

Iris knew she was on a roll, but seeing the numbers in black and white hammered Baxter's point home. She'd been around long enough to see it happen. Sooner or later, the confluence of random events conspires to help you make more than a few lucky picks, and there were plenty of off times, too. But she hadn't realized how hot her picks had been. In over 80 percent of the cases, she had made the right guess. What were the odds of that happening?

"Of course, you're right, Baxter, it's highly unlikely. In fact, now that I see my trades all listed one after another . . . I don't know what to say. I didn't realize I was on such a streak or I would have made some changes in my own portfolio."

Iris's attempt at levity fell flat. What else could she say? She had no rational explanation and was damned if she was going to be goaded into being defensive. She did nothing wrong—her backup would prove that—and in the meantime, she would suffer through an audit with her head held high.

"Look, Iris, we truly hope there's no problem here. Management wanted me to talk with you and to make sure nothing funny was going down," he said, trying to soothe her ruffled feathers. The last thing Baxter wanted was a screaming she-bitch freaking out on a Friday afternoon. He needed her to be calm and compliant, a willing collaborator as he investigated her activity.

"Look, you're making some good calls. We don't want that to change, you can understand. We want to make sure everything is on the up and up," he concluded, sounding sensible and soothing.

After assuring Baxter she was as clean and straight as a new broom, Iris went back to her office. *Let them pull all the backups, and I have nothing to hide*, she confirmed to herself. But the extra work and office gossip would be a huge pain in her ass. No one likes to have every move investigated, and Iris was dreading the coming week. Sitting at her desk, she glanced again at the list of stock trades. She still couldn't believe her probability threshold was over 80 percent. A part of her was thrilled—who the hell wouldn't like to guess right 80 percent of the time? As she was reading the list, one of the stocks caught her eye: ChemoCo, a large chemical producer of pharmaceuticals and agricultural products. She had counseled a couple of her clients to sell when it was at 24 and an eighth. But there was something about the stock that niggled at her, and she couldn't put her finger on it. Closing her eyes, she tried to remember what she had seen. Was it a stock analysis, an article in the *Wall Street Journal*, or a Bloomberg report? The connection eluded her. But regardless of what triggered her intuition, Iris felt deep down that NOW was the time to buy. In some weird way, she KNEW the stock was going to rocket up. Did it really matter HOW she knew?

So strong was her feeling that Iris put in a buy order for 300,000 shares in her own account. "Why not put my money where my mouth is?" she reasoned. "Come Monday, if the stock goes up, I'll call a couple of my big clients and see if they want in." Strangely, Iris thought of this as a kind of test, but exactly what this was testing she couldn't answer. In her mind, she thought the stock would rise nine points—an unlikely scenario for this type of traditional chemical company. Making a note on her calendar, Iris wrote to sell the stock if it hits 48. That one transaction would net her almost $2 million. Taking a chance on a chemical stock was unlike her. But this didn't feel like a chance; it felt like a sure thing.

A phone call from Brett interrupted her thoughts. Looking forward to a weekend at home with her son, Iris spent the rest of the afternoon tying up loose ends. Come Monday morning, she knew there would be little time for the day-to-day chores of running the office. Logging off, Iris had another strange feeling. It was as if this would be the last time she would use her office computer. Packing her things for the weekend, she couldn't shake the sense she was leaving for a lot longer than two days. Iris had always respected her feminine intuition but never spent a lot of time thinking about it until now. She sensed a new voice rummaging around her psyche. It was confident and straightforward, and it was telling her she should collect all her personal items because this was likely to be the last time she'd sit in her office.

***

Monday morning arrived before she knew it, and Iris was getting ready for work while listening to her favorite business show. One of the anchors was reporting on a breaking business story. At the mention of ChemoCo, she abruptly stopped what she was doing to stand in front of the TV.

"ChemoCo, the giant chemical manufacturer, announced over the weekend they are rolling out a new class of fertilizer," the anchor reported.

"Take a look at the premarket trading," commented his co-anchor. "ChemoCo shares are sure to open much higher on this news. We're witnessing the waking of a sleeping giant."

Iris was in shock as she watched ChemoCo's stock shoot up in real time on TV. The talking heads had not only projected a rapid rise in price but were using words like "This is ushering in a new era for the company." The word on the Street was BUY. By the time the news report was over, Baxter had called, suggesting she take a leave of absence while they went through her files. He told her to sit tight for a week or two until the compliance boys sorted everything out. And, by the way, he asked, how did she know about ChemoCo? He heard it was a closely guarded secret.

Chapter 13

The bell rang, signaling the end of the morning session. It caught her by surprise, and she was disappointed that time had passed so quickly. Onawhim was having the most wonderful day. Gathering her lunch, she walked to the teacher's room feeling more satisfied than she had in a long time. Over the last couple of weeks, she had noticed a gradual change in her students' behavior. Each successive day, they seemed more attentive and better behaved. Not wanting to devote too much time analyzing it, Onawhim figured the months of reinforcing the same routine had finally sunk in. But she couldn't help feeling today was different. This Tuesday had started out normal enough. She arrived at her classroom before 8 a.m., like always. The children filed in at 8:05, the way they did every day since school began in September. As was her custom, she told the children to stow their coats and get their writing notebook out. Again, this was something she had been saying each morning without exception. On a typical day, Onawhim would start writing the day's lessons on the board, killing time until everyone was seated and ready.

A good number of the kids were always slow to follow her directions—shuffling papers and books, dawdling to their seats, talking, and acting out. Ordinarily, she'd have to reprimand one or two, fighting to be heard over their loud voices while trying to project more of a commanding presence. But today, the boys and girls promptly responded the first time she asked, and without her having to bang on her desk to hurry them along either. A brief word in her normal voice was all it took for her students to be seated, attentive, and quiet. Onawhim smiled to herself at the thought of it.

Arriving in the teacher's lounge, Onawhim walked over to her regular table, taking the remaining seat. As usual, the room was buzzing with conversation and activity. Teachers were reviewing papers, grading tests, gossiping, eating, and drinking. Sue Mooney looked up from the newspaper to catch Onawhim's arrival.

"You look like you're in a good mood," Sue remarked. Rarely did Onawhim show any emotion, but today, she looked positively happy. "Is it that boyfriend of yours?" Sue asked with a smile, fishing for some personal information. Most of the teachers were a gregarious group, but Onawhim was different. A self-described private person, Onawhim preferred keeping her personal life to herself.

"I'm having the most rewarding day," Onawhim offered. "The kids were so well-behaved. They seemed to have matured overnight! I was able to cover my entire lesson in half the time," she described incredulously. "And the students understood it. They answered all the questions. Even the more challenging kids had no problem. It was fantastic."

Her words escaped before she knew what was happening. And not only did she have Sue's undivided attention, but the other teachers at the table stopped what they were doing and looked up to listen as well. Her colleagues set aside their papers, lunches, and knitting and turned to Onawhim with undisguised interest. One after another asked questions, wanting to hear more, wanting to learn Onawhim's secret: Just what was her technique?

The rest of the day continued along in the same way. Onawhim's quiet, melodic voice seemed to float in the air. Each syllable rang with clarity. Her students couldn't be more engaged. But what was even more amazing was that they were listening, they actually HEARD what she was saying. She was getting through, making a difference, having an impact—they were getting it. This was every teacher's dream: to stand in front of a classroom of children and explain a new concept or idea, whether it was math, social studies, or English, and have every eye trained on your movements and every ear on your lesson. She had their attention for the entire time, and it seemed the more she spoke, the more attentive they became! It was so rewarding; Onawhim was sorry when the last bell rang.

After class, she had a round of parent/teacher conferences. It was all part of the school's "partnership for a better learning program," geared toward helping remedial students. Teachers were expected to meet with parents regularly and devise a learning plan. Onawhim had a number of children who fit into that category, and according to school policy, she had to monitor each child's progress and call meetings with the parents when necessary. This was her least favorite task. No parent wants to hear their child has special needs or is not performing up to standards. Typically, the parents were pricklier than the kids and would offer excuses as to why extra work shouldn't be assigned. She always had a hard time getting them to listen, and observed that the parents shared many of the same learning disabilities as their children.

Tommy Swope's mother was the first appointment after school. A loud, heavy-set woman, she always tried to bully Onawhim into revising her evaluation. It didn't matter how many examples of Tommy's work Onawhim provided; Mrs. Swope simply overlooked the obvious. Every meeting felt like a battle, which usually ended in a stalemate. Onawhim took a deep calming breath and steeled herself as the woman took her seat.

"Hi, Mrs. Swope, so good of you to come. Let me review Tommy's recent work," Onawhim began, getting right to the point. Small talk seemed to distract people and make it even harder for them to focus on the real purpose of the meeting.

"Yes, it's good to see you too, Ms. Young. Sure, let's see what my Tommy has been up to," Mrs. Swope replied pleasantly.

Her positive response took Onawhim by surprise. Typically, the woman would start each session by complaining: there was too much work, she didn't think this was what Tommy needed, and why he had to do more than the others, she'd demand. Then, when Onawhim got down to specifics, Mrs. Swope would get louder and even more defensive. Most of the time, it was an effort to keep control of the meeting, but that was not the case today.

Instead of speaking to a woman who wouldn't listen, Onawhim found Mrs. Swope interested and engaged. When it was time to review the next steps in helping Tommy understand the lessons, Mrs. Swope was in complete agreement. And when Onawhim handed over a pile of worksheets to be completed over the next couple of weeks, Mrs. Swope smiled and said. "Thank you."

Onawhim was in shock. What was even more fantastic was that the next two meetings went exactly the same way. Onawhim showed each parent their child's classroom work, explained the problems, suggested solutions, and offered additional homework as extra help. Without exception, the parents were calm and respectful. They listened, agreed with her assessment, and offered to do whatever she suggested.

On the drive home, Onawhim couldn't stop thinking about her day. It was utterly amazing. From the children in her classroom to her colleagues at lunch and even the parents after school, everyone was actively listening—they seemed to be absorbing her words directly into their brains. Not only was she being heard, but she was also influencing minds.

Chapter 14

Penna was sitting at her desk sorting through the mail—the bills in one pile, the checks in another, and the junk mail tossed into the circular file by the side of the desk. It was as routine a chore as one could imagine. The last couple of days had been pretty scary, and sitting in her familiar chair at the familiar desk in Uncle Dominic's familiar office was comforting. She was trying to remember when those unusual feelings started to happen.

The first time was two weeks ago. Coming home from work, Penna found her mother acting strangely again. It wasn't anything specific, but Penna had a sense that something about her wasn't right. Repeated questions were brushed off.

"It's nothing," her mother said. "Everything's okay. It's you, Penna. You're the one who's on edge."

But a little voice inside her head wasn't buying it. Penna KNEW it had to do with her health.

The odd thing was she couldn't for the life of her figure out why she was so certain. She asked after her mother's back, her knees, the mole on her left shoulder . . . Penna quizzed her mother about every ailment she could think of.

"Everything's fine," came her mother's reply, but something inside Penna's head couldn't let it go.

It wasn't until the next day that Penna learned the truth. Her mother had been to the doctor and was given a prescription to lower her high blood pressure and high cholesterol. The doctor told her mother to lose weight and exercise more. The harsh words and unpleasant consequences were so upsetting Penna's mother didn't want to talk about it. But what was different this time was Penna KNEW her mother's silence concerned a health-related issue. At first, she thought it was nothing more than one of those déjà vu premonitions. Penna got them fairly frequently and figured this to be another one of those unexplained hunches.

But that incident was nothing compared with those that followed. One can be expected to have an intuitive suspicion about close family members, maybe even a series of them. For example, Penna knew at one glance when something was wrong with her kids. Mothers around the world all share that innate sense. No, these other incidents were different. In the beginning, she thought them to be a series of odd coincidences, like the time 15 years ago she had watched an old movie on TV, one she had seen with her high school sweetheart. And then, out of the blue, she ran into him at the drugstore a couple of days later. That was weird, she remembered. But these episodes weren't like what she was experiencing either.

More recently, one happened when she was sitting at the desk going through the mail, like now. The door opens, and in comes Pauly, one of Uncle Dominic's regular bookies. Something didn't seem right.

"So what's doing, Pauly?" Penna asked.

Pauly looked her right in the eye and told her a story about his friend Chi-Chi, who got in trouble with the law and was arrested over the weekend. He went through all the details, right down to describing the cop who arrested him and how long he'd be in jail.

Since working with Uncle Dominic, she'd heard hundreds of these stories. She'd always listen politely and consider the facts with a grain of salt. Then she'd commiserate with Pauly or whoever was telling the tale, offer her sympathy, maybe even suggest sensible advice. After sharing (and refining) the story with Penna, Pauly would typically hurry along to Uncle Dominic's office and repeat the whole tragic tale, appealing to her uncle's well-known generosity.

But on that day, she KNEW exactly when Pauly was telling the truth and when he was making things up. "Pauly, it wasn't Chi-Chi that got arrested, was it?" she asked knowingly. "It was for dealing, not possession, right? Wait a minute. Didn't that guy get locked up with no bail because this was the third strike?"

Each question hit the mark, and before long, Pauly was shifting nervously, trying to square his version with the specifics she was outing. It was an amazing coincidence. As Pauly was telling the story, Penna seemed to KNOW all the facts.

"You want to see Uncle Dominic for some money, and you made up this whole story about needing to help a friend make bail to gain his sympathy," she stated. The words were out of her mouth before she could stop herself. Pauly looked at her in disbelief, but it would have been difficult to tell which of them was more surprised. It was bad enough that one of Uncle Dominic's friends would be looking to take advantage of his good nature, but the fact she saw through all the bull and KNEW the real story was simply unexplainable. Of course, it shook Pauly to the core. He couldn't believe she made him. With a look of utter confusion, Pauly turned and hurried away.

Later in the day, she asked Anthony, her eldest son, about his day at school. Typical with most boys, he would hardly reveal any details and more likely would offer the timeworn "Nothing happened." But this time, as he started to speak, she KNEW what he was going to say, knew what happened to him in the classroom, at the gym, during recess, and on the bus. With her son uttering a few words here and there, Penna was able to fill in all the details. She recounted what he did, right down to pushing Richie Santos off the swing. Anthony figured she had been following him around. How else would she have known Mrs. Pinkerton got mad when he wasn't paying attention? That his mother seemed to know all about his day didn't seem odd to the nine-year-old. Anthony was convinced this was merely another example of his mother's all-seeing abilities. But Penna was shocked into silence.

During the past few days, these events became more frequent. Penna noticed her insight was more pronounced as soon as someone spoke directly to her. She began experimenting with her newfound gift. Each day she'd flex her ability, like exercising a muscle—zooming in to focus on the speaker and tease out the information they were not so willing to share. As time went on, Penna learned to fine-tune her lie detector. Lately, some people simply opened up to her unbidden, sharing a torrent of information just by being in her presence, as if filling a need to get something off their chest. It was mostly a case of Too Much Information, necessitating more practice at controlling the flow.

Chapter 15

"Raychie, where are you? Come on, honey, or you'll be late," called Sollie from the bottom of the stairs. She glanced at her watch, thinking they were running behind schedule as usual, but to her great delight, she was early, much earlier than she could ever remember.

"I'm coming," her daughter replied with a hint of surprise in her voice.

Back in the kitchen, Sollie surveyed the counter and ran through a mental list of items. She had already packed her bag and had the sales folder for the meeting.

Could it be I'm ready to go? Sollie marveled. It seemed a bit farfetched, like snow in summer. Raychie bounded into the kitchen like a whirlwind, ready to complain and criticize her mother's tardiness, but was brought up short at the sight of her mother standing by the garage door, pocketbook in hand, waiting patiently to leave.

"Mom, are you really ready?" Raychie asked with a surprised tone.

"Of course, I am. I guess sometimes pigs do fly," was the only comeback Sollie could think of. This unexpected punctuality wasn't lost on Sollie either. After years of running late, she had forgotten what it was like to be on time—not to mention early.

Mother and daughter got in the car and had a pleasant drive to school. Sollie even remembered the correct drop-off point, and Raychie slid out of the car, pleased to arrive on time for once. The whole morning turned out to be so agreeable Sollie wore a smile the entire way to work. Traffic was lighter than usual, and she made every light. Arriving at the LISP parking lot, Sollie pulled into her favorite spot. She had 15 minutes to spare BEFORE the meeting was scheduled to begin! *This is a first,* she thought to herself. With a quick glance in the mirror, Sollie was pleased the dark circles around her eyes looked lighter, and the puffiness was not as pronounced. A quick smear of lipstick and she was ready for the morning meeting.

Strolling to her desk, she greeted some of the agents who were clustered around the coffee pot, waiting for it to finish the first of many brews of the day. Sollie called this group the Prep Squad—the office superwomen who drove expensive foreign cars, had gleaming nails, and were always perfectly coiffed. A surprised look grazed their semi-awake faces.

"In early today," Rosalind Cornwall observed. Sollie considered her the leader. Rosalind was one of those women who always looked as if she stepped out of a photo shoot for *Town & Country* magazine. Dressed in a starched, striped, buttoned-down shirt, khaki pants, and a navy blazer with not a single hair out of place, Rosalind was type-A personified.

Sollie never had much to do with the Prep Squad. Right from the beginning she had sensed their disapproval. Did they think she couldn't hear those snide comments about her scattered behavior and rumpled clothes? But today, she was getting a different vibe. Maybe it was because Sollie had been able to do her hair, put on a bit of makeup, and still had enough time to touch up her dress with an iron. Looking fresh and poised, she stopped at the coffee pot in time to snag the first cup.

"Hi," Sollie answered with a smile.

"Nice dress," Rosalind remarked, thinking Sollie must have lost some weight or got a new haircut or something. "Is it new?"

"Thank you, Rosalind," she replied, meeting the other woman's inquisitive stare. "I had forgotten all about it until I was cleaning out my closet. You can't believe the stuff I found hiding in the back. Well,

I think I'll go in and take my seat. Are you girls coming?" Sollie's effortless reply was so genuine it took Rosalind—and the rest of the Squad—by surprise. This was a side of Sollie they had missed, and they were intrigued enough to follow her into the conference room.

A few minutes later, Myra swept into the room. Setting her books and handouts on the table, it took a full minute before she noticed Sollie sitting across the way. But it was more than her presence that surprised the office manager. Sollie looked different. Unconsciously, Myra stopped in her tracks to stare at the woman she thought was the office's biggest loser. Sollie was sitting at the table chatting with Rosalind, Sheila, Brooke, and some of the other top agents. Was this the same Sollie Gold she had figured would never arrive on time?

"Oh, hello, Sollie," Myra called out, not able to let the moment pass. "I'm so glad you were able to make it. Is that a new haircut? Looks nice." Myra smiled. It was the best she'd seen Sollie look in years.

Once the meeting was over, Sollie took a moment to confer with Myra about her upcoming schedule. Sollie was expecting her current customer, the Lis, to make an offer on the Church Street house. This was a huge coup, as the property had been on the market for a while. Over the weekend, she was planning an open house on Saturday, along with taking out a new couple on Sunday. And then there was the presentation Myra and Sollie were making for a new house listing that afternoon. The facts about each transaction and appointment seemed to appear inside her head as if by special delivery. She came prepared with her notes but found she didn't need them.

"Would you like to go over the comps I found?" Sollie asked.

Myra stood in shock. "Uh, yes, let's go over the presentation in my office. Give me a couple of minutes to get myself organized," she stammered, staring at the poised, self-assured woman.

"Sure, no problem. Will be there in a few," Sollie replied as she gracefully turned to walk back to her desk. She was feeling GREAT! Sollie couldn't remember the last time Myra looked at her with respect: no snide remarks about mismatched shoes or rumpled clothing and no targeted barbs about her tardiness or lack of preparation.

Things seemed to be working out lately, and Sollie had no idea why. She noticed it had started a few weeks ago. Initially, she began arriving home from work earlier than usual. Those 35 minutes seemed to make all the difference in getting dinner on the table, and she had a little more time to clean up, too. Being on top of things had put a spring in her step.

A day or so later, Sollie woke before her alarm went off a full hour earlier than usual. Those additional minutes gave her plenty of time to organize the kitchen, pay some bills, and have the kids' breakfast ready when they got up. Even Stewie was impressed.

Then things started to snowball. More time meant she didn't have to rush and could remember things more easily. Instead of feeling scattered and under the gun, she was more composed and self-possessed, able to accomplish more tasks than at any other point in her life. It was amazing! Time seemed to stand still.

Over the weekend, she hit her stride. Tired of not being able to see inside her closet, Sollie finally changed that light bulb. One thing led to another, and her Saturday morning flew by as she cleaned and organized. For the first time in all their years of marriage, Sollie arranged her clothes and then Stewie's. From the shoes on the floor to the boxes piled on the shelves overhead, Sollie found dresses, skirts, and a host of other long-forgotten items that had been hidden from sight, creating a helluva lot more space than she ever thought possible.

By the time Sollie finished, the once cluttered and overcrowded closet was the picture of precision. But the real surprise was how quickly she completed the reorganization. At one time, she would have dreaded this job, and it would have likely taken days to go through everything. Not only was her closet organized, not only did she accomplish this thankless task in record time, but she felt great—both physically and emotionally!

After working on the closet, Sollie found time to prepare a nice lunch of potato salad and wraps using a variety of cold cuts she had in the fridge. Afterward, she went into the office, called a bunch of potential new listings, made an appointment with a new customer for Sunday, reviewed her plans for the week ahead, and still had time left over for food shopping. That evening, Sollie crafted another meal from scratch. Her dinner of Tuscan chicken smothered in a tangy wine sauce won raves from her family. By the time 8 p.m. rolled around, Sollie was still going strong and looked over at Stewie for a little marital excitement.

Thinking about the last couple of days, Sollie wondered what caused this incredible transformation: where once she was always late, now she was on time or even early. Where once she had been forever misplacing things, now she could put her hands on her keys, work notes, bills—without missing a beat. Where once her appearance was always rumpled, her hair unkempt, clothes wrinkled, now she was neat, pressed, and attractive. Her kids stopped complaining, and Stewie went to sleep with a smile on his face for the first time in months. She felt composed, competent, and in control for the first time in her life. It was incredible.

Glancing at her watch, time seemed to have stood still. A mere six minutes passed, and she had already cleaned her desk and was ready for the day. Sollie decided to fill her cup with more coffee on the way to Myra's office. It was a pleasant coincidence that another pot happened to finish brewing just as she walked by. Settling in across the desk from Myra, Sollie waited patiently until her manager finished a phone call.

"Yes, not to worry, I'll tell her. You did the right thing. We always want to hear feedback from our customers. As a service business, we rely on the goodwill of people like yourself. You can count on me to pass this information along to the team," Myra replied smoothly into the phone. No one could tame the savage beast like Myra, who was at her best when dealing with difficult clients.

Hanging up, Myra's typically intense look melted into a smile. "Sollie, you're never going to guess who that was! The Lis, your customers on the Church Street house. Well, they called to tell me personally what a wonderful agent you've been and how smooth and painless the whole transaction went. They couldn't say enough—the compliments came gushing out. In fact, they are sending some family members over for you to work with and are planning to recommend you and LISP to everyone they know," Myra said, beaming with approval.

"I don't think I did anything different than any other time." Sollie blushed, looking pleasantly surprised. "I helped them the best way I knew how. I'm honestly surprised they took the time to call." It was a special moment for Sollie. It had been a long time since she had been on the receiving end of Myra's esteem, and it felt good.

"Whatever you did these people think you're some kind of deity." Frankly, Myra couldn't believe it herself. The woman sitting across the desk looked composed and self-possessed. Was this the same Sollie Gold who, for the last four years, arrived late to every sales meeting, showed up in mismatched shoes, and always looked like an unmade bed? "I don't know what you're doing, but keep at it. It seems to be working beautifully," she concluded.

Chapter 16

Gil found Glynn at her office inside the law library, surrounded by a pile of reference books and typing away in front of an active computer screen. So engrossed in her project she didn't hear him enter. Standing off to the side, he watched his wife furrow her brow and stop for a minute as she gazed unfocused at some faraway point before returning to her prose. With a pencil clenched in her teeth and notepads strewn across the table, Glynn's quiet determination permeated the room. He relished this brief moment, able to watch her undetected. Checking to see if they were alone, Gil quietly strolled over and gave his wife a lover's kiss on the neck.

"Oh!" she exclaimed at his touch, looking up from the computer into a pair of light-brown eyes. Before another sound escaped, Gil covered her lips with his, thoroughly enjoying their surreptitious encounter. He wanted to undo her blouse but satisfied himself with an illicit feel, rubbing a nipple that reflexively popped to attention. The sound of someone outside the door caused Gil to pull away, but he remained leaning over, pretending to read what was on the computer screen, thankful no one could see the blush on his wife's cheeks or the growing bulge in his pants.

"I thought I'd stop in and see if you were almost ready to leave," he said. It was rare that Gil ever left the office before 6 p.m. But today was different.

"You mean you're done for the day?" she asked incredulously. "It's only Friday, moments from 5 p.m."

Her sarcasm hit its mark. "I know, I know, half a day?" he mimicked in a voice capturing her inflection perfectly. "I could stay and work a couple more hours, but I thought we'd celebrate." He was hinting at something big. Before she could respond with questions of her own, Gil delivered the news.

"Guess who received the LIMBO invite?" he teased, slowly drawing his hand out from behind his back.

"It came? You got the letter? Let's see," Glynn squealed, almost grabbing it.

Glynn fingered the letter gingerly. The distinguished LIMBO swinging-door logo was engraved on a fine white bond with the list of current officers and board directors displayed down the left margin. An invitation to sit on the LIMBO executive board was highly coveted. Members almost never relinquished their seats, and it was rarer still for an attorney to be asked to join.

"Dear Mr. Patrick," she read, "By unanimous vote, we are pleased to invite you. . ." her voice trailed off as if it were a sacrilege to read the rest out loud.

"Oh, Gil," she exclaimed after she finished. "I'm so proud. This is wonderful," and gave her beaming husband a congratulatory kiss, indifferent to who may be walking by.

"It's great, isn't it?" Gil said with pride. "I called Quint and Lowell to see if they wanted to join us for a drink. I thought we'd celebrate with a romantic dinner at . . ." Gil paused for dramatic effect, The Barge."

"You got reservations at The Barge?" Glynn exclaimed.

"Perks of the position," was all he would say, but the look on his face did most of the talking. "Did I mention I spoke with Arnie Holtzmann personally?" Glynn looked dumbfounded. "He called to extend the invitation. Dinner at The Barge was his idea, and by the way, it's their treat!" Gil relayed, beaming as if light were radiating out of his pores.

"Are you sure? I can throw together a couple of grilled chicken breasts . . ." Glynn teased.

"You mean you don't want to go?" Gil asked in a mocking tone.

"I didn't say that," she said, smiling before turning serious.

"Look," she said, speaking slowly as her idea started to gel. "Maybe I can help out at LIMBO. I'm sure the board wouldn't mind if you offered the services of your law firm's head researcher. There might be projects to investigate or proposals I could review—you know, behind-the-scenes stuff. No one need know," Glynn suggested.

Gil laughed. He not only welcomed her support but couldn't help thinking how cute she looked promoting her earnest proposal. "I'm sure there will be more than enough time for that, but I thank you on behalf of the LIMBO board just the same," he said in his mock trial voice. "So, what are you working on? You looked pretty involved when I walked in."

"I got this new project. It's for one of Marshall's clients, Crystal Clam Wineries."

"Are they the ones with the clam shell on the label?" Gil asked. "They have a pretty good white if I remember."

"Right. We had one of their wines at dinner on February 10th," Glynn replied.

"Really, it was February 10th? You sound quite sure of the date?"

A perplexed expression crossed her face. "Yes, and I can even recall the exact bottle and what we ordered. Crystal Clam is not only popular. They've won numerous awards in California and Europe. If it wasn't for Crystal Clam, there probably wouldn't be a wine industry on Long Island," Glynn finished.

Surprised, Gil couldn't believe she was recalling all this trivia. "So, what's Marshall doing for them? Is there a lawsuit or something?"

"It seems Crystal Clam and the other wine growers have been testing this new type of fertilizer. They love the stuff. It's supposed to be highly effective in addition to being environmentally friendly."

"Sounds almost too good to be true."

"No kidding. The product, SCAB (<u>S</u>elective <u>C</u>hemical <u>A</u>gricultural <u>B</u>ioproducts), is made by ChemoCo, the giant agricultural company. It's been in field tests for a couple of years and has an impressive track record of success. The wine growers can't get enough of it.

"Now that the tests are complete and the results are in, everyone on the East End is waiting for LICE to proclaim SCAB safe and approve it for agricultural use. But the scuttlebutt is LICE's Director, Bill McCleary, is holding things up. Possibly not granting approval at all. Needless to say, the wine growers are not happy."

"Yeah, I've worked with some of those GRowLers (Wine Growers League.) They can be a vocal bunch, and pretty well-connected too," Gil interjected.

"Ted Landis, owner of Crystal Clam Winery and also president of the Wine Growers League, came to Marshall for help. The GRowLers are looking into every angle to push through SCAB's approval. ChemoCo's claim is that the product does not fall into the traditional category of chemical fertilizer because it is all-natural. And the GRowLers are piggybacking on the all-natural claim, alleging that because SCAB is biodegradable, LICE's environmental regulations shouldn't apply."

"So let me get this straight—Marshall thinks that because SCAB is biodegradable, we should be able to do an end-run around LICE?"

"Well, yes. That's what I'm researching," Glynn replied. "Marshall told Ted and his GRowLers that we're exploring loopholes. Maybe it'll be enough to leverage LICE so the wine growers can continue using the product as we wait for the testing results and LICE's approval."

Gil knew all about LICE (Long Island Conservation and Environment) and their militant director, Bill McCleary. Gil had met McCleary a couple of times and found the man bright, passionate, and more than a little self-righteous. After running LICE for almost 30 years, McCleary had made as many enemies as friends, partly due to his famous take-no-prisoners tactics when it came to protecting the environment. In fact, there was a rumor circulating that the governor was looking to ease McCleary out and replace him with someone who was on better terms with local businesses.

"Do you think there's a way to circumvent LICE?" Gil asked, thinking that could create quite a brouhaha.

"Marshall thinks so. If not, there's a chance the GRowLers will file a lawsuit against LICE. Then there's his plan to snag ChemoCo as a new client. They have a huge stake in getting SCAB approved. You know how it is when Marshall smells a business opportunity. There are sure to be some big fees if this goes to court. Who knows where it could land?

"He's pulled me off other projects so I can devote all my time and attention researching the whole SCAB/LICE issue. I'm not sure yet, but it may be possible to do an end-run around LICE. There appears to be nothing in the Long Island Conservation and Environment's charter that allows them to regulate nontoxic, biodegradable chemicals. Anyway, LICE is sitting on their report, and it's one of this year's best-kept secrets."

Gil remembered Arnie Holtzmann mentioning something about SCAB and ChemoCo at lunch the other day. "If LICE bans SCAB, it'll piss off a lot of people on the East End—not the least of which would be the Wine Council," Gil mused, thinking about ten steps ahead. "This could be a pivotal issue, especially because McCleary may have few friends left in high places."

"There was no shortage of articles and editorials both praising and lambasting the powerful environmentalist. The time may be right for SCAB," Glynn suggested, "and this could be a battle McCleary might end up losing."

Gil loved it when Glynn was passionate about an issue. He knew if anyone could find a way to get ChemoCo and SCAB around LICE's requirements and nitpicking, it was Glynn. Underneath that cute, perky exterior, she could be a powerful force, wielding details and unearthing statistics with deadly accuracy. She had a razor-sharp intellect and always investigated an issue from all sides before taking a position. You had better be prepared when debating Glynn—something Gil had learned firsthand.

Reluctant to leave his wife, Gil could see she wasn't ready to go. "Come to The Legal Pad when you're done," Gil suggested on the way out. She barely lifted her head to say goodbye.

Part 3
Revelations

104

Chapter 17

Sollie was the first to arrive at Kuriko, the quiet little Japanese restaurant Onawhim chose. She couldn't believe it was only a month since their last book group meeting—it felt like ages ago. Sollie finished reading *The Generous Geisha* in record time. In fact, she had completed two other books as well. *That is a first*, she thought. *One more eerie instance of my new talent* . . . the results of which Sollie still couldn't believe. Her kids had developed a new appreciation for their mom, work was great—she was on track to win the salesperson of the month award—and Stewie was the beneficiary of her newfound increase in sexual energy. And now, 20 minutes early, she had plenty of time to kill.

"Hi, Sollie. I had a feeling you'd be the first to arrive. Strange, huh?" commented Iris upon entering from the parking lot. "I guess it's not as strange as some of the other stuff I seem to know." Iris delivered this last remark without thinking. She'd been so surprised by recent events that knowing Sollie would be early didn't even strike her as odd. But that wasn't what stopped Iris in her tracks. The once-frumpy Sollie Gold was transformed. She looked well-rested, well-groomed, and even thinner as if Sollie had returned from a month at an upscale spa.

"You look great," Iris complimented her. "What have you been doing?"

"My life has totally changed since our last meeting. You wouldn't believe the new me! I'm a hundred times more organized, always punctual, and even have time to cook and clean—unheard of," Sollie replied, beaming. "What's going on with you?"

"It seems we both have changes to report. This past month, I've been on an unplanned sabbatical from my office, which has turned into the most welcome vacation. But the best news is I've been on some sort of lucky streak with my stock picks. It's like I know which stocks will be going up and when they'll go down. I've made more money in the last couple of weeks than in my entire career!"

Before they could continue, Penna and Onawhim arrived. The four girls were immediately shown to a table in the back. Even though the restaurant was empty, they continued talking in hushed tones.

"You'll never believe what's been happening," Penna blurted out. "I've gone through some sort of transformation. People come into the office and tell me things, like personal stuff, you'd only reveal to a close friend or relative, and without me asking, as if I'm some sort of magical confessional. All it takes is one look, and a profusion of details comes spewing out. But there's more! I can tell if the person speaking is giving me honesty or a load of bull. It happens at the office with Uncle Dominic's cronies, at home with my kids, and with my mother, too. I can even remind them of things they forget to mention! At first, it freaked me out. 'What the hell is this?' I thought. It wasn't until I tried to tune in and control my focus that I finally got a handle on things. Gradually, I've learned how to zero in or pull back while concentrating on what the person was saying, like a mental yo-yo. Thankfully, it worked because I was afraid I was losing my mind. Now I can tell when someone is embellishing a story, outright lying, or simply leaving things out. Let's say it's been useful in dealing with Uncle Dominic's offbeat friends and clients. I'm calling it 'mind-dropping,'" Penna concluded with a smile.

Glynn arrived at the end of Penna's story. She noticed immediately how different each of her friends looked, and not because they were all staring wide-eyed after hearing Penna's astonishing account.

"Yes, I too have noticed something extraordinary," Onawhim declared. Her clear, sparkling voice caused all four women to turn.

"It's my voice. It has a power I've never known before. When I speak, whether it's to my class, to other teachers, or even to parents—anyone, really—I notice they are focusing on me, truly listening to what I'm saying. But it is more than merely hearing my words. I'm able to imprint my ideas, thoughts, advice, or whatever directly on the listener's mind.

"For example, I've observed each of my students paying attention in class. Their parents are following the recommendations I offer and even agree with me. Friends and strangers alike take my offhand remarks seriously; they are acting on the littlest things I say." Onawhim's velvet-coated voice mesmerized the table. As if in a trance, each of her friends KNEW at once what she was describing.

Both Iris and Sollie shared their special gifts and unusual experiences, too. Glynn listened raptly, considering the probability this was some sort of extraordinary coincidence.

"If I understand correctly, each one of us has recently identified some sort of unique talent," Glynn suggested. "Sollie is super productive—shifting time, even—allowing her to devote more time to herself, her family, and her job. Iris is able to predict stock prices. Maybe only in the short term, but with surprising accuracy. Penna zeros in on the truth and the intentions of the speaker, sort of like a human lie detector. And Onawhim's quiet, disarming personality has become more persuasive than she ever thought possible," she summarized.

"What about you?" Iris asked, already guessing what the answer would be.

"Well, I seem to be able to connect the dots. Everything I read, hear, or see—every iota of information somehow becomes imprinted in my brain. I'm able to remember enormous bits of unrelated facts, sort of like a data download, and am then able to put it all together. I can almost feel my brain cataloging and categorizing information, being able to draw inferences and develop conclusions, sometimes in topics I never would have considered. It's like I'm the smartest person in the room," Glynn admitted quietly, not as thrilled with her gift as the others.

"In fact, I was working on a project for the head of my law firm. It entailed doing a lot of legal research, but also understanding chemical properties. I spent a couple of evenings reading college chemistry textbooks—fascinating!" Glynn noticed the surprise in four pairs of eyes.

"Reading about chemistry was easy. I taught myself enough to provide valuable insights about a key chemical formula. My report was pretty comprehensive, if I do say so myself," concluded Glynn, glowing with pride at the complexity of her work.

The four other women were stunned at the enormity of Glynn's new ability. Glynn paused for a moment before continuing. "It's obvious something profound happened to each one of us, and I think I know what it is.

"Do you remember the cloud we saw in the parking lot of The Good Grill after our last meeting? I can still recall that distinctive smell—it was the most intense aroma of freshly mowed grass. It filled the air, permeated my hair and skin as I inhaled great lungfuls deep into my body," she said, looking around the table. As Glynn's gaze rested on each of her book group friends, they spoke in turn about the unique aroma each of them experienced. One by one, they described a fragrance different from the others but no less exceptional. And each was able to trace the start of their new abilities to that night.

"How did this happen?" Sollie asked. "Why us?"

"I believe there was something in that cloud that affected us, each in a different way," Glynn suggested. "I don't know how or why, but I'm sure it has something to do with the building across from The

Good Grill. That's the LIQuID research facility, an incubator for upcoming biotechnology companies. If I had to guess, I'd say that cloud was a gas composed of escaped chemicals from some research experiment, and we happened to be downwind at just the right time."

"I wouldn't be surprised if it could happen again," offered Iris. "Maybe even tonight."

"I don't know about you, but another cloud of unknown chemicals being released into the atmosphere affecting unsuspecting people, like we were affected, is distressing," Onawhim said. "I don't think we should sit by and allow that to happen. We must do something." She placed an increased emphasis on her suggestion, and others nodded silently in agreement.

"Let's see a show of hands," Glynn suggested. "Who's up for going to that plant tonight to see what's going on?"

It was unanimous. No one considered that the place might be closed or they might be more successful during business hours. In fact, Iris recommended they leave right away in order to arrive in plenty of time before the next accident.

Chapter 18

All five stood as if on cue. Dinner was forgotten. The book discussion on *The Generous Geisha* would have to wait. Glynn offered to drive, as she was best informed about the plant. What started out as a fairly routine evening turned into a public service mission to protect the community. On the way to the LIQuID facility, they took turns describing some of their recent experiences. Each story was laced with feelings of bewilderment, amazement, and implausibility, but they also felt profoundly transformed and believed they were better for it, whatever it was.

"Look, I don't know about the rest of you, but I'm kind of happy this happened," Sollie said. "Don't get me wrong. I'm not in favor of breathing in unknown chemicals, even if it did smell like chocolate, but I have to admit the new and improved Sollie is better."

"I feel that way too," Onawhim chimed in. "I think we all can relate. But this is about a larger issue. Why should people be allowed to release chemicals into the atmosphere and not be held responsible? What if it affects our health? What if we get sick from it?" She was pretty passionate about the moral implications. A single mental thrust went a long way toward influencing the group.

"I may be benefiting from some unexplained change in my brain, but I wasn't unhappy before. I didn't ask for this or to be under investigation at my firm, although it's hard to complain after making a boatful of money," added Iris. "I want to know what I inhaled that night, but more importantly, I want to know who these people are."

"We can't allow them to get away with this. We need to uncover the truth and get to the bottom of whatever happened," Penna concluded.

Driving, Glynn was content to listen to the others as she thought about the building they were going to visit. An article about LIQuID appeared in her mind unbidden. She could picture the article and see the actual page as if it were right in front of her.

"This place was developed under a program from LIMBO, Long Island Metro Business Organization, in order to support biotechnology incubators," Glynn announced as if reading directly from the article. "It's called LIQuID—Long Island Quality Intellectual Development—a nonprofit entity that gets some of its funding from the government. LIQuID is charged with supporting startup technology companies and independent researchers. The goal is to nurture these biotech startups and give them guidance and business expertise to help them get up and running. By bringing them together under one roof, each entity would realize financial benefits based on the economies of scale and allow their projects to progress more easily. LIQuID would reap the rewards should one of their discoveries become a commercial success."

Turning the corner, the LIQuID facility loomed directly in front of them. It was a large, imposing structure taking up two square blocks. Glynn continued her explanation as she drove into the parking lot.

"Built in the late 19th century, this building was formerly known as the Wallace Fabric Mill," Glynn recited. "In its hay day, the old Wallace Fabric Mill churned out miles of fabrics sold by the yard and shipped around the world. But by the mid-twentieth century, fabric manufacturing in the US was on the decline and the mill's operating expenses were fast outpacing its revenues. The place was hemorrhaging money. Rising costs, along with cheap foreign labor, turned the Wallace Fabric Mill into the classic manufacturing white elephant. Finally, sometime in the '60s, it was abandoned and boarded up, sitting vacant for decades, a sad example of changing economic realities. In LIMBO's search for a new technology campus, the old

Wallace Fabric Mill fit the bill. Purchased on the cheap, LIQuID received grants to gut and renovate it, turning the building into a state-of-the-art, high-tech incubator," she summarized, still surprised at being able to access all those details so readily.

The car fell silent as Glynn drove into the entrance and passed the now-vacant guardhouse. The place looked deserted, except for a few lone cars scattered across an empty parking lot. Thankfully, working streetlights dotted the property, illuminating the vast unfriendly exterior. Glynn swung into a convenient spot and turned the engine off. The girls sat for a minute, contemplating their next move. No one rushed to exit the vehicle, preferring the warm interior to the cold of the unknown outside.

"Come on. Let's go find out who we can talk to," suggested Onawhim.

The women herded themselves along the path to the main entrance. Reaching a series of front doors, Iris expertly chose the only unlocked door, ushering everyone inside. The barren, inhospitable interior did little to take the chill out of the early May evening. Fluorescent lighting gave the unimpressive lobby an institutional feel. Two dozen or so modern metal-and-vinyl chairs outlined a seating perimeter punctuated by a few randomly placed chrome end tables to break up the monotony. They walked toward a huge greeter's counter constructed of black stone, which seemed to grow up from the floor. An open book on top reading "Please Sign In" had a few visitor names scribbled below. The place was dead quiet, the only sound coming from the click-clack of their heels as they walked across the cold stone floor.

"Helloooo! Is anyone here?" Sollie called. She was comfortable entering buildings thought to be empty.

"Here comes someone now," Iris mentioned.

A young man emerged from a side door. He was dressed in a security uniform and sported a mildly annoyed expression.

"Excuse me, ladies," he began. "We're closed. Come back tomorrow and someone will be able to help you."

Penna ignored his remarks. "We know the place is closed to visitors, but you are the person we need to speak with. You're Kevin, right?" she asked, reading his name tag.

Kevin stared. "Right now, there's no one here for you to speak with. The place is closed. I'm not the one who can help you."

"We know there's a biotech group here. We have a few questions for them. Once we satisfy our curiosity about the research they're conducting, we'll leave and you can go back to watching TV," Penna replied matter-of-factly.

He looked as if he saw a ghost.

"Could you please explain what is being researched here?" Onawhim asked with some intensity. Her self-confident tone rang around the barren lobby.

"The work here is highly classified," Kevin replied, unable to stop himself from answering, "and very technical. We're not allowed to discuss what's going on in some of the labs. I wouldn't want you nice ladies getting into trouble. I'm going to have to ask you to leave now."

Onawhim decided to keep pressing for more information. "We believe there was some gas released from here about four weeks ago. We must know more about this event, especially the kind of chemicals in that gas."

"You said four weeks ago," Kevin repeated, tilting his head, unable to resist responding to her request. "Let me think. There's been a number of biohazard ventings over the last couple of months." He couldn't believe he was revealing information to this small, unassuming Asian woman. She reminded him of the guys in Lab 8.

"Kevin, what about the guys in Lab 8?" Penna asked as if she had read his mind. "Aren't they doing some sort of research concerning the brain?"

Again, he was shocked at her inside knowledge. How did these women know so much about this top-secret facility? "Are you investigators from the government or something?"

"Look, Kevin, it's obvious we know the people in Lab 8 are still here working. We're concerned there may be another problem—a venting, as you said. All we want to do is prevent this from happening . . . again," Glynn said, summing things up.

"Time's wasting. We need to speak with those guys now before there's another accident. What the hell kind of research are they doing?" Sollie asked, trying to impress a sense of urgency on the guard.

"I know it won't be a problem if we went back there now. Why not show us the way and make the introduction?" Onawhim suggested pointedly in her composed, serene voice.

Chapter 19

Even though it went against established procedures, Kevin decided it was easier to go along than resist.

The five women followed behind a perplexed Kevin through the security door as he led the way to Lab 8. The long, brightly lit hallways were painted a mustard yellow and gray. The place was spotless. Everything looked identical except for discreet dark gray signs identifying every door they passed. The hallways seemed endless. They walked in silence except for the women's heels echoing on the floor, but this time, the clacking was joined by the rhythmic squish-squash of Kevin's rubber soles. The security guard took them through a series of checkpoints, sliding his ID through multiple scanners and holding open heavy security doors. Finally, they arrived at the entrance to Lab 8. The door appeared more heavily reinforced than any they had passed. Two different security checks were required.

Kevin immediately keyed the intercom. "Hey, guys, Kevin here. I have some visitors that need to speak with you."

They waited in silence for a response.

"What? We don't have time for this now. Tell them to come back in the morning," an anonymous voice barked.

Onawhim gently stepped up to the speaker and pressed the Talk button. "Tomorrow will be too late. We need to speak with you now. Please, won't you take a minute to hear what we have to say?"

A short second passed before the intercom came to life again. "It looks as if the reaction may be in hyperactivity again," they heard. "Shut things down for now. I'm breaking the seal to see what's going on," the voice on the other side of the door said. The intercom fell silent as they waited for the door to Lab 8 to open. Meanwhile, Sollie closed her eyes and thought about speeding things up.

"It'll be a minute until they can shut down the experiment," Kevin offered. "These guys are here around the clock. They're always working," he chattered, trying to break the oppressive silence.

"It's something to do with brain research, isn't it?" Penna asked.

"I wouldn't be surprised if they're close to making an important discovery," Iris offered. "Do they have a name for their company yet?"

In less than 30 seconds, the heavy door swung open to reveal someone clad from head to foot in protective lab suit. He reached to remove the face mask, goggles, and other gear that protected him from exposure to their chemical experiments. As he stepped forward, Onawhim was immediately struck by his fine features and serene manner. Their eyes locked for a moment and she felt strangely drawn to this unknown man.

"My name is Ray, short for Tang Rae-Chung, and I'm the team leader. What's so important that you need to interrupt our experiment?" he asked in a quiet, determined voice.

Glynn stepped forward, assuming the role of spokesperson. "I'm Glynn Patrick, and we believe we've been affected by something vented from your lab a month ago. We want to know what you're working on."

Ray looked at each of the women, lingering a little longer on Onawhim until he settled his stare at Kevin.

"Hey, man, don't look at me," Kevin volunteered defensively. "They wouldn't take no for an answer."

"Tell me what happened," Ray asked the group, unwilling to allow them inside until his question was satisfied. Each of them took turns describing what they experienced in that parking lot across the street, going into particular detail about the cloud and the unique aromas they inhaled.

Onawhim spoke last and summed up their recent experiences and new abilities. "We cannot deny we have benefited from these changes, but that's beside the point. We have a right to know what you're working on," she concluded with quiet intensity.

"Yes, you are right," Ray said, unable to look away. "Won't you follow me inside and my colleagues and I will show you."

They entered a large room filled with all manner of scientific equipment, from computer terminals displaying complex 3-dimensional images to machines containing medical samples to sophisticated microscopes. The other members of Ray's team had already unmasked and stood silent as introductions were made. The next 30 minutes passed quickly as Ray explained, mostly in complex scientific terms, their background and research theories. When he finished, the room fell silent as the female visitors slowly digested Ray's dissertation.

Glynn was the first to speak. "Let me make sure I understand what you're saying," she began, unable to resist summarizing and clarifying his remarks. "Your research hypothesis starts off theorizing that the brain uses only a small percentage of its capacity. Meaning most of us utilize a fraction of what our brains are capable of, leaving behind a wealth of unused brainpower. Your team has identified certain powerful chemicals, found only in the brain, which are responsible for turning on brain function, like a chemical On switch. For the past six months, your research has been aimed at investigating these special enzymes. But success has been elusive, and isolating those particular chemicals proved difficult. They are volatile, which caused the problems experienced in many of your experiments. The unpredictable nature of these chemicals resulted in your loss of control, requiring venting to expel the vapors and thereby releasing these unknown and possibly volatile elements into the atmosphere. Am I correct so far?" Glynn asked dryly, already certain she didn't leave anything out.

Ray nodded as she continued.

"It seems one of these unplanned events happened about a month ago, and Kevin here," Glynn gestured toward their security guard guide, "hit the Vent button, sucking all these complex chemicals outside, where they coalesced and floated over the parking lot of The Good Grill to ultimately become inhaled into our bodies." Glynn gave a questioning look at Penna, wanting to make sure there was nothing Ray had left out.

"I might not have understood everything they said, but I know they're giving us the whole story," Penna affirmed.

"So, in other words, we're some kind of real-life guinea pigs, breathing in a bunch of unknown and possibly harmful gases because your experiment got away from you." Sollie fumed, pissed off that the ineptitude of a bunch of kids could have such far-reaching consequences.

"I seem to be able to guess at the future with a degree of certainty that defies the odds," Iris volunteered. "I may not have an advanced degree in bioscience, but I feel certain we will continue to be influenced by those chemicals for the foreseeable future," Iris declared.

"It seems your experiments were successful," Onawhim remarked quietly. "We have developed new and powerful abilities, each unique, individual, and different from the others. Can you tell us what else we should expect, and what the health risks are?"

"We do not know why or how these results were produced and do not have a clue as to how we can reverse them," Ray added apologetically, speaking for his team. "This is uncharted territory. We can't say what the risk to your health will be, whether in a day, a week, or even a year. But we will not leave you to fend for yourselves. Please let us work with you toward finding some answers. More research is the only way to better understand these mystery enzymes and their effect on the body." This was the best suggestion Ray could offer.

Glynn led the girls into a corner to discuss their options as they considered Ray's proposal. For all their schooling and smarts, those scientists seemed as surprised and clueless by the outcome as their unwitting subjects. In the end, there didn't seem to be a choice. Glynn, Onawhim, Sollie, Iris, and Penna reluctantly agreed to become human test subjects. Ray took out his marker and penned "LIQuID 5" on a new folder.

"We should get your information now," Ray suggested, marshaling the other researchers, "along with a blood sample from each of you. We will need you back here in two weeks."

Glynn responded for her friends. "Look, we don't want to worry our families or call attention to ourselves at work. I think it would be better if we came at night, around this time. Everyone will think we're going to another book club meeting."

Ray agreed, and it was arranged the women would return in two weeks at 7:00 p.m. The scientists would devote their efforts to analyzing the data and individual blood samples, and the five subjects would return to their everyday lives, acting as if nothing had happened. Kevin was sworn to secrecy. No one wanted word of the accident to leak, whether inside LIQuID or out.

As the women prepared to leave, Onawhim's eyes met Ray's, and she said in her most persuasive voice, 'I know you will do your best.'

His solemn expression conveyed only half of what he was thinking. The other half, Ray decided to keep to himself.

Chapter 20

"Hi, Rose. Is Marshall around? I'd like to meet with him when he has a minute. I think I've found something on McCleary and LICE that he'll find interesting," Glynn said, standing in front of Marshall's secretary's desk instead of calling on the phone for an appointment.

Usually protective of her boss, Rose generally kept people away, but she knew he was waiting for Glynn's report. In fact, not only was Marshall waiting, but both his client Crystal Clam Wineries, along with his golf buddy and LIMBO honcho A Holtz (the nickname for Arnie Holtzmann, which was widely used around the office), were anxious to hear her report, too. Rose didn't know all the details, but she was smart enough to put two and two together. It had something to do with a potential new client—ChemoCo, remembering one of Marshall's phone conversations. She overheard Marshall state he hoped ChemoCo would open a new office on Long Island. Rose made it her business to pay close attention to all Marshall's calls. She prided herself on being well-informed. But it was beyond her imagination as to how Glynn's research played into things.

Seeing a smug smile on Glynn's face as she stood in front of her desk, Rose guessed the report would make her boss happy. "One minute, dear," Rose purred as she intercommed Marshall, interrupting a phone conversation with his wife.

124

Chapter 21

Marshall Matlock was one of the founding partners of Shuster, Yleskin, and Matlock and the primary force behind its success. It didn't matter if he was on the golf course, playing tennis, searching out the latest high-tech gadget, or handling the firm's prestigious clients; winning was all Marshall cared about. Shrewd and cunning, Marshall had a well-earned take-no-prisoners reputation. He specialized in corporate law, successfully representing some of the biggest companies on Long Island.

In their younger days, Marshall Matlock and Arnie Holtzmann would run into each other at various political fundraisers. They were both ambitious, driven young men looking to make names for themselves. Marshall was seeking to build his law firm and ingratiate himself with judges and politicians, while Arnie was scouring the landscape for business leaders to recruit for his new Long Island Metro Business Organization. The two hit it off and had been competitive golf players and business colleagues for more than 30 years.

Over the years, Marshall had heard all about Arnie's continual confrontations with Bill McCleary, the head of LICE. McCleary was known to be stubborn, especially when defending LICE's policies; he could dig in like a real lice infestation. The environmental group always seemed to be stonewalling every new business initiative Arnie's LIMBO would champion. Lately, during their weekly golf game, Arnie expressed renewed complaints about LICE's stall tactics concerning a new fertilizer/weed killer. "Tough luck" would have been Marshall's typical blasé response . . . until about three weeks ago. That's when he received a call from his client, Crystal Clam Wineries, looking for legal help regarding the SCAB issue.

Crystal Clam was one of the oldest and most successful wineries on Long Island's environmentally fragile East End. They had been experimenting with ChemoCo's new eco-friendly fertilizer for the past couple of years with stellar results. Now that the testing phase was over, Crystal Clam wanted unrestricted access to SCAB, as did almost everyone else in the agricultural field. Unfortunately, there seemed to be a problem in the approval process. Not only was LICE dragging its feet, but McCleary had given some interviews lately hinting that SCAB might not meet LICE's environmental guidelines.

Talk on the street suggested LICE was not going to approve SCAB, creating an uproar from the Wine Growers League, better known as the GRowLers, whose members could be pretty vocal. The GRowLers, Crystal Clam, and every other significant agricultural operator on the East End were up in arms. Tremendous pressure was being exerted on anyone who could influence the approval process, with Arnie Holtzmann's LIMBO topping the list. It was a no-brainer when Arnie turned to his old friend for help.

Marshall listened with half an ear as A Holtz ranted about his personal battle with McCleary. These animated outbursts were nothing new. But when Arnie mentioned that ChemoCo was considering Long Island as a home for a new R&D plant and may be looking for legal representation, Marshall took notice. The ChemoCo board was considering many locations. It seemed obvious that getting SCAB approved by McCleary and LICE would tip the scales in favor of Long Island. There was no doubt landing the ChemoCo account for Shylock would be another feather in an already impressive headdress for Marshall. And this was exactly what Arnie Holtzmann was counting: on a fired-up Marshall Matlock would commit the resources of his firm to finding a way around McCleary and LICE. Moments after Rose signaled Glynn's arrival, Marshall Matlock was striding out of his office with a broad smile and a welcoming arm as he smoothly ushered Glynn into his office. "Glynn, come in. Let's sit over by the windows."

Marshall escorted Glynn to a lovely sitting area arranged in one corner of his expansive office. It was much more informal than peering over his enormous mahogany desk. The classic carved wood furniture was elegant and expensive. The couch and chairs were upholstered in muted tones of burgundy and gold.

"Can I get you anything? Something to drink—coffee, soda?" Marshall was known for his hospitality and style. The next couple of minutes were taken with social pleasantries and polite inquiries into family and mutual acquaintances.

"I was talking to Arnie Holtzmann about you," Marshall said. "You know who he is, right? The head of LIMBO. Of course, he's thrilled to have Gil on their board—we all are. It's a big honor. Gil will get great exposure," Marshall said, feeling chatty. Finally, when the right amount of time had passed, he was ready to learn the real reason for her visit.

"So, what did you find out about McCleary and LICE?" he asked, fixing Glynn with his signature intense stare, a well-known, get-down-to-business tactic.

The head researcher blinked and looked away before beginning her report. "As you know, I've devoted the past week or so to uncovering everything I could about Bill McCleary and the Long Island Conservation and Environment. I went back as far as 1968, the year they were formed, and while it's been more than 50 years, there have been almost no changes made to their charter." Glynn prattled on, compelled to provide her boss with all this vital background information.

"Back then, the first head of LICE was a political appointee, a hack who was owed favors: Foley "Bud" Gray. Gray had no background in environmental policy and, as it turned out, no aptitude or interest in it either. After a number of years of mismanagement, with little real effort made to solve some fairly substantial environmental problems, there was a loud demand from a vocal environmental lobby demanding Gray be replaced by a young and idealistic William McCleary."

Glynn continued with her history lesson, apparently unaware of Marshall's increasingly bored expression.

"At the time, this proved to be the right move. McCleary had sound educational credentials, with advanced degrees in both chemistry and wildlife biology. He had been doing research on acid rain and air pollution and was familiar with many of the state's hazardous waste sites. Aside from being a darling of the Sierra Club, McCleary knew his way around Albany, having advised many of the state's key legislators. His appointment was widely hailed as a change for the better."

Glynn paused for a moment. Marshall noticed she spoke without notes or other aids and radiated an air of quiet confidence. He settled himself more comfortably into the couch and nodded for her to continue.

"Over the years McCleary built LICE into his own private feifdom. He took on tough battles, fought against large polluters, and supported the creation of state parks and the protection of large tracts of land home to endangered species. Of course, his activities were both praised and attacked, making McCleary some powerful friends and enemies. It's a miracle he's been able to stay as Director of LICE for this long. But in truth, it was because those in power knew the public supported McCleary's work. It was so easy for politicians running for reelection to take credit for LICE and its good deeds, thereby ensuring McCleary a steady stream of support. As you know, this has gone on for years. No one looked into LICE's charter; there was no need to. The public was happy to have cleaner air and water, bad polluters were forced to pay to clean up their mess, politicians could shout about their wonderful environmental record, and

McCleary was left alone to run his ever-expanding and influential organization."

"All very interesting, Glynn," Marshall interjected at the next break, starting to wonder if she had anything he could use. This history lesson was starting to wear thin. "What can you tell me that has relevance today?" he asked with a touch of impatience.

Without skipping a beat, Glynn continued her dissertation. "McCleary has been head of LICE for so long, garnering years of press and publicity as an environmental champion, he's been thought of as a permanent fixture. Falling somewhere between the Pied Piper and the Pope, no one has wanted to challenge McCleary for fear of public backlash. But the permanence of his appointment, one he's successfully promoted, is an illusion. Lately, McCleary's popularity has been waning and many of his former supporters are no longer in office."

"Glynn, what are you saying?" Marshall asked, sitting a little straighter as his mind was trying to work out the angles.

"It's all in the original charter. It clearly states the director of the <u>L</u>ong <u>I</u>sland <u>C</u>onservation and <u>E</u>nvironment serves at the discretion of the governor. There is no specified beginning or end to his term."

"Do you mean the only thing keeping McCleary in that job is Governor Harris?" Marshall questioned in disbelief.

Glynn was unruffled by the intensity of Marshall's statement and resumed her relentless presentation. "If I understand the problem correctly, our client Crystal Clam Wineries is asking us to help get a new environmentally friendly fertilizer approved. From what I've been able to read, SCAB is used after the first month of planting. It does two things at the same time: it covers the ground, suppressing weed growth, while simultaneously acting as a plant fertilizer. ChemoCo's literature alludes to a proprietary process where all-natural plant nutrients encapsulated in time-release pellets are scattered throughout the ground cover. These pellets are dissolved by water—whether through irrigation or naturally occurring rain—thereby enriching the growing crops. While LICE's final report on SCAB has not yet been released, ChemoCo's preliminary data looks promising."

Getting even more restless as Glynn droned on, Marshall stood, stretched, and started pacing about his office. If he didn't need her results so badly, he would have had Rose draft a summary of the report.

But even seeing her boss pace the floor didn't distract Glynn. "I did find articles containing bits and pieces of LICE's soon-to-be-released report. It appears LICE is claiming there are issues concerning chemical runoff. From what I've been able to glean, McCleary is suggesting SCAB is polluting the Long Island Sound. It does seem likely McCleary will press to reject SCAB, thereby preventing its use by Crystal Clam and everyone else on the East End. While I've not been able to uncover anything definitive, this does run counter to all the data that has been published to date."

Marshall stopped and turned toward Glynn, silently hoping she would have something more to add. Something he could use.

"In order to best serve our client, I have two recommendations," she prattled on single-mindedly. "First, we need to get a complete copy of that report as soon as possible. There is a real possibility LICE is overstepping its charter. Nowhere does it say they have regulatory control over biodegradable or 'natural' fertilizers. Second, and we don't have to wait on this one, we can put pressure on our elected officials, especially the governor, to replace McCleary. The time seems ripe for a replacement to be named for a number of reasons, not the least of which is McCleary's growing unpopularity with the public and his lack of support in the legislature. Getting SCAB approved could simply be a matter of the governor appointing someone else."

Marshall stopped pacing and stared at Glynn. "You mean to tell me LICE doesn't have jurisdiction over SCAB?" he asked, wanting to make sure he wasn't mistaken. It seemed too simple to be true.

"It seems so," Glynn replied confidently. "I reviewed the ChemoCo literature on SCAB you sent, analyzed the chemical compounds, and compared those to the technical specifications outlined in LICE's operating charter. The LICE charter is clear as to exactly what chemical elements need to be present in order for a substance to be considered a chemical fertilizer. Basically, it appears SCAB does not fall into this category because it's made of naturally occurring elements."

Marshall was not ready to celebrate. He had one more question, a detail nagging at him. "Glynn, this is great work. I mean, you did an incredible job investigating all the angles. It would appear SCAB's approval may depend on its classification. And you did say you reviewed all technical materials, the chemical structures, etc.? How can you be so sure? Did you show this stuff to a chemist, or an authority on chemical fertilizers? I didn't realize you had a background in chemistry. Shouldn't we get a corroborating opinion?" Marshall asked, fixing her with another intense stare.

Uncharacteristically, Glynn fell silent, unable to answer right away. "Err, you're right," she stammered. "I did give the material to a friend I know at the biotech incubator—you know, LIQuID?—where he's a chemist. He looked everything over and confirmed my suspicions. I can get you his name if you'd like?" Glynn offered sheepishly, glad of the spur-of-the-moment idea but sorry to have to use Ray in her white lie. She didn't have any choice. How could she tell Marshall the truth? Breathing in an unknown chemical substance caused her to develop powerful cognitive abilities, enabling her to understand chemical composition and analysis in a matter of hours?

A long second passed as Marshall held her gaze before he was satisfied by the response. "Okay, I'll go along with this. If your friend is a chemical expert, and he was the one who made this discovery, we can trust his abilities, right?"

Glynn nodded, not wishing to verbally incriminate herself anymore.

"So now the ball's in my court," he said, walking over to the phone and buzzing his secretary.

"Rose, get Arnie on the phone. Tell him I have some important information on LICE." Hanging up, a supremely happy Marshall turned to Glynn. "You've done a superb job. This could mean a lot to the firm," he said while ushering her out of his office. He made a mental note to ask Rose to purchase a $500 gift card at her favorite store—a small price to pay for what could be a large return.

Before Marshall closed the door on the retreating Glynn, Rose announced Arnie Holtzmann was on the phone.

"Arnie, how are you today? Hear anything more about McCleary's report?" Marshall asked coyly. He could feel the tension emanating from the other end of the phone.

"Marshall," Arnie barked, "I was in the middle of a conference call with the county supervisor's office! I hung up on them for you. What's going on? Did your girl find anything? This better be good."

Marshall was expecting Arnie's reaction. It was the reason Arnie's nickname, A Holtz, fit so perfectly.

"Are you ready to listen?" he countered, not in the least intimidated. As the other end of the line went silent, Marshall used the next five minutes to summarize Glynn's report.

"Look, Arnie," Marshall concluded, "on behalf of Crystal Clam, I plan on attacking the LICE report directly—now, before its release. I'll be contacting some of the other wineries to get a class action going, and then file a motion claiming LICE has overstepped its bounds and doesn't have jurisdiction over SCAB. That should keep McCleary busy. We could even alert the press and get them to cry holy hell about LICE's abuse of power. McCleary will be so busy defending himself he won't know what hit him."

"I've got one even better," Arnie said, barely able to get his thoughts out fast enough. "I'm attending a fundraiser for the governor tonight. It's no secret he's dissatisfied with that nitpicker lately. I think the time's right to introduce a little bug control of our own," said Arnie, positively gleeful at the idea of exterminating McCleary.

"According to my girl," Marshall added, "the political timing could be right for LICE to get a new head.

"Fighting LICE over the SCAB approval is part of the picture. I want assurances on getting the inside track to ChemoCo's legal business," Marshall reiterated, not wanting any misunderstanding that he expected nothing less than legal exclusivity.

Arnie knew he had to keep Marshall properly incentivized. If Marshall found a way to get SCAB approved, Arnie felt certain he could find a way to convince the ChemoCo board to approve a new Long Island plant. A deal like that would solidify his image as a powerful and effective dealmaker. It could be the perfect springboard for his next move, a run for state or even national office. The sky's the limit, Arnie thought.

"All right, Marshall, you'll get your shot," A Holtz affirmed. "But you're not the only one with a lot at stake. Let's not get ahead of ourselves; we have a way to go before it's a done deal. By the way, I'm planning on throwing a little shindig for ChemoCo and Kingsley when he comes in for a visit. He's pals with Stan Piper: old school buddies, in case you didn't know," Arnie revealed.

Part 4

Exploration

136

Chapter 22

Penna was in the kitchen washing up after a typical weekday dinner of macaroni and cheese for the kids and leftover meatloaf for the adults. The TV was on so she could catch the news. *This evening's meal had been interesting*, Penna thought.

Today's dinner conversation started out by asking her children about their school day. Penna "learned" things using her new ability that they would never have revealed, such as quarrels with classmates and incomplete answers on a quiz. When Frank related a story from his current plumbing job, she was able to fill in some of the details he had overlooked. But when Penna asked whether her mother remembered to take her pills, she knew the answer before hearing the reply.

When she first became aware of her gift, Penna would blurt out new insights, unable to hold back. Many of her remarks so shocked her family that they wondered if she had been spying on them. As time went on, she became more judicious, carefully picking and choosing the information she revealed. There were times she felt being privy to their little omissions was less of a blessing. *Sometimes, it's better not to know.*

Watching the news was no different, but here, Penna enjoyed having a front-row seat to the news reporters' unspoken information. Penna quickly deduced not everything a reporter learned when covering a story made it on air. Once the anchor introduced the story, like some good-looking mannequin, the camera would switch to the reporter on the street to deliver the details. That's when things got interesting, and Penna's premonitions started pinging like a radar signal homing in on a solid object. She 'knew' the reporter was leaving out key pieces of information, maybe glossing over certain facts or emphasizing others, thereby influencing the story's slant. Penna would compare her awareness of the story with the reporter's version. If there were clips of a newsmaker being interviewed, so much the better. All it took was a mere five-second sound bite from the newsmakers themselves, and Penna would know the truth in no time. It amazed her that much of what was considered "news" was merely the repackaging of preconceptions.

Tonight, she was watching an interview with Arnie Holtzmann, Director of Long Island Metro Business Organization. Holtzmann was claiming victory for the people of Long Island and their beleaguered agricultural industry. "The time has finally come to exterminate LICE, the all-powerful Long Island Conservation and Environment, a bloated government organization that is responsible for costing Long Islanders jobs and income," Holtzmann was saying on camera.

Holtzmann answered the reporter's question about a new natural fertilizer—SCAB—some sort of wonder chemical that was sure to grow better crops without hurting the environment.

"Who could be against that?" Holtzmann asked the reporter, inferring only an idiot (like LICE's Director) would be. But when he neglected to reveal that SCAB's parent company, ChemoCo, might open a plant on Long Island, Penna sensed there was a lot more at stake for the LIMBO director. *The television-viewing audience will never hear the whole story.*

Next, there was a cut to a press conference featuring a red-faced McCleary pounding the podium, defending his record as he angrily responded to charges that he was purposely blocking SCAB's approval. *There's something about his stand against SCAB that doesn't ring true.* He explained that LICE was still examining SCAB's chemical formula, but Penna could sense there was something missing. Surprisingly, it didn't stop him from citing results from a report he wouldn't or couldn't produce. For Penna, it felt all wrong. *There is no doubt McCleary is 100 percent committed to doing all he can to block the use of this new fertilizer, but why isn't he presenting the supporting facts?*

The reporter left out any mention of the obvious animosity between Holtzmann and McCleary or why McCleary was dragging his feet on releasing the SCAB evaluation. She sensed Arnie Holtzmann was angling to get McCleary fired. Could SCAB really be the next wonder fertilizer, as Holtzmann asserted, or was it a dangerous product being deceptively marketed, as McCleary charged?

The TV screen once again featured the reporter quickly summing up the need for business organizations like LIMBO to keep an eye on what's important as they helped local companies navigate the minefield of inefficient government agencies like LICE. The story ended with the news anchor offering hope that sane minds would prevail. *Amazing,* Penna thought. *There's so much more going on behind the scenes than what we see in these news reports.*

Chapter 23

At the sound of the phone, Iris glanced over at the clock, wondering who could be calling her this early on a Monday morning. In the old days, when she was "working" for a living, she would have been in the office by 7:30 a.m. at the latest.

Picking up the receiver, she was surprised to hear Baxter's voice.

"Have you seen the cover story in today's business section?" her boss asked abruptly.

"No. Since I've been home, I'm not on top of the headlines like I used to be," Iris replied. She was trying to control the annoyed tone that had crept into her voice. "I thought you'd be phoning sooner, telling me when I could return to work." *The nerve of this guy*, she thought. *No contact for weeks, and when he does, it is to ask if I read the paper.*

"Look, Iris, I'm sorry I haven't called sooner. The investigation is progressing, and I don't have anything new to report—until now. Do you have the *New York Times* handy?" Baxter was determined to put her through the paces.

"I'm getting it right now. What's the big deal?" Iris asked as she unfurled the paper from its plastic delivery sleeve. Right on the front page, above the fold on the right side, was the headline LICE FOILED IN ATTEMPT TO PICK SCAB APART. Skimming through the article, Iris read all about McCleary's boneheaded decision to try to block SCAB's approval for use on the East End and the subsequent lawsuit alleging he'd overstepped LICE's charter.

"Okay, I've read it. What does all this LICE/SCAB stuff have to do with me?" Iris asked, trying to make sense of Baxter's call.

"You mean you don't know?" Baxter asked incredulously, wondering what had happened to the old Iris, who would have put the pieces together by now. "Put aside the fact that McCleary was cut down a notch or two, and his agency is looking like a head case. The real story here is about SCAB. Now that LICE is out of the picture, it is likely SCAB will become the fertilizer of choice for most, if not all, of the wineries on the East End. This is a huge deal," Baxter emphasized, waiting for Iris to catch up.

"Of course," Iris whispered. "SCAB is made by ChemoCo."

"Bingo! Do you have any idea what this will do to ChemoCo's stock? Iris, do you have any idea what this does to the investigation?"

She had no doubt as to ChemoCo's new stock price by the end of the day and was mentally preparing her sell order. Iris quickly figured out her new net worth. She'd make her investment back a hundred-fold.

"So what are you saying, Baxter? Does the company think I've been involved in insider trading? I didn't even know about this."

"It doesn't look good . . . not good at all. So far, we've reviewed most of the activity in your account and do you know what we found? A probability threshold of over 90 percent!" Baxter's voice had started to rise, but instead of getting louder, it got higher. He was sounding like a schoolgirl shrieking about Taylor Swift's new album. "Add in this new ChemoCo situation and . . . Well, how can you explain it? It smacks of impropriety! It won't do Iris, won't do at all."

"Are you saying I'm out? After over 20 years, I'm getting the boot?" This didn't come as a shock—she had known this would happen. But a part of her did feel bad. She honestly liked her work and didn't know yet how she'd replace it. "Look, I'll be in later and we can finalize my termination." She hung up.

Chapter 24

Gil and Glynn were having dinner at their favorite Italian restaurant. It was a habit they had started early in their relationship. All week long, they were like two ships passing in the night, barely having time for anything more than brief snatches of conversations. But on Friday, they made a commitment to sit down and catch up.

"So, what did he say next?" Gil asked as the salad arrived at their table.

"That he had to call Arnie Holtzmann. It was obvious he was happy with my report. I did a pretty thorough job. It was simple. I spent the first part of the meeting detailing LICE's charter and McCleary's history as Director. Then I moved onto the SCAB formula itself. Based on the specs from ChemoCo, it is obvious SCAB doesn't fall under LICE's purview. Therefore, McCleary was overstepping his authority," Glynn concluded smugly before taking a sip of wine. She couldn't stop herself from explaining all the details, even though she sounded like a know-it-all.

"Well, Marshall was impressed. Especially the part about your showing the SCAB specs to some chemist at LIQuID." Gil had been surprised his wife knew people at the LIQuID facility—she had never said anything about them before.

Glynn covered her discomfort at the mention of LIQuID by concentrating on moving her salad around the plate. "Well, yes, I do know a team of biotech researchers. I met them through one of the girls in my book group. You know, Onawhim Young, the teacher? She's seeing one of the guys, and, well, we all met him one evening," Glynn replied, digging deeper into her food. It was not like her to withhold details about her book club, but she wasn't prepared to clue him into her changes just yet.

"Well, it was a stroke of genius to make the connection between SCAB's chemistry and LICE's charter." Having come from the LIMBO board meeting, Gil knew how pumped Arnie was about ChemoCo. "According to Arnie Holtzmann, there's a lot riding on getting SCAB approved—it's tied into LIMBO's annual goals. And you must know that Arnie Holtzmann is about as subtle as a train wreck. Whatever he can do to promote his agenda is a priority. Have you seen some of the media coverage? Arnie's plastered all over the news aggressively promoting SCAB, discrediting LICE, and smearing McCleary. He's a one-man media circus."

Glynn hadn't been paying much attention to the news lately and didn't know the Holtzmann/McCleary feud was playing out in the papers and on TV. "I can't help but get the feeling something more is going on," Glynn said, trying to figure out what made this different from other arguments. "They've had disagreements before. Why is this one so virulent? Why can't these things be worked out over breakfast, or during lunch in some conference room?"

"You're right—there is more to this than meets the eye," he admitted, taking a forkful of salad into his mouth. "This is about more than merely getting SCAB approved for use by Crystal Clam and other wineries. McCleary had been rubbing people the wrong way for a long time, and over the years, he's lost much of the political support he once enjoyed. Arnie Holtzmann smells an opportunity. This is a guy who eats raw meat for breakfast. And now may be the right time for a change. After all, Arnie is presiding over a business development agency this close to generating business development," Gil explained, gesturing with his hand how close "this close" was. "It's pretty evident the public strongly supports the creation of more and better jobs, and maybe the environment is now taking second place to economic growth."

"Do you think Marshall shared my report with Arnie?" Glynn asked, feeling uncomfortable that someone outside the firm would have access to it.

Gil loved it when his wife was perplexed: a rare occurrence. "No doubt about it. Both Marshall and Arnie want ChemoCo to open their new R&D plant on Long Island. And they both think getting SCAB approved for use is the only way that will happen. Word is there's a lot more at stake than just SCAB's approval. The rumor has Arnie angling for McCleary's job," Gil said quietly as he looked around to ensure he wasn't overheard. "This could be the start of a whole new environment policy for New York—a radical departure after years of McCleary's embedded dominance. Arnie Holtzmann is an incredibly astute businessman, and now may be his best chance," Gil finished in almost a whisper.

All of a sudden, Glynn realized she wasn't hungry any longer.

Chapter 25

Sollie was the first to arrive. Being early was something she was still getting used to. Like the others, she had been experimenting with her new skills. Adjusting time was a form of compression, squeezing vs. stretching. If she squeezed, time sped up; conversely, if she stretched, there was more time for important activities. Each was a purposeful act requiring a burst of intense concentration. She could do it only briefly but with stunning results. Having 20 minutes to kill, Sollie decided to practice. She closed her eyes and visualized the hands on a clock moving forward: two minutes, five minutes, nine minutes, and then one last push. Taking a deep breath, she opened her eyes and looked at her watch. In the space of what felt like three seconds, time had elapsed by almost 15 minutes. One by one, her friends were pulling into the LIQuID parking lot.

The women didn't want to linger outside for a variety of reasons, not the least of which was their fear of being spotted. They all shared the same craving for anonymity as they hurried along the concrete path, mumbling quick hellos and pleasantries. As soon as they arrived in the empty reception area, Kevin appeared by the side door to usher them inside. It felt like a reunion of sorts. Walking the enclosed and protected hallways was strangely comforting. In what seemed like no time, they were standing outside the door to Lab 8. Kevin keyed the intercom and announced their arrival, and moments later, the door opened.

"Ah, so nice to see you all again," Ray said as he ushered them inside. "Have you enjoyed the past two weeks?" It was more of a pleasantry than a question he expected answered. "We've uncovered some interesting information and are anxious to continue our investigation of your, err—" He paused, not knowing the proper phrase. "—Your recent changes and condition." It was the least offensive label he could think of.

For the next 20 minutes, Ray took the women through all the steps he and his team performed on their blood chemistry. It was a detailed and technical explanation, including caveats and warnings that the results were not exact. They were counseled there could be other unknown elements or factors outside the scope of their tests that may affect the results.

"The field of brain chemistry has identified certain key chemicals used as markers for brain function. Remember, this is an emerging area of scientific inquiry, much like the discoveries in blood chemistry 100 or more years ago." Ray paused to note the rapt attention of everyone in the room.

"We're looking at certain enzyme levels: Ga1, Tc3, R2Bh5. When a person is in a stage of advanced Alzheimer's, for example, their Ga1 levels are low—between 0.3–0.6. It's the same with the Tc3s, which register between 0.5–0.9, while their R2Bh5 levels are high, around 4.2–4.9, in some cases over 5.0. This indicates impaired brain function. As I mentioned last time, our team has been researching ways to improve brain function by adjusting these levels, and it seems we were successful. There is no doubt your brains are operating substantially above the normal range.

"I'm confident, very confident, our conclusions could be . . . are, in effect, the only way everything makes sense," Ray explained. "So as not to confuse the situation, it is best for you to sit and view a prepared slide presentation. One picture is worth a thousand words, so to speak, and after that . . . Well, it might be a good time to answer questions." Ray could have continued rambling on till morning if Glynn hadn't stepped up.

"It's okay, Ray. We want to see your results. We want to know," she confirmed.

The PowerPoint presentation took seven minutes, but due to its complexity and unfamiliar language, it seemed twice that long. Each slide melted into another as Ray narrated in his flat, matter-of-fact voice. He began by giving an introduction to the field of brain research, specifically those areas that deal with higher cognitive functions and memory. Then Ray got into the meat of things. He outlined the research hypothesis they were testing for and how they measured and decoded the results.

The last three minutes were devoted to unraveling, for the layperson, intricate molecular models. Ray created captivating analogies rooted in everyday life, which helped better convey their theories. He reviewed the results of their blood chemistry, described the theory behind their computer models, and drew attention to various relationships and unexpected occurrences. It was an impressive and thorough presentation. After a brief pause, Ray turned off the machine and sat with his team across from the five female experimental subjects in the darkened room, with only the under-counter lights for illumination. As they were treading in murky territory, everyone seemed more relaxed under the cloak of darkness.

"Do you have any questions?" Ray asked before going on to the more difficult part of this meeting. "We've brought you up-to-date. We will try to make the connection between what we are studying in the lab and what happened to you the other evening.

"Our research is based on the supposition that humans use only a small percentage of their available brainpower. Think of brainpower, your brain, as if it were a gas tank. Each day, we wake and start off filled with gas—100 percent capacity. But over the course of the day, humans, men and women alike use a small amount of our gas to fuel cognitive output. That leaves a surplus in storage. At the end of the day, some of us may have used 45 percent, some as high as 60–65 percent if we've been really challenged. It's true our usage rate fluctuates from day to day, and what may be normal brainpower usage for you may be different for me. That's what makes us all unique. Like a fingerprint, our brainpower signature is exclusive to each of us. But, you may ask, what about Alzheimer's patients or people with brain disease or impairments? These people have a distinctive brainpower graph, too. In many cases, what's available could be high, but something internally is blocking access, causing them to use little of their available brainpower. We wanted to uncover that anomaly, to identify why the brain is not tapping into its available power." Again, Ray paused for questions before continuing. "We thought we had the answer. In Alzheimer's patients, we found a series of proteins strung together, forming a kind of barrier preventing the brain from drawing upon its power reserves. If we could unlock this obstruction and find the right 'key,' it would allow the brain's natural mechanism to operate, and we believe normal brain function could be restored.

"Unfortunately, our theories did not prepare us for what happened. We found difficulty in unlocking the barrier's molecular code. Then we had a surprise event one evening: a mistake in our calculations—a very simple error that created a chain reaction, something we were not prepared for. We were able to unlock the barrier, but the decoded key exposed an opening, like a crack in a dam. And just as water would leak or gush out of a hole, so too did the backed-up, unused brainpower come flooding out. It happened so quickly. As we were monitoring the chemical values, the Lab filled with gas. Before we knew it, the gas triggered an alarm in the main control room and our friend Kevin hit the exhaust fan and vented everything outside. Normally, these chemicals break down and dissipate rapidly, which is why we haven't been affected. But this time they coalesced, floating in the calm evening sky. That is what you breathed in—the chemical codes that unlock the brain's storehouse."

Ray finished speaking, and the darkroom was quiet with a thousand thoughts.

"But that's not all, is it?" Penna asked. *He was holding something back—something that had to do with their future.*

"You are right. I have forgotten your special abilities," said Ray apologetically. "It is a fact you breathed in our experimental molecular formula, and it did affect your cognitive capacity. The past we understand. At present, we can monitor and study—we will keep records and track the effects. But it is the future we cannot predict."

"You mean you don't know how this will affect us tomorrow, next week, or even next year?" Iris questioned. "Could it get stronger? Will it disappear? What can we expect?"

"That, as they say, is THE question. We simply don't know what will happen to you, or your brain function. You have crossed over into an area where we simply do not have any data—nothing, not even animal experiments have been performed," Ray added.

"Look, things have been great for me lately. I don't know about the rest of you girls, but this brainpower thing has changed my life, for the better. I don't want to go back to the old Sollie. I'm lovin' the new me. And as time has passed, I'm finding it easier to direct and control my new gifts," said Sollie, needing to get her feelings out in the open.

"That brings me to the next area. We need a detailed, moment-by-moment account of all that has happened. Once we create this history, we will ask you to come in periodically for monitoring and further study. We are breaking new ground here—this is uncharted territory, and you are, excuse the reference, our guinea pigs." Ray wanted to be clear he not only needed their cooperation now but would need to see them on a regular basis for the foreseeable future.

"I, too, have been enjoying my newfound influence. It seems my words, sometimes even the merest suggestion, can have a profound effect. I'm happy to do all I can to aid your research, but I must insist on anonymity. I do not want to be identified or identifiable in any way, and I feel strongly about that," emphasized Onawhim, who understood how influential her statement was. She had felt particularly affected by her new gift. The pendulum had swung to the other extreme, and while she was enjoying her enhanced ability, it frightened her. To have harnessed the power of persuasion, so elusive and so often wished for, was an eerie dream come true. One she still hadn't come to terms with. Onawhim, naturally cautious, felt better taking things slowly.

"Of course," Ray confirmed. "Our interests are the same. We have no intention of revealing this research and have much more work to do before we can even come close to understanding what is going on in each of your brains." Ray's assurances were a formality—after Onawhim's strongly worded request, it was unthinkable that their private files would be made public. "Each of you will sit with one team member who will be your key contact. He will get to know you, understand your thinking, and will chronicle your life. Please answer all questions honestly and completely. We need your cooperation, and you have our assurance all will be held in strict confidence."

The researchers and subjects paired off, and the rest of the evening was spent as described. Glynn found herself with Ray, reliving the past month as he recorded the events of her life day by day. It was toward the end of her recitation that she thought to ask for his help on another matter.

"Ray, I was wondering if I could ask a favor. I've come across the technical specs for a new fertilizer. It is of particular interest to one of my firm's clients. Because I'm able to read and understand vast amounts of information, I was able to teach myself about chemistry. But now I'm having doubts about my ability to interpret this chemical formula and its impact on the environment," she confessed, feeling a bit uncertain about her analysis. "My firm is relying on my evaluation, and I'd like a second opinion to be on the safe side. Could you look at the specs and verify my conclusions?"

Ray smiled. "Of course. Leave the information with me and I'll review it. Do you need an answer right away?" Glynn nodded as she slipped ChemoCo's technical sheets on SCAB out of her case and handed them to Ray.

"I'll read it through tonight and give you a call tomorrow. Will that be soon enough?" he offered.

154

Chapter 26

"Oh, hi, Ray," Glynn answered, cradling the phone in her hand. "Yes, this is a fine time to talk," she added, glancing around to see if anyone was nearby to capture snippets of her conversation. "I'm glad you were able to get back to me so quickly," more than ready to hear his confirmation of her conclusions.

While Glynn's abilities to process incredible amounts of data had expanded, she had no formal training as a chemist. After all, what was a couple of days of intensive study compared to years of practical experience? And with so much riding on her recommendation, Marshall Matlock's reputation, the East End's agricultural prosperity, LICE's integrity, and ChemoCo's revenue stream from sales of SCAB, it was comforting to have someone of Ray's stature confirm her findings. Glynn had no doubt he would arrive at the same conclusions as she: that SCAB was an environmentally friendly weed suppressor/fertilizer that would increase crop production without harmful chemicals or damage to the environment. Exactly as ChemoCo had warranted.

"Glynn, where did you get these specs?" Ray asked with a touch of concern.

"They were given to LICE—you know, Long Island Conservation and Environment. LICE is using them to evaluate ChemoCo's claim that SCAB would not harm the fragile ecosystem on the East End," she replied. There was little reason to explain her boss' connection with Arnie Holtzmann, who had received ChemoCo's documentation from Stan Piper, a longtime friend of CEO Bennett Kingsley.

"Based on the pages you gave me, I'd say everything looks fine."

"Oh, that's a relief," Glynn replied, exhaling in a rush, not even realizing she had been holding her breath. Merely as a formality to be

100 percent certain, she got it right, Glynn asked, "So, then everything with SCAB is as ChemoCo has—"

"Wait a minute," he said, interrupting her. "Yes, the formulas and supporting documentation do look fine based on the pages you supplied. "But . . ." Ray paused for a moment, adding a bit too much drama for Glynn's taste. "The materials are incomplete. They describe a piece of the SCAB chemical composite, a substantial part of it, but not the whole compound. There's a part missing."

"What?" was all she could manage. Glynn was speechless and had stopped breathing again. Silence engulfed the phone line as she struggled to process Ray's words, not wanting to believe what she had heard.

Ray's voice filled the silent vacuum as he continued SCAB's chemical assessment. "Based on what they supplied, the product does appear to be comprised mostly of organic elements. But that's not the whole story. To evaluate SCAB, you'd need the complete chemical formula in order to replicate the substance in its entirety. Only then will you have an independent test to verify their claims," he finished.

"Do you mean to tell me we can't corroborate ChemoCo's claim?" she blurted out, hoping she'd misunderstood him.

"Look, Glynn, it's perfectly understandable to have mistaken the formula for being complete. It's not something a chemistry novice, or maybe even someone without advanced chemistry experience, would have picked up," he added. "Frankly, I'm impressed you were able to make an evaluation at all, especially without any formal training. Your cognitive functions seem to be accelerating," he said, giving her accomplishment all the credit it was due.

"You're saying we don't know if SCAB is safe, right?"

"That's right," he replied, wondering why she was having such a hard time with this simple concept. "We have no way of knowing based on the information you gave me."

Once again, there was a loud silence on the line. "I don't know of any way you can make an evaluation of a substance without all the relevant documentation," Ray repeated. "There would be no way to replicate SCAB without independent testing. It's impossible to accurately prove or disprove ChemoCo's claim that SCAB is environmentally friendly," he concluded matter-of-factly. "When you get the rest of the specs, send them over, and I'll be happy to make a complete evaluation."

Left with nothing else to say, Glynn replied that, of course, she'd follow up with him as soon as possible. Barely able to find her voice, she thanked him for his time and hung up.

For all her newfound abilities and God-given smarts, Glynn was scared and clueless as to what to do next. Here, she had confidently given Marshall her assurance that SCAB was safe. And based on her report, Marshall was doing his level best to push LICE into approving SCAB. Acting on behalf of Crystal Clam Wineries and their lobbyists from Long Island Agricultural Resources (LIAR), who believed the East End desperately needed this new, improved fertilizer, Marshall Matlock would do everything in his power to represent his client's best interest. There was no doubt Marshall would not rest until he obtained LICE's go-ahead to have SCAB become THE approved fertilizer for Long Island's burgeoning wine industry. The resulting fallout from a mistake like this—her mistake—could be devastating.

Racing through all sorts of tragic scenarios, Glynn imagined everything from an environmental disaster and agricultural ruin to embarrassing public disclosures and monumental lawsuits. Not only had she jeopardized her job and quite possibly her husband's position, but she placed Marshall and the firm in an indefensible position of supporting a product that could be an environmental nightmare with ramifications affecting Long Island's ecology that could last for years. All because Glynn Patrick, Head Researcher of Shuster, Yleskin, and Matlock, got caught in the headiness of her new "powers" and had the audacity to think she knew how to decipher complex chemical compounds. How could she say SCAB was safe when she didn't know? Glynn became physically sick at the magnitude of her foolish error.

Self-recriminations didn't stop there. Glynn remembered Gil's gossip about McCleary being under siege as Director of the Long Island Conservation and Environment. It was no secret Bill McCleary was in a political dogfight due in no small part to his growing unpopularity. The rumor was that Holtzmann was preying on a friendless McCleary, calling attention to his stonewalling of SCAB's approval in order to force McCleary out. And if what Gil said was true, the next director could be none other than A Holtz. It was enough to give Glynn's already unsettled stomach an unpleasant lurch. She thought she was going to lose her lunch.

It was her research report that set all these events in motion. Feeling smart and smug, she gave her assurance SCAB was clean. Oh, if only she could turn back time, like Sollie, and do it all over again! *"Pride goeth before destruction, and a haughty spirit before a fall," or something like that*, she thought—although she knew the proverb was correct. Glynn closed her eyes and wracked her brain for a solution. The best she could do was to go home. She had to get out of the office and find a quiet, safe place to close her eyes and figure out how to set things right. Glynn left work, claiming a touch of stomach flu. It wasn't far from the truth—she felt sick to her stomach and looked the part, too.

Curling up on the couch to watch the evening news, Glynn hoped some mind-numbing television would allow her higher cognitive functions to work things through. Obsessed by a thousand and one details, she almost missed the lead story on the six o'clock news: "After almost 30 years, the director of LICE, Bill McCleary, has resigned," the TV anchor read.

Glynn bolted upright and focused her attention on the screen. "The embattled director of the Long Island Conservation and Environment, Bill McCleary, today has tendered his resignation, clearing the way for the governor to make a new appointment—the first time in almost 30 years—to this important and powerful agency. Bill McCleary was a pioneer in protecting the environment and a fearsome champion in the fight to enact landmark conservation legislation. A fixture on Long Island, McCleary is credited with many of the state's most effective environmental policies. The governor's office released a statement late this afternoon praising McCleary's years of service in protecting the environment."

Glynn was shocked. She couldn't believe the news report—it was an uncanny realization of her worst fears. Not surprisingly, there had been no mention of ChemoCo or SCAB in the news report. It was entirely possible the press didn't know of the controversy or had simply failed to connect the dots. With McCleary gone, there would be no one standing in the way of SCAB's approval—a clear victory for Marshall's client Crystal Clam Winery and the GRowLers. She could picture Marshall celebrating the news over drinks with his LIMBO buddy, Arnie Holtzmann. There was no doubt Holtzmann had a hand in McCleary's resignation. They had battled on many issues over the years, and A Holtz wasn't shy about publicizing how much he hated the powerful head of LICE.

One question flew through Glynn's brain. Who, besides her and Ray, knew the materials ChemoCo handed over to LICE for review were incomplete? She had to believe McCleary was aware of ChemoCo's deliberate omission. Is that why he was reluctant to approve SCAB? Otherwise, why risk his job stalling on SCAB's approval? Did A Holtz know? Doubtful, Glynn figured. The guy didn't want to know the truth about things: "Don't confuse me with the facts," she could almost hear him say. LIMBO's mission was to promote business growth, and A Holtz was the strong arm, the hired gun committed to obtaining SCAB's fast approval before the next planting season passed. He was the conquering hero, the savior of the popular, fashionable, and highly profitable wine industry on the East End.

The newscast continued. "In a prepared statement, McCleary was quoted as saying the time was right for him to step down. After years of fighting the good fight for a better and cleaner Long Island, McCleary explained, he was growing weary of the political battles that took an ever-increasing amount of his time. It is no secret that McCleary and the governor have been butting heads over key environmental issues lately. McCleary's resignation paves the way for the governor to handpick someone for what is widely considered one of the most important and powerful nonelected positions on Long Island." The news segment ended as the station cut to a commercial.

Glynn sat and stared at the TV. Even though the report suggested a number of candidates were being considered as McCleary's replacement, she had no doubt Arnie Holtzmann would be the next head of LICE. And with A Holtz as LICE's new Director, SCAB would get swift approval, killing all hopes of an objective and comprehensive review. Glynn prayed SCAB was everything ChemoCo claimed. But what if it wasn't? What if SCAB was harmful? Then she, Glynn Patrick, would have to live with the guilt of being a contributor to Long Island's growing environmental problems—that SHE was a polluter! This was not acceptable. Glynn needed to find a way out, a course of action to set things right. She needed to get a complete, unbiased, independent, and scientific evaluation of SCAB. If it was determined SCAB was safe, well, then everything would be fine. Yes, poor Bill McCleary would be out of a job, but things were going in that direction for him anyway. BUT . . . if SCAB was found to be environmentally damaging, that would put everything in an altogether different light. Glynn was starting to get queasy thinking about it. She had to find out the truth.

Part 5

Investigation

162

Chapter 27

Laughter filled the crowded dining room as four of the five women seated at the round table in the corner responded to the punch line of Sollie's latest story. Sollie was a natural storyteller, regaling the book club with descriptions of her self-important, overdressed coworkers. Her knack for calling attention to their absurd characteristics enlivened her tales and never failed to entertain. And, of course, her timing was impeccable. Lately, though, her accomplishments at work were garnering the kind of appreciation she could deposit in the bank. Sollie was on track to become salesperson of the month and a likely shoo-in for one of the company's prestigious annual awards. *Now, this is a story I could get used to telling*, Sollie thought.

It had been two weeks since the girls last got together. And with the passage of time came both an increase in their abilities as well as a rising degree of confidence. Iris found being free from the yoke of corporate responsibility was more empowering than she once thought possible. Not to downplay the financial rewards—Iris was making more money than ever with less work and stress. Life couldn't be better. But the real benefit was measured in the increased time she was spending with her son Brett. *When one door closes, another opens*, Iris thought, having the time of her life picking one winning stock after another.

Meanwhile, Penna had been enjoying her front-row seat at the most fantastic character showcase imaginable—it was like watching The Sopranos and Sex in the City combined, only more outrageous. She was mesmerized listening to the parade of misfits and ne'er-do-wells dropping by her uncle's office on a daily basis. Able to read between the lines and then some, she uncovered their small lies, large deceits, deep dark secrets, and predatory behavior, all culminating in a tour de force of convoluted plots and misguided motives. Penna was privy to gossip, which could make even Uncle Dominic blush.

For Onawhim, each day, she grew more comfortable with her new power to influence others. In class, her students were actively soaking up all she could teach, hanging on every word. Her colleagues found Onawhim's opinions and ideas interesting, even impressive. The impact of her words, the ability to persuade, the sway of her thoughts, the authority of her arguments—it was simply incredible. Onawhim was living her lifelong dream, which, thankfully, took away some of the sting left from her breakup with Tru.

Unfortunately, Glynn was the only one having a tough time these past two weeks. Plagued with guilt, she spent almost every waking moment reviewing and researching her options. These included confessing her error to Marshall and offering herself to whatever recriminations and reprimands he thought appropriate, blowing the whistle on ChemoCo's deliberate withholding of important information on SCAB, and last but not least, explaining all of the above to Gil. She shuddered to think about the impact these actions might have on their marriage. After all, how could she account for learning years of chemistry in a couple of hours? Or justify her arrogance that a cursory review could substitute for an expert's evaluation of a complex formula? Gil was so honest, so straightforward, so decent. What would he think? Yes, just what would he think about her newfound abilities? Would he see her as a freak? As damaged? Would he still love her? All this kept her occupied while awake and unable to sleep at night. After days of purposeful thought, she finally decided to bring her predicament to the book group and clue them in before their scheduled visit with Ray and his staff at the LIQuID building.

"Glynn, you've been unusually quiet tonight," Penna remarked, able to sense discomfort in her friend.

"I think she's going to tell us something important," offered Iris knowingly.

Glynn smiled as she looked around the table at her friends. They're making this easy for me, she thought.

"I need to ask a favor," Glynn started, figuring it was better to come right out with it and not beat around the bush. "Lately, things for me have been pretty rocky. The thrill of my new ability to read and absorb all sorts of data has been both a benefit and a burden. There's no denying it's helped me do a fantastic job at work—it's incredible how much more information I can process. But the flip side has put me in an unexpected predicament."

"You mean something backfired?" Sollie asked incredulously.

"Yeah, that's a good way to put it. Something did indeed backfire," Glynn remarked dryly, "and it might splatter all over my firm." She'd been so uptight and worried lately that it felt good to imagine a cartoon-like consequence.

"I unwittingly gave our top partner misleading information," she confessed. "It was for one of our bigger clients. And if that weren't bad enough, it could have larger repercussions, like affecting agriculture on the East End, or possibly polluting the water. I don't even know if the recommendation I made is correct or not, and I've not been able to figure out a way to set it right."

Glynn detailed all that had happened, from her intensive self-taught chemistry lessons to her misguided assurances outlined in a report for Marshall Matlock and her ill-advised assumption affirming SCAB as safe for the environment. She described her conversation with Ray and her distress as he declared her inferences inconclusive. In fact, all of them were equally shocked when she revealed the sad truth—it was impossible to make an evaluation of SCAB, as the formula was incomplete. Finally, Glynn reviewed the events on the news concerning McCleary's resignation as Director of the Long Island Conservation and Environment and concluded with an expectation that Arnie Holtzmann would be announced as the new head of LICE.

When finished, she let go of the breath trapped inside her lungs. Looking around at the faces of her friends, women she had grown immeasurably closer to over the last month, Glynn felt more relaxed than she had weeks. "After days of soul searching," Glynn confessed, "I've tried to figure out how to set things right. I have two choices: 1) Do nothing and let the chips fall where they may, hoping SCAB is all that ChemoCo claims—effective, biodegradable, and safe for the fragile East End environment, or 2) Confess all and go public."

At this point, Glynn was on a roll. Her rapid-fire delivery freed all those imprisoned thoughts that had been bouncing around her brain.

"Maybe I should take this to the press. After all, public attention might force ChemoCo to release the complete chemical documentation," she reasoned, "or even shame LICE into an investigation. You know, greater oversight to hold ChemoCo accountable."

"There's no doubt I'll lose my job, and there's even a strong possibility this may destroy my marriage. I mean, what could I possibly tell Gil but the truth? And I have no idea what his reaction to all this will be." The strain she had been under was painfully evident.

"Don't worry, I'll keep you out of anything I say," Glynn added, looking around the table at each of her friends in turn. "I'll say it was me who was affected, that I was alone when the cloud appeared; no one need know about any of you." She lent special emphasis to this last statement, wanting to assure her friends they'd be safe from discovery. If anyone had to suffer consequences from her mistakes, Glynn wanted it to be her and her alone. There was no way she could live with herself if her friends' lives were ruined as well.

"Glynn, I can see you're feeling guilty about this. You were doing your job, trying your best, acting innocently and honorably. There is no need for self-recriminations. Even smart people make mistakes," Penna soothed, hating to see her friend in such pain.

"I agree," Iris seconded. "Look, we didn't ask for this change—to have supernatural abilities, or whatever you want to call it. As I learn to trust my newfound instincts about the future, I feel certain—very certain—this will have a positive outcome." While she could offer little in the way of specifics, Iris "knew" it would all work out for the best.

"I went from failure to favorite in a couple of months—not only with work, but at home with my family, too. I know more than anyone what it's like to be on the wrong side of a bad decision. Glynn, honey, I may not be able to see into the future like Iris, but I do know we will help you work this out. We're behind you 100 percent," concluded Sollie.

Glynn was profoundly moved by their kindness and generosity. "Thank you. I don't know what to say," she croaked, unable to hide the lump in her throat. "But I don't think you know what you're getting into," she added. "SCAB could be more than a benign crusty cover—it's possible there's an ugly sore underneath, something which could fester and spread. There is a lot at stake here as this could have an impact on the wine industry, the economics of the region, and not to mention possible environmental issues. And then there's my firm, Shuster, Yleskin, and Matlock. They're well-connected and have friends in high places—to say nothing of ChemoCo, a large and powerful corporation." Glynn had to make sure they understood what they were getting into.

"We are in this together," Onawhim interrupted before Glynn could continue with her doomsday monologue. Her quiet voice rang out like a bell, cutting through the noisy restaurant like a knife through soft butter. "It's true this is a potentially disastrous problem," Onawhim summarized. "That doesn't mean you should go through it alone. There may come a time when one of us slips or stumbles. I could easily be the next one standing before you looking for help. But all this is beside the point because you've left something out. There is a third option," she stated matter-of-factly.

All eyes stared at small, unassuming Onawhim as she let the silence serve as an unadorned set before her words filled the stage. "What if we worked this through together—as a team? You won't need to make any personal confessions, whether to Gil or your boss, if we help you uncover the truth." It was a simple statement offering a reasonable option.

"It seems to me we must ascertain SCAB's true nature. Other issues might end up being irrelevant should SCAB be all ChemoCo claims. It's conceivable that ChemoCo has been acting responsibly—we don't even know for certain whether they held back parts of the LICE formula. All we know is the information your boss gave you was incomplete. It could be an innocent mistake—he could have misplaced some of the pages, or maybe he wasn't given the complete set," Onawhim concluded.

Chapter 28

"Your appointment is here," the receptionist said.

"Thanks, Misty. I'll be right there." Glynn quickly replaced the phone and straightened her desk. She took a deep breath, hoping it would settle her nerves. This was the beginning of their bold plan. Even though they had debated various alternatives, discussed all the pros and cons, and arrived at a unanimous decision, so much was at stake she couldn't help being nervous—it felt spooky to act covertly inside her own company. Glynn made an effort to walk normally as she navigated the warren of hallways toward the reception area.

The dark-haired visitor stood, and, after a moment came forward to give Glynn a friendly hug. The two girls smiled. A casual observer wouldn't have noticed the knowing look they exchanged.

"Misty, this is my friend Penna," Glynn said, offering an introduction.

Penna walked over to the attractive 30-something sitting at the large wooden greeters' desk. "Nice to meet you," she responded with a smile. "We have something in common," Penna continued. "I also greet people who come into my Uncle Dominic's office, but my surroundings are not as attractive as this . . ." She gestured with her arm toward the beautiful furniture and décor. Misty was immediately disarmed by Glynn's friend.

"Why, thank you. Yes, I enjoy welcoming everyone coming through those doors. It gives me a chance to check them out," the receptionist replied. "I pride myself on knowing everything that's going on at Shylock. It's one of the reasons I like sitting here, and it also helps me avoid getting bored."

Glynn was shocked at Misty's blunt remarks. Of course, everyone knew she was a busybody—they took it for granted that, as a receptionist, she would have the skinny on all the office gossip. But Glynn had never heard her be so open or bold—and to a stranger!

"That's how I am at the office, too," Penna chirped. "I'll bet you keep track of everyone's whereabouts."

"I know who's out visiting clients, who's eating lunch, and who's enjoying a nooner." Misty winked. "That reminds me—Gil wanted me to tell you he'll be home late tonight, around eight."

"Thanks," Glynn replied. "I guess it's work on that case he's involved in."

"Well, he didn't tell me why he was going to be late. That husband of yours is pretty tight-lipped, although you probably already know that," Misty suggested with a sly smile. "I know he's going to be late because there's a last-minute LIMBO meeting tonight. Heard it from Arnie—you know, A Holtz?—he calls here regularly, sometimes three or four times a day. He's best friends with Marshall, and I've gotten to know him too." Misty couldn't resist explaining. "Sometimes we talk dirty to each other—you know, trash talk. It's not easy doing that in the open, but I've gotten pretty good at it. We even have a secret language I use if someone is sitting here. It turns him on, so I'm told, and every now and then he sends me a present."

Misty continued prattling on, happy to share some of the highlights from their sordid phone sex encounters.

Glynn was dumbfounded. She had never heard Misty talk this way before and glanced over at Penna to see if she registered the same surprise. But her friend looked as if Misty were discussing shoes and pocketbooks. It took half a second for Glynn to put two and two together. Somehow, being near Penna affected what Misty chose to make public. It was as if she lost her sense of reserve. The receptionist seemed unaware that she was revealing private, even intimate details. Things better left unsaid.

Penna flashed a knowing smile and gave her shoulders a shrug, effectively confirming Glynn's impression. Oh my God, Glynn thought. Just standing near Penna has an effect. Hopefully, the real work ahead of them will go as easily.

"It was nice meeting you," Penna said, having heard enough.

"Same here. Will see you on the way out," Misty replied with a smile.

"Thanks again, Misty," Glynn mumbled, shaking her head, wanting to get away before poor Misty realized what she had revealed.

Penna followed Glynn out of the reception area. It took a supreme effort for Glynn to keep a straight face all the way back to the law library. Only when her office door was closed did the two friends laugh out loud.

"Is this what's it's been like for you?" asked a wide-eyed Glynn. "Unbelievable! I've known Misty for years, we've shared many lunches and plenty of after-work drinks together, and I've never heard her open up so. I mean, she'd make a couple of suggestive remarks, or give up a couple of juicy stories here and there, but nothing like that!"

"Misty was unusually open. Not everyone reacts in the same way," Penna explained. "In fact, it depends on the person. I haven't figured out why one person will spill all their beans, while someone else would offer only a hint of what's on their mind, but I think it has to do with their personality. I also noticed that the closer I stand and the more I concentrate on the person, the more they volunteer. It's been pretty incredible," she admitted.

"Time to go," Glynn said as she checked her watch. "Rose will be getting ready for lunch, and we don't want to miss her."

Penna and Glynn chatted amicably as they wound their way to Marshall's office. Penna was suitably impressed with the Shuster, Yleskin, and Matlock workplace. They walked on plush burgundy carpet past traditional paintings of landscapes hanging in between rows of offices. Some doors were open, and Penna couldn't help looking inside. They were filled with expensive mahogany furniture, accent chairs, sophisticated window treatments, and brass light fixtures, and occasionally, she got a peek at a handsomely dressed executive or two.

"Wow, I had no idea what an attractive company you work for," Penna whispered. "Everything is so dignified—it's nothing like Uncle Dominic's office. Even his attorney Sal's office is low rent compared to this place. When I visit Sal, it's two flights up a dark staircase. His office is a mess, with piles of folders stacked on every available surface. You can't even see his furniture. But the worst part is the smell," Penna related. "Sal rents two rooms above a deli. Every time I've gone there, the kitchen downstairs always seems to be making sauce for the meatballs and spaghetti. You can't believe the odor coming up through the floor!"

Glynn smiled at the vivid description. The only smell she ever noticed at Shylock was lemon furniture polish.

The girls made the final turn into the partners' corridor. Only the very important had an office in this area, which meant either your name was on the front door or you were billing in the seven figures. Glynn knew Gil had his eye on occupying one of the corner offices, and she had no doubt he was on track to make senior partner. It was almost unbearable to think all his hard work would mean nothing if she didn't set things right. They were about to take their first step toward that goal: a friendly chat with Marshall Matlock's secretary, who had an altogether different personality from the trash-talking receptionist Misty.

Rose Mantle was right out of another era—a time when women took dictation, served coffee, made appointments (business or otherwise), and protected their boss from unwanted phone calls, unpleasant employees, and annoying spouses. She believed in Miss Manners' rules of etiquette and practiced an old-fashioned work ethic—she was never late, rarely sick, and expected a high degree of deference from others. A call from "Mr. Matlock's office" required a prompt reply, and you'd better make sure all the I's were dotted, and the T's crossed because she enforced a high standard.

Rose had created the office handbook, which carefully outlined all approved procedures. There was a large section covering typing, filing, and the proper storing of reports prepared by secretaries and legal assistants. It specifically required the preparer's initials and current date to appear on the bottom of each page of every document. At such a large and diverse law firm, Rose made it her business to be able to trace each report and know the origination of every document.

After all, she was Mr. Matlock's right hand, in charge of enforcing their firm's standards, and as such, took her responsibility seriously. That included leading by example and offering herself as the model of appropriate behavior. Protocol dictated proper respect and adhering to boundaries, especially from the younger associates and clerical staff. To the senior attorneys, Rose was friendly but in a standoffish way—everyone knew she always kept a sharp eye (or ear) out for any "talk" Mr. Matlock might need to know.

Glynn enjoyed a good relationship with Rose, mostly because Marshall respected Glynn's abilities. "Hi," Glynn said as she stopped in front of Marshall Matlock's outer office. Rose Mantle looked up from her desk and did a quick glance at Penna before turning to look into Glynn's eyes. A 50-something-ish matron, Rose dressed like she belonged in another era too. Her straight brown hair was pulled back into a bun at the nape of her neck. Standing around 5' 4" in her kitten-heeled black shoes, her figure could be described as pear-shaped. Short legs, a large bottom, and a flat chest made clothes shopping a real chore. Holding court from behind her desk suited Rose just fine.

"Why, Glynn, I didn't know Marshall was expecting you," Rose said, surprised that the librarian had showed up without an appointment . . . and with a stranger in tow. "He already left for his lunch appointment, and I don't know if he'll be able to see you later. His schedule is pretty tight this afternoon. Is there anything I can do?" Rose inquired in her all-too-familiar way.

"As a matter of fact, yes. We didn't come here to see Marshall," Glynn replied. "I was giving my friend Penna a tour. I thought he would be out to lunch by now and we might be able to peek inside his office. He has such a wonderful view."

A long three seconds passed as Rose sat quietly, staring at Glynn. There was nothing else for her to say until an introduction was made. A stickler for etiquette, the office was filled with stories about Rose's prim and formal behavior.

"Please forgive me," Glynn promptly responded. "This is my friend, Penna. She came for lunch. Would you care to join us?" Glynn knew there was a better chance of Rose doing a jig on her desk than to step out with them.

"Thank you for the invitation, Glynn, but not today. There are some reports for Mr. Matlock I need to finish," Rose replied, using one of her standard excuses. She liked Glynn well enough, but the only lunch date she'd seriously consider was one from Gil. Tall and handsome, Gil Patrick was a hunk who didn't even know the effect he had on women—especially her. The day he announced their engagement, Rose put on a happy face, but her insides felt like they had dropped 20 stories in a freefall.

Everyone knew about her standoffish attitude when it came to socializing with the female employees. Rose was partial to the company of men—a well-known secret. There was even talk she and Marshall had a thing going. "Nice to meet you Penna," said Rose, turning to greet Glynn's friend. She stared deep into Penna's fathomless clear brown eyes. There was a sense of familiarity, a strong feeling they had met before. They were connected in an important way, maybe as friends in another life . . . drawn in, comforted, relaxed. She couldn't put her finger on it, but it was hard to look away.

"Hi, Rose, nice to meet you," replied Penna, extending her hand. "You have a lovely office," she complimented sincerely. "It's going to be difficult going back to mine after spending time here. You guys are lucky to work in such beautiful surroundings. Do you think we'll be able to take a quick peek out the window?" Penna asked, concentrating on Rose's face. Penna could see the older woman's struggle to decide if she should let them into Marshall's office. *Would it be proper? What are the rules for this? Glynn's been in there a hundred times, and her friend seems nice enough. What could they do? What's the harm?* These were the thoughts running through Rose's mind as she considered Penna's request.

"Uh, I don't see why not," Rose concluded, pushing her chair away from the desk. "He does have the nicest office on the floor— after all, he is the head partner." She was proud of the fact she worked for the top guy, and his office was by far the most lavish. Walking over to the door, she inserted a key into the lock and turned the knob. The heavy door swung open with surprising ease.

Penna walked right behind Rose, happy to keep their conversation going. "Wow, it is impressive! Look at this view. Why you can just about see Manhattan from here." Penna was taking her time glancing around, all the while peppering Rose with questions. So fully engaged in replying, Rose didn't even notice Glynn hadn't followed them inside.

Penna heard all about Rose's involvement in decorating Marshall's office. She learned Rose was instrumental in choosing the colors and arranging the furniture. There were questions about her years of working for such an admired attorney—obviously successful—which, of course, couldn't have been accomplished without her. Penna kept eye contact with Rose, smiled in encouragement, nodded, and listened with rapt attention.

In the meantime, Glynn went to work searching for the SCAB files. Knowing Rose was anal about details like filing, there was no doubt it would most likely be in the large cabinet behind her desk. While Penna kept Rose distracted, Glynn quickly pulled open one drawer after another, rapidly scanning all the file folder tabs until she came upon the one titled ChemoCo. Removing it, Glynn examined every page. Her keen photographic memory recorded every detail— she was as good as any copier and without the telltale paper trail. She learned all about ChemoCo's plans for their new office, read about an upcoming golf outing, and even found the letter thanking Marshall for offering his legal services, putting the decision to retain Shylock off until the SCAB approval came through. Glynn found everything EXCEPT the SCAB documents. She next looked in the Crystal Clam Wineries folders, but while they contained interesting details, the SCAB formula wasn't to be found there either. Pressed for time, she decided to look for LICE.

Packed into three folders, the LICE file was huge. Glynn paused for a moment to listen in on what was happening with Penna. Thankfully, Rose was engaged and happy to respond to Penna's questions, meaning there was still time for her to pick through LICE. Halfway into the first file, Glynn came upon the original SCAB formula, which had been given to her. There was a cover letter attached from the CEO of ChemoCo, Bennett Kingsley. Horrified, Glynn read the letter twice. Here was proof of a link between ChemoCo and her own law firm. Not wasting a moment, Glynn flipped through the rest of the LICE file. After absorbing all the materials, she carefully replaced each page and closed the file drawers.

Glynn took a deep breath, composed her face, and walked into Marshall's office in time to hear Rose tell how she came to be hired by Marshall some 18 years ago. Signaling to Penna that her work was complete, Glynn waited for Rose to finish her story.

"Are you sure you don't want to join us for lunch?" Penna asked again. This time, Rose paused before she responded. The pull to stay in Penna's company was powerful, but so was her commitment to her job.

"Thank you, Penna, but no. I've work to complete. Mr. Matlock has an important meeting this afternoon. Maybe another time," Rose replied, wishing it could be otherwise. Turning to leave, Rose followed Penna out of the office. She noticed Glynn was there too. It was odd she hadn't remembered seeing her standing there before. *But, of course, Glynn must have. Where else would she have been?*

"Oh, before I forget," Glynn turned to Rose as if remembering an important business question. "I was wondering if you could give me the phone number for your contact at ChemoCo."

"Marshall's ChemoCo contact? Why is that necessary?" Rose asked, automatically suspicious of Glynn's request.

"I'd like to follow up with them. You know, as an addendum for my file," Glynn replied, hoping Rose wouldn't think too hard about this.

"Keeping the files up-to-date is so important," Penna added. "I do that all the time. In the end, it makes life so much easier."

There was no doubt Penna was doing her utmost to help Glynn get all the information she needed.

"Yes, of course it's important to keep your files complete," Rose said, repeating Penna's words. "But what kind of matter are you referring to?"

Even Penna's powerful presence wasn't enough to wipe away years of habit. Rose didn't think Marshall would want Glynn calling the CEO, Bennett Kingsley, for God's sake.

"Oh, I'd like to make sure I have all the info on the SCAB compound—it's pretty technical stuff, and you know how Marshall likes to make sure we have all the facts," countered Glynn. Sometimes, dealing with Rose was like walking a tightrope. One tiny slip . . . *There is a risk Rose might mention the request to Marshall, but so what?* Glynn thought. *He would think I am being thorough.*

"Hmmm," Rose muttered under her breath, thinking Marshall wouldn't mind if Glynn contacted someone in their R&D department. Rifling through her rolodex, Rose came upon the name she was looking for. "Here it is. Call Carl Hammerling, Vice President of Research & Development."

Chapter 29

"Excuse me, sir, are you finished?" asked the immaculately dressed dining room attendant at the Gold Coast Golf Club. The dining room was three-quarters filled with male-only members dressed in the club's permitted attire for lunch: collar shirts, no shorts, no sandals, and absolutely no jeans. The servers were kept to an even stricter standard: starchly pressed navy slacks, a cream-colored buttoned-down shirt, and a striped bowtie in the club's signature green and purple colors. There were no women working the lunch shift—in fact, women weren't allowed in the clubhouse between 11 a.m. and 3 p.m., a tradition held over from a bygone era. Calvin, a veteran waiter, smoothly removed the luncheon dishes, scraped the table clear of crumbs, and asked for the coffee and dessert order. The three gentlemen sat silently, waiting until the attendant departed before resuming their conversation.

"This was great, Stan. The food here never disappoints," Marshall said as he leaned back in the upholstered club chair to better digest his large lunch. While not a member of the GCGC—the club was too stuffy and the rules too oppressive for his taste—Marshall nevertheless always enjoyed visiting.

"My pleasure," Stan Piper replied. A founding member and Gold Coast trustee, Stan was one of a core group who voted to maintain strict adherence to the old rules, preferring to spend the day in the company of men of similar status and disposition. He had decided long ago to use whatever influence necessary to ensure the proper separation of the sexes. He liked it that way. Even with such unpopular, old-fashioned rules, the club had a long waiting list to get in. Stan believed continuing the customs from an earlier era was more important than ever, especially when Wall Street millionaires were a dime a dozen.

Privately, Stan was thankful he didn't have to dodge membership questions from his guests. The GCGC wasn't the sort of place for everyone. And anyway, Marshall and Arnie would never make it past the nominating committee, no matter how much money they amassed. The Gold Coast Golf Club was one of the few places left on the North Shore where some members could remember what it was like when $10 million and a seat on the board really meant something.

"I'd like to review ChemoCo's timetable for relocating to Long Island, if you wouldn't mind?" Marshall asked, wanting to get down to business. Lunch was nice, but it didn't mean shit next to the untold dollars in future revenue he was anticipating.

"Next week ChemoCo's legal department will be signing off on a three-year lease for 3,500 square feet of lab space at the LIQuID building," Stan replied. "This is the latest information, and comes straight from Bennett Kingsley."

"A lease?" Marshall responded in a voice a little too loud for GCGC standards. "I thought they were locating a major plant here, doing some serious construction. What's going on? Arnie, did you know about this?" The news was not good as far as Marshall was concerned. What kind of legal fees could he expect if they were leasing a couple of offices at the LIQuID plant?

"Calm down," Arnie soothed. He had already had a "heads-up" from Stan and knew Marshall wouldn't be too happy with the news. "Bennett is coming to Long Island next week and we'll nail things down with him then."

"Kingsley's a cautious man," Stan added, "and he has a split board to answer to, which, as you can appreciate, is not easy to manage. You know how it goes—one of the board members was angling for a new plant in Columbus, or somewhere. Bennett's got to go slow; he doesn't want to piss that guy off."

"So, explain this to me," Marshall demanded, glaring at Arnie, trying to keep control of his indoor voice. "I rounded up the GRowLers on the East End and got them to rally around SCAB. The formula was analyzed with an unofficial recommendation for approval. The Wine Growers League and LIAR joined forces to put pressure on LICE, working to discredit that louse McCleary. They even complained to the press that LICE was holding things up, causing an agricultural bottleneck and possible economic problems. Why I even did a couple of off-the-record interviews." With each statement, Marshall's voice got progressively louder. "All to help smooth the way for ChemoCo to locate to Long Island.

"Things couldn't have worked out better for you, Arnie. Word is you're on the shortlist as LICE's next director. And what do I have? A new client leasing office space half the size of my house! Tell me, how are you going to make this right?" Marshall was spitting mad, his lunch lying in his stomach like a slab of sludge.

"Look, Marshall, of course, I understand you're pissed off. But let's get things straight," Arnie counseled, using both hands to calm the waves of intensity shooting out from Marshall's eyes. The key was to distract Marshall from seeing red and get him to focus on all the green he'd be making. "Everyone knew it was a matter of time before McCleary would get the boot as Director of the Long Island Conservation and Environment. And there's no denying you did a fantastic job—it probably sped things up, too. As for your client, Crystal Clam . . . Well, they're already using SCAB now, right? They think you've done another wonderful job representing their interests. Have I summarized things correctly so far? Finally, it's not as if ChemoCo is using another firm for its legal work. There is no one else—you're their guy."

Marshall was slowly calming down. The deal with ChemoCo would happen, only now it would be later rather than sooner. At least all that money he had been mentally counting wasn't evaporating if you could trust what Arnie was saying.

"Look, Marshall, I talked with Bennett about your firm already," Stan explained reasonably. "He's committed to using you—their move here is just a smaller step than originally planned. Come on, they're taking it slow. These things happen. Only the timetable has altered, that's all," Stan counseled, looking around to see what effect Marshall's temper tantrum was having. Thankfully, the dining room had emptied and the few members present were otherwise engaged.

"That's nice talk, Stan," Marshall spat, his eyes bulging in anger. In the twilight of his career, Marshall wanted to go out with a big win, and being chief counsel to a major ChemoCo division was going to be it. This was his entrée into one of America's leading chemical and manufacturing companies. "There's no way I'm going to be at the beck and call of some junior exec sitting in a closet-sized cubical at LIQuID," he emphasized.

"ChemoCo's advance team is arriving next week, all their top guys. Of course, we'll be meeting with them—the first chance we can. In addition, I plan on hosting a LIMBO reception at the Sunset Haven Club. You know, to give them an official welcome." Arnie was doing all he could to turn things around for Marshall. "I'll be inviting all the usual suspects on my A list, as well as some key pols. And we'll include whoever you want—like those agricultural guys on the East End and, of course, Crystal Clam Wineries.

"Even Bennett is planning on attending. Let's face it: he's not making the trip for any other reason than to square things and set their plans for a bigger move later next year. Think of this as a dress rehearsal," Stan said with finality. Calvin appeared at his elbow with a pen. Stan barely looked at the chit as he scribbled his initials with annoyance. In the old days, they would automatically charge his account. But with a new computerized system and an expanded membership, controls were needed.

"What day's your shindig?" Marshall asked, resigned that expending any further energy on this situation was fruitless. As the steam that powered his fury dissipated, he knew it was only a matter of time before his digestive system would relax and unknot.

"Thursday, June 30," Arnie replied, satisfied Marshall was finally on board.

Chapter 30

Glynn was relieved to hear the door to their apartment close; she had been patiently waiting for Gil to return from his LIMBO meeting.

"Is that you?" she called from the living room couch. "How did the meeting go?"

"You know those things—20 minutes of networking, 20 minutes of rules and association business, and 45 minutes of Arnie Holtzmann outlining his plans for the next six months. You'd never know the guy was about to be leaving to head up LICE.

"So, it's official?" Glynn asked.

"Yeah, it seems his appointment to become Director of LICE wasn't much of a secret. Arnie was ready for a new challenge—at least, that's what he said tonight."

Glynn nodded as she listened.

"Well, I can tell you everyone at the meeting toasted and congratulated Arnie on his appointment. It was Christmas in June for LIMBO—there's no doubt it'll be a boon to business with Arnie heading both organizations. It's what we're all about."

"You mean Arnie is staying on at LIMBO?" Glynn asked, astounded he wasn't relinquishing this role.

"He's in no rush to leave. Said he wants the change in leadership to be smooth and is taking time to find the right replacement. In fact, everyone liked the idea of a slow transition. After all, the guy practically gave birth to LIMBO. It's been his baby for almost 30 years. It's gotta be hard to walk away from that," Gil explained.

Glynn was appalled. "Don't you think it's a conflict?" she asked. "How can you run oversight on issues concerning <u>L</u>ong <u>I</u>sland <u>C</u>onservation and <u>E</u>nvironmental AND promote business investment at the same time? It's inevitable disputes will arise. Where will his sympathies lie?"

"Why does supporting the environment have to be at odds with business growth and prosperity? Oh, I wouldn't worry, Glynn," Gil soothed. "I think Arnie wants what's best for our region. We're in for some exciting times at LIMBO and I'm glad to be a part of things."

Gil left for the bedroom to change out of his suit and missed seeing Glynn's unhappy expression. She wasn't going to challenge her husband's view of these new developments. It was clear Gil was buying into the whole LIMBO mumbo jumbo. She couldn't imagine what Gil would say if he found out Arnie knew ChemoCo was less than honest about SCAB. What if SCAB was harmful to the environment? It made her sick to think Arnie Holtzmann, a guy Gil all but idolized, would have sold out to ChemoCo. This was a money deal, pure and simple. Glynn hoped she was wrong about the potential health problems, environmental pollution, and crop damage. Of course, they'll need a high-powered attorney like Marshall Matlock should the negligence lawsuits start rolling in. She prayed it wouldn't come to that.

Chapter 31

Glynn took a deep breath and lifted the phone receiver to make the call according to plan.

"Hello, Carl Hammerling, please," she asked.

"One moment and I'll see if he's available," said the female on the other end of the line. Glynn held her breath, hoping she'd get to speak with Carl and have this whole SCAB issue put to rest.

"Hammerling," said the voice.

"Hi, this is Glynn Patrick from Shuster, Yleskin, and Matlock."

"Yes?" came the quick reply.

"I'm calling about SCAB. My company represents Crystal Clam Wineries, an agricultural company here on Long Island, which has enjoyed great success with SCAB. We're actively lobbying our elected representatives, hoping SCAB will be quickly approved by our local environmental agency." Glynn paused to catch her breath. It felt as if she were speaking to herself.

"Yes?" he replied.

"As you must know, the whole approval process hinges on having SCAB pass an environmental evaluation. Well, we'd like to do everything in our power to speed this process along." Her goal was to position them as allies, working toward a common goal.

"Yes?"

"It seems our files are missing a key piece of the formula. We need you to forward a complete version. I can give you my email address or fax number, whichever works best for you," she concluded, glad to have put the request on the table.

Silence.

"Hello, Mr. Hammerling?" She felt the need to address him formally. "Are you there?" Glynn asked, feeling more uncomfortable by the minute.

"Yes."

"Well, what works best, email or fax?" Glynn was trying to keep her nerves from showing in her voice as she was having trouble breathing.

"You are sorely mistaken, Ms. Whateveryournameis. While we appreciate your efforts on behalf of SCAB, we cannot release company documents of this sensitive nature to just anyone who makes a phone call. Please type a request—on letterhead, of course—and send it to our customer service department. Only by following our established protocols will we be able to evaluate your request and determine if it is legitimate."

Glynn's mind went numb as she listened to Carl Hammerling drone on about company policy. Sadly, she realized there was no way she was going to get the SCAB info easily, at least not from Carl Hammerling. This was the dead end she had feared.

As she was hanging up from her call, Glynn spied Marshall Matlock striding purposefully toward her desk.

"Morning, Glynn," Marshall began seriously.

"Hi, Marshall," Glynn replied, wondering what monumental event could have brought the firm's senior partner to the law library first thing in the morning.

"Rose tells me she gave you the name and phone number of Carl Hammerling at ChemoCo. She couldn't explain why you needed to call him . . . something about tying up loose ends. Whatever it is, I think it's best we limit our contact with ChemoCo. There are important, and delicate negotiations going on between our firm and ChemoCo, and I wouldn't want to mess things up because of unauthorized contact."

"Of course, Marshall," Glynn readily agreed, wondering privately what the hell was going on.

"I tell you this confidentially: ChemoCo is planning to open a satellite office here on Long Island in the LIQuID building. I believe it's the start of what could be a new plant—a boon for our economy and this firm. I'm confident we'll be able to lock up most, if not all, of ChemoCo's legal work. In any case, we're hosting . . . LIMBO, I mean, is hosting a reception for some of ChemoCo's advance team in two weeks. The invitations are going out today. I'm proud to say you've earned an invite, regardless of what your LIMBO husband has to say. I don't have to tell you how crucial your research on SCAB was in helping bring all this about. If we didn't put pressure on LICE, none of this would be happening," Marshall concluded, happy to give credit where credit is due.

Glynn was speechless, all the while staring back with a pleasant smile, nodding her head in agreement.

"Now, I know you want to make sure your files are tidy, but in this case, I'm telling you to let things alone. As soon as LICE gets a new director, I'm confident they'll approve SCAB. After all, you said it was environmentally safe, and I'd take your evaluation over that nut McCleary's any day. This is a win-win-win-win scenario," Marshall continued. "A win for Crystal Clam having access to SCAB's superior agricultural benefits, a win for ChemoCo with SCAB opening up new agricultural markets, a win for LIMBO by landing a new major employer for our area, and a big win for us. We need to take a step back and let LIMBO work out the details between LICE and ChemoCo. Now that McCleary's out, things should move along pretty quickly, but ChemoCo's a bit skittish. We don't want to do anything that may spook them or cause a pullback—that would be a major disaster," Marshall summarized, outlining his rationale as much for himself as for Glynn.

"So, you understand how important it is we steer clear of ChemoCo for the time being?" There was no mistaking Marshall's meaning as he lowered his gaze and fixed Glynn with one of his hairy eyeball looks. This last line was more than a simple request. An implied threat hung over her ominously.

"Of course," Glynn replied. There was little else she could say as she fought to regulate her breathing and appear calm. Marshall was a shark in designer clothing. She couldn't mistake the vibe radiating across her desk—Marshall Matlock would swallow her whole if she screwed up his deal. And not just her, but Gil, too. GULP!

"All right," he concluded. "Let Rose know if you need anything."

Glynn watched her boss turn and walk briskly away. Marshall's intensity and win-at-all-cost style were well-known around the office. But this was the first time she had been on the receiving end, and it rattled her. Further contact with ChemoCo was now out of the question, meaning her chances of getting a copy of the complete SCAB formula were next to nil.

What is the real story of SCAB? Glynn wondered. Is it the world's best fertilizer or an environmental nightmare? Maybe a little of both, she surmised. In any case, Marshall made it perfectly clear she was to drop the whole thing. After all, she had a wonderful relationship with Gil and a great job. Why not simply let LICE, ChemoCo, LIAR, LIMBO, and Marshall Matlock work it all out?

Unfortunately, this was one SCAB Glynn was itching to pick.

Part 6
Complications

192

Chapter 32

Arnie came back to the office feeling better than he had in a long time. The blood was flowing through his limbs, pumping confidence and power with each stride. The visit to LICE headquarters left him eager to move in. He decided to make an unannounced stopover, wanting to see what was going on inside. *After 30 years of McCleary's mismanagement style, I may have to fumigate the place*, Arnie thought, not without some glee. His impromptu arrival took everyone by surprise, even the Head Louse himself.

Wish I had a photo of that look on his face—now, that would be something I'd hang on the wall for dart practice. Arnie chuckled to himself.

The tour left him cold: room upon room of gray metal file cabinets, gray metal desks, and gray metal chairs. The place even smelled depressing—it had that institutional odor of neglect, except for the labs. Those areas were spotless. You could eat off the floor; they were so clean, the complete opposite of the offices, which were cluttered and dusty. A young functionary named Bruce showed him around. The poor kid looked to be no older than 15, although he mentioned he'd graduated with a master's in environmental engineering from some fancy college.

But the highlight of the morning was walking into McCleary's office. *If looks could kill, I would have been lying on the floor with my legs in the air like a dead beetle. But instead, I'm the top bug at LICE.* Arnie laughed out loud. The animosity between the two men was so great McCleary could barely perform the basic social custom of shaking Arnie's hand.

"Came to see your new office?" McCleary barked as Arnie strolled in like he was already installed. "I'll be moving my stuff out over the weekend, if you can wait that long?" This last line was delivered with undisguised venom, and Arnie loved every minute of it.

"I guess you'll be finding another host," Arnie remarked snidely. He couldn't resist one last jab. McCleary had been sucking the blood of the people of New York for far too long. Arnie didn't feel one ounce of regret in having had a hand in forcing him out.

Arriving back at his office, Arnie walked to his secretary's desk. He couldn't wait to put his plans into action.

"June, I need you to arrange for a cleaning crew to go over to the LICE building next week and clean out that office—the corner one. In fact, I'm going to knock down a wall and grab the associate director's office too, so we'll have to get a paint crew. Also, call that decorator we used, Eileen What's-her-name, and get her up here for an appointment. That place needs lots of work.

"Oh, and call Ted Landis and have him send over a case of Crystal Clam wine for the staff. That should put those nitpickers in a good mood." Arnie chuckled to himself. *It's ironic; that's what it is. It is ironic to toast the end of an era with wine that benefited from the very substance they were trying to ban.*

"Next, contact the governor's office and find out if there are any rules or stuff in the bylaws concerning the transfer of power from one director to the next. You'll need to get a roster of LICE employees, too. Then I want you to prepare a memo asking for each person's work and education history. Time to do a little nitpicking myself," he concluded with glee.

"Those poor bastards at LICE," June mumbled under her breath. "They'll be surprised when the exterminators show up." Before she could look up and ask if there was anything else, Arnie had one last request. She rolled her eyes at his rapid-fire impersonal style.

"Oh, and get Stan Piper on the phone. I don't care if he's in the crapper with his pants around his ankles—I need to talk with him right away." He then abruptly turned, walked into his office, and closed the door.

June sighed and once again wondered if the money was worth it. Arnie was a tough, gruff, street-fighting loudmouth who couldn't tell good manners from bad. He simply had no manners. Being accustomed to his work style, and paid exceedingly well, kept her at a job she had begun to loathe. It hadn't taken her long to stop helping him discover his kinder/gentler side. Instead, she became very good at damage control. Lately, she had even stopped working at that.

"Mr. Piper is on the line," June reported to her boss.

"Stan, I just got back from LICE. I'll be moving in within a week. What a dump that place is. Give me a month and you won't recognize it." Arnie barreled through the details. "And you'll appreciate this—I asked Ted to send over a case of wine as a parting farewell gift." He chuckled.

Stan was holding the other end of the phone as if it were nuclear waste. *What happened to the protocol of pleasantries?* he wondered. The man was a bull in a china shop, and Stan felt like all the fancy plates were being shattered into bits. He had to listen to Arnie rant a full five minutes before he could get a word in edgewise. It was so boorish and impolite. But he needed this uncouth man, and Stan sucked up his displeasure.

"Yes, I see, you'll be cleaning house over at LICE. Of course you should," Stan agreed, trying to respond in a civilized fashion. "Look, Arnie, I just got off the phone with Bennett—they're all set to come to Long Island in two weeks for the reception. In fact, they plan on relocating ChemoCo's R&D unit immediately. He asked again for assurances that SCAB has LICE's approval. He wants to do a conference call this afternoon—now, if you have a minute?"

"Sure, sure, whatever," Arnie replied, wondering why Bennett was so worried. "What more can I do? Once I'm installed as the new director, I'll stamp APPROVED on Bennett's forehead if he wants."

On the other end of the phone, Stan rolled his eyes. "Hang on, Arnie. I'll patch us into Bennett now."

A minute or so went by, and the sound of a phone being answered could be heard.

"Is that you, Stan? You always did have impeccable timing. I'm getting ready to chip into the 15th—hang on a second, will you?"

Thursday afternoon was Bennett's golf day, and he was supposed to be inaccessible, even with today's technology. Bennett had been around plenty of men like A Holtz: big talk, lots of hot air, promising the moon—or, in his case, the coveted LICE approval. When the chips were down, and you HAD to make the putt for par, the guy would choke. Bennett had to make sure that the LIMBO guy didn't leave him in limbo, hanging from his own petard.

"Give him a minute, Arnie," Stan explained. "He's made our conversation a priority."

Pacing in his office, stopping every minute or so to look at the view, Arnie couldn't believe HE had to wait until Bennett completed his golf shot—a not-so-subtle reminder he was still one rung from the top of the food chain.

"Thanks, Stan," Bennett huffed into the phone. "I had a bit of a tricky lie but knocked it in in two."

"Bennett, I have Arnie Holtzmann on the line," Stan said.

"Oh, yes, that's right. Good of you to wait. We're having a helluva day here at Spruce Hill. You'll have to come out for a round once all this LICE business is over. Stan tells me you're a scratch golfer. I look forward to a friendly wager when we get together."

"Yes, I look forward to it too," Arnie replied, twitching with pent-up energy. He fought against his high-octane nature, trying to calm down and allow Bennett to control the pace of the conversation. And it was damned difficult, too.

"Stan, I'm trying to make time for a round when I come to town," Bennett drawled on. "There's a lot on my agenda for this trip, but nothing some prioritizing couldn't fix. In any case, where do we stand with LICE, Arnie? I'm relying on YOU," Bennett delivered forcibly as he changed the subject. "We've made a lot of plans based simply on your assurances. Now the deal must be done. The board needs proof SCAB has the go-ahead—our marketing and distribution plans are relying on this. A newspaper headline reading LICE IS OFFICIALLY APPROVED on Monday should do the trick. Pick any paper you'd like—the *New York Times*, *The Post*, even *Newsday*, and alert my office. Don't disappoint me, Arnie." This last part dangled quietly in the air.

"Right, Bennett. We'll talk again next week. Drinks at the Safari Club Monday night as usual when you get in. Regards to Cynthia." Bennett rang off.

Arnie was fuming. He felt like some low-level administrative assistant taking orders from an arrogant boss. And where was Stan in all this? Hiding on the other end of the phone, letting Bennett-fucking-Kingsley walk all over him—the new head of LICE, the chairman of LIMBO, who had hundreds of people all over the island competing for his favor. It was galling, but Arnie knew he needed to keep Stan's goodwill a little longer.

"Well, Arnie, you heard Bennett: time to deliver the goods," Stan reiterated. "Bennett can be a bit bossy. Always was at school. He'll need that headline to convince his board, which isn't unreasonable when you think about it."

Stan was prattling on as Arnie double-marched the same path from one end of the office to the other.

"Stan, there's one little problem—I'm not going to be installed as head of LICE until later in the week. How the hell can I get that headline BEFORE I take office?"

"Well, that is not my concern," Stan shot back. *Just who the hell does Arnie think he's talking to?* "Let's not forget who came to me begging for an introduction to my school chum. Who was it that guaranteed approval? Who is getting a new ChemoCo R&D department coming to Long Island, which LIMBO can take credit for? Look, Arnie, now it's time for you to keep your word."

By now, Arnie was raging mad. Who the hell did that pantywaist Stan Piper think he was dealing with? "Look, Stan, all I'm saying is it's a bit unreasonable for Bennett to expect the approval before I'm sworn in. I simply won't have the authority on Monday," he croaked. Sweating and red-faced, Arnie loosened his tie and opened the top button of his shirt.

"Well, that's not our problem, is it?" Stan countered. "Don't get cold feet now, Arnie—it's not becoming. Bennett and I have every confidence you'll pull this off. We look forward to Monday's paper," he closed, choosing to use the royal pronoun.

Arnie was fuming as he slammed the phone. His mind raced through all sorts of alternatives, one worse than the next. There was no way he could allow the whole ChemoCo deal to slip through his fingers, not when he was this close. He'd look like the biggest jerk on the planet. Yet, how was he to get SCAB approved when he wasn't the head of LICE? *There's no way I'll get access to those SCAB files,*

Arnie thought, *and I'd sooner eat SCAB than ask McCleary for their results.*

That left only one alternative.

"Get me, Marshall Matlock," Arnie barked to June. If there was one person who had as much to gain as Arnie, it was Marshall. *Without SCAB, Marshall will have a lot of unhappy clients. And without Bennett Kingsley, there goes ChemoCo's R&D move to Long Island and all those fat legal fees Marshall is dreaming about.*

"Mr. Matlock on the line," June announced. She knew something was up—her boss's good mood had quickly been replaced by a foul one.

"Marshall, I need your help," Arnie began, all pleasantries aside. "I'm . . . No, WE'RE in a bind."

Marshall was used to Arnie's brusque style, but even by his standards, this was unusual. "You know I'll do what I can. What is it?" Marshall looked at the ceiling, waiting for it to fall. Chicken Little had nothing on A Holtz.

"I need to leak that SCAB report to the press. You know, the one where your research girl said SCAB was environmentally safe?"

"Her report is proprietary information. She's not working for LICE; she's my employee. She can't approve SCAB—only LICE can do that," Marshall explained as if he were talking to a high school civics student.

"I know," spat Arnie, losing his patience. "Look, I have to have the SCAB approval in the newspapers on Monday—MONDAY!—before I'm to be sworn in. If that story doesn't appear, Kingsley pulls out, which means no ChemoCo on Long Island, no fat fees for Shylock, and no fertilizer for your wine friends on the East End."

The other end of the phone was silent. "Come on, Marshall, don't you see? We've come this far already–what's one more thing to clinch the deal?" pleaded Arnie. "Would it be horrible if that report made it into the press a day or two early? I'll be approving SCAB as my first official act as the new director of LICE. What's the worst that can happen?"

Marshall was fuming. He had already put himself out on a limb with his client Crystal Clam Winery, assuring them privately that SCAB was environmentally safe, based on Glynn's report. They were such a bunch of nervous ninnies, afraid it wouldn't be approved, afraid it would have a negative impact on the soil, or afraid it would contaminate their precious vines. He told them it would turn out all right, and they paid him a lot of money for that advice, too. Marshall was getting a knot in his gut—the premonition of a bad feeling.

"Look, I'll leak the report to the press Sunday," Arnie offered. "I know someone who'll be more than happy to get this scoop. We'll take your report and slap a LICE logo on it. Who's to know? McCleary's out. And those other LICE nitpickers—they're a bunch of nobodies if I ever saw. Who's going to challenge us?" Arnie ranted, convinced beyond a doubt of the rightness of his position.

"All right, I'll drop it off later today," Marshall volunteered against his better judgment. "But I'm going to remove all traces of my firm's name. There better not be a fuck up here, Arnie," threatened Marshall.

"June!" barked Arnie. "Get me that reporter Roger Haddit from *Newsday* right away! Oh, and make a golf reservation at the club for Sunday."

Chapter 33

Marshall hung up the phone and grabbed a bottle of antacid from his bottom desk drawer. Lately, every conversation seemed to end with acid reflux. *This better not be another screwup, with Arnie promising more than he could deliver, juggling ChemoCo, LICE, LIMBO, and his own law firm like so many marionettes on a stage.* Marshall hated the feeling of having his strings yanked.

"Rose, get me a copy of Glynn's report on SCAB, please," Marshall requested into the intercom. At least, this was one thing he could count on—there was no reason for him to doubt Glynn's research or her conclusions. "Clear my schedule for the rest of the day."

After a discreet knock, Rose walked over to Marshall and handed him Glynn's report on SCAB, neatly typed on company letterhead inside one of those report covers with the firm's name embossed on the front—a professional presentation befitting the head partner, Rose thought.

"Oh, this has our letterhead and name all over it," Marshall remarked. "This won't do, Rose. I need the report on plain paper: no letterhead, no presentation cover. Nothing. And put it in one of those unmarked manila envelopes."

Not ten minutes later, Rose returned with the report inside the plain envelope. Marshall slipped out the top half to satisfy himself that all evidence of Shuster, Yleskin, and Matlock, Attorneys at Law, was removed. "I'll be back later," Marshall said as he exited.

"Goodbye, Mr. Matlock," Misty called from the reception desk as Marshall marched through the door. Have a good weekend."

Marshall offered a quick wave and curt nod. He had much more important things on his mind than an exchange of pleasantries with the receptionist.

Chapter 34

Picking up the phone, Misty pressed the top speed dial button. "Hi, June. Is he in?" Taking out a nail file, Misty gave her index finger a careful review as she waited to be connected.

"I'm getting ready for a snack," Misty delivered in a quiet, breathless voice.

"What do you feel like today?" the male voice at the other end of the phone asked.

"I need a pick-me-up," she continued, leading up to the game they played.

"Would you be more comfortable lying on top of the desk?" he asked, rubbing himself with pleasure, imagining her lying right in front of him.

"A vanilla cone," came the reply, code for his penis. "I can't wait to get my lips on the cool ice cream top."

"You mean you'll be licking the entire cone?"

"I love to lick ice cream," Misty breathed into the phone, making slurping sounds.

Hard as a rock, Arnie released himself from the confines of his khaki trousers as he relaxed into his desk chair.

Through the phone, he heard Misty say goodbye to a couple of associates leaving for the weekend. The thought of her talking to them as she ate the ice cream cone spread-eagled on top of the desk was an even bigger turn-on.

His phone rang as June tried buzzing in unsuccessfully. She knew he was talking to someone at Shuster, Yleskin, and Matlock and normally would have figured it was Marshall Matlock, except it was Marshall who was calling, saying he'd be dropping by in a couple of minutes. "I'll let Arnie know, Mr. Matlock. He's on an important call right now," she explained, wondering who her boss was tied up with.

Arnie ignored a couple more interruptions as he enjoyed listening to Misty finish her ice cream cone, especially when she asked for his sweet syrup to top things off.

Chapter 35

Strolling into the LIMBO executive office, Marshall went right to the chairman's door. "Hi, June. Is Arnie in?" Marshall asked as a mere formality, all but ready to turn the knob and let himself in. He had never been denied access, and with his company's SCAB report, Marshall figured Arnie would have met him out front with open arms.

"He's in all right, but on the phone right now. I've been buzzing him since your phone call. I don't know who he's talking with, but it's someone at your firm," June offered, not thinking she was revealing anything top secret. After all, everyone knew Marshall and Arnie went way back.

In one swift move, Marshall reached over to the phone and announced himself before he had the handset at his ear.

"Marshall," Arnie croaked. "Give me a minute."

"Is that you, Rose?" Marshall asked, thinking he caught the tail end of a female voice.

"No, it's me, Misty, Mr. Matlock," the receptionist replied. "I was, um, telling Arn . . . Mr. Holtzmann about a um, you know, a place to get great ice cream."

Marshall listened as the girl bumbled on, talking nonsense. He always thought she was an airhead, but now he was even more convinced. He'd have to talk to Rose about her and find out what the hell she was doing talking to A Holtz.

"I'm here, Arnie. Why am I waiting outside while you're talking to my receptionist?" Marshall asked, allowing his annoyance to flare.

Releasing the phone to its rightful owner, June simply returned Marshall's stare. An uncomfortable moment passed. Both adults allowed the silence of Arnie's outer office to cushion their thoughts.

In the minutes it took for Arnie to straighten himself out, Marshall's stomach had turned itself into an amazingly tight ball. If the envelope contained any other information, he would have left it with June and walked out. But there was no way he'd turn over this report and possibly implicate himself to anyone other than Arnie.

"Marshall, thanks for coming over," Arnie offered expansively as he marched out to meet the attorney. Face flushed, eyes averted, jacket buttoned, he looked like a well-dressed shoplifter running from the law.

"Look, Arnie, I don't know what's going on, but here's that report we talked about. I wanted to deliver it myself, no mix-ups. Take care of it and keep me informed," Marshall advised. He couldn't wait to get out of there. In fact, he wanted to put all this SCAB/LICE/ChemoCo bullshit behind him.

Chapter 36

"Mr. Haddit?"

"Yes,"

"Hold for Mr. Holtzmann," June announced.

Roger rolled his eyes. *Doesn't this guy know we are in the twenty-FIRST century?* He couldn't believe A Holtz couldn't pick up the phone and press the phone buttons himself. *Who did he think he was?* Roger had no patience for these old white guys, a bunch of throwbacks, men who still thought they ruled the world. After years of covering everything from police corruption, political scandals, mob rubouts, and all sorts of predatory sex and money laundering cases, Roger had HADD-IT. His name was an all-too-appropriate description of the cynical backpack he carried.

"Roger, I have a good one for you," Arnie said.

"Yeah?" This was not the first time Roger was the beneficiary of Arnie's nonexistent social skills. "So what is it this time?" Roger asked, allowing a dose of sarcasm to creep into the conversation. He didn't want Arnie to think he was sitting around waiting for his phone call. There had been times when Arnie's "news flashes" were nothing more than self-serving press releases.

"I don't want to get into it on the phone. What are you doing on Sunday? How 'bout meeting me at the club for a round of golf? Say 10:30?"

Roger perked up. "What's all this about?" He didn't want to seem too easy. "If I have to give up my Sunday, I need a little more to go on." Roger could play hardball with the best of them.

"You've heard of SCAB, right? You know there's a lot riding on its approval. Well, I've got the report. You know the one I mean," Arnie teased, dropping hints to whet Roger's curiosity.

"You mean you have the LICE report? How did you get your hands on it?"

"All I'll say is I was over there this morning. Do I have to connect the dots for you? Meet me Sunday morning and all your questions will be answered."

This was an offer Roger couldn't pass up. But he didn't fully trust A Holtz either. He had a friend at LICE and called over to check Arnie's story. Sure enough, the soon-to-be-installed new director was telling the truth. Roger went to see his editor—this could be big. Front-page news is big.

Chapter 37

Roger Haddit had one busy Sunday afternoon. His golf game with Arnie was cut short as he excused himself to make a beeline into the office. He spent the rest of the day writing and researching an article that not only impacted the lives of countless Long Island residents but may have clinched him a Pulitzer Prize. Roger left no stone unturned. He reached out to Bill McCleary, the soon-to-be-former head of LICE, whose responsibility it was to issue the report. "No Comment," was all he got.

Of course, he had Arnie Holtzmann's quote: "Great news for the East End, LIAR, and the Wine Growers League. A big win for the Long Island economy in general, and of course, LIMBO in particular. I look forward to taking LICE into uncharted territories."

Arnie was all too happy to take full credit for the report, even though he had nothing to do with it. Roger considered it one big egocentric rant. Then he reached Bennett Kingsley, ChemoCo's CEO, for a quote. Beaming with praise for all those LICE workers—so diligent, so impartial, so right. Why shouldn't he be thrilled? That report put millions into his pocket and billions into his company's coffers.

210

Chapter 38

"Thanks for coming out on such short notice," Glynn said, glad they all could make it. The gratitude she felt eased the tightness around her mouth and eyes. The strain was taking its toll.

"I have to come up with a better excuse to explain where I'm going than an emergency Tupperware party," joked Sollie. "Stewie gave me a funny look, like I was getting some, you know, sex on the side."

A little levity was what the room needed. Even Ray blushed.

"We've all seen the story?" Iris asked rhetorically. She had almost spit out her morning coffee upon unrolling the paper. An early riser, Iris, called Glynn at 5 a.m. This news couldn't wait for a more civilized time.

Copies of *Newsday* were arranged on the counter in Lab 8. The front page was filled with huge letters that screamed: LICE APPROVES SCAB. But that wasn't what caused Glynn to ask for an emergency book club meeting. She had figured SCAB would be approved sooner or later. It was worse than that.

Glynn spent the day hiding in her office in the law library, fending off phone calls by shocked coworkers. Too worried that returning home would reflect a guilty conscience, she stayed and toughed it out. By the end of the day, she was exhausted and didn't think anyone believed her protestations and explanations of innocence anyway. Why should they? She thought. Even Rose called on behalf of Marshall Matlock, wondering how her report made it into the paper. Rose made some vague threats about looking into firm security and hinted at an official inquiry.

"We can only imagine what you've been going through today," Penna soothed as she put her arm around Glynn's shoulders. "It's natural everyone would think you leaked the report, but I know they're more shocked than anything. Even Gil. He doesn't think you had anything to do with this. Your husband loves you and is looking for answers. He wants to come to your rescue, but doesn't quite know how."

Penna's words were what a frightened Glynn needed. From the moment Glynn saw the paper's reproduction of the LICE report and noticed the GOP at the very bottom of each page, her life forever changed. The minuscule letters were barely discernible, but they were her initials: GOP, standing for Glynn Olsen Patrick. It didn't matter if the report was on LICE letterhead or if the story was credited to a high-level LICE informant. Whoever stole the report simply forgot to remove her initials from the footnotes on the bottom of each page, where they automatically appeared as part of Rose Mantel's procedural rules on office reports.

"I was hoping the SCAB assessment I wrote would never see the light of day," Glynn confessed to her friends. "It was a mistake, written out of pride and ignorance. Maybe there is a LICE report, one that evaluates the full SCAB formula. But now I'm not so sure."

"ChemoCo's stock shot through the roof today," Iris reported. "I had a feeling it was going to go up, but even I had no idea the full effect this leak would have on the stock price. That reporter did his homework."

"Don't fret so, Glynn," Onawhim said. "Only your coworkers think you're associated with this report—they will forget all about it in a day or so. In fact, you'll probably be considered a hero." Her assessment was hard to counter. "There are two issues which we must consider. The first has global consequences: Is SCAB safe? The second question is of a more personal nature: How to clear your name? In my estimation, you must solve the first in order to correct the second."

"I know, I know," Glynn replied with a sigh, thankful to have her friends come to the same conclusions. "But in order to prove SCAB safe, we need to get the full formula. And I've tried—there's no way they'll release it. Regular company channels are a dead-end. Especially now that everyone thinks the full formula was approved."

"Who says we need to go through regular channels?" Penna asked. "Why I've heard of countless stories from Uncle Dominic's friends who operate on the fringe. We need to figure out where the formula is kept."

"That would most likely be with the head of R&D," Ray suggested. "I would guess it's in a protected computer file."

"Hey, didn't that article say ChemoCo is opening up an R&D office here at LIQuID?" Sollie asked. "Wouldn't the formula be assessable from here?"

"They're moving in next week," Glynn confirmed. "In fact, there's a reception for them on June 30th, which also happens to be Arnie Holtzmann's not-so-farewell to LIMBO gala."

"Everyone who is anyone on Long Island is being invited. Even I got an invitation," Iris volunteered. "I heard the chairman of ChemoCo, Bennett Kingsley, will be attending."

"And I wouldn't be surprised if their VP of Research and Development, Carl Hammerling will be there as well," piped in Glynn.

"Are you suggesting we break into the ChemoCo offices and get a copy of that formula? What is this, Watergate? We're not plumbers," Sollie blurted out, "we're housewives. How are we supposed to lift a SCAB while being inside a LIQuID? It's a comedy skit if you ask me."

"I'm with you, Glynn," Onawhim said, her voice leaving a pleasant echo inside Lab 8's concrete walls. "I believe these special gifts require us to make some sacrifices, a type of payback, if you will. How perfect for us to do something worthy like helping determine whether SCAB is real or simply a nasty cover-up."

"I know we're all uneasy about snooping around, searching for information that's been locked away," Penna explained. "And believe me when I tell you, the cops are out there looking for the bad guys. But they're not looking for us. Not a couple of sweet middle-aged. . ."

"Hey, watch who you're calling middle-aged," Sollie shot back.

"You know what I mean. I see this all the time with Uncle Dominic's associates. Sometimes, they get caught, but not as much as you'd think. And the police won't be looking for us, believe me. They'll be trailing those characters," Penna concluded. "But this won't mean much without help analyzing SCAB from Ray and his team," Glynn explained.

All eyes turned toward the researcher. "Not to worry, we will do our best to provide an accurate evaluation of this chemical," Ray confirmed. "Just be advised it may take a week or two before we have conclusive results."

Chapter 39

When Sollie left for work, her kitchen was clean, the laundry was folded, and the house straightened. She was even marinating chicken for their evening dinner. This would have been unheard of six months ago. She now had more time to spend servicing current customers and developing new prospects, and was currently on track to win Broker Of The Month for the second time in a row. Inhaling those chemicals might not have been something she'd have volunteered for, but the benefits were undeniable. Even the snobby Prep Squad did a 180, and she was now included in their gossip gatherings.

"Sollie, can I see you for a minute?" Myra called from her office. Sitting patiently behind her desk, she watched Sollie Gold, once the most disheveled, disorganized agent in her office, take her seat. The woman staring back appeared 20 lbs. thinner and almost unrecognizable. From the top of her new haircut to the color-coordinated outfit, she was styled and fashionable. If the changes hadn't happened before her eyes, Myra never would have believed them.

Over the years, Myra had been patiently employing various management skills to shape her wayward charge, and she took her job as a motivator and molder very seriously. So, of course, she accepted a healthy share of responsibility for her agent's transformation. Thankfully, the turnaround came just in time. The home office only wanted winners on their team, and Myra had been running out of ideas. During company management meetings, she'd use Sollie (name withheld) as a sample problem, asking for possible solutions. Time was ticking, and Myra was being forced to make the hard choice of putting the slacker on probation. But now, with Sollie's transformation right before her eyes, Myra believed the change was the result of her years of time and effort. Proud of this not-so-minor accomplishment, Myra felt justified in her unofficial title of 'agent of change.'

Amazingly, this all happened when she had been on the verge of giving up! If there was one lesson to be learned, it was hard work, and patience paid off—proof positive even the most difficult cases can be saved.

"Hi, Myra, how can I help?" Sollie asked.

"Home office called. You may have heard that ChemoCo, a large chemical engineering company, has decided to open an office here. There's a couple of relo's for us to handle. Some ChemoCo executives are moving to Long Island," Myra explained. "I thought I'd have you handle one."

"All right," Sollie exclaimed, still not used to her newfound success because, in the past, Myra would have given this plum assignment to either Cynthia or Brooke. "I know they're taking over space at the LIQuID facility," Sollie replied. "In fact, I think there's a LIMBO reception next week welcoming them, if I'm not mistaken."

Once again, Myra could only shake her head, staring back at her charge as a proud mother would after her toddler took its first steps.

"The man is the head of research, the top guy in their R&D department: Carl Hammerling. He's single and looking for an upscale bachelor pad. ChemoCo is guaranteeing the mortgage and all the fees. I'm told he works around the clock—one of those tech nerds who has little social skills. I thought of you right away. If anyone can get him to relax and open up, you can," Myra said, using a newly learned management technique aimed at guiding Sollie to the next level.

"Here's his number and a brief customer profile. He's expecting your call. Good luck." Myra pushed the materials into Sollie's waiting hands.

Back at her desk, Sollie couldn't believe the coincidence. Here is the profile of ChemoCo's R&D guy! It must be the same one Glynn had been talking about. Picking up the phone, Sollie could barely contain her curiosity.

"Hammerling," the voice said.

"Carl Hammerling?" Sollie asked. "This is Soledad Gold from LISP. I'm the realtor who will be helping you find your new Long Island home."

"Oh, yes, the realtor," he replied curtly. There was no reason to get happy about a move he never wanted.

Sollie felt the frosty reception immediately and didn't want to spend any more time on the phone than necessary. Compressing her few questions into as many seconds, she got all the information she needed to identify possible houses for him to visit next week.

Carl was surprised when he got off the phone. She had interrupted an important calculation, and he figured the phone call cost him a good 15 minutes. But when he glanced at his watch, it appeared they had been talking for less than half that time. House hunting was a necessary evil, and hopefully, this woman was organized. The less time spent, the better.

Chapter 40

Sollie pulled into the first empty space closest to the main entryway. "Who would have thought I'd be back at LIQuID so soon? Two months ago I didn't even know this place existed, and now I'm here once a week!" she said to herself.

Climbing out of the car, Sollie gathered her materials and marched off to the main reception area. The place was different in daylight. For one thing, the reception desk was manned, and there were people in the lobby. She also noticed an indefinable buzz, an energy that wasn't there at night.

"Soledad Gold for Carl Hammerling," she said to the guard behind the massive counter.

"I don't recognize the name. What company is he with?"

"ChemoCo," she replied.

"One moment."

Sollie waited patiently while the guard searched through papers and binders.

"I'm sorry, but I don't show anyone with that name listed."

"He's new—ChemoCo recently leased space here," she offered. "Here's his extension. Maybe this will help."

The guard gave her a funny look. It was his job to know the occupants and protect them from unwanted guests.

After doing some brief research, the guard replied, "Mr. Hammerling will be right out."

At the strike of 3:00, Carl Hammerling lumbered into the lobby. He was a tall fellow with rounded shoulders and muddy brown hair, which could have used a good shampooing. His clothing looked soft and fuzzy like they had been washed too many times but not pressed. Sollie wouldn't have been surprised if he slept in his clothes. Brown eyes darted from behind brown-framed glasses. Even his teeth looked brownish.

"Ms. Gold," he said, addressing Sollie as he extended a limp hand. It could have been either a question or a statement. "Follow me back to my office. We obviously can't talk here."

After barely shaking his hand, Sollie did as she was told. Not another word was spoken until they arrived at his office. The hallways at LIQuID had a typical institutional feel. World-class research might be happening in their labs, but the hallways looked like an inner-city high school without the graffiti. Sollie tried to keep track of their route, but it became almost impossible as one corridor blended into the next. Only when they rounded the last corner did the color change to a burnt orange right before they scooted into Carl Hammerling's office.

"Please have a seat," he said, gesturing to the lone metal office chair directly across from his desk.

"Oh, I see you have Western exposure," Sollie commented, noticing the afternoon sun streaming through the window behind him. She always tried to start off a meeting by saying something positive—unfortunately, that was the only constructive observation she could make. His office was a small, cluttered space with folders, binders, and books littering the desk and floor. There were piles of computer reports stacked about. Some seemed to be growing toward the ceiling. Glancing upward, Sollie noticed a mass of cables and wires hanging from a hole in the ceiling tiles. The electronic spaghetti wound its way into various connections on his computer.

"Yes, the glare on my computer screen is maddening," Carl mumbled, slightly impressed this woman made an intelligent observation. He caught her eyeing the wires dangling overhead. "This is a temporary hookup. My move here was sudden, and it was the best they could do. It's my lifeline to the mainframe," he explained, delivering the last line with a lopsided smirk.

Oy, thought Sollie, *I think he just made a joke.* Clearing her throat, she decided to move things along. "I've brought some homes for us to review based on your remarks over the phone the other day." Luckily, she had guessed right about this guy—he'd prefer darkness to light, was something of a loner, and wouldn't care about his neighbors or if he lived on a busy street.

Sollie went into her presentation and took notes on the various homes Carl seemed to be interested in. He wasn't talkative, so she had to read his nonverbal cues. They decided to meet on Sunday, and she'd drive him around to visit those he chose. She could pick him up here, he suggested.

"Well, Mr. Hammerling, I'm sure we'll find you a nice home in no time," Sollie affirmed, giving those nasty wires a cold look. She could imagine them coming to life, entwining unsuspecting humans in some sort of electrical chrysalis.

"I'm sure too. Thank you for your help. See you Sunday."

Sollie couldn't wait to get out of there.

Part 7

Intensification

224

Chapter 41

It was unusual for the book club to meet on a weekend—there were always so many chores to catch up on after a whole week of work, not to mention various family and social obligations. But the importance of the upcoming LIMBO reception outweighed all other concerns.

Iris agreed to host the club. Working at home had given her access to Brett 24/7, so what did missing one Saturday afternoon matter? Mrs. Bambino was available, and the two went off to a museum program. Iris decided to bring in some food, keeping the menu light and casual.

Adjusting her lifestyle from being a high-powered stockbroker/finance mover-and-shaker to working from home was not as difficult a transition as Iris once thought it would be. While she wasn't officially terminated, Baxter Wright made it clear they didn't want her back. It was too risky. The thought of the SEC crawling all over their files was a consequence no one needed. Iris was smart enough to realize it wasn't healthy to sit in front of her computer all day making trades, even if it did yield her vast sums of money. She had been looking for a way to combine her knowledge and special talent for picking stocks with her newfound free time, and had finally come up with the perfect solution.

The sound of the doorbell interrupted her thoughts. Sollie was the first to arrive.

"It's been a while since I sold you this place," Sollie remarked as she walked into Iris's beautifully decorated foyer.

"I'm here five years," Iris replied. "And what changes have happened during that time!" *Not the least is my investment abilities,* she thought.

"It's beautiful," commented Sollie, marveling at what unlimited financial resources can achieve.

The rest of the book club began arriving. Meeting at a member's home was a new experience for the girls. Iris was proud to show off, pointing out various paintings and objects d'art sprinkled throughout. After a brief house tour, everyone settled in the living room. As the unofficial leader, Glynn stood to start things off.

"Now is a good time to summarize our plans," Glynn began. "This Thursday is LIMBO's reception welcoming ChemoCo's executives. LIMBO has invited a Who's Who of the region's rich and powerful. It's also Arnie Holtzmann's first official LICE event, so I'd be surprised if it wasn't well attended."

"Even Uncle Dominic got an invite," Penna said with a twinkle in her eye. "Too bad he doesn't plan on attending."

Glynn smiled and continued with her review. "My firm's partners will be going, and not surprisingly, I got an invitation of my own. I guess that little article in Newsday wasn't a total loss," she remarked dryly. "Our primary goal is to gain access to the SCAB formula. But I'd also like to find out exactly who at the law firm leaked my SCAB report to the press. The thought of a spy in my office is unsettling."

"Couldn't the formula be with LICE?" Sollie asked. "After all, weren't they evaluating it before McCleary got sacked? It might be easier to reach out to Bill McCleary and see if we can get access."

"And why should Bill McCleary turn that over to us?" Iris interjected. "He could have spoken out to the press countless times, but didn't. I don't think he has the complete formula, and admitting to it publicly would further tarnish his already cloudy legacy."

"I agree," concluded Glynn. "We have to assume LICE has the partial version, the same as I found in my company's files. Otherwise,

McCleary would have made an announcement that could have saved his job. I believe the entire SCAB formula is a closely guarded secret, one that has never been released in its entirety." The rest of them nodded in agreement.

"Is everyone set?" Glynn asked.

"I'll pick you up at 7:30," Sollie said to Onawhim. "Can you believe I've turned down free food and drinks to sneak around that old dungeon in the dark? What would Stewie think?"

"Well, that leaves you, Iris. How can we get you in?" Glynn asked.

"No need," Iris replied, brandishing her invitation.

"I've recently formed a new consulting service: Investor Relations and Insider Services—IRIS. I'll be monitoring corporate boards as a stockholder and have decided to start with ChemoCo," Iris announced to the delight of her guests. "Bennett Kingsley himself has extended a personal invitation, along with a select few of their major stockholders, to a private pre-reception reception. It's all about thanking those who have stuck with the company, allowing us to bask in their soon-to-be success with SCAB."

Glynn nodded approvingly. Things were coming together. Now, all they needed was a little luck.

228

Chapter 42

It was one of those picture-perfect early summer days. Even the membership committee couldn't have arranged a more ideal weather forecast. The sun illuminated the golf course from a cloudless blue sky. The greens were fast, and the fairways were breathtaking. The relaxed foursome was finishing their round and ready to enjoy a leisurely lunch. A casual observer would have figured the group as two aging brothers hosting a morning of golf with their adult sons, as they appeared familiar and at ease with each other. But the relationships went deeper than simple family ties, and there was more at stake than kinship and harmony. This seemingly casual reunion was the latest in a series of clandestine meetings held over the past year.

Today's golf round had Stan Piper paired with Ted Landis, the current president of Long Island Agricultural Resources (LIAR), owner of Crystal Clam Wineries, and a man with the good fortune to be standing on the precipice of a monumental change—one that would revolutionize his industry. But it was more than luck that favored Ted. It didn't hurt that his mother was Stan Piper's sister or that Uncle Stan had bankrolled Crystal Clam. Conversely, Bennett Kingsley partnered with Carl Hammerling, ChemoCo's R&D guru and son of Bennett's first cousin.

These SCABees, as they called themselves, had been planning this very moment for years. The fact that they all got along so well was beside the point. Their association began with a chance meeting almost seven years ago during a private ChemoCo holiday party held for top management and select family members in New York City. Bennett happily invited his old school buddy Stan Piper. But when Stan's wife was unable to attend, Stan extended the invitation to his nephew Ted.

The two had become business partners in the up-and-coming Crystal Clam Winery. Their business relationship started when Ted approached Uncle Stan to borrow money for some gambling debts. Not willing to simply throw good money after bad, Stan was intrigued by Ted's interest in starting a winery. Wine growing on Long Island was a new concept at the time, and Stan always liked getting in on the ground floor of new ventures. It didn't hurt that he had a knack for picking winners. After careful research and a no-nonsense business plan, Stan gave more than his blessing—his $8 million investment bought him majority ownership in Crystal Clam Winery and brought his nephew under Stan's protective wing. Stan was happy to keep his involvement quiet. He gave Ted a long leash, one with a retractable button, to more easily keep an eye on things. A savvy businessman and shrewd investor, Stan's original $8 million was worth triple now.

Ted was considered one of the region's wine experts. He became an active member of the GRowLers (Wine GRowers League) and its big brother, LIAR (Long Island Agricultural Resources). All this involvement gave him a certain notoriety, which he drank up. His personality was perfectly suited to the limelight as he partied his way through East End social events. Despite age and personality differences, Stan and Ted's personal and business relationships bloomed as their enterprises expanded and diversified.

The ChemoCo party proved to be fruitful territory for their interests. After a brief introduction to Carl Hammerling, the two young men immediately clicked. It was easy to cultivate Carl's interest in the wine industry as Ted complained about the need for a high-yield fertilizer. Carl realized they had much in common, too, especially since ChemoCo was starting research into a weed suppressor that could also fertilize crops.

As CEO, Bennett had been able to quietly divert company resources to fund Carl's research, thankfully turning this discreet gamble into a scientific breakthrough. It took longer than he had thought, all the while getting assurances from Carl that a formula was forthcoming. Meanwhile, Ted rallied the GRowLers and kept up the pressure with LIAR, insisting there was a real and urgent need.

It fell to Stan to figure a way around the many local regulations and environmental roadblocks a new agricultural product must navigate. Stan quickly learned any new fertilizer would need the approval of Bill McCleary's LICE, a difficult process at best. That's when he decided to join LIMBO and become an ally of Arnie Holtzmann, McCleary's sworn enemy.

"Four club specials," Stan ordered after the steward brought their drinks.

"Here's to SCAB," Ted announced as he raised his glass of Crystal Clam merlot for a toast.

"To SCAB," the other three SCABees intoned as they clinked glasses.

"We're at the 18th tee," Bennett summarized. "We should be sending the first shipment to LIAR in two weeks. Our stock price is up 80 percent, and ChemoCo is on track to have our best year ever. But the credit must go to Carl and Ted."

Stan was okay with that. Credit was something he gave to his wife. Between reaping the benefits in his portfolio from ChemoCo's higher stock value to the increase in profits from Crystal Clam's improved wine production, Stan felt the smug self-satisfaction of success. He quietly acknowledged his own invisible handiwork: Who helped incite the "war" between A Holtz and McCleary? Who got Bennett to open a ChemoCo office on Long Island? And who was the shrewd negotiator dangling rich legal fees in front of Marshall Matlock in exchange for a priceless and utterly false SCAB evaluation? The full-page Newsday article touting LICE's approval of SCAB leaked to Roger Haddit was icing on the cake. *This is how business should be done,* Stan thought. *The quiet exercise of judgment and power, the unseen hand pulling the strings. There are no nosey regulators, no curious board members, or high-and-mighty watchdog zealots to answer to.*

While Stan had been on the front lines smoothing the road for SCAB's approval, Carl was the man behind the scenes, working tirelessly on a product that could deliver for Ted's GRowLers. A high-yield fertilizer AND an effective weed suppressor—it was a worthy challenge. It had taken years of research and a couple of close calls, times when it looked as if the whole project could have tanked before he hit upon the right formula. Lurking in the background, like a sore that wouldn't heal, was the chance SCAB might not fulfill its creator's intentions. It didn't help to have the CEO breathing down his neck, either. That he was related to Bennett Kingsley didn't seem to matter. Results were all Bennett cared about, and Carl was not going to let his efforts fail. That was never an option. Even naming SCAB—<u>S</u>elective <u>C</u>hemical <u>A</u>gricultural <u>B</u>ioproducts—was inspired.

"It's Carl who deserves the credit," Ted replied. "Without his hard work, his total commitment . . . Well, we wouldn't be celebrating today."

"Yes, quite right," Bennett acknowledged. "There's no doubt Carl's future is secured as ChemoCo's 'Crusty Golden Boy.'"

"How're things going?" Ted asked, redirecting the conversation to cover the project's few loose ends.

"The LIQuID facility is under construction, and the work should be done in a couple of weeks," Carl replied. "In the meantime, I've installed a temporary computer link to the mainframe back at HQ, but it's not as secure as I would like. It was the choice between the lesser of two evils—risk pushing back our production timetable as we wait to install a slower yet more secure computer connection vs. going for speed," Carl explained, trying to keep the frustration out of his voice.

Obviously, with the SCAB report leaked, McCleary shitcanned, and the eyes of the stock market staring at the ChemoCo stock price, Carl chose expediency over security. So close to approval, he was unable to imagine what could derail the SCAB delivery timetable at this stage.

But despite everything, Carl was still pissed off about the move to Long Island. *What a bitch*, he thought when he learned about his department's relocation. *This is the last thing I need,* he complained mostly to himself. But it was out of his hands. Not even a personal appeal directly to Bennett made any difference. It was the price ChemoCo had to pay to get the coveted approval from LICE, or so he was told. Did he want to leave the company and see years of his life go down the drain?

"Long Island is a great place to live," Bennett had said. "Don't worry, Stan and Ted will set you up, take you under their wing. You'll forever be known ChemoCo's 'Crusty Golden Boy,' with an immediate appointment to LIMBO," Bennett promised.

"I think you made the right choice, Carl. Security is not much of an issue anymore," Stan confirmed, trying to smooth the researcher's ruffled feathers. "There's nobody left to worry about: McCleary's been neutralized, A Holtz and LICE are on board, even the press is thrilled with the prospect of ChemoCo bringing more jobs to goose the local economy. Who's left to stand in our way?" Stan crowed, finally voicing his innermost thoughts.

"We still have LIMBO's reception on Thursday. I'm especially looking forward to shaking Arnie Holtzmann's hand," Bennett admitted slyly. "There's also a special Investor Relations meet-and-greet earlier in the evening before the official party starts. Some of our larger stockholders who live in the area have been invited, I'll be personally meeting and glad-handing those investors who have supported our stock," Bennett announced.

"There are a few others you need to meet," reminded Stan. "Let's not forget about Marshall Matlock and his girl who wrote that report. Marshall is expecting a signed legal contract in the next week or so."

"I've invited Roger Haddit, the *Newsday* reporter who broke the story," Ted offered, barely suppressing a grin. "There will also be the usual local politicians and business leaders. LIMBO is inviting everyone."

"Oh, and I've arranged for a special surprise for the evening," Stan concluded. "It'll be a knockout."

Carl sat quietly as the others discussed plans for the reception. *This is one event I won't mind missing*, he thought. It seemed even a "crusty Golden Boy" had obligations.

"By the way, have you started house hunting yet?" asked Ted.

"I've met with the broker Sunday. She showed me a couple of places. I'm deciding between two of them," Carl replied, wishing for a last-minute reprieve. "I hope to make a decision in time for the reception." There was something poetic about having all the loose ends tied up at once.

"That's an ambitious schedule. Let me know when you've decided and I'll see if I can help," Stan said. He couldn't resist stepping into a deal.

Chapter 43

Walking into the sumptuous Sunset Haven Club, Iris felt like Cinderella at the ball, minus Prince Charming. She had dusted off one of her designer cocktail dresses. The black silk hugged her trim figure, accentuating her bosom, with a thigh-high slit revealing a shapely leg. Four-inch pumps a couple of diamond baubles sparkling on her wrist and ears, Iris was dressed to impress. After years of hobnobbing with the rich and richer in New York City, going solo to a suburban shindig on a Thursday night was child's play. It was her secret agenda that infused the evening with anticipation. Head high, shoulders back, Iris glided to the greeter's desk. She produced the coveted investors' invitation and was quickly checked in.

The violet-hued Twilight Room was awash in a thousand tiny lights, which would resemble stars once the sun slipped below the horizon. A tuxedo waiter offered her a glass of champagne as she surveyed the room. Right away, she caught the eyes of a couple of the guys from her office and, of course, Baxter Wright. Walking over to her former boss, Iris was warmed by the surprised look on his face.

"Hi, Iris, good to see you," intoned a curious Baxter. Only superior breeding saved him from showing discomfort. *How the hell did she get an invitation?* He wondered to himself before he quickly put two and two together. *Of course . . .* It confirmed his original suspicion that she had access to insider information; otherwise, how could you explain her incredible run of success with the ChemoCo stock?

"Baxter, yes, it's good to see you, too," Iris replied, barely suppressing a grin as she raised her glass in a mock toast. She knew what he was thinking. It was a logical conclusion, after all.

"You must introduce me to some of your ChemoCo friends," Baxter suggested in an undisguised assumption of her illegal activity.

"Oh, I've never met the ChemoCo folks," Iris brazenly replied. "Have you?"

Confused, Baxter stared, unable to form an appropriate retort. He didn't believe her. How could she have received the necessary information—which would explain her stupendous run-up in ChemoCo stock—without a personal connection? But years of ingrained social training prevented him from challenging her statement in such a public setting.

"As you say," was all he could manage before being interrupted by none other than Stan Piper.

"So good to see you," Stan said, offering Baxter his hand.

"Of course, I wouldn't miss this," Baxter replied, knowing the firm expected him to represent their interests. Caught in the web of social customs, Baxter had no choice but to introduce Iris to his largest client.

"Stan Piper, this is Iris Carmichael," Baxter said, all but mumbling her name. "Until recently, we worked together." Baxter didn't want his client to think they were still colleagues.

"Iris, have we met?" the old fox asked, always one to appreciate a good-looking woman.

"Not that I can recall. I'm sure I would remember," she replied sweetly. Of course, Iris had heard of Stan Piper. Who on Long Island hadn't? He had a reputation for being an "old school" charmer—someone who'd been involved with big business dealings for over 50 years, as well as being one of Long Island's most generous philanthropists. He knew all the players—had you out to his club if he liked you. This charming elder statesman could be as tough as nails if even half the stories Iris heard were true.

"But you're not associated with Baxter's firm anymore, is that right?" Stan asked. He had to have all the facts.

"No, I've recently gone out on my own. I'm sure Baxter is doing a fine job on your account, Mr. Piper. But in case you'd like another perspective, I'd be happy to do a review."

Burning with rage, Baxter could barely keep a civil tongue. "Stan Piper is an old friend of my dad's—we go way back." This was as much as Baxter could claim without sounding like a braggart.

"Well, Ms. Carmichael, thank you for your offer. As Baxter says, we do have a long and profitable relationship. I'm guessing you're here because of your prior association with his firm?" Stan asked, giving a nod in Baxter's direction.

"After leaving, I've recently invested heavily in ChemoCo," Iris offered with a slight smile. "And thought it would be fun to meet Bennett Kingsley and his management team."

"I'm an old school chum of Bennett's. Why don't I make the introduction? You won't mind if I take Ms. Carmichael away?" Stan asked a fuming Baxter.

Stan was never more on his best behavior than when escorting a beautiful woman, and Iris Carmichael was striking. He was the gallant knight to her damsel in success. A light touch on the small of her back guided Iris in the right direction.

"So, Ms. Carmichael, how invested are you?" Stan asked smoothly.

"About 9 percent," Iris replied, watching Stan Piper's expression change.

"Of your family's account, I assume. Is your husband here, too?" Stan was surprised he didn't already know the guy. Maybe they belong to the Brightwater Bog Club, which would explain things. He'd lost count of how many Brightwater Bog members first applied to get into the GCGC and were subsequently turned away.

"How about you?" she asked, steering the conversation away from herself. "We have a lot to celebrate. Bennett Kingsley is a genius, and I can't wait to show my appreciation."

Stan scanned the room for a glimpse of her husband, expecting the guy to stroll over any minute, looking for an introduction. Of course, the husband would recognize Stan. After all, he had appeared in the news countless times as Long Island's elder statesman of industry.

"Er, well, I'm not as well-invested as you," Stan said, giving her an appreciative look. "Baxter tries to keep me diversified, but maybe there's room in my portfolio for another approach," he suggested, figuring ChemoCo represented less than 3 percent of his investment portfolio.

Their conversation was interrupted when Stan's nephew appeared.

"Allow me to introduce Ted Landis, member of Long Island Agricultural Resources and owner of Crystal Clam Winery. Ted, this is Iris Carmichael." Stan wanted to finish the introduction with her business title or family's accomplishments, or husband's associations but realized he had no further information.

"Pleased to meet you," Ted offered with a smile.

"Will we be enjoying your wine this evening? Crystal Clam is a private company, yes?" Iris asked, twirling her glass. She took a moment to study the youthful-looking vintner. He reminded her of a California surfer: blond hair, even tan, and a naturally relaxed attitude. She imagined him having a snack in his board shorts at a local burger shack.

"Yes, on both counts. We're longtime members of LIMBO, and whenever they host an event, they try to promote their members' products and services."

"Tell me, Ted, what's your take on SCAB? Is it as good as they say? Do you think it will make a difference?" Iris asked, looking forward to getting his insight on the product.

"Crystal Clam was one of the wineries that took part in the test. SCAB was amazing. It almost doubled our yield, and we didn't have to do any weed control either," Ted explained. "We're a small operation, and SCAB improved our production at a fraction of the cost. It was invaluable. SCAB is important for all agriculture on the East End, not just for the GRowLers."

"GRowLers?" Iris repeated. "Some East End music group?"

"GRowLers is what we call the Wine Growers League, our local industry association. We're part of LIAR–Long Island Agricultural Resources—members of LIMBO and big supporters of ChemoCo and SCAB," explained Ted.

"We have a lot at stake," Stan added. "Unless you're involved with agriculture, you may not fully appreciate ChemoCo's impact. Ted and I are on the front lines, so to speak," Stan clarified, wanting to make sure she knew which side of the SCAB debate he was on.

"You must be pretty pleased with the LICE approval?" Iris asked, already knowing the answer.

"You bet," Ted replied. "That nitpicker Bill McCleary could have ruined everything. Everyone on the East End cares about the environment, but we need to balance that with making a living. New products should be encouraged, not stifled. We finally have someone who has our business interests at heart running LICE. I'm proud that Stan had a hand in helping."

"Really?" Iris exclaimed. She was getting the strong sense Stan Piper was more than an old-time business busybody and couldn't resist getting confirmation on her suspicions. "Do you have a business interest in Crystal Clam?" Iris asked Stan, all but knowing his answer.

"Right you are, Ms. Carmichael," Ted replied, smiling at her quick assessment. "Without Stan's help, we wouldn't be one of the leading grape growers and wine producers on the East End. Stan believed in the wine industry before we even produced our first bottle."

Iris gave Stan a smile and nod of appreciation. The old gentleman deserved his reputation. She had a feeling things were going very well at Crystal Clam. "You wouldn't be looking for additional investors?" Iris asked. Maybe she could buy in. *Why not?* she thought. *This may be an opportunity to keep close tabs on what's going on.*

"Well, Ms. Carmichael—" Stan started to reply.

"Please, call me Iris."

"Okay, Iris. We can set a date for further discussions," Stan offered. "What type of investment were you thinking?"

"Oh, I don't know. I would consider somewhere between 10 and 20 . . . it would depend. Of course, I'd have to review your books," she explained, glancing over at Ted.

Stan's thin smile barely masked his paternalistic air. She may be able to talk a good game, but she couldn't run with the bulls. There was no doubt he'd need to discuss any deal with her husband.

"Ten to twenty thousand dollars wouldn't even cover the expenses of this year's harvest," Stan replied, treating her with the deference he used when talking to women about their golf game: polite but in a superior sort of way. "We'd be happy to invite you and your husband over to the club to discuss things. You know, the Gold Coast Golf

Club." He couldn't resist getting in a social dig. Maybe she should stick to playing bridge when making bids.

"Oh, Stan, you're mistaken! I didn't mean $10–20 thousand—I was talking about $10–20 million dollars." Iris laughed. She was taking great pleasure in watching Stan's expression change from one of condescension to enlightened self-interest. They were making a lot of money, Iris surmised, and she'd be surprised if they'd tell her where the books were, let alone allow her to look at them. Ted didn't say anything. She wasn't sure if the GRowLer liked the idea of bringing another investor in, or maybe he didn't want to let on that his relationship with Stan could use a little shaking up. There was more going on here than calculating a return on investment, Iris surmised.

Before further investment talks could continue, Stan was clapped on the back by a stylishly dressed middle-aged man. From the perfectly positioned handkerchief in the charcoal-gray suit pocket and the sharply knotted Countess Mara tie all the way down to the knife-creased pants and the smartly shined Bally loafers, Marshall Matlock extended a manicured hand to Stan. The gold Patek Phillippe watch peeking out from behind the monogrammed shirt cuff was overshadowed by a large diamond school ring.

After paying respects to Stan, as protocol would demand, Marshall turned to his client. "Ted, good to see you, too," Marshall added, pumping the GRowLer's hand.

"I understand Shylock had something to do with the SCAB evaluation making it into the press," Ted stated, hinting at the public story. Of course, he knew Uncle Stan pressured Arnie, who then put the squeeze on Marshall.

"Glad we could help," Marshall replied, shifting his stance. His first instinct was to remind his client of all the legal services his firm continues to provide, but the circumstances of the "leak" left him distinctly tongue-tied. "It goes to show you can never be too secure," an uncomfortable Marshall replied. He hated seeing his company's private documents appear in the press. An anonymous leak was one thing, but it was especially unpleasant when his company was identified as the source of the documents. Damned unpleasant! But it had happened, and there was nothing he could do about it. He might as well try to find some way to come out ahead.

This exchange was the intel Iris was looking for. She picked up right away that it was Marshall Matlock, the head partner, who had arranged for the SCAB report to find its way into the press. *I wonder what Glynn would make of that?* she thought.

"I was thinking maybe we should draw up a liability statement," Marshall suggested to both Stan and Ted, "in case something goes wrong. Why not protect yourself? Of course, SCAB is great, but well . . . An Act of God is one thing, but what if this chemical ground cover ruins your vines? Where are you then? Think of it like an insurance policy, only you don't have to pay any premiums. This way should something go wrong with SCAB . . . Not that anything will, but you never know. A statement of liability will assign risk to ChemoCo upfront. You can talk to Kingsley about this, right, Stan?"

Marshall was out for bear. Someone had to pay for the breach in his firm's security, and he always looked to the guy with the deepest pockets. And because Crystal Clam benefited the most, and Stan not only owned Crystal Clam but was Bennett Kingsley's best friend . . . Well, he could connect the dots as well as the next guy. Why the hell shouldn't his company get some money for drawing up some legal docs: a small price to pay for his firm's unexpected exposure?

"Of course, Shylock is indispensable," Stan concurred. "We couldn't do it without you. We'll talk next week."

"Let me introduce you to Iris Carmichael. She's one of ChemoCo's major stockholders," Stan said, happy to change the subject and not averse to using Iris—as a matador would his cape—to draw the bull's attention.

"So, you're a ChemoCo stockholder?" Marshall asked, eyeing the attractive woman. Unlike Stan, Marshall held women in high regard and prided himself on not underestimating them. He learned long ago if you want to be successful, surround yourself with women. They work harder than men, care more, and you can even pay them less.

"What kind of work are you in?" he asked, not one to beat around the bush.

"I'm in my own business now, and trade in stocks and bonds, which is why I was invited," Iris said.

"Iris is one of ChemoCo leading investors on Long Island," Stan announced, wanting to make sure Marshall knew who he was talking to.

"How many shares do you own?" Marshall asked, needing to put a number to her face.

"Somewhere around 9." Iris blushed.

"Nine shares?" Marshall repeated, quickly figuring the value at a couple of hundred dollars. No big deal.

"No, my shares represent about 9 percent of the company," she replied sweetly, secretly enjoying the change in Marshall's expression. "I'm particularly bullish on ChemoCo."

"Yes, we're all pretty bullish on ChemoCo," parroted Marshall, always one to adopt an interesting phrase.

"Tell me, Mr. Matlock. What did your firm do for Crystal Clam that concerned ChemoCo?"

"My firm represents Crystal Clam. They have a lot riding on SCAB, hoping it'll cover over a host of problems."

"Oh, yes, Ted Landis mentioned how his East End GRowLers were itching to get their hands on SCAB. Could it be your firm has been involved in this regard?" Iris asked.

"Yes, we were helpful in discovering the true nature of the formula. How the press got hold of our internal report I'll never know, but it resulted in a real win-win for everyone. And we're in the win business," Marshall emphasized. He was always selling, always trying to close the deal, even if there wasn't one.

"If I'm not mistaken, Shylock has a reputation for being successful," she continued. "It's always good to know where one can find a lawyer who will put his client's needs first."

Her not-so-subtle suggestion that she may require the services of a high-powered attorney like Marshall Matlock, coupled with his revised calculation of her net worth, kept Marshall interested in the conversation.

"Here comes Bennett now," Stan announced, glad to use Bennett as another distraction; Marshall was getting that leering look in his eye.

So far, Iris has been picking up bits of information about ChemoCo and learning about Stan, Ted, and Marshall's interconnectedness.

"Bennett, this young lady has been looking forward to meeting you all evening," Stan said in his ultrasmooth voice as he again touched the small of her back to propel her toward ChemoCo's chairman.

"Hi, Mr. Kingsley, I'm Iris Carmichael," Iris said as she offered her hand, confidently stepping inside his inner circle of associates, leaving Stan, Ted, and Marshall to look on.

Bennett was momentarily taken back. He had been briefed on all the stockholders, but no one told him Iris Carmichael, one of ChemoCo's largest, was an attractive young woman.

"Well, Iris, we had hoped you would come," said Kingsley in his best royal flourish. The woman-owned more shares than he did and almost half of what was held by the entire Board of Directors. It was hard for him to think she was anything but exceedingly lovely and, of course, exceedingly lucky. The Investor Relations Department had done a quick calculation of all the shareholders they invited, and her ChemoCo shares alone were worth close to $80 million. Sure, there were a couple of big fund managers in attendance, along with some pension investors who controlled more shares, but she was the single largest shareholder in the room.

Falling into a familiar role, Iris allowed the engaging Bennett Kingsley to speak about his vision for ChemoCo. He was at ease taking credit for ChemoCo's recent success and dropped hints of what she could expect in the future. Iris laughed to herself at that last remark. The future was something she didn't need any help understanding. To hear Bennett Kingsley talk, you'd think he alone developed the SCAB formula. She pressed him with her desire to meet their crack research team, wanting more than anything to extend her congratulations to those who discovered the answer to creating the next Garden of Eden. Reluctantly, Bennett waved over a tall, pasty-faced, uncomfortable-looking underling.

"Let me present Carl Hammerling, head of our R&D team and developer of SCAB."

"Carl, nice to meet you. I think you created my fortune single-handedly," Iris purred, as she delivered one compliment after another, setting about to charm this gawky, socially awkward man.

Iris's gift was not that she knew the future, only that she could get a sense of things. It was easiest with numbers, especially stocks. She'd simply get a feeling of whether she should buy, hold, or sell and then act on those sensations. There was no doubt Carl Hammerling would be accessing the SCAB formula over the next couple of days—you didn't need to have a heightened awareness to know that. But where would he be? And could they remote in? As Iris focused all her attention on Carl, peppering him with questions and listening intently to his answers, eventually, she began to get an awareness of his next actions. She knew he'd be logging on to ChemoCo's mainframe later that evening. Yes, it was at the LIQuID facility–of course, he'd have an office hookup, even if it were only temporary. There was more, too, something about great quantities of SCAB. She figured it was a delivery of sorts.

Carl was warming to the attention of this attractive investor. Glad to talk about himself to a willing listener, she was even smiling at his responses. He didn't realize how lonely he'd been. Not that he needed a girlfriend—there was no time to date. But he wasn't a monk, either. Iris laughed at one of his favorite anecdotes, the one about staying late and getting locked in the chemistry lab for the weekend. She asked about his schooling and where he got the inspiration for SCAB, things he hadn't articulated in a while. He found himself loosening up.

"Excuse me, Ms. Carmichael," Bennett Kingsley interrupted. "Can we borrow Carl for some introductions? I promise to bring him right back."

"Of course. I hadn't meant to monopolize him," Iris replied, offering the gentlemen a dazzling smile. "We can finish our conversation later," she said casually before turning to leave.

Bennett's interruption couldn't come at a better time. The violet Twilight Room was filling up as the LIMBO invitees began arriving. There was a palatable excitement in the air. From her bird's-eye view of the second-floor gallery, Iris spotted Glynn and her husband Gil enter the room. Wearing a soft pink suit, Iris could detect a flash of sequins on her collar and cuffs. The outfit accentuated Glynn's proportioned figure, hinting at her amble bosom and tight butt.

Iris watched as Glynn and Gil wound their way through the room, greeting acquaintances as they headed toward the grand staircase. They made a handsome pair, and Iris could see by the way Gil took on a protective air that he was very much in love. Glynn's arrival was her cue to leave. Iris got what she came for, and it was time to pass the baton. They slid by each other silently while Glynn exchanged a knowing nod. All the while, Gil's focus was on Marshall Matlock as he made a beeline to intercept his boss.

Chapter 44

Glad to be outside, Iris took a deep breath of clean air. She stood off to the side, watching the steady stream of Long Island's rich and powerful enter the Sunset Haven Club. It was time for Phase 2 as she pressed the programmed contact number in her phone.

"Team Alpha," the woman answered.

"Team Alpha?" Iris replied, unable to keep the surprise out of her voice.

"Yeah, I thought it would sound more exciting than a simple hello," Sollie explained, laughing. "So, what have you got? Can we move to position tango, tango, mango yet?" Sollie couldn't resist taking a stab at keeping the tension in perspective.

"Carl will be accessing the formula later tonight from his new ChemoCo offices at LIQuID. I don't think he'll be going there for at least three hours. Good luck." Iris ended the call. Her job was complete, and she handed the parking ticket to the attendant. Waiting for him to retrieve the car, Iris offered a slight nod to Penna as she walked by.

Chapter 45

As a member of LIMBO, the host organization, Gil and his guests had access to the exclusive area above the increasingly congested main floor. LIMBO members were identified by the LIMBO logo pin: a yellow bullseye with bright blue LIMBO letters all superimposed on top of a black outline of Long Island. There was no doubt where LIMBO was—smack dab in the center of everything.

On the second-floor gallery, Glynn had no problem spotting Penna's arrival. Her friend was wearing a forest green tunic and pants made of some sort of silky-flowy material. Penna glided through the crowd like a brightly colored bird, her long, dark hair perfectly coiffed over her right shoulder. Gold bangles adorned her arms, and an antique enamel and gold pendant nested below her throat.

"Penna, what a surprise," Glynn exclaimed, not letting on this prearranged rendezvous was part of the plan. "Let me introduce you to my husband."

Gil Patrick was as attractive and charming as his wife. "It's nice to finally meet you. I had been thinking the book club was a cover for Glynn's extracurricular activities," Gil joked.

"And I feel as if I already know you," Penna said with a knowing smile. It wasn't a stretch either, as Penna's intuitive abilities confirmed what she had surmised about Gil Patrick.

"Let me introduce you to our firm's head partner," Gil offered, turning to bring Marshall Matlock into their circle.

Standing off to the side, Glynn watched the exchange between Penna and her boss. Penna was calm and confident, while Marshall looked transfixed. Glynn didn't think his eyes even blinked. So far, so good, Glynn thought as they chatted, hoping Penna would be able to intuit something important.

Suddenly, the noise in the room grew louder, coinciding with the arrival of the guest of honor, Arnie Holtzmann. All eyes turned to see him march in like a king leading a procession, stopping every few feet to shake some politician's hand or offer a slap on the back to an old crony. Everyone who was anyone was there to pay homage to his years of successful wheeling and dealing. As the new head of LICE, the night was Arnie's triumph. Everyone wanted a piece of him, and he had more than enough to go around.

Finally making his way to the podium, Arnie grabbed the microphone and stood looking out into the crowd. He wanted to savor the moment, to breathe in the sweet smell of adulation and attention. It had taken him years of hard work, arm-twisting, and backdoor negotiating to get to this point. He knew every face, and they all knew him. There wasn't a business exec, political aide, or power broker in the room that hadn't owed him a favor or benefited from his "invisible" hand. His years in LIMBO perfectly prepared him for this next move, and as the new head of LICE, he was ready to wield the full power of that important agency. The SCAB deal was just the beginning.

"Thank you all for coming," Arnie said over the thunder of applause, motioning for the troops to quiet down. "I'll forever remember my years at LIMBO . . ."

While everyone turned to hear Arnie speak, Glynn took that moment to inch over toward Penna. "Marshall was the one who leaked the SCAB report," Penna whispered.

Glynn nodded, not trusting herself to say anything. The only thing she cared about now was getting the complete SCAB formula over to Ray for analysis.

"Today, we celebrate a huge victory for our community," Arnie continued. "And make no mistake—this is something each and every one of us will benefit from. SCAB is no longer a dirty word!" he shouted. "We've fought a tough battle and won, and now I say this: I pledge to never rest, to fight on, so our children can look back on this pivotal moment with pride in their hearts.

"Way back when, we all had high hopes for LICE as a champion of environmental responsibility. But it has degraded over the years, and most recently became a parasitic agency. Lately, we've watched LICE suck the blood out of our region's economic development and growth. No longer. Tonight, I pledge to restore LICE to its proper place of prominence in the business community." This last line elicited a round of applause.

He went on for a couple more minutes, praising his staff at LIMBO and taking credit for years of business growth and success. Many thought he was going a little too far, famously living up to his nickname A Holtz. But they were happy to cheer him on as they ate his free food and enjoyed the free drinks.

"Finally, I want you to meet the newest members of our business community—Bennett Kingsley and his staff at ChemoCo. Please, Bennett, Carl . . . everyone come on up." Arnie offered glowing praise to the brilliance and ingenuity of the ChemoCo R&D team and to the foresight and vision of its chairman. "Don't worry, guys, you've made it to LIMBO, and we'll take good care of you. I'd like to present you with the official door, a symbol of our organization."

The coveted LIMBO door was a doll-sized version of a wooden door attached to a frame. Turning the doorknob freed the door, allowing it to swing both ways, clearly demonstrating that it didn't matter which side of the door you were on; you'd always be in LIMBO.

While Arnie was wrapping up his praise of ChemoCo, Glynn took a minute to survey the room. The crowd seemed impatient and bored with all the self-congratulations. Glynn sensed people were more than ready to resume their own conversations and networking. It was time to party.

Glynn's premonition was uncanny. In that split second, a man dressed in military camouflage with "war paint" covering his face elbowed his way through the crowd to the front of the stage. He threw down a large duffle bag and began to heckle the speaker.

"THAT'S RIGHT YOU PIECE OF SHIT—KEEP TALKING. THE WHOLE EAST END WILL TURN INTO ONE BIG DUNG HEAP AND YOU'RE GONNA BE THE KING: THE KING OF THE SHIT PILE. HEY, ASSHOLE, OR SHOULD I SAY A HOLTZ? PEOPLE WILL BE CLEANING UP AFTER YOU FOR YEARS, MAYBE GENERATIONS, YOU STINKING, FESTERING, PUS-FILLED BLOWHARD!"

The man continued yelling curses while those closest moved off, giving him a wide berth. Everyone was rightly shocked; it was so outrageous and over-the-top that some thought Arnie had arranged for the harassment by an actor. It would be just like A Holtz to organize his own send-off and engage some sort of avant-garde theater. Expressions of surprise turned into smirks of disbelief as people slowly got the joke. But then things turned ugly.

In less than a blink of an eye, the street performer bent down, unzipped the duffle bag, and whipped out an assault rifle. Taking point-blank aim, he leveled the weapon right at Arnie's chest and squeezed off round after round. The echo was deafening as the rifle's sound ricocheted around the room. Not content with one target, the lone gunman next turned his attention to the others on the stage. After a quick magazine change, he pivoted and sprayed the room with gunfire, pointing and shooting indiscriminately. Pandemonium erupted.

"I guess you can hear that, Arnie?" the intruder yelled as the man brandished his weapon.

The once semi-bored partiers in their high heels and shiny shoes morphed into a mass of frightened victims. Some froze, others dropped their food and drinks and bolted. It didn't take long before a full-scale panic ensued, transforming the sophisticated attendees into a terrified stampede. The party erupted into bedlam. People ran for cover, only to realize there was no place to hide—the room was as wide open as a prairie. Women in gowns and cocktail dresses teetered and slipped, trying unsuccessfully to move with speed and purpose. Those nearest the doors were caught in the crush as everyone tried to push their way to the exits. Some fell on the ground and were trampled; others continued to push and shove, disregarding anyone in their way. Caught unawares, the security team fought against the stampede of escaping partiers as they tried to reach the gunman. More shots rang out, and those still on the podium collapsed and fell to the ground.

On the second-floor gallery, Glynn, Gil, Marshall, and Penna were out of harm's way and had a clear view of the perpetrator: Bill McCleary, covered in warrior war paint with a half-crazed look in his eyes as he leveled his weapon for another round of shots. The noise in the ballroom was so loud and the scene so chaotic they could barely make out what he was saying. Glynn caught bits and pieces— something having to do with a disaster of biblical proportions if SCAB was released.

After what seemed like an eternity, the security detail was finally able to tackle McCleary to the ground, but not before he got off one last shot, aiming his gun right at Arnie Holtzmann's head.

"There's something wrong with McCleary," Penna announced.

"Well, isn't that obvious?" a shaken Marshall Matlock snapped back. "Of course there's something wrong with him. The guy shot up a party and tried to kill the host."

Police and security flooded the room; they handcuffed and dragged Bill McCleary from the scene. An ambulance arrived, and then another. EMS teams ran inside with stretchers rushing to assist the fallen. People were trampled. A man collapsed, grabbing his chest. There was even a woman screaming she was having her baby. Food and drink littered the floor, making running dangerous. A couple of women in high heels slipped and fell, twisting ankles and damaging limbs in their haste. But the group on the stage suffered the worst. Bennett Kingsley had collapsed—some fearing a life-threatening bullet wound—and was one of the first to be put on a stretcher. Others had fallen or were pushed off the stage only to scamper underneath, hugging the floor. A smattering of blood confirmed everyone's worst suspicions.

Penna pulled Glynn aside. "McCleary was drugged," Penna whispered. "He isn't in his right mind. Someone gave him a powerful hallucinogen, one that interfered with rational thinking, and set him loose in the room. The outfit, camouflage paint, and gun were props. This wasn't McCleary's intention—I don't think he even knew what he was doing."

Gradually, the police got the scene under control. The sick and injured were identified for medical attention. Everyone else was herded into groups to be questioned by the authorities. No one was allowed to leave until they gave their name, address, phone number, and a statement of what they saw and heard. It was a long, exhausting process.

Over the next hour, word leaked that McCleary's gun was a fake, which was why no one suffered any gunshot wounds. Not that a crime wasn't committed, but it obviously wasn't mass murder. Arnie and the

ChemoCo group were placed under a heavy security detail and escorted out separately. Gradually, the place quieted as people gave their statements and left.

Marshall was outraged. "What the hell just happened?" he fumed, marching over to the police, explaining who he was and why he should be allowed to leave. "I'm part of the ChemoCo group," he announced, sounding like a petulant boy. "Let me through," he demanded. How was he going to schmooze Bennett Kingsley now?

"I'm sorry, sir, but we have instructions to isolate only those on the podium. You'll have to wait your turn," the officer explained, too busy to spare any further time addressing Marshall's concerns.

Not one to be put off, Marshall grabbed his cell phone and frantically called A Holtz.

"Arnie, what's going on? How's Kingsley? Was he shot?"

"We're all okay, Marshall. That idiot was firing blanks! Some sort of sick joke, huh? Bennett has a heart condition, and the whole scene triggered some sort of heart palpitation. He's going to be fine. We're rendezvousing at the Hilton's lobby bar—stop by if you can," Arnie suggested. "Bennett will likely spend the night in the hospital, so you have one more day to practice your sales pitch," Arnie said in this last line with sarcasm.

Marshall practically threw the phone on the floor, spitting mad. You didn't have to have special powers of insight to appreciate his frustration. Pacing and complaining until his turn came, it took Marshall a good half hour to calm down.

Wound up from all the excitement and not yet ready to end the evening on a complete disaster, Marshall announced he would be meeting with Arnie and the ChemoCo folks at the Hilton. Turning his attention to Gil, the unspoken invitation was hard to resist, especially since it was the senior partner doing the asking. Of course, Gil, being a newly installed full-fledged member of the LIMBO board, supplied additional motivation, making his attendance even more of an obligation.

Watching her husband leave with Marshall, Glynn followed Penna as they walked out of the Sunset Haven Club, both still trying to control their adrenaline-spiked sensibilities. It felt like the stakes got amplified by a factor of ten. Sollie and Onawhim were likely in the middle of their part of the evening's plans, as Penna had given them a go before all the disruption. Glynn could only hope they would be unaffected by recent events.

Chapter 46

Marshall was itching for a drink and could barely wait for the bartender to take his order.

"Glenfiddich on the rocks—and make it a double," he barked. Gil ordered a Stella Artois. He never did acquire a taste for hard liquor and had stopped trying years ago. Waiting to be served, Gil surveyed the room and saw the refugees from the LIMBO party camped out at a large table in the back corner. Arnie Holtzmann was there, along with Stan Piper, Ted Landis, and the rest of the ChemoCo crew.

"Hey there, Marshall, Gil—over here," yelled A Holtz, clearly much more relaxed than when Gil last saw him.

"What an asshole," Marshall sneered under his breath. He was fast losing any love he had for his old buddy.

The two men walked over to the ChemoCo table, where the partiers shifted their chairs to make room for the newcomers.

"You know how to throw a party, Arnie," Marshall joked. "Just as I was losing interest in your speech, you found a way to keep my attention."

That comment elicited a good-hearted laugh. Because they had all been whisked away right from the beginning, everyone at the table wanted to know what had happened after they left. Marshall and Gil began fielding all sorts of questions—who was injured, what were the police saying, and how was the press handling things—but mostly, they wanted to hear about the perp: that head case, McCleary. There were plenty of theories flying around, whether speculating about McCleary's motives, his goals, or his misguided attempt to block the greatest fertilizer since manure. That he lost his mind when he lost his job garnered universal agreement. Everyone had something to say—

everyone except Stan Piper. Gil noticed Stan sat listening intently, with an almost imperceptible self-satisfied smile.

Marshall held court, regaling the group with observations and commentary like a sports announcer. He was in his element. Even so, Gil was surprised to hear Marshall add unnecessary bits of embellishment and exaggeration, especially since the real events were dramatic enough. But this was Marshall's personality; he couldn't help himself, Gil realized, watching Marshall play to the crowd as the center of attention.

Turning to Stan, Gil inquired after Bennett Kingsley.

"Oh, Bennett has a bit of a heart condition," replied Stan. "Who could have guessed this evening's experience would have triggered it? He's under observation at the hospital overnight, and will likely be released in the morning."

Gil nodded, thinking it odd the way Stan referred to the terror they lived through as an "experience," like going whale watching.

"Why do you think he did it?" Gil asked, putting his question directly to Stan.

"Pride," Stan replied. "The man couldn't accept being wrong, couldn't face being out of a job, being the laughingstock. He was so powerful for so long his ego couldn't deal with the loss of control, that he would no longer preside over Long Island's Conservation and Environment," Stan stated.

It was a smug assessment, delivered with Stan's barely disguised superior tone. But it didn't square with Gil. No, there was something missing. No matter what you may have thought about his politics or judgments, it would take more than the loss of his job—one he was rumored to be losing for a while—for a man of McCleary's intellect and experience to go off the deep end.

"If he was so off his rocker, why didn't he use real bullets?" Gil asked, realizing too late that he should have kept this question to himself.

"The guy was crazy," Stan declared, staring Gil in the eyes so intently it was as if he were trying to imprint that one thought onto Gil's feeble brain. "Why else? Can you explain a crazy man's actions rationally? And anyway, he botched that job too." Stan delivered this last line with a barely concealed snort.

Yeah, he botched shooting up a room full of people. Wouldn't that be the one thing he'd try to get right, at least partially? Gil thought sarcastically to himself.

"You know, Gil, we'll be looking to find a replacement for Arnie as Director of LIMBO. I don't have to tell you how important that position is. A couple of years as director and you can write your own ticket. I'd consider it one of life's game changers," Stan said.

Gil nodded. There was nothing for him to say. He never even considered that position for himself, having been a LIMBO board member for less than a month. But Stan was fixing him with a pretty direct look.

"We're going to ask for applicants shortly. The whole process will take some time. Time a young man could put to good use. For example, I'm sure the LIMBO board would like to know exactly what kind of evidence McCleary had on SCAB. Uncovering that kind of intelligence could only help LIAR, especially the GRowLers, like your client Crystal Clam Winery."

There was something about the way Stan was looking at him. The way he spoke about McCleary was like he was still some sort of threat. It felt odd. And suggesting he might be considered for the director job was even stranger. Gil would never have thought himself a possible candidate. Hell, he was their newest board member.

"Someone from LIMBO is going to have to go over to jail tomorrow," Stan continued. "The organization is involved, especially since we're the victim. We need to be on top of things to look out for our interests, to make sure that head case gets what he deserves. And you're LIMBO's only attorney on the board, right?" he asked, already knowing the answer.

"I hadn't considered the legal issues for LIMBO," Gil replied, trying to choose his words carefully. "If the board wants me to monitor the legal proceedings and report back, well, I'm sure they'll let me know."

Chapter 47

"Got it, over and out," Sollie chirped into the phone. She was sitting in her car in the darkest corner of the LIQuID parking lot with a quiet Onawhim in the passenger seat. "Project leader confirms the mission is a go."

"Sollie, do we need all the melodrama?" This was all Onawhim had to say to get the realtor into the proper frame of mind. After all, they were two respectable, law-abiding citizens out for a night of breaking and entering. It was time to get serious.

"Okay, Iris thought Carl wouldn't be back to his office until after ten. But now that the whole party got shot up by a deranged gunman firing blanks into the crowd, Penna thinks we may have even more time. I'm sure I could push the time frame up if we need to. There's no time like the present to trespass and burglarize," Sollie said. Even with Onawhim's pointed remark, she couldn't help herself.

The two ladies drove to the side entrance and parked far away from the parking lot lights. They were dressed in black–a cross between going to a funeral and working in the garden. Somber but comfortable. They were familiar with the LIQuID entrance and reception area and were prepared to have a complicit Kevin escort them through the ChemoCo offices.

The building was dead quiet and felt empty. Sollie and Onawhim waited in the lobby for Kevin, who was sure to notice them on the closed-circuit security monitor. A slow ten minutes passed, and he was still nowhere to be found. How were they to get past the locked security door without him? Afraid to make too much noise and alert the real guards, Sollie tried to shift time forward in the hopes of hurrying Kevin to the lobby.

"I don't know how we'll make our way inside and to the ChemoCo offices," Sollie said, worried they wouldn't be able to complete their mission.

Thankfully, the security door opened. Getting ready to walk through, they almost bumped into a not-too-friendly guard.

"Excuse me, but what are you doing?"

Neither Sollie nor Onawhim had expected to see anyone other than Kevin. This guard was tall, bearded, and soft around the middle. His steely blue eyes held their gaze and didn't waver. He meant business and expected an answer—a worthy answer, or there'd be trouble.

Caught unaware, Sollie was the first to speak. "Oh, thank God you're here. I didn't know how we were going to get inside." A strong offense is always a good defense, Sollie figured, and after all, she had years of practice. "My son left some of his papers in the office and he needs them for a big meeting tomorrow. We were driving by, on the way home from our book club meeting, and I told him we'd get them."

"Step away from the door," the guard said. He wasn't buying any of their bullshit. Thankfully, he'd looked up from his girlie magazine at just the right moment to see them trying to break in. If her story was true, he'd know soon enough. If not, he figured the cops would earn their paycheck for the evening.

"Look, Mister, what's your name?" Sollie asked in her most nosey and annoying voice.

"Mr. Guard will do."

"Yes, Mr. Guard, you are right. We have no business being in this building after dark. But as my friend has said, we must get into her son's office and retrieve those important papers." This was the first time Onawhim had spoken. She focused all her attention on his face, looked him square in the eyes, and delivered her request with such force and conviction the guard was caught unawares.

He blinked a couple of times, forgot what he was doing, then promptly inserted his keycard into the door. Sollie took the lead, followed by Onawhim, with the guard trailing. Setting off down the dimly lit corridors, Sollie tried to remember the way Carl had walked to his office the other day. It was a right turn, then another, past the green door; she was remembering minor landmarks. Thankfully, the guard merely followed along like some lost shaggy dog hoping to get a meal.

They wandered around the silent building, barely making any noise themselves. There were a couple of wrong turns, but eventually, Sollie spotted the orange corridor and knew Carl's office was nearby. Meanwhile, Onawhim kept close to the guard, whispering confirmation he was doing right by allowing them access.

"This is the office we need. Use your key card to allow entry," Onawhim stated firmly. "Wait here and we'll be out shortly." Mr. Guard simply blinked and waited patiently as if he were commanded to stay.

The door opened to reveal a cluttered office with a window facing west. The desk was positioned in front of it with the computer screen aligned perfectly to receive the annoying western sun glare.

Sollie quickly called Iris on her cell phone. "We're in position," Sollie said, this time in a more serious tone.

"Have Onawhim take a photo of the wires coming out of the ceiling and where they connect to the computer, then send that to me," Iris asked.

After reviewing the photo and identifying the proper wires, Iris knew exactly what to do.

"Now listen carefully. You're going to disconnect the large circular white wire from the computer. You'll need to turn it to the left until it comes loose," Iris explained.

Sollie repeated the directions to Onawhim, who performed each task with precision. They had to turn on Carl's computer and install a special program that would capture his keystrokes, reconnect the cable, and test the newly installed program. The whole process took less than 10 minutes, maybe even less when compressed by Sollie's intense concentration.

"We're done," Iris declared. "Get out of there now. There's nothing to do but wait for Carl to log on."

Sollie couldn't leave fast enough. All this spy stuff had caused her to break out into a cold sweat, and it was making her damned uncomfortable.

"Thank you, Mr. Guard," Onawhim said on the way out. "We're leaving now. I don't think our little visit is worth remembering, do you?"

"No, ma'am. You weren't here long. Not worth mentioning, if you ask me," the guard agreed.

Part 8

Obstruction

Chapter 48

"I've got to get myself a life," Carl said to himself as he entered the LIQuID building. Half-drunk, he couldn't stop shaking his head. "I can't believe I'm moving here," he said for the hundredth time. Being the focus of a terrorist plot at his welcome reception did not bode well for the relocation. Of all the employment papers and disclosure forms the company mandated employees to sign, he was sure there wasn't one which required him to serve as target practice for a crazy man. No way did he remember any papers suggesting he'd hold the company blameless for putting his life on the line.

He'd have to talk to an attorney about this–"Crusty Golden Boy," be damned. There's no glory in a title if you can't live to enjoy it. "Maybe I'll give Marshall Matlock a call. Marshall seemed to know the way of things—at least he spoke a good game. I need someone like that," he figured, even if he couldn't quite identify what exactly he'd have Marshall do.

Carl stumbled his way down the industrial corridors toward his office. The place was even more depressing at night. It had a kind of disinfectant smell about it—a little too clean, maybe.

He slipped in his key card and opened the door to his office. *Why buy a house when I can live here? It's not like I'm bringing any girls home,* he thought morosely. He remembered meeting that pretty girl investor earlier in the evening—it seemed like a million years ago. But he quickly dismissed that thought. *She is out of my league—way out. Way, way out,* his addled brain kept intoning.

Turning on his computer, he noticed the screen did a brief lurch. "That damn connection," he cursed, turning to look at the mass of wires hanging from the ceiling. His computer was not the same here; it was slower, like it, too, was dragging its feet, wanting to go back home. Finally, the logon screen appeared and he keyed in his passcode. It was a bit of a rinky-dink security setup, but it was that or wait, and word had come that waiting was not an option. Now—they wanted it NOW. The other SCABees were adamant. No risk, no reward, he figured.

The first thing he looked at was the production schedule—right on time. ChemoCo was churning out 10,000 gallons of SCAB a day for immediate delivery. That should be ready next week, he figured. Next, he checked on the QC reports, a series of random tests performed throughout the production cycle making sure the formula was followed to the letter. He scanned the QC report but wasn't satisfied. Nothing took the place of going through the data line-by-line, something Carl was particularly good at.

Carl could recall the formula like a schoolboy reciting the alphabet, but there was more to SCAB than its chemical signature. The manufacturing process was complicated. The mixture went through multiple stages, heating and then cooling. It even needed to ferment and rest for a time—the whole process had to be followed EXACTLY. Years of his life and those of his coworkers went into defining the process, and with one wrong step along the way, the whole mixture would have to be scrapped.

The production of SCAB, like its discovery, was a miracle. He had been staying late one night, one of many, going over that day's lab results–checking and rechecking the output numbers when he noticed someone had left the heater on. The mixture was solidifying—it literally turned from a liquid into a solid and looked like something completely different. Carl was intrigued and performed a series of tests and experiments on the new substance, and voilà-SCAB! A complete accident. That's how many things are invented, he remembered reading somewhere. It'll all come out in the history books, he figured, once the benefits are formally documented. There is no doubt when they write the chapter on chemical innovations for the early 21st century, Carl Hammerling will be forever linked to this turning point in crop production, a boon for mankind. He could visualize SCAB covering the earth like some sort of protective layer. "I AM 'Crusty Golden Boy,'" he crowed.

272

Chapter 49

Iris's hands were shaking as she turned on her computer. She had entered uncharted territory, but things had been like that for a while. A mere eight weeks ago, if someone had told her she'd be able to pick stocks with almost 90 percent accuracy, lose her position with the company after 20 years, and she'd be hacking into the mainframe of a publicly traded company in search of a secret formula, she'd have thought they were crazy. Certifiably crazy.

She clicked the Re-ReedIt icon on her screen and the program immediately began to work. It downloaded information, creating folders and subfolders at an incredible speed. Iris was barely able to catch some keywords as the program finished its task. Once it stopped, she found herself staring at a blinking cursor, daring her to click Next. One deep breath, some tentative pressure on top of the mouse, and there were all the files she downloaded as neatly organized as could be. There were emails, spreadsheets, corporate memos, QC reports, and a single folder labeled SCAB. Opening the SCAB folder, Iris read through a couple of documents until she came upon it: the formula. Without wasting another minute, Iris called Glynn.

"Hello," came the whispered voice.

"Glynn, its Iris. Are you at your computer?"

"Yes," came the one-word reply. Glynn was too afraid the phone call and her conversation would wake Gil. How would she describe this early morning activity—a driving desire to do research at 5 a.m.?

"We got IT!" Iris exclaimed. The last minutes were too nerve-wracking to contain herself. "Shall I send the email now?"

"Yes, send it now," was all Glynn could say. Her hands were sweating. She was truly afraid Gil would walk in any minute.

Iris composed a brief email and attached the SCAB file. It was so easy, point and click, and off it went, silently delivering information from her computer to Glynn's. Iris had been told the Re-ReedIt program was basically invisible, operating undetected in the background. It enabled her to share Carl's screen in real-time while it captured and saved everything to a file on her computer. Iris could let the program do its work and come back later to review. I'm glad she didn't have to stay put the whole time, like watching some boring nerd movie hunting for an Easter egg. There was even a self-destruct feature that, when activated, would wipe out all traces it ever existed. She wasn't ready to use that feature yet, feeling the program might still come in handy.

Quiet moments passed as Glynn reviewed the formula. Iris all but bit her lip, trying to hold back from asking if this was what she and the others had put themselves at risk to obtain. "I recognize the part I had copied from our files, the part I originally sent to Ray. Now I see the formula continuing on for four more pages and includes specific steps and directions. This is it." Glynn exhaled. "Thanks," she whispered into the phone.

Hanging up with Iris, Glynn quickly composed an email to Ray. *Now we'll see*, she said to herself.

Chapter 50

"I'm fine and I'm leaving," declared Bennett Kingsley, glad to be changing out of the hospital gown. The staff at County General had been extremely helpful. When they wheeled him in last night, he was in quite a state. He remembered being at the LIMBO party feeling tired and bored—that Arnie Holtzmann could drone on. He had been looking forward to a quiet drink with Stan. Then the whole place disintegrated into a scene of mass confusion: gunshots, screaming, pandemonium, It had sent his heart into overdrive, as if it would beat right out of his chest. That was the last thing he remembered before waking in the ambulance.

"Am I shot?" he asked the EMS gal. They had restrained his arms, so he couldn't feel for wounds.

"Lay still, Mr. Kingsley. You're gonna be all right—you fainted. Don't worry, we'll see you get the right care," she replied.

"What about the others?" Bennett managed to ask as he closed his eyes and dozed off. *They must have given me something,* was his last thought before waking in the ER.

After speaking with the on-call doctor and his personal physician, Bennett was satisfied he'd see him in the morning. There were no bullet wounds but a nasty bump on the head. They also gave him something to get his heart beating normally again. He learned the whole thing was a hoax, some sort of madman's revenge. Thankfully no one was shot, although he was surprised to learn he was the worst casualty of the evening.

Bennett didn't mind the overnight hospital stay—better safe than sorry—but now he couldn't wait to leave. He had a big day planned, one helluva busy agenda, and was itching to get the show on the road.

"Get Arnie Holtzmann on the phone," he barked to his assistant. "Tell him I want to call a press conference. Then call Stan and have him meet me at the LIMBO offices." Bennett commanded a small army of assistants, both in person and on the phone. There was the board to reassure, the PR folks to direct, and his health to manage. *No one takes shots at Bennett Kingsley without consequences,* he thought, proof positive that he was feeling much better and more like his feisty self.

Once outside and safely in his limo, Bennett went into further action. He had his office arrange for a press conference. He demanded a full report on McCleary, an update on SCAB production and delivery, and a review from legal on his options. Like a bear when cornered, Bennett could be dangerous when provoked, and he had never felt more provoked than now.

"Jeez, Arnie, just call the damn press conference for one o'clock. What's to prepare? Your life was threatened—he shot up your party, for Christ's sake. No, I don't want to wait. Now's the time to make our statement and call for action," Bennett insisted. He couldn't understand why Arnie was dancing around things, No wonder they call him A Holtz. *How the hell did he run LIMBO for all those years?* Bennett thought after suffering through all of Arnie's mumbo jumbo.

Meanwhile, as Bennett was heading to his hotel to wash and freshen up, Arnie's office phone was ringing off the hook. June could barely keep up with the calls.

"Marshall on line 2," she yelled as he hung up with Bennett.

"What?" Arnie's usual brusque manner had gotten even worse.

"Look, Arnie, I want a meeting with Bennett Kingsley today," Marshall demanded.

"You're kidding, right?" Arnie replied. "The guy is just now leaving the hospital, and you want to discuss why he should pay you a retainer? Do you really think this is the right time?"

Marshall had a tough night's sleep. His OCD was acting up—he wanted the ChemoCo deal so badly that it was all he could think about. Like a laser-guided missile, Marshall couldn't disengage, couldn't let it go. He was fully committed and unstoppable.

"Bennett is out for Bill McCleary's hide; that's what he wants," Arnie continued. "If you can deliver that, he'll lick milk from your hand. Look, he's arranging for a press conference—he's got us jumping through hoops," Arnie explained, hating to have someone from outside call the shots in his backyard, but he had no choice. He wooed ChemoCo, sucked up to Kingsley, and now had the dubious misfortune of hosting the worst social event of the century. No one was ever going to forget that Bill McCleary upstaged him on his big night, no less. It was galling, and Arnie felt like he had swallowed more bile than was humanly possible.

"A press conference," Marshall mumbled, tuning out Arnie's self-absorbed rant. "I'm coming, what time?"

"One o'clock," he snapped and hung up.

"Stan Piper, line 1," June called out.

"Jesus, Stan," Arnie spat into the phone. "This is a disaster."

Stan was in no mood for Arnie's hysterics. He didn't give a shit about Arnie's bruised ego. "Look, Arnie," Stan began as if Arnie had answered the phone and simply said hello, "we talked about this last night, don't you remember?" Stan couldn't believe Arnie had forgotten their whole conversation. *The guy has the memory of a day-old bird.*

"Of course I remember. We talked about arranging to have someone from LIMBO go into the jail and monitor what's happening with McCleary's case. We didn't talk about throwing a press conference for the media!"

"I just hung up with Bennett, and he is furious. He's questioning their move to Long Island. His board is having a fit. Legal is drawing up papers to sue the shit out of everyone from you and LIMBO to the Sunset Haven Club. They're ready to walk away," Stan said, hoping this last bit of news would get through.

"Whoa, what do you mean, walk away? Do you mean not come to Long Island? Not relocate their plant here? Not bring jobs? Is that what you mean?"

"Bennett is a little upset right now—wouldn't you be if you were attending your first party at your new location and the evening's entertainment included a madman shooting at you with a gun? He needs to know we have his best interests at heart. He needs to know we're on his side," the old fox soothed. "We've worked so hard, don't blow it now. If we keep our heads, we'll all get what we want."

"Okay, so what's the plan?"

"We hold the press conference. Bennett makes his statement and then answers questions. You, as party host, offer to make sure McCleary gets a fair trial. You want to see justice done and that he's not hanged in the press. You're taking the high road, feeling sorry for the poor bastard, and when the facts come out, he'll be completely discredited."

"All right," Arnie snarled. "What do you want me to do?"

"Call that kid from Shylock—you know, Marshall's boy—and get him to visit the jail and keep an eye on things for us. Let him converse with McCleary, get his side of the story. It'll help us counter any crazy claims we're ramming a conviction through."

"What do you mean, 'crazy claims'?! McCleary's out, gone, retired. He shot up my party and is in jail as a nutcase. Just who do you think will pay attention to his crazy claims?"

"No one. I'm sure everyone will simply dismiss his ranting as someone who's lost his way. We need to keep an eye on things, it wouldn't do to get blindsided, you know," Stan fibbed. He couldn't go into detail with Arnie. This was a need-to-know situation, and Arnie did not fit into that category. Anyway, it was an insurance policy. Bennett was anal when it came to loose ends and insisted McCleary be rendered inert—ChemoCo lingo for inactive, which Stan understood to be secure. "See you at one," Stan said before the phone went dead.

"June, get me Marshall," Arnie bellowed, popping two antacids as he paced around his desk. Back on the phone with his old buddy, Arnie explained what he wanted. "Stan and Bennett already know about this. In fact, I got the feeling it may help your cause, if you know what I mean?" Arnie said, happy to throw Marshall a bone. "I'll messenger over something official."

280

Chapter 51

"Gil has a letter at the desk," Misty chirped into the intercom. She noticed it was from LIMBO and decided to give Arnie a call. Now seemed like a good time to continue their ice cream cone conversation, she thought, looking at her watch.

"He's busy right now," June said, taking it upon herself to screen this call from her boss. "We're getting ready for a big press conference. Maybe try him later." June rolled her eyes as she hung up the phone.

"Now that's a first. Maybe that's where Marshall was heading," Misty figured.

Gil came out to the reception area to retrieve the letter himself. He took a minute to open and read the contents, compose his expression, and marched off to the law library.

"This is exactly what Stan Piper suggested last night," Gil commented.

"What do you mean?" Glynn asked. She had been so consumed with her own agenda that she missed that part of their conversation.

"I was talking with Stan Piper in the Hilton bar last night. He thought someone from LIMBO should be a visible presence at the jail—you know, to look out for our interests. And here's the letter on LIMBO stationery authorizing me to go over there and do just that," Gil explained, still surprised he was the one they chose.

"So, what does this mean?" Glynn asked, trying to understand why her husband was involved.

"LIMBO was victimized, and the board wants someone to keep an eye on what's going on."

"Keep an eye on who? McCleary? The guy's locked up—he's not going anywhere," Glynn replied, still not getting what Gil was supposed to do. Ironically, she was the one who had a particular interest in talking to McCleary. There are a couple of things only he can set straight, but that will have to wait—at least until the report comes back from Ray.

Glynn had called Ray when she arrived at work to make sure he received the formula, and it was, in fact, the complete version. Yes, he said, it was all there. He reminded her to be patient: an accurate test result could take 14 days or so. Pick up a good book, he suggested. But that was the last thing Glynn was going to do.

"What are your plans tonight?" Gil asked, wondering what had been occupying his wife's time. "I'll call you when I'm done downtown. Maybe we could meet for dinner," he suggested.

Chapter 52

"Thank you for coming," welcomed Arnie, standing at the lectern and speaking loudly into the microphone. The feedback was deafening. He had commandeered the building's auditorium, effectively kicking out a class on safe driving. It turned out to be the right decision, as the LIMBO conference room would have been way too small. By one o'clock it was standing room only, and people were still coming in.

Behind him sat Bennett Kingsley, CEO of ChemoCo, along with his team. Stan Piper sat in the reserved section in the front row, along with Marshall Matlock, the chief of police, some local politicians, as well as a couple of his LIMBO board members.

Arnie surveyed the room. He recognized a number of reporters covering the Long Island beat, including Roger Haddit from *Newsday*. The national press was there as well: CNN, MSNBC, Fox News, *The New York Times*, to name a few.

"Before I turn the microphone over to Bennett Kingsley, I'd like to make a brief statement." Arnie paused for effect, smiling into the lights and cameras. "It's been no secret Bill McCleary and I have had our differences—we've been on the opposite side of most issues. But I'm sure if he were standing in this spot today, he'd agree that civil dialogue works best in our democracy. I don't understand what's going on in his mind—whether he thought pretending to shoot up a room full of people was a harmless prank, or that we'd see it as good fun. But I can tell you we hope he gets the best medical care and fair representation from our impartial judicial system."

Arnie continued to talk well past what most would consider brief. The national media were the only ones surprised—those who knew Arnie didn't expect anything less. Finally, after a plug for LICE, he ended with the hope that ChemoCo wouldn't hold this fiasco against

Long Island, the region, its elected officials and people, or LIMBO, and, most especially, him personally.

"Thank you, Arnie, and the good people of LIMBO," Bennett began. "I don't mind telling you I had a very different expectation of my visit to Long Island than what happened last night." He paused, listening to a few chuckles from the largely silent room. "First, I must commend the police and emergency teams for their quick response. I would also like to acknowledge the expert care I received at County General. Thankfully, no one was truly hurt, but we cannot consider this event victimless.

"Not only were the innocent bystanders at last night's party traumatized, but an attack like that puts everyone on edge. These are dangerous times; I don't need to tell you that. We at ChemoCo understand the need for prudent behavior. We believe our responsibility is to the community, to provide safe, helpful products that solve problems and offer solutions to people around the world. This is not because we're a public company and have to answer to our stockholders. We take our role as a good corporate citizen seriously.

"Now, many of you may have heard ChemoCo was considering opening a plant on Long Island. Believe me when I tell you the Board of Directors was vigorously questioning the wisdom of that decision in light of yesterday's events. But I told them ChemoCo is NOT going to be scared away by any random act of terror. We thought Long Island offered fertile territory for the expansion of our product lines with new opportunities for our employees, and I still believe it's the right move for us.

"Let's see this unfortunate act in a positive light, a chance to start from scratch and build something ChemoCo and Long Island can be proud of. And our first order of business is to announce the first shipment of our new product, SCAB. We've had only positive results from various local test sites, and I understand your environmental group has approved it for use. Next year, at this time, we'll be toasting to its success with wine grown using this wonderful natural fertilizer and weed retardant.

"But before I hand the microphone back to Arnie, I want to address anyone else who might be thinking of using ChemoCo as a target, or those who may expect us to retreat home with our tail between our legs—" Bennett paused for emphasis. "We cannot and will not be frightened or bullied. We intend to pursue justice for this crazy act, make no mistake about that."

Bennett ended his speech, noticed the silence after his last words bounced around the walls, gave a brief nod as if to thank everyone for listening, and took a step back, allowing Arnie to return to the microphone.

The room erupted with shouts and an explosion of hands springing up. Everyone had a question.

"All right, all right," Arnie soothed as he motioned for quiet. "Bennett has agreed to take a couple of questions. Roger," he said, motioning to the *Newsday* reporter.

"Mr. Kingsley, why do you think Bill McCleary was so against your company?" Roger Haddit asked.

"I never laid eyes on Mr. McCleary until last night. If he had a beef with me or ChemoCo, I would have been happy to address his concerns, whether on the phone, by email, or in person. Frankly, I'm not sure what his objections to SCAB are. And if his actions last night were any indication of his mindset, I'd say Mr. McCleary's opinions on important matters should be seriously questioned, and quite possibly dismissed."

"We understand McCleary was dragging his feet on giving the approval to SCAB. Have you considered if he left notes or other papers which might explain his position?" asked the man from Fox Business.

Bennett was expecting this: that McCleary might have left a paper trail or worse. Those thoughts kept him up at night. "We honestly don't know what the holdup was. He never explained it, nor asked us for more information."

"If you recall, LIMBO was pushing for approval." Arnie couldn't stay quiet.

"Why was it important to get this done so quickly? Isn't it better to be safe than sorry?" asked CNN's female anchor.

"We're in a tough economy. Creating jobs is a priority. We need those high-tech, high-paying jobs ChemoCo is bringing," Arnie responded, reluctant to step away from the mike. "Why he couldn't fast-track the approval is the reason he's no longer in that position."

"Last question," Arnie announced.

"Exactly what's your commitment to this region?" inquired the WABC TV reporter.

"ChemoCo is looking to expand, and we've been researching various locations that fit with our business plan. This is a test situation for us. We're dipping our toe in the water, so to speak. We have relocated the SCAB team here and hope to add to that with some highly qualified local applicants. As I said, this time next year we hope to be toasting the groundbreaking on a new ChemoCo lab. Thank you again for coming," he said, then turned to walk off the stage.

Much to Arnie's disappointment, the auditorium immediately emptied out. Everyone had stories to file, and they figured there was not much more Arnie would add.

With the press conference over, Stan Piper left his seat to meet Bennett offstage, followed closely by Marshall Matlock.

"Hello, Stan," Bennett said as he greeted his friend with a handshake. "So how was it? Do you think the press got the message?"

"You were brilliant. Of course there will be investigations and questions, but I think you stressed what's most important, and hopefully that's what'll make the evening news," Stan confirmed.

"I think everything went well," intoned Marshall, nudging closer to Bennett. "Glad to see you're all right. What a damned idiot! I always thought McCleary was tightly wound, but never expected this!" Marshall thought if he kept talking, things would go his way.

"I'm sure you have a lot on your plate after last night's fiasco, but I wanted you to know one of my associates, Gil Patrick, is at the jail right now, looking out for our interests." He didn't need to confuse things by saying Gil was acting on behalf of LIMBO. "You know, some of our clients have a vested interest in SCAB, like Crystal Clam Winery."

Bennett knew all too well the relationship between Marshall's firm and Stan Piper's business interests. He saw the hungry look in Marshall's eyes and liked that from his attorneys. "You know, Marshall, over the next couple of days I'd like to carve out some time to go over our needs for legal representation here. I'll have my assistant call you and set something up."

After a brief handshake to show he was serious, Bennett turned and walked out the side door with Stan Piper for a late lunch at the GCGC.

Chapter 53

"Thank you again for coming," Bennett Kingsley said, signaling the end of the press conference. Gil had arrived at the jailhouse as it was winding down, and he was amazed to find everyone staring at the TV.

"Gil Patrick, representing Long Island Metro Business Organization, to see Bill McCleary," Gil declared to the officer behind the glass partition.

"Sign in here on the last line," the guard said as he pushed the clipboard toward the attorney.

"I see there have been others," Gil stated after perusing the sign-in list.

"Yeah, there's been a steady stream this morning: the doctor, legal aid, a couple of local reporters . . ." the guard commented. "Have a seat."

Gil was prepared to wait; he knew the routine. He made himself comfortable along with the others in the waiting room as all eyes turned to the television. At the close of the ChemoCo press conference, the screen shifted to the anchors, who were busy weighing in on Bennett Kingsley's remarks, as well as discussing the events from last night's party. They showed clips from interviews with some of the partiers, along with selected snippets from Arnie Holtzmann and the lead police investigator. It seemed the verdict on McCleary was already in:

- He lost his mind . . .
- Out of control . . ."
- He was wrong about SCAB
- . . . too power-hungry . . .

Comments like these were being tossed around the anchor desk.

"I think we have to give Bennett Kingsley a lot of credit," the anchor on the right said. "He was in direct line of fire last night, and not 24 hours later is standing up to his board to keep ChemoCo on track, pushing for their new Long Island location. That says something about this guy—like a bull," he remarked, referring to his manly parts.

"Yeah, but you have to wonder what kept McCleary from approving SCAB. I mean, the guy headed that environmental group for years." The comment hung on air for a brief second right before they went to a commercial break.

"Mr. Patrick," the jailhouse guard called.

Gil stepped to the fortified door, waiting to be buzzed in. He walked through a metal detector and was scanned while his briefcase was opened and its contents inspected. He followed the guard down a long beige corridor to another fortified door and was buzzed into one of the small, windowless interrogation rooms. Moments later, a shackled Bill McCleary shuffled in and was directed to sit in the chair across from Gil.

This McCleary looked nothing like the man Gil remembered from the party last night. Shoulders slumped, head down, arms cuffed in front with his legs shackled: This was a broken man. His complexion was pale and tinged green, a shadowy leftover from the camouflage paint. Falling into the chair, a beaten-down Bill McCleary lifted his red-rimmed eyes, exposing a vacant look, almost as if he wasn't quite sure where he was.

Gil instantly felt pity for the man—someone who, a week ago, was one of the state's major power players. "I'm Gil Patrick from Shuster, Yleskin, and Matlock," Gil said, reflecting oddly that he'd left out the fact he was acting on behalf of LIMBO.

"Oh, I know that firm," Bill replied, perking up. "That's Marshall Matlock's firm isn't it?"

"Yes, but I'm here—" He was interrupted before he could add his LIMBO credentials.

"You're here because you want to make a name for yourself like all the others. I have a good mind to walk out right now," McCleary threatened in a surprisingly strong voice for a man who looked so weak.

"That would be a mistake, Mr. McCleary," Gil said. "I don't know if you realize the amount of trouble you're in, or what type of help you need."

Bill's eyes shifted. He looked tired but not quite beaten. There was still some life left.

"Are you aware of what happened last night?" Gil asked. It was a shot in the dark.

McCleary looked down; he rubbed his stubbly chin, his shoulders curled inward. "Not really," he whispered.

The answer surprised Gil. Like everyone else, he assumed McCleary's terrorist attack was a planned event, even if it was executed by a madman. But now he was getting the sense that this broken man didn't know what happened at all. Could it be he really wasn't in his right mind?

"Can you tell me what you remember of last night?" Gil asked, slipping naturally into his lawyer mode.

Bill McCleary closed his eyes and fought to recall the events of the last 24 hours.

"Let's start with what you can remember," Gil suggested.

"I spent yesterday morning cleaning out my office—you know, going through papers, collecting my personal effects, packing some boxes. There's more than 30 years' worth of hard work and memories there. I had lunch with some of the LICE staff. We went to my favorite restaurant, Tully's Tavern."

Gil knew the place. It had a reputation for good solid food: burgers, club sandwiches, steaks, and one of the best selections of tap beer in the area. He remembered seeing McCleary on TV and in photographs holding court from his favorite table in the back.

"There were five of us all together, Chris Brandt, Andy Weiss, Jill Winkle, Marty Howell, and myself. We were at my regular table, eating and having a couple of beers. You know, toasting to the good old days." He said this last line with regret.

"Then what?" Gil asked.

"Lunch was over. They went back to work and I drove home. I felt tired, drained—you know, like someone let all the air out of my tires. I wanted to lie down and close my eyes. I guess it was the strain from the last couple of days, and drinking a couple of beers helped too. That's it."

"What do you mean, 'That's it'?"

"I don't remember anything else until I woke up in jail."

The room was silent, not a sound except the low-level hum of the fluorescent lights. Gil's first reaction was shock. He thought maybe McCleary was giving him a load of bull. But there was something about the way he talked, how he looked, his body language . . . Something Gil couldn't put his finger on had him thinking McCleary might be telling the truth.

"Look, believe me or not. Frankly, I don't give a shit," McCleary spat, clearly sick of telling this same story to one skeptic after another. "I know what they tell me I did. I don't have any memory of it."

"Do have representation?" Gil asked, not sure where he was going with this.

"Yeah, some legal aid guy was assigned my case. I met him first thing this morning. He looks about 14 and just graduated from law school."

"I'd like to help you," Gil offered, surprising himself.

"Are you offering to represent me?"

"That's right," Gil replied. Once he was Bill McCleary's attorney, everything fell under attorney-client privilege. He wondered briefly what Marshall and the folks at LIMBO were going say before brushing those thoughts aside.

"So does this mean you believe me?"

"I don't know what I believe just yet, but I can tell you I'll do my best to uncover the truth."

Gil scribbled an agreement on a blank legal pad for McCleary, formally acknowledging their new legal arrangement. Bill McCleary signed after Gil, and the guard was the witness. Once that was done, Gil left McCleary with a set of instructions—primarily that he should talk to no one without Gil being present. Lastly, Gil suggested he submit to a comprehensive blood test and a complete physical.

"Before you go, I need you to do something for me," Bill McCleary asked, motioning he'd like to say it in private, without the guard present.

Once the two men were alone, McCleary looked Gil squarely in the eye, dropped his voice to just above a whisper, and spoke about important files still at his old office. He didn't want to go into detail about the files—that they would be incriminating to various government and business leaders—he only focused on the SCAB report.

"I was going to get them after lunch. I didn't want them sitting around with my other boxes. One file, in particular, you must locate and keep it safe—away from A Holtz and the folks at ChemoCo."

Gil nodded, not knowing where his client was going with this.

"It's LICE's preliminary report on SCAB. Research documents and various test findings about the ecological impact on East End waterways. There's a likelihood SCAB could be an environmental nightmare, wreaking havoc on the fragile ecosystem.

"The files are stored in the safe behind the aerial photo hanging in my office. You'll need both the code and a key to open it. I keep the key hidden underneath a loose board in my bedroom."

McCleary went on to give Gil the eight-digit code to the LICE safe, and described in detail where Gil could find the key. Without the SCAB file, McCleary would find it difficult to prove he was anything other than a deranged man hell-bent on revenge. The file would prove how far ChemoCo was willing to go to get SCAB to market.

Chapter 54

The meeting with McCleary turned out differently than anticipated. Gil knew there were precious few hours before the world would learn he was Bill McCleary's attorney. He mentally checked off a to-do list: inform LIMBO of his new role in the case, give Marshall Matlock a heads-up, convene his first press conference, and call Glynn to arrange their meeting for dinner. But before all of that, Gil had one important task to perform. He needed to get into Bill McCleary's house, retrieve that key, and open the safe at LICE. He had to get that file.

McCleary's house, a small, well-cared-for cape, was nestled in the middle of a quiet suburban block off Route 25 and set comfortably back from the road. The shrubs were neatly trimmed, and the lawn was freshly mowed. The light-gray siding was fairly new, as was the roof. *This is the house of a tidy and orderly man,* Gil thought as he walked up to the policeman on duty.

"I'm Gil Patrick, the lawyer representing William McCleary. I need to have access to his house," Gil said, looking the cop straight in the eye.

The officer took a minute to review McCleary's signed legal authorization. He called over to headquarters before unlocking the front door. Gil asked the policeman to wait outside.

It took a minute for his eyes to adjust to the dim light inside. Gil noticed everything was clean and precise, from the placement of the couch and chairs to the pictures on the wall. There weren't many items on the coffee and end tables aside from lamps and a couple of well-placed magazines. The floor was partly covered by an area rug complimenting the colors of the drapes and furniture. It didn't look lived in, more like something staged for a photo shoot. Gil remembered his own bachelor apartment, it looked nothing like this.

Straight ahead was a small hallway that led to the bedrooms and bathroom. Unlike the living room, he found McCleary's bedroom a complete mess. His bed was unmade, and clothes were thrown on the floor. A couple of the dresser drawers were opened, and Gil could see the insides were pulled apart. There was no denying someone had been scrounging around. Turning toward the bed, Gil bent to locate the loose floorboards McCleary had described. He found them easy enough, as they had already been moved aside. Gil stared into an empty cavity. Someone had found and removed the key.

Gil left the house quickly and hurried to the LICE offices before they closed for the weekend. He arrived as the last of the staff was filing out. Gil introduced himself and met two of McCleary's coworkers—Andy Weiss and Jill Winkle. The other two, Marty Howell and Chris Brandt, had left early for the weekend. Andy had worked with Bill McCleary the longest, almost 15 years. He was their chief researcher and was intimately familiar with the SCAB testing. Jill handled press for LICE and advised McCleary on PR issues. Both were given pink slips earlier in the week in preparation for A Holtz's arrival.

"Can you spare a couple of minutes now? Why don't we go directly to Bill's office?" Gil suggested as both staffers seemed genuinely interested in helping their former boss.

Gil closed the office door and walked over to the aerial photo hanging on the wall. He tried moving the picture, but it wouldn't budge.

"Press the top right corner and the bottom left corner together," Andy offered, clearly familiar with the picture's secrets.

Gil did as he was told, and silently, the picture slid upward, revealing the safe. Gil typed in the code, which caused a green light to appear. Directly below was where the key should be inserted. Clearly, he could do nothing more.

"This place is scheduled to be painted next week," Jill mentioned. "Likely they'll find the safe. I heard they might be taking down this wall, creating a bigger office for A Holtz."

"As you can see, the safe cannot be opened without both the key and the code," Andy said. "All our work is in there. Bill made me promise to destroy any copies or other records—he was paranoid about leaks."

"For what it's worth, we have a difficult time believing Bill shot up the LIMBO party last night. It was no secret that he and A Holtz hated each other, but Bill would never do anything like that. It's not like him," Jill finished, shaking her head.

Gil asked about their lunch yesterday, specifically if they noticed anything odd or unusual. Both thought it strange Bill went home right after they ate. Bill McCleary was known as a high-energy workaholic—they couldn't recall a time when he was tired enough to go home and nap. "Leaving to go home in the middle of the day was not typical of Bill," Jill commented, "but stress does strange things to people and Bill was under a lot of stress."

298

Chapter 55

Penna was wrapping up the week at Uncle Dominic's office. She always stayed late on Friday. She liked to have everything just so when she left. Despite her best efforts, chances were good Uncle Dominic would come in over the weekend. More times than not, she'd walk in on Monday morning to find the place a mess, no matter what straightening she did Friday afternoon.

Looking up from her desk, Penna was surprised to see one of her uncle's "associates" coming in the front door. Penna considered Pauly, her uncle's least appealing visitor. Scruffy hair, chin stubble, mismatched clothes with the whiff of garbage around him, Pauly's beady eyes darted about as if looking for a rabbit to jump out from behind her desk.

"Hi, Dominic in?" Pauly asked. A lopsided smile creased his face, offering his best imitation of being friendly.

"He's on the phone," she replied, glancing to see his phone button lit. "Is he expecting you?"

Pauly gave her a sheepish look, one instantly conveying more than he expected.

"You're looking to borrow some money, right?" Penna asked, unable to help herself, praying her uncle would end up kicking the guy out. "Money for a ticket out of town. Someplace like Florida?" Penna continued matter-of-factly as she caught the look on Pauly's face.

"Yeah, how'd ya know?" He couldn't keep the surprise out of his voice. He already felt jittery, and Penna's questions aggravated a tightening in his throat, making him cough. He repeatedly tried to clear his throat.

Penna was getting all sorts of information streaming into her brain like music from a radio.

"What are you running from?" Penna asked, confronting him head-on. "You had something to do with the shoot-up at the LIMBO party last night, didn't you?" It was more of a statement than a question.

Pauly was staring at her now, wide-eyed with fear. He always thought Dominic's girl was weird, but now she was freaking him out. He would have run out the door if he didn't need the money so badly.

"Look, I don't know what you're talking about. I was nowhere near that party—you can ask anyone."

Penna couldn't help herself. "What did you do to Bill McCleary?"

"Bill who?" Pauly barked, coughing up a storm.

"You saw him before the party, didn't you? Were at his house, too. You know something about what happened last night. Something important." Penna was staring at him now, her eyes boring into his. Try as he might, Pauly couldn't look away. He was squirming and hacking uncontrollably.

"Don't try lying, I'll know. You slipped him a drug, didn't you? Something to alter his mind. It was at that tavern he likes. You went to that tavern and put something in his beer. Isn't that right?"

Pauly was shaking as he fought to look away, fairly choking during each one of Penna's statements. *How did she know?* If he was freaked out before, he was crazed with fear now.

"Who's there?" Uncle Dominic called out from his office.

"It's me, Pauly, I need to see ya right away," he squeaked, tearing himself away as he pushed past her.

There was one more nugget of information Penna gleaned as Pauly disappeared into Uncle Dominic's office. It had something to do with a key.

The minute Pauly disappeared behind Uncle Dominic's door, Penna called Glynn.

PATRICIA RUTH

Chapter 56

"Where are you?" Glynn asked as she spoke into her cell phone, wondering why Gil was not calling from the office phone.

"I'm on my way to pick you up," Gil replied. "I thought we'd go to dinner at Wine on Vine. Be outside in ten minutes."

This is a change, Glynn thought. *He was usually the one working late at the office.*

Gil was waiting at the curb as Glynn exited the building. She could tell right away something was different. Face flushed, he leaned over and gave her a sweaty kiss. There was an air of excitement about him—something she couldn't put her finger on.

"I have some news to share with you," he said, charging right into things.

"So do I," Glynn replied, but she could tell he wasn't listening.

"I'd like to wait until we're in the restaurant," he said, and then he quickly changed the subject. "Did you catch the ChemoCo press conference?"

"We all watched it at the office. Marshall was there. He wants to get Bennett Kingsley's business in the worst way. He asked me to do a complete workup on ChemoCo—he wants to know everything from the day they opened their doors. Most of it is in the public domain, but I did uncover a couple of juicy nuggets," Glynn mentioned.

"Some juicy nuggets, huh?" Gil replied absently.

Glynn prattled on about the report she put together, and how Rose has become even more protective of Marshall, causing renewed speculation in the office about their on-again/off-again affair. Glynn even recounted some of the comments circulating about A Holtz and the LIMBO party, especially after seeing the photos in the newspapers.

Finally, they arrived at Wine on Vine, left the car with the parking attendant, and were escorted to their table. The restaurant was an oasis of calm. The décor was rustic, a takeoff on one of those turn-of-the-century wineries. Even the air felt cool like you were sitting in the cellar with the wine barrels. Instrumental music floated in and out of the various dining rooms, providing the quiet seclusion Gil was looking for.

After the waiter took their drink orders, Glynn sat back and gave her husband a look, communicating the time had come.

"All right, there's no easy way to say it: I'm Bill McCleary's attorney."

Glynn blinked.

Gil smiled, glad to render his wife speechless.

"I thought you were going there to observe, check things out, and report back. What happened?"

Gil recounted the time spent at the jail and what he felt about McCleary. There was something not quite right with the story circulating in the press. He told Glynn about his visit to McCleary's house and the missing key. Finally, he explained what he learned about LICE's report on SCAB.

"When are you going to tell Marshall?"

"I'm not worried about Marshall; he's an attorney, after all, and will be calculating the increase in fees once this hits the papers. No, it's Arnie Holtzmann who could do the most damage. The guy's an asshole and I'm sure to be smeared. I wouldn't be surprised if I were branded a traitor and drummed out of LIMBO before the new stationery listing my name comes back from the printer."

Glynn spent the next half hour quizzing Gil on his meeting with McCleary. She had already put two and two together after her phone call from Penna. There was no doubt McCleary had been drugged, robbed, and set up, but not by that lowlife in Penna's office. This was a sophisticated operation. Someone had to know where McCleary would be, that there was a safe, and its key hidden in his bedroom. But why go through all that effort unless you were certain there was a damning report locked in the LICE safe?

Glynn thought about all this new information, trying not to jump to conclusions. She didn't want to repeat her mistake by coming to an incorrect inference, like what happened with the SCAB report she fed Marshall. The thought of working with her husband to expose the truth about SCAB and uncover the events leading up to McCleary's shootout at the LIMBO party was tempting. No doubt they would make a formidable team. Glynn loved her husband and hated to keep something so important from him. But she had made a pack with the girls—their experiences at LIQuID would not be mentioned unless they all agreed. Her hands were tied. The best she could do was to listen and offer her support as Gil did the job of defending McCleary. Hopefully, in the process, she'd discover whether SCAB was a blessing or a curse and maybe see some bad guys get punished.

Chapter 57

"I hope I'm not catching you at a bad time," Gil said, trying to sound considerate before he dropped a bomb in Marshall's lap. "I need to make you aware of some new information regarding the McCleary case."

Marshall was on his way home from dinner with his wife and another couple. They had polished off a couple of bottles of wine, and that was after two rounds of cocktails. If he were home, he'd be asleep in front of the TV.

"Did you catch the press conference today?" Marshall asked. One thing was on his mind: getting Bennett Kingsley to sign on the dotted line. "I spoke with Bennett, and he's looking forward to setting up a meeting; I'll close that deal yet," Marshall boasted.

"That's great," Gil agreed, allowing his boss to prattle on.

"You went over to the jail today," Marshall said. "Did you see that creep McCleary? What could he have to say? I mean, the guy is nuts, right? It'll be interesting to watch him squirm during his trial. So, what did you want to tell me?"

Gil took a deep breath. "I've agreed to represent McCleary," came whooshing out.

The line was silent. "Did you hear me?" Gil asked. "By tomorrow morning it'll be in all the papers and on TV, if it isn't already. I thought I'd give you a heads-up."

"Are you fucking nuts? Arnie sent you over to the jail so you could keep an eye on things for LIMBO, NOT to become his freakin' counsel," Marshall yelled, moving beyond whatever lingering effects the alcohol had in his system.

"Oh, this is great, just great," Marshall continued sarcastically. "Here I am sucking up to Kingsley and we're this close to a deal, and you decide to sign with Bill McCleary—a nobody. A crazy man who's out of a job and shot up a party in front of hundreds of people. People who are our clients and would-be clients. I don't know who's more irrational! You or that nutjob sitting in jail!" Marshall had pulled over and was shouting into the phone.

Holding the phone away from his ear, Gil let Marshall unload. There was no chance of explaining until the senior partner got it all out of his system. Not that Gil had anything to defend—part of his employment contract stated he was fully entitled to represent whoever he wanted. There was even an obligation to do pro bono work. But given the nature of events, there was no way he could allow his boss to read about this in the papers. That would have been a bad move.

Finally, the phone fell silent. "Look, Marshall, McCleary was drugged. He was given some sort of powerful substance and brainwashed, and he was robbed too. I know it sounds crazy, like science fiction, but his house was ransacked. The robber took a key, the key to his office safe." Gil didn't want to say anything more.

Marshall didn't need a road map to follow where all this was going. "You mean you think McCleary was set up?"

"It looks that way."

"Kingsley," Marshall breathed. "But Kingsley doesn't yet know you're McCleary's attorney. How could he? So, what does he want? He doesn't have to pay $1,000/hour to have me review office rental agreements."

Gil listened. He had the same thoughts Marshall was now expressing: Why would Bennett Kingsley need to hire Shylock?

The wheels were turning in Marshall's brain. He was feeling better about Gil's surprising announcement. There'll be plenty of press, he thought, and the names of Shuster, Yleskin, and Matlock will be splattered across the media. Good for business no matter what the outcome.

"Have you arranged a press conference yet?" Marshall asked. "Use our conference room. Check with Rose—she'll help you set everything up. Make it for first thing Monday morning. Have you told A Holtz?"

"No, you're the first one. I'll be calling Arnie when we hang up."

"Keep me posted," were Marshall's last words as he ended the call.

Gil took another deep breath and punched in the numbers of A Holtz's cell phone. This was the first time Gil was initiating contact. He was so new the letter from the LIMBO board authorizing him to monitor the McCleary case didn't even have his name listed as a board member.

"Gil Patrick," Arnie answered after the second ring. "Reporting in, I see." He didn't want to tell this young pup he no longer needed to receive updates; Gil's report should be made to the board. But why confuse the boy?

"I'm not disturbing you or anything?" Gil asked, trying to keep the conversation as polite as possible.

"No, tell me what you've got," came back the demand.

"I'm afraid I won't be able to fulfill the LIMBO board's request to monitor the McCleary case."

"Why is that?"

"I've signed on as Bill McCleary's legal counsel."

Silence rang out on the other end of the line; Gil could just about make out the voices from some TV program in the background.

"Sonofabitch. Do you know what the hell you've got yourself into? A stupid move boy, and you had so much promise. That man's crazy, a nutjob, and you've made the worst decision of your career."

The call ended abruptly as Gil sat staring at the phone.

Chapter 58

Marshall was pulling the car into the driveway when his phone rang.

"Do you know what that jerk associate of yours has done?" Arnie said, not even giving Marshall a chance to say hello. "He's McCleary's attorney, for God's sake! It's a stupid move, Marshall, damned stupid, and it'll ruin your firm. Do you think Bennett Kingsley will hire you now?"

"Why not?" Marshall asked. "What should my associate's client have to do with ChemoCo and Kingsley?"

"You're as crazy as he is! Don't you get it?" A Holtz yelled. "ChemoCo is committed to Long Island, Bennett said so himself at the press conference today. I know for a fact he's considering Shuster, Yleskin and Matlock—he's ready to sign with you. And now THIS! Your idiot associate has screwed things up, don't you see?" Arnie couldn't believe how dense Marshall was being.

"I figure we'll have the inside track to what's happening with McCleary," Marshall suggested. "Why would he want his business elsewhere?"

Not even bothering to reply, Arnie ended the call instead.

Part 9
Combination

PATRICIA RUTH

Chapter 59

Sollie found herself walking the halls of the LIQuID building again, this time first thing in the morning. She had an appointment with Carl to take him house hunting at 10:00. But first Ray and his team asked to meet with her in Lab 8.

"Open up, Ray, it's me, Sollie," she said into the intercom.

The door buzzed open as Ray ushered her into the lab.

"Glad you were able to come this Saturday," Ray said with a welcoming smile.

"I had to come here anyway. I'm taking a customer to see some houses. Have you've met Carl Hammerling yet? He's one of the ChemoCo guys that recently moved here."

"I've heard about them, but we don't mingle with the other companies," Ray explained.

Sollie wasn't surprised. She didn't think the guys ever left the lab, yet they were always clean and looked freshly pressed. It was a mystery.

"We're interested in testing your ability with time alteration," Ray started without much preamble. "I've modified the interval invigilator to capture the exact amount of time change. The whole process shouldn't take long—time well spent," he joked.

Sollie stared at Ray. "You mean you didn't invite me over for breakfast?"

Ray paused a minute, not quite certain how to respond. He was still getting used to dealing with these women.

"You're going to capture me invigorating the sample? Stewie might get jealous," she continued.

Ray smiled past this joke, too.

"My theory is this: maybe we can get the results of the SCAB test sooner if we speed up time," he suggested, nodding in Sollie's direction.

"I've set up a secure area over here," Ray said as he walked over to the thick door in the back of the lab. He opened it to reveal a room the size of a closet with a large table in the center. On top of the table was a series of containers, some sitting on top of burners, each filled with liquid; it was the SCAB formula cooking and coagulating. Next to them was a large gray box with three dials and three windows. Each window featured a different readout–one was an arrow-like gauge, one showed digital numbers, and the third had horizontal lines that fluctuated up and down in yellow, red, and green.

"You want me to go in there?" Sollie asked, eyeing the tiny room with suspicion.

"It's safe, but also self-contained. You can perform your time altering inside and it shouldn't have any effect outside its walls. Right now we have been preparing the SCAB formula for two days. The chemicals need to cook and cool at least seven days to complete all the steps. If you can speed up time, we'll have the results much sooner, and we'll know for certain whether SCAB is benign or harmful."

"So, I'm the experiment on the experiment. Is that it?"

"I wouldn't have thought of it that way, but yes."

Sollie didn't like going into the small windowless room with only a bunch of chemicals and some electronic equipment to keep her company, but she shrugged her unease off as she entered.

"Now I want you to concentrate, concentrate very hard on moving time forward. The interval invigilator is set to record the time fluctuation. When you're done, open the door—you're not locked in or anything."

Sollie nodded and closed the door behind her. Left alone in the tiny room, she felt cut off from the rest of the world. It was a bit scary but also exhilarating to finally be measuring the effects of her newfound ability. Sollie stared at the chemical soup on the table, focused her attention on it, calmed her breathing, and allowed her brain to fixate. A little push to start and then another. She decided to make one more effort and took a deep breath, closed her eyes, and thrust her mind forward. This last push was more powerful than any she had ever tried, and its residual effects were felt immediately. She leaned against the table to steady her balance. Glancing at her hand, she noticed her fingernails had grown, and her hair seemed longer too.

Opening the door, Sollie felt the clean, fresh air of the lab hit her face. Funny she hadn't noticed the room was stuffy when she entered, but it felt that way now. Ray was standing exactly where she left him when she entered the room, which was odd because she thought he would have walked away.

"You're done?" Ray asked, clearly surprised she'd emerge so soon.

"I did it. Three times. The last was the most powerful. My nails are longer." Sollie felt a little lightheaded and found a chair. "Do you have anything to eat, a bagel or something?"

Ray walked into the room to retrieve the interval invigilator. "This is amazing," he said, scribbling the readings on a pad. "The time in that room advanced by almost five days, and it looks as if the SCAB chemical process is five days further along."

"I'm guessing I aged five days as well," Sollie stated, not happy about getting older.

"Yes, you aged five days, too, but I believe you can easily fix that. Take a break. I have some power bars. Rest for a bit, and we'll put you back in and see if you can move time backward." Ray was beaming—this was unbelievable. He'd have to spend time analyzing the interval invigilator's readings and cross-reference with the other gauges, but he knew what the answer would be. Sollie did, in fact, shift time, and she moved it considerably.

After her rest, Sollie went back into the room. Ray had removed the SCAB chemical apparatus and reset the interval invigilator. She concentrated again, this time pulling instead of pushing. It took as much energy, and again felt weak and drained afterward.

Once back outside the room, Ray read the gauges. This time, they showed time had reversed a little more than four days. "You're not back to where you started, but pretty damn close," he confirmed.

"At least that's good," Sollie replied. "I'd never forgive myself if I was using this gift to make myself older. Then I'd really need my head examined!"

Sollie's test was the first real empirical data on her time-shifting ability that Ray's team was able to compile. Ultimately, his research would have to be independently confirmed, but he had no doubt what the results would be. The conclusion was undeniable. After years of long hours and almost total devotion, his theory about brainpower was proved beyond a shadow of a doubt, and all in the span of mere moments.

Sollie felt as if she had put in a full day's work doing something physical like cleaning her house, but the clock on the wall showed only 20 minutes had passed since she entered the lab. Ray ordered a bagel and coffee from the shop across the way and escorted her to one of the lab's more comfortable chairs to rest. Twenty-five minutes later and feeling stronger, Sollie left for her meeting with Carl Hammerling.

Chapter 60

"Arnie, good to see you," Ted said as he extended his hand, surprised to see the former LIMBO boss.

"Arnie is a last-minute addition to our foursome after Carl bowed out," Stan explained, suppressing the urge to say anything more.

"Carl's loss is my gain," Arnie commented, not comfortable with making small talk.

"I'm sure Carl would rather be here too," added Bennett. "He was none too keen on house hunting, but we all have to do our part."

Inviting Arnie was Bennett's idea. Stan would have been more than happy to play with whoever the club would assign to round out their foursome. But Bennett had a special job for Arnie and wanted to make his request in person. The whole situation was giving Stan a headache. What started out as a simple plan to ensure SCAB's approval now seemed to be getting more complex by the day.

Stan still felt bad about Bennett's health scare the other night. How could he have known his old friend would end up passed out on the floor and whisked away in an ambulance? Of course, the experience could have scared the shit out of anybody. But he had to keep Bennett in the dark, needed to protect him from the truth, like in the old days. And now this latest news about the Shylock attorney representing McCleary? It was a surprise, all right. Clearly, no one had considered that.

So, on Bennett's insistence, Stan had called Arnie with the golf invite. As usual, the conversation was one-sided, with Arnie ranting and raving. Arnie actually expected Stan to be more enraged at the thought of McCleary getting a high-priced defense attorney, or that McCleary held up the SCAB approval—a clear jobs creator, or that

McCleary was derailing ChemoCo's next big product launch. *All the screaming in the world is not going to alter the facts. Why can't Arnie just get it?* Stan thought. Now, it seems he was doomed to listen to Arnie's rantings for the rest of the day.

"I don't know about you, but I'm still steaming about this whole McCleary mess," Arnie declared, unable to keep his thoughts to himself. "Who would have thought the kid would sign on as his legal counsel?"

"Yes, we agree," Stan replied in his most soothing voice. He was already regretting Bennett's decision to include Arnie, and the day was just beginning. The man had no manners, was insensitive to his surroundings, and couldn't keep his feelings under control.

"I wouldn't worry too much," Bennett offered. "We think McCleary will be discredited. Two hundred people saw him shoot up that party. I'll wager there's plenty of evidence floating around to send him away for quite a while. But our real concern is getting into that safe."

"Yes, the safe is our next target," Ted parroted, fingering a chain around his neck. "We still don't have the code, but maybe Arnie could help us?"

Stan mentally rolled his eyes at the thought of Arnie being able to do anything requiring finesse.

"So Arnie, have you settled into your new LICE office yet?" Bennett asked innocently enough.

"I was there the other day—checked it out. My girl is arranging for the place to be fumigated, if you know what I mean?" He meant it as a joke, but no one laughed.

"A new coat of paint, yes, of course," Bennett confirmed. "Did you happen to take anything off the walls?"

"No," came the one-word reply.

"So, you went to the LICE offices but didn't poke around McCleary's desk or anything?" Bennett reiterated.

"What are you talking about? McCleary was there the whole time. What was I supposed to do, tie him up?" Arnie couldn't see where all this was going.

"Bennett, I think it would help things if you told Arnie the plan," Stan stated, sick of the cat-and-mouse game Bennett loved to play.

"Tell me what?" Arnie demanded, getting angry at being manipulated. He was the one who did the pushing around, not the other way around.

Red-faced, Arnie waited, not trusting himself to speak.

"All right," Stan offered, unable to watch the spectacle any longer. "We know the SCAB report is in McCleary's . . . I mean, your LICE office, in a safe located behind an aerial photo of Long Island. We believe McCleary's SCAB results were not complete; there were missing pieces. It must have been what he was waiting for and why he didn't publicize the results or try to discredit SCAB. McCleary simply didn't have all the proper documentation. As it turns out, the timing has worked in our favor. Too bad for him." Stan paused, wanting to make sure Arnie was following his narrative. It wouldn't do to have the whole world see the LICE report. The revelation that there were missing parts of the formula would create a scandal and fuel questions as to why ChemoCo didn't provide all the information. It could vindicate McCleary and LICE's decision to withhold approval, and no one wants that to happen.

"To open the safe requires a key and the code. We feel certain we can get the key, or at least have a copy made. We need your help getting the code," Stan finished.

Arnie looked from Stan to Bennett to Ted. "So you're saying you have the key already?" he asked, wondering what they were leaving out.

"Don't get hung up on the key. You're missing the point," Stan reiterated, calmly trying to have Arnie focus on what was important. "We'll get it, you don't need to worry about that." It was not necessary to give Arnie too many details, and knowing the location of the key was on a need-to-know basis.

"I know a guy, my ex-bookie, who says he'll be able to get someone who can pick that lock for a couple of bucks," Ted teased as he fingered the chain hanging around his neck.

Arnie simply stared at Ted. "You want to break into McCleary's safe?" Arnie asked, not believing what he was hearing. The vintner was the last person he'd expect to have underworld connections. Ted always struck him as a surfer dude suffering from one too many wipeouts. In fact, the idea these three would even contemplate breaking and entering seemed bizarre.

"It's not McCleary's safe anymore," Stan said, "it's YOUR safe. You should have access to it. You're the director, for God's sake. And I'm sure I don't have to remind you that you've already approved SCAB. It was front-page news."

"We want to make sure your approval doesn't contradict whatever McCleary has stashed away. Hell, man, you don't want to look like a fool should the press get access to the contents of that safe and find a bunch of reports which disagree with your approval, do you?" Bennett emphasized.

"You can always ask McCleary for the key and code. Maybe he'd give it to you because he feels bad for shooting up your party," Ted suggested, wanting to lighten things up a bit.

"The code is an eight-digit number, which when combined with the key will open the safe. Just eight digits stand in the way of getting that report," Stan reiterated.

"You're tight with Marshall Matlock, right?" Bennett asked rhetorically. "He's Gil's boss, the kid representing McCleary, and Marshall is head of the firm. If anyone can get that code, it'll be Marshall. We need your help, Arnie. I don't have to tell you how much is riding on this," Bennett added, wanting to drive home the point.

Arnie let the conversation pause—it was a lot to consider. "You're right, I am the director. It is my safe," he acknowledged slowly.

"Well, if that's what you want, you'll have to do your part too," Arnie countered. "Let's start with transferring some ChemoCo stock."

326

Chapter 61

Sunday morning found Arnie pacing around his living room. He couldn't stop thinking about that safe. He felt the fool learning about it from that pansy Ted Landis. "You have to give Bennett Kingsley credit," Arnie repeated to himself for the hundredth time. "The guy knows more about what's going on at LICE than me. He must have quite a network." Sure, he told those boys he'd get the code and told them exactly what they wanted to hear. Why not? He was in possession of the safe now. It was part of the office of the director of LICE, his office. It didn't hurt that they provided an attractive incentive—10,000 ChemoCo shares to be transferred to a private offshore account . . . once he delivered the code. The first thing he did when he got home was look up the closing price. The next thing he did was to go over to the LICE offices and see things for himself. He spent nearly two hours combing every shelf, drawer, and file cabinet, but the eight-digit code was nowhere to be found.

"We need to talk," Arnie barked into the phone, not able to delay a moment longer.

"It's Sunday morning. Can't this wait?"

"Meet me for coffee. I promise it won't take long. The place down the street from my office, the LIMBO office. I'll see you in 20 minutes." He was itching for this meeting, it had been on his mind since yesterday's golf game.

Hanging up, Arnie went into action. He arrived at the Donut Hole early, commandeered one of the tables in the back, ordered a black coffee and a glazed donut, and reviewed his plan yet again.

Marshall strolled in ten minutes later. Seeing Arnie at a table in the back, he ambled over. "Why couldn't this wait?" Marshall asked as he eased himself into the chair. He gave Arnie a hard look.

"I need a favor," Arnie began.

Marshall called over the waitress and ordered a coffee.

"You have to talk to that kid, Gil. Tell him I need to speak with McCleary."

Marshall stared back. "I can't believe your nerve. Tell me, why should I do that?" The anger vibe shooting out from Marshall's eyes could have burned through cinderblock.

"I called the jail yesterday—no go. They have orders to pass all requests through his attorney. There is no way anyone can speak with McCleary. It was a long shot, but I tried."

"What do you want to tell him? It's okay he shot up your party? That he's forgiven and now you want to be friends?" Marshall asked sarcastically.

Marshall's words hung over the table as the waitress served the coffee.

"I need some information—it has nothing to do with the criminal charges. As the new head of LICE, I require something only my predecessor knows."

"Why bother me? Ask Gil, he's the attorney."

"He's not going to give it to me. But a request from you is a different story."

Again, silence. Marshall sat very still, waiting.

"Look, it's the code to the safe in McCleary's office . . . my office now. I'm the head of LICE and in order to do my job, the job I was appointed to, I need access to all materials, papers, files and yes, the safe in the office."

"That's it? Nothing more?"

"By the way, I'm sure you'll be happy to know you'll be getting a nice fat retainer check from ChemoCo this week," Arnie dropped this lure, certain it would get Marshall to seriously consider his request. "Look, the safe is part of LICE. I'm in charge of that organization now, I should have the code. It's unfortunate all this other stuff had to happen," Arnie said, sounding conciliatory.

"What's in the safe?" Marshall asked.

"How would I know? That's why I need the code."

Marshall sat quietly for a moment, considering.

"I'll look into it," was Marshall's terse reply.

Chapter 62

Normally, Gil would have slept in on July 4th. He always took Independence Day as a vacation, but not this year. He was up at the crack of dawn, writing and rehearsing his speech, crafting answers to the inevitable questions . . . at least to the questions he could anticipate. Thankfully, Rose had arranged everything over the weekend, including opening the offices, readying the conference room, and ordering coffee, etc., for the media. What a help. He didn't care what the gossipers said about her and Marshall or if she didn't have a life outside the office—the woman was there when you needed her.

Glynn was up, too. She sat and listened to his prepared responses, offering comments and suggestions. If it had been a regular workday, she would have been in the office, maybe quietly observing from the back of the room. But today, she would be watching the press conference from the comfort of their living room as the firm planned to stream it live on their website.

Gil would do just fine—no one could be more prepared. But things weren't going to be easy. Hundreds of people saw McCleary brandish a weapon and fire shots at the party; the fact that they were blanks made things only marginally better. The press was having a field day. You'd think the guy was responsible for global warming and the 2020 pandemic the way they were characterizing him. Glynn hoped Gil wouldn't be tarred and feathered along with his client.

Life was going to be different for them now. The press was camped out in front of their apartment building. Gil had been at the jail conferring with McCleary all weekend and would be spending even more time there as the legal process lurched forward. Marshall was calling three times a day, wanting constant updates. Gil hired a doctor to give McCleary a full exam—urine, blood tests, the works.

He also called in the services of Manny Dawkins, a private investigator the firm uses. Glynn thought she wouldn't be hearing much about the case, as Gil is typically close-mouthed, but this was different, too, as he wanted to make sure he wasn't overlooking anything. She had become his sounding board.

Normally, she would be happy—flattered, even—to have his confidence and be part of such a big case, but not now. The whole chain of events was odd, Glynn thought. While they were both working toward the same goal, they were going about it in two different ways. Gil was out front with every move being scrutinized. Glynn was working to uncover the truth, too, but through the back door. It killed her, keeping Gil in the dark about her activities. She had considered telling him what happened in the parking lot that night of her book club meeting, wanting to confess her abilities and how they led her to wrongly endorse SCAB. But not now. Now, she'd do what she could to help as his dutiful wife and pray the rest would remain a secret.

While Gil was off at the jailhouse or working at the office, Glynn had been busy all weekend, too. On Saturday, her first call was to Ray shortly after his test with Sollie. The researcher was so animated Glynn could hardly believe she was talking to the same reserved guy.

"Sollie was amazing," Ray exclaimed, unable to keep the excitement from his voice. "We should have the SCAB test results as early as Thursday. I wish I had an actual sample from their lab to compare it to. It's hard to know if Sollie's time push will affect the chemical process."

Learning they'd be getting the results early was a huge weight off her mind, as Glynn couldn't wait to see the final SCAB data. Documenting Sollie's time-shifting ability was another plus. Maybe if Ray could understand how their new abilities worked, he could figure out exactly what altered inside their brains. Ray's good news lifted her spirits, and for the first time since this whole thing happened, Glynn was feeling positive, like maybe things would work out after all. But that good feeling lasted only until she checked in with Iris, who was still monitoring Carl's computer.

"Carl received confirmation that the first SCAB shipment is to leave ChemoCo on Wednesday, July 6th. You won't believe the delivery address—Crystal Clam Wineries. Aren't they one of your firm's clients?" Iris asked. "And another thing that's interesting: Who would have thought Carl Hammerling and Ted Landis would be so buddy-buddy? It appears Ted is more than a ChemoCo customer. The two of them seem to be friends, close friends. I get the feeling Ted is part of the whole SCAB thing, and has been for a while."

"Curious," Glynn thought, as she remembered Crystal Clam was one of the first SCAB test sites, and Ted Landis had been active in pushing for its approval.

"What else is going on with Carl?" Glynn asked.

"You mean aside from the fact he likes to visit porn sites? He has three or four he alternates between," Iris offered with a laugh. "There were some other emails back and forth yesterday about getting a code. Ted was talking up the fact he held the key to opening the safe, and all they need now is the code. Carl asked if there was a plan, and Ted replied Stan was taking care of it. Do you know what they're talking about?"

"I think they're referring to the code for McCleary's office safe. According to Gil, someone stole the key from McCleary's house the night of the LIMBO party," Glynn replied.

"Well, Ted did write about fingering something precious when he sleeps—I assumed he was referring to his penis, but maybe not. Maybe he was talking about the key."

"I can't believe it, but I think Ted Landis might have it," Glynn exclaimed, unable to envision the affable vintner involved in breaking and entering. "We need to get that key," Glynn said as she hurried off the phone, quickly placing her next call to Onawhim.

Chapter 63

"That's all for now. Thank you for coming," Gil said as he concluded the press conference. He had been expecting a decent turnout, but it was even bigger than anticipated. Rose had done a great job setting everything up. *"Glad that's over,"* Gil thought, thankful he took the time to prepare and had his answers ready without any delay. Now, he had to get on with the business of defending his client, with the first task trying to get McCleary out on bail. Exiting the room, Gil glanced over at his boss.

"Good job," Marshall said as he walked over to the younger associate. "I think you gave the press something to chew on other than the obvious 'disgruntled employee going postal'," Marshall remarked.

"Yeah, well, now the real work starts," Gil replied, hustling back to his office to review papers and check in with his client.

"How's McCleary holding up?" Marshall asked, walking along. "It's got to be tough being locked up in jail."

"He's doing okay, better every day," Gil replied, wondering why his boss was asking the same question he just answered for the press moments ago.

"Does he ever say anything? You know, like what he was thinking or why he did it?"

"No, he doesn't talk about that night. He can't remember much." Again, Gil got the feeling he was repeating himself. Early on, he had mentioned to Marshall the possibility McCleary might have been drugged; Gil had left it vague and never spoke of it again.

"Tomorrow Arnie will be starting his first full day as Director of LICE," Marshall remarked, changing the topic. "He wanted me to offer his apology for the way he talked to you the other night. You know he can be a bit of loose cannon at times."

"Really? I didn't think the word apology was in Arnie's vocabulary."

"I know the guy can be a bit gruff and uncouth, but he's done a lot for the region. He doesn't get the credit he deserves. I guess he wants to start his new job off on the right foot."

Gil nodded, not knowing what to say. *If Arnie felt bad, maybe he should have called me himself,* was one thought.

"I don't mean to be making excuses for him, but you know Arnie and I go way back. I guess I know him better than most people," Marshall explained, looking for his opening. "He's human, like the rest of us. Wants to do a good job, has his heart in the right place, even if his mouth goes off in another direction sometimes." This last line Marshall delivered with a bit of a smile.

"In fact, he's especially concerned about starting his job at LICE under the cloud of the whole McCleary case. Typically when government workers change jobs, the incumbent helps the incoming chief. You know, they turn over files, computer passwords, that kind of thing. But with McCleary locked up, that didn't happen. And of course, under the circumstances, getting them together for a chat wouldn't be appropriate."

"So, what does Arnie want?" Gil asked, wondering why it was taking his boss so long to come to the point.

"The code to the LICE office safe."

The question stopped Gil in his tracks. Arnie must know that to open the safe, you need both the code AND the key. If he wants the code, it must mean he has the key.

"Oh, the code to the safe," Gil replied, turning to face his boss, stalling for time. "Yes, Bill mentioned the safe in one of our discussions. He didn't have a chance to clear out his private papers before the party, and we all know why he couldn't afterward."

Marshall had stopped walking, too, and turned. He was giving Gil one of those looks that said, "Don't make me do something nasty to get this information."

"Let me see what I can do." Gil got the message, all right.

PATRICIA RUTH

Chapter 64

Gil hustled over to the jail as fast as he could; he didn't trust this conversation on the phone. It took a good 10 minutes to be checked in and have McCleary buzzed out to one of the interview rooms. As it was, Gil still felt like the walls had eyes and ears. He and McCleary were developing a sort of code using a combination of written and spoken words, just in case.

"How did the press conference go?" McCleary asked as soon as he sat. "Some of the guards caught it on the internet—they thought you handled yourself well."

"Fine, it went off fine. Mostly the typical questions, like why'd you do it, what was your state of mind, and are you crazy? That's not why I came today. I have something more important to discuss."

McCleary stared at Gil, waiting for him to talk. His life was in this man's hands, so if his attorney had something important to say, well . . . Mother McCleary didn't raise no fool.

"On the way over here, I called Manny for a progress report. He's gone through your house with a fine-toothed comb, found a couple of hairs, a footprint, maybe there's even a partial fingerprint on one of the tables. But that's it—not much to go on. In other words, for now he's run out of leads."

McCleary nodded, taking all this in. It wasn't surprising. He didn't think the private dick would find anything, anyway. The guys that did this to him had been very careful.

"I was given a request to pass along to you, and as your attorney I'm duty bound to do so," Gil explained, talking in his most official lawyer voice.

Now McCleary was sitting up and paying closer attention.

"I've been asked for you to supply the code that will open the LICE safe in your old office. The request came from my senior partner Marshall Matlock, but he was simply the messenger. The man asking is Arnie Holtzmann."

Bill McCleary almost jumped out of the chair. His face turned red, and his eyes hardened even more than they were.

Bill wrote one word on the pad in front of him: *key*.

"Arnie has every right to gain access to that safe," Gil continued as if he were speaking to a class of freshmen. "He's in charge of LICE and should be able to review all the files, even those locked in that safe."

Gil continued on in this vein for another couple of minutes, as he was sure their conversations were taped. After he said his peace about the importance of cooperating and how it would look to the judge, etc., the room fell silent.

"I'll need to think about it," was McCleary's reply, but his eyes spoke volumes.

Gil nodded. Glancing at the pad, he watched his client draw a circle around the word key with a diagonal slash through the middle. The answer couldn't be clearer: he would not be providing that code anytime soon.

"And what will you tell Marshall?" McCleary asked, recognizing his young attorney was being caught in a squeeze play.

"That I'm working on you, and as we all know, you're a tough sonofabitch." What Gil didn't say but wrote one word on the pad— Manny. He'd direct the private investigator to look into A Holtz's personal and professional life. That should be interesting, Gil thought. It's not something he'd run back to share with Marshall.

McCleary nodded again. The last thing he wanted was A Holtz's grubby hands inside his safe. He knew everyone was focused on the LICE report, but inside were also reams of notes on just about every project LICE handled. Not to mention scores of documents incriminating past and current politicians and businesses. He didn't want to share all this with his attorney; Gil had enough on his mind. Those documents are my personal property, McCleary thought. Calling attention to them will only muddy things up.

Even though LICE's report would support his public stance that SCAB could be an environmental disaster, in truth, it contained precious few facts. Gut feelings and decades of experience were hard to document. He could imagine the smirk on A Holtz's face after reading a report that was inconclusive. It might even corroborate the current public opinion that he was crazy. He figured it was better to keep quiet and let events play out. He hoped young Gil had an iron backbone because he was going to need it.

PATRICIA RUTH

Chapter 65

Gil walked through the front door, looking like he had run a marathon. His face was sweaty and red, his hair disheveled, and his crumpled clothes looked like he'd rolled on the ground. Glynn stopped what she was doing and went to greet her husband. After a brief kiss, Gil slumped into a kitchen chair and asked for a beer. He took two long pulls before he felt like talking.

Glynn was expecting this. The guy was pushing himself harder than she had ever seen—burning the candle at both ends was bound to catch up with him. She filled the silence with details of her carefree day puttering around the house, catching up on paperwork, doing some cleaning, and everyday chores that needed to be done. Typically, they would have been away lounging at the beach or around a pool. Those days seemed very long ago.

"Sorry I didn't call back today, I was running from one thing to the next, didn't have a minute to think straight," Gil confessed.

"Don't worry, I wanted to tell you how proud I was and what a great job you did at the press conference." Glynn had called afterward; they spoke all of two words before he got rushed off the phone. Gil said he'd call back but never did. While she understood, it did sting a little. Gil was always good about returning her calls—another example of how things had changed.

"So let's hear the latest. What's happening with the case?" Glynn asked, eager to get all the inside information.

"Marshall came down hard on me today," Gil replied. "He's acting as A Holtz's messenger boy, relaying an apology from A Holtz for the way he talked to me on the phone the other night. It was odd, to say the least. But the big news is he wants me to get McCleary to give up the safe's eight-digit code, citing Arnie's right to it because he's now the director of LICE."

"Jeez," Glynn whispered. "Everyone wants to get inside that safe. What do you suppose is in there?"

"The SCAB report, for one thing. Beyond that, I haven't a clue. McCleary won't say too much, and he's the only one that knows. And my efforts to uncover who ransacked his home and took the key have dead-ended. Manny came up with next to nothing. Thankfully, due to Tully's Tavern's closed-circuit TV, we were able to identify the guy who slipped something in McCleary's beer. He turned out to be a known lowlife named Pauly—not your sharpest tool. It's unlikely he was the mastermind behind all this. And he seems to have skipped town ahead of our investigation." Gil took another long swallow of beer, removed his tie, and undid his belt.

"Well, what are you going to tell Marshall?" Glynn asked, holding her breath. "Are you going to give him the code?"

"That's the last thing I'm going to do. The materials inside that safe can help my client in ways Arnie Holtzmann wouldn't appreciate, I'm sure. But what's almost worse is the thought of having Marshall working this case, directing me, using me. Who knows what his real intentions are? If I had to guess, Marshall only cares about getting Bennett Kingsley to sign on as a new client."

"But what about the charges? Can the contents of the safe help with that?" Glynn asked, even as she knew the answer.

"Well, I'm working on that too. Whoever has the key was behind drugging and setting up McCleary, that much is certain. The tricky part will be finding them and then proving it."

Chapter 66

"Glynn, Mr. Matlock would like you to come to his office," came the call from Rose, "Now, if you're free." It was said as a request but meant like a command.

The long walk to the partner's wing had Glynn wondering what her boss wanted. Typically, his research projects came as printed memos or email messages from Rose. Only when the project was sensitive or involved an enormous sum of money did he speak with her directly. This must be a big deal, Glynn thought as she walked to Rose's desk.

"He's waiting for you," Rose said and spoke Glynn's name into the intercom, announcing her arrival.

Usually, Marshall would be standing in front of his desk and would walk toward her as she entered, extending a friendly arm around her shoulder and ushering her to a seat on the couch. Today, he was sitting behind his desk and motioned her to take a seat in front of his desk. He looked grim like a big dose of bad news landed on his lap.

"I'm sure you've been hearing about the McCleary case," Marshall said. No welcome hello, no inquiry after her well-being. "I'm guessing your husband has been keeping you apprised, yes?"

"Well, he does mention things from time to time. But I'm not involved," Glynn replied, not wanting to give the impression she was working on a project and not billing. "You know Gil, he's used to handling work on his own."

Marshall's eyes were boring into her, and she was feeling uncomfortable. He kept staring at her, expecting her to say something else, even though there was nothing else to say.

"I asked him for something, something important to me and this firm. But he hasn't responded yet. Can you think of a reason why he hasn't?" Marshall asked slowly, standing. "Can you tell me why I have to ask his wife to follow up?" He was raising his voice now, staring down at her, directing the full force of his power vibe into her face.

Glynn felt as if she were shrinking, becoming smaller and weaker by the moment.

"Maybe if I knew what you wanted, I could help," Glynn asked, trying to sound reasonable. She knew what he was getting at: the code to McCleary's safe.

"Look, you tell Gil to contact me before the end of the day. I will not be jerked around. You tell him your job depends on it." Marshall spit those words out with such force the spittle flew across the desk and nearly landed on her. "I'm done, you can leave."

Glynn rose slowly from her chair, almost afraid to turn her back. She had heard about Marshall's temper—there were stories floating around the office. But they were mostly tales of conquest and valor, where Marshall was the good guy vanquishing his opponent. Never did she think she'd be on the receiving end of his nasty venom. It felt as if she were infected with some malignant virus attacking her insides.

Outside his office, Glynn could barely meet Rose's eye as she scurried back to the law library. Rose had seen people leave Marshall's office like that before—an unpleasant business, but necessary, she assumed. Marshall always had his reasons, and they were good enough for her. If he had to dress down Glynn, she probably deserved it.

Shaking and on the verge of tears, Glynn found her desk and slumped into the chair, crying. She knew what he was doing. That bastard. He was using her to get to Gil, and get him to turn over the code. But it stung just the same. She was being set up. It didn't matter that she liked her job, was good at it, or had made a positive contribution to the firm. Nothing mattered except Marshall getting his way. The whole thing disgusted her.

After a few minutes, she was able to compose herself. A couple of tissues to blow her nose and a quick look in a mirror to fix her makeup worked wonders. Squaring her shoulders, Glynn picked up the phone.

"Hi, Ray, got a minute?" She outlined her idea to the researcher, and he agreed. Glynn had already discussed the matter with Onawhim. Glynn told Ray to expect Onawhim's call. So much for Marshall's threat, Glynn thought.

Knowing her plan was in the works, Glynn called her husband.

"Yeah, honey, what's up?" Gil said as he balanced the phone on his neck while flipping through a bunch of papers. Glynn knew he was camped out at the jail, fielding interview requests from the media in between meetings with his client.

"I just came from a meeting with Marshall."

"That's nice," he replied, not focusing on what she was saying.

"Gil, he threatened my job!"

That got his attention. "He threatened you?" Gil switched gears in a flash. "What's this about?" But Gil knew the answer just as he asked the question.

"It's the code, he wants the code," Glynn repeated. "He never said what he wanted, only that you hadn't responded to his request."

"I know what he's doing, turning up the heat. Using you to get to me."

"Look, I don't care. I can get another job. Maybe I'll take some time off, maybe we can start working on that baby we talked about. I'm not sure I want to continue working here after this," Glynn admitted.

"Take some vacation time—put in for the rest of the week, at least," Gil advised. "You must have plenty of days saved. If Marshall wants to fire you, let him write you an email. Just get out of the office for a while. I'll handle his request, not to worry."

Chapter 67

"Mr. Matlock's office," Rose answered. "Oh, hi, Gil. Yes, he's in. Hold a moment."

Rose punched some buttons and spoke in the intercom. Marshall picked up the call before she could hang up her phone.

"Well, Gil, thanks for getting back to me." Marshall's sarcastic tone came through loud and clear. He had been waiting for this call . . . about eight hours longer than he thought he should.

Gil was silent. After hearing Marshall's oily voice and mocking attitude, he wanted to hang up. But that wouldn't do anyone any good, and Gil was nothing if not practical. He gathered his thoughts and calmed his anger.

"I hear you've had a busy morning," Gil started. "Your plan worked—you got through to me, although I have to admit threatening Glynn was one of the most underhanded ploys I've witnessed."

"Well, I'm ready to take down the code now," Marshall continued as if Gil hadn't said anything.

"You're quite sure of yourself. I can see where it has served you well in the past. But it's not going to work this time. Bullying my wife to pressure me . . . Well, that just backfired. I'll resign and smear your name in the press if you ever threaten anyone I know again. As for the code, I don't know why you think I would give it to you, or Arnie, or ChemoCo for that matter. Not after that little stunt you pulled—"

"I may have come off as gruff and demanding—I'm her boss after all—but I didn't threaten her. I want the code and you weren't cooperating. She overreacted. We all like Glynn, she does a fine job here. I simply needed you to take my little request seriously, and I see you have."

"Listen up, Marshall, because I'm only going to say this once," Gil shot back, too furious to control his temper. "My client has instructed me to not—let me repeat: NOT—divulge the code to that safe. Its contents will remain a mystery until such time as the court will direct otherwise. Now I've instructed Glynn to go home and take the rest of the week off. And I would suggest you write her a note of apology offering to double her pay this week for the emotional distress you caused."

"Now wait a minute," Marshall bellowed into the phone, getting ready to lash into his young associate and set him straight.

"NO," Gil shouted, louder even than Marshall. "You will do as I say or I WILL take this incident to the press. Don't worry, I'll be sure to mention your cozy relationship with Arnie, and his with ChemoCo. Oh, and I'm guessing ChemoCo will likely find another law firm to strong-arm once I'm done. I've no doubt the rest of your clients will want to read all about this," Gil threatened as he ended the conversation.

"Get me Arnie," Marshall demanded into the intercom.

Rose did as she was told, not liking the foul mood her boss was exhibiting. At first, she held Glynn responsible, but now he was even angrier than before. She concluded it must be something to do with Gil. As far as Rose was concerned, it was better for everyone if you kept romance out of the workplace. This is what happens when you allow employees to marry, she resolved.

"Did you get it?" Arnie asked.

"That little shit turned me down," Marshall replied, truly unable to believe he got outmaneuvered by an associate.

"What?! You assured me it wasn't going to be a problem!" Arnie was pacing mad and popped two antacids right away. It was galling to sit in the office and stare at that safe and not be able to get inside.

Part 10

Implications

354

Chapter 68

It was a picture-perfect day for a drive to the East End. Ray was behind the wheel of his Jeep having a thoroughly enjoyable conversation with Onawhim. A casual observer might assume they were a romantic couple out for a day of wine tasting and relaxation. Until this trip, Onawhim and Ray had only been in each other's company a few times and always in the presence of the other LIQuID researchers and subjects. He had been forced to admire her flawless complexion and her beautiful, lilting voice from a distance. Of course, he was aware of her powerful ability to influence people, but like the others, it seemed to work only when she "turned it on." Timid Onawhim and shy Ray were hitting it off during the 90-minute drive.

"We're almost there," Ray announced after checking their location on the GPS. "Are you ready to do this?"

"Yes, I'm certain we'll be successful. Don't worry," she replied with a warm smile. Onawhim was enjoying his company and was already looking forward to their ride back home when it was all over.

"Here we are. Let me do the talking first," Ray said as he pulled up to the restored farmhouse, which served as the winery's main office.

Crystal Clam Winery wasn't one of the first vineyards on Long Island's North Fork, but it quickly became one of the largest. They not only grew their own grapes but did the fermenting and bottling, too, and even supplied those services to neighboring vineyards. It was a large operation with hundreds of acres under cultivation.

Ray and Onawhim walked through the screen door, causing a little bell to announce their presence. They found themselves in a charming country store, well-stocked from floor to ceiling, with items ranging from wine bottles in gift cases to napkins and corkscrews. The windows were framed by red gingham-checked curtains, and braided rugs dotted the hardwood floors. Every item for sale had either a grape or wine theme.

Continuing further into the building, the back of the store opened into a much larger room dotted with individual tables and chairs. Sunlight streamed in from large picture windows overlooking acres of vineyards, with the sparkling bay in the distance. On the right was a long bar topped by a Lucite countertop featuring tiny crabs suspended in clear plastic. Behind the counter on the wall was a huge tin sculpture of a clam painted in a sparkling white glaze, gripping a bottle of wine in one claw and a glass in the other. This was where customers came for a round or two of wine tasting. But today, the place was empty as they were closed on Wednesdays.

"Hello, can I help you?" called a cheery woman wearing an apron over her t-shirt and jeans.

"We have an appointment with Ted Landis," Ray said. "Sky and Laurel Greenleaf." Ray and Onawhim had researched and rehearsed their fictitious identities. They were posing as a couple who wrote a wine column and online blog for wine lovers and who just happened to be taking a brief vacation on the North Fork.

Ray smiled at Onawhim, clearly enjoying their undercover identity.

"Oh, you're from GrapeToGlass. Ted mentioned your organization. Wait here and I'll get him."

Onawhim found setting up the appointment was easy, as everyone was looking to expand their online presence. Ted happily agreed to a private tour of the winery, along with a special wine tasting, in exchange for an article and the free publicity that comes with it.

"Hi, Ted Landis," Ted said, walking purposefully out of the back room, hand extended to greet the visitors. He looked every inch the gentleman farmer, wearing crisply pressed jeans, a city version of cowboy boots, with a deep blue Polo shirt tucked into his pants framed by a brass belt buckle, a smaller replica of the clam sculpture on the wall. Ted had bright blue eyes, sandy blond hair, and the lithe body of a tennis player. Tan and fit, Ted exuded the benefits of living the good life, which included making and drinking wine.

"Tell me about your newsletter," he asked, hoping there would be some value to this tour. Not that it even mattered—he was available and never tired of talking about wine. Ted loved being a vintner and was a believer in taking small steps toward success. So far, that business philosophy and Uncle Stan's capital had served him well.

Ray described their newsletter and blog using the wording they had carefully rehearsed. When Onawhim suggested she was anxious to begin the tour, Ted quickly moved off his stool.

The tour started innocently enough. Ted was charming as he showed the couple around the various rooms and equipment they use for making and storing wine. Initially, Ray asked most of the questions, focusing on the technical aspects, like the fermentation process, filtering, and aging, and even asking about the various blends they sell. Occasionally, Onawhim would comment or ask a follow-up question, but she mostly kept her thoughts to herself. When she did speak, Ted seemed captivated by her voice and would even stop walking to look at her.

The tour ended in the tasting room, and Ted was happy to have them sample several of the wines that were for sale. Once the three of them got comfortable, Onawhim subtly took control of the conversation.

"This is such a lovely setting. I see the water in the distance—does your property extend all that way?" she asked, gesturing to the far-off coast.

"Yes, now it does," Ted replied, happy to tell the story of his humble beginnings and rapid expansion. "Crystal Clam fronts over 2,000 feet of Peconic Bay coastline, and we're committed to keeping it undeveloped and pristine." It didn't hurt to get in an environmental plug.

"I seem to have read somewhere about a new environmentally friendly fertilizer being tested out here. Do you know anything about that?"

Ted eyed the diminutive girl closely. He had a brief sense of discomfort when she posed the question, but after looking at her eyes, that worrisome feeling melted away. He was more than happy to expand on SCAB and the important role Crystal Clam played in getting the final approval.

"In fact, we're expecting our first shipment sometime this week. The stuff is amazing! It almost doubled our crop yield and cut in half the amount of weed killer we had to use. It's the wave of the future."

Onawhim's next words were delivered very quietly. Looking into Ted's eyes, she repeated and paraphrased a series of statements taken from the remarks he had made throughout their tour. She started with the wine-making process and purposefully interjected comments about SCAB and its effect on their crops. Little by little, she mentioned the ChemoCo product as she slowly directed the conversation toward LICE's controversial holdup of its approval. Finally, she concluded LICE probably commissioned a report about SCAB and asked if he knew where the report was.

Thoroughly enjoying Onawhim's interest, Ted gladly responded to all her questions without reserve. He seemed mesmerized by her calm, quiet manner, her soft voice, and the depth of her knowledge. It was refreshing to speak to someone so intelligent and attentive. He felt he could talk to her forever, and was happy to tell her whatever she wanted to know.

Finally, Onawhim got around to the whole point of their trip.

"It's been so interesting talking to you about SCAB's wondrous effects. What's surprising is why LICE was holding up its approval. It doesn't make any sense. Don't you agree?"

"I know," Ted exclaimed, all too happy to harmonize with her. "McCleary, the former head of LICE, is in jail now. He was the one who was holding everything up."

"In jail? You're kidding. They arrested him for not approving SCAB?" Onawhim asked innocently.

"Not really. He went to a party with a gun loaded with blanks and shot the place up. No one was hurt, but he sure showed everyone that he had a couple of screws loose."

"Were you there? Did you see it?"

"You bet I was there. I even had a role in making it happen," Ted replied absentmindedly. "We had no choice but to discredit him. The guy was holding everything up, and there was no way around it."

"What you mean?"

"Well, earlier in the day, I arranged to have his drink spiked at lunch. Afterward, he went home and we drugged him some more. That's when we learned about the LICE report in his office safe and the key hidden in his bedroom. It was like taking candy from a baby," Ted boasted.

"Go on," Onawhim encouraged.

"Stan said McCleary had to be discredited; otherwise, people would think he had a good reason to hold up the SCAB approval. So we decided to have him go to the LIMBO party dressed as a terrorist—like some kind of unhinged Halloween reject. I put the camouflage makeup on myself," Ted explained. "We loaded the rifle with blanks and Uncle Stan administered the drug. Without the hypnosol, I doubt if McCleary would have done it. That stuff is incredibly powerful."

"Hypnosol, what's that? I've never heard of it."

"Oh, Stan got it from Bennett. ChemoCo makes it as part of their drug division. I don't know too much more—it might not even be approved. I think it's still in the experimental stage," Ted said, trying to remember so he could answer her question accurately.

"Who's Stan?" Onawhim asked, concentrating intently on Ted's face.

"Stan Piper," Ted exclaimed. "You do know who he is, right?"

"Oh, yes, of course I know of Stan Piper," Onawhim replied, pushing Ted a little harder.

"Without Uncle Stan's help, I couldn't have built Crystal Clam into what it is today," Ted bragged.

"So did you get the report? What does it say?"

"No, that's the frustrating thing—we still don't have the report."

"You're kidding," Onawhim said, 'encouraging' him to continue.

"We went to the LICE office, found the safe and used the key, all fine. Only thing we didn't realize was to open the safe you need both the key and a code: an eight-digit code. Without the code, the key is useless."

"Unbelievable," Onawhim whispered, shaking her head in understanding of his predicament. "So what did you do with the key now that it's useless?"

"It's not going to be useless for long. We have a plan to get the code, and then we'll open the safe. I'm waiting on a call from Uncle Stan, then I'll be leaving to meet him."

"Why do you have to go? Can't Uncle Stan handle things without you?"

"He can't do it without me because I have the key," Ted replied proudly, reaching around his neck to pull out the chain.

"What if I told you I knew the code?" Onawhim was really concentrating now, and she could see the change in Ted's eyes. They were unfocussed and glassy. His face took on a vacant expression even though he was still smiling and appeared happy.

"You have the code?" Ted asked, unable to believe his good fortune. "That means with this key, you could open the safe and get the report."

"Yes, you're right. All I need is the key. If you hand it over, I will get that LICE report and you could stay here and tend to your grapes and wine." Onawhim suggested as she held out her hand and pushed him a little harder still.

"Well, of course. Here it is. I'm happy to help. It'll help me and be a big help to Uncle Stan too. He'll be grateful to have the SCAB report, that's for sure." Ted was starting to repeat himself and had a more confused look. He took the key from around his neck and placed it in Onawhim's open hand.

"Thank you, Ted. You've been a wonderful host." Onawhim motioned to Ray it was time to leave. "I don't want you to worry about a thing. We'll take care of getting that SCAB report to Uncle Stan. I think it would be a good idea if you went back into your office now. You'll feel better if you don't remember our conversation, like we were never here."

"Great. Thanks for coming, but I've work to do and need to get back to my desk. Enjoy the rest of your day," Ted said as he walked away.

Slowly but with purpose, Ray and Onawhim exited the building, got in the car, and left for home. Ray was speechless. If he hadn't witnessed what happened, he would not have believed it. Onawhim sat looking at the key, turning it around in her hand, undeniably proud she was able to get it so easily.

"That was amazing," Ray said, in awe of Onawhim's ability.

"It was like figuring out a puzzle—similar to working through Sudoku, but easier. I knew where I needed to go and all I had to do was execute the correct moves to get there. I do feel a bit worn out. I don't think I ever pushed anyone that hard before, or for that long a period of time."

"Do you think he'll remember who he gave the key to?"

"Maybe he'll have some idea, like an elusive dream image he can't quite put his finger on. It's possible he could remember more if he sees us or speaks to us. But otherwise, I doubt he'll be able to tell anyone. It's not as if he'll be reporting it missing to the police. He might not even realize he doesn't have the key until someone asks for it."

"I can't believe Ted admitted Stan Piper's involvement, and that they were both responsible for drugging McCleary. I wonder if the police know?"

"Yes, what an awful man. Poor McCleary was set up and didn't even realize it."

"Before we head home, I have a hunch. Let's see if we can drive over to the bay so I can get a sample of the soil and water bordering Crystal Clam property," Ray suggested. "I want to compare it to the SCAB sample brewing in my lab."

Onawhim was more than happy to agree. They drove down many streets as they wound their way to the coast, sometimes turning around and doubling back until they were within walking distance of the water. Ray got out some sample jars and led the way through the brambles and weeds. They could see the Crystal Clam farmhouse in the distance and knew they were in the right place.

Ray noticed the vegetation was stunted and dying in spots. There was also a foul stench, depending on the wind direction. The water had a sickly opaque look. Onawhim gazed at the unspoiled coastline: there wasn't a single man-made structure for miles. Yet the water and surrounding plant life appeared diseased and polluted. Ray gathered his samples, and they turned to drive back home.

364

Chapter 69

Glynn was fidgety, constantly looking at her watch and then up at the door from her strategically placed table at Cafe Blue. The interior was composed of various shades of blue, from pale sky blue to bold turquoise. But she couldn't focus on her surroundings. All she cared about was Onawhim and Ray's visit to Crystal Clam Winery. She didn't even want Onawhim to say anything on the phone when they called in, only to give her the time when they would arrive back. And now she was sitting on pins and needles, hoping for some good news.

Glynn's sabbatical from work was both a blessing and a bust. Gil was out of the house early and worked late into the night, consumed with the biggest case of the year. This gave her plenty of time to wait: wait for the SCAB concoction Ray was brewing in his lab, wait to see if SCAB was harmful or not, wait to get into the safe at LICE . . . In other words, wait for their plans to come together. Left alone and away from work, she tried to fill her day with distractions. The meeting with Marshall still stung but was slowly receding, especially after she received a large bouquet of flowers. The note thanking her for her contribution to the firm was appropriate, but the real surprise was a nice fat check. Money does have a way of making things better, Glynn concluded.

Finally, Onawhim and Ray walked through the door. Glynn waved them over to the corner table where she was camped out.

"I have the key," Onawhim declared before she sat.

A smile of instant relief spread across Glynn's face as she leaned back in the chair and took a long drink from her mojito. Onawhim placed the key gently on the table as three pairs of eyes considered the prize.

Staring at the oddly shaped object, Glynn was struck by the enormity of what it represented and how much was at stake—for the environment, for the life's work of a once-important public servant, for the fortunes of a powerful company, and for the reputation of all those pushing through the approval of a new chemical product. It was a power grab, all right, and now Glynn had the key to the kingdom.

While Ray and Onawhim ordered their drinks, Glynn made a couple of calls. The first was to Gil. He would be coming home late, she learned. Tomorrow was a big day in court, and he was spending every waking moment preparing. The proceedings were open to the public, and Glynn planned to be there to lend moral support. But she had an ulterior motive as well. The next calls were made to Penna, Sollie, and Iris, as each had a part to play as she finalized their plans.

But she didn't want to get ahead of herself. Glynn put down her phone, leaned back, and was all ears as Onawhim and Ray described their encounter with Ted Landis. She couldn't help but notice Ray's supportive manner and the deference he displayed to Onawhim. His interest was charming to watch as he revealed a side of himself Glynn hadn't seen before. But it was Onawhim's description of "pushing" Ted in her calm, matter-of-fact voice that Glynn found the most fascinating. That he and Uncle Stan were responsible for McCleary's ill-fated terrorist scheme was chilling. A man of Stan Piper's stature hiring some thug, drugging a public figure, breaking and entering, and arranging to set loose a would-be terrorist in some shoot 'em up scenario at a party filled with innocent bystanders . . . It was beyond mind-boggling. The lengths some people were willing to go— respectable business leaders, no less—to forward their cause.

Ray told her of their side trip to get soil and water samples, which he planned to test when he got back to the lab. He also thought the SCAB test would be done by tomorrow and hoped to get the results to her late in the day. All good news, Glynn thought. Things were coming together. The three of them enjoyed a relaxing dinner as she reviewed the plans for the next day. It's important to get a second opinion, Glynn had learned, and she wanted to make sure all the angles were covered. Onawhim approved and gave Glynn a direct look in the eyes, told her to go home, get a good night's sleep, and said everything would work out fine.

Chapter 70

"I don't give a flying shit what Marshall says. You're the one we're relying on, Arnie. No more excuses. Do what you need to—just get me that code." Stan slammed the phone so hard he thought the delicately crafted federal-era side table would crack. He couldn't believe his use of expletives either. It goes to show how difficult this whole project had become. Days had passed, and they were still no closer to getting inside that safe. The only good news was the other side couldn't open it either—a small consolation.

Bennett had confirmed the first shipment of SCAB, so things on that end were moving right along. *Now, if only we could get the code.* Relying on that clown, A Holtz was going nowhere, and it was time he took matters into his own hands. Stan knew the judge presiding over McCleary's case—a fellow member of the GCGC. Even though Stan didn't socialize with Judge Leland Gorman, they were club friends, and now seemed like the right time to call Lee and make a few pointed inquiries.

"Hi, Lee. Stan Piper here."

"Hello, Stan. Don't worry, I've made out my check to the foundation. It'll be in the mail in the morning," Judge Gorman explained, wanting to save the venerable GCGC president emeritus the trouble of having to ask for his donation. Stan Piper sat at the top of the pyramid at GCGC and belonged to the cream of Long Island's social scene. Judge Gorman may be all-powerful in his courtroom, but Stan had that distinction almost everywhere else.

"Oh, yes, your check. So good of you to contribute. It's a worthy cause, as you know, and we appreciate your help. By the way, how's Evelyn and the kids?" Stan asked, wanting to give a more social feel to the call. Conversations today are so rushed—it's as important as ever to observe the social niceties, he believed.

Being a club member for nearly 20 years, Judge Gorman rarely, if ever, had much personal interaction with Stan Piper. They didn't travel in the same social circles, and he was surprised and curious to learn the reason for this call. Stan directed the conversation over a variety of topics, from the state of the golf course, to the induction of new members. He wanted to share with the judge some of the inner workings of the club, information only a few of the board members were privy to.

"We'll be looking to add one or two new members to the board in the coming year," Stan revealed. "Not many know this as yet. So, if I might make a suggestion, now would be a good time for a whisper campaign. I could see you on the board, Lee. You more than Sam or Franklin. Give it some thought," Stan suggested.

"Yes, yes, I will," Judge Gorman replied, already thinking about what being a board member would mean, all the benefits, and, of course, the status that position would confer. Evelyn would be pleasantly surprised, too, he figured.

"Oh, there's one more thing. You're presiding over McCleary's hearing tomorrow, right? Gee, wouldn't it be nice to have this whole unfortunate LICE thing put to bed?" Stan sighed and waited for Gorman's agreement before continuing. "We need to move on and get the economy going again. I understand from the new director that he can't even get into his office safe. That doesn't help anyone, if you know what I mean?" Stan mentioned smoothly. "We could sure use some levelheaded thinking about now, like giving the new director access to his agency's information. Just a thought," Stan concluded.

The call to Lee Gorman went exactly as Stan envisioned. Why use a hatchet like A Holtz when a few subtle suggestions will do? But he didn't want to leave things to chance. After all, he wasn't 100 percent certain how the judge would rule, and he believed in having a backup plan just in case. Stan picked up the phone to make his final call of the night.

"Hello?" Ted whispered groggily as the ring intruded into his deep sleep. He went to bed early with a pounding headache and had been sound asleep for the better part of three hours.

"Ted, is that you?" Stan asked. "Are you all right?"

"Tired. Thought I'd get some sleep."

"Look, no need to stay on the phone. Drive over tomorrow morning, early, I can talk to you then. Feel better."

Chapter 71

"I'm leaving," Gil said to his wife as he bent to give her a kiss. He was surprised to find her awake when he got home after midnight. They had a brief chat before he passed out, and now she was asleep. "I'll see you in court later. It's Judge Gorman's room, around 10:30," he whispered in her ear.

Glynn stirred as consciousness inched its way into her sleeping brain. She had been up into the wee hours of the night, unable to fall asleep, going over and over the plans for the following day. There would be a lot of unknowns, which was worrisome. She had learned the hard way that stuff happens.

Chapter 72

Ted woke feeling energized and refreshed. He couldn't remember when he had such a great night's sleep. He vaguely recalled a phone call from Uncle Stan asking him to drive in today, but he wasn't sure if it was real or a dream. In fact, he had a number of strange dreams, most of which he couldn't quite recollect, though they had something to do with the LIMBO party and McCleary. No matter. He quickly brushed them aside and decided to check in with his uncle.

"Hi, Ted, how are you?" Stan asked.

"Great, really needed that sleep yesterday. Don't know why I was so tired, but it did me a world of good," Ted replied.

"I need you here today. Meet me at the courthouse, in front of Judge Gorman's room at 10:00. And don't forget the key," Stan reminded as he hung up.

Chapter 73

"Anyone home?" Sollie joked as she waited to be buzzed in. The lab was a beehive of activity. Sollie found Ray hunched over his computer screen with a stack of papers at his side. The other researchers were in the process of moving the SCAB experiment into the little time-shifting room.

Ray looked up from his screen. It took a moment to refocus his eyes on Sollie's face. "Great, you're here. We need you for another time push," he said without much preamble. "Are you ready?"

"I was born ready," Sollie replied, groaning inwardly at using such a cheap line.

"Go into the room, like before. Only this time I need you to watch this dial on the interval invigilator." Ray pointed to one of the gauges. "Push only until this arrow goes to here, right before the number four. It's very important—we don't want to go too far."

"Got it." Sollie nodded her understanding.

Ray closed the door. Not a moment had passed when Sollie emerged from the room.

"You're done?" he asked, surprised again at the time differential. The other lab techs and researchers came over to collect the specimen and examine the equipment.

"I did as you requested. It gets easier each time. I barely started when the needle hit the spot. How much time was that?"

"Only four days, and you don't seem to be affected." Ray noticed, writing more observations into his notebook. "Maybe you're able to project out from yourself a little better and not be included," he suggested.

Ray walked around the lab, checking with his colleagues on the results. Thankfully, he felt certain they accurately replicated the SCAB formula—no small task, as it was a complex and time-consuming process that had to be followed exactly. There were two more tests he wanted to conduct. The first would tell him how well the product worked with real seedlings. The second involved the plant and water samples he took from the Peconic Bay the day before.

"We're ready for the next test," Ray said as he appeared at her side. "We want you to move time forward a week, after this line," Ray explained as he pointed to the gauge again. "There are two test containers: one is the newly created SCAB product interacting with freshly planted seedlings. The other is the water and plant samples we took from the bay. If you feel you can push for a longer period, fine. The interval invigilator will record the amount of time, so it doesn't matter. Ready?"

Again, Sollie walked into the little room and, in mere moments, came out. Ray hurried past her to check the readings—18 days. Unbelievable! And Sollie didn't look any different either. This time, she felt tired and asked for a drink. Ray and the other researchers poured over the samples, entering data into the computer and running all sorts of checks.

"So tell me, Ray, what's all this about? The other tests had me speeding up the SCAB sample to get the results sooner. What are we doing now?"

Ray walked over with his laptop. "We want to see how the SCAB formula we created interacts with small seedlings. Part of the product's claim is that SCAB's a powerful fertilizer, so we wanted to see how the plants would react after a couple of weeks. Here, take a look at this," Ray said as he showed her the computer screen. "You see this green line, it represents typical plant growth. Now take a look at the growth for the SCAB seedling—the blue line. It's almost vertical, which indicates incredible . . . No, I'd say almost unnatural growth."

"Does this means your SCAB concoction worked?" Sollie asked.

"Yes, it worked. But even more important, the plants are growing at such an accelerated rate, I fear it may change their molecular chemistry."

"You mean they're not—what they were?"

"We planted carrots."

"You mean they're not carrots now? They're something else—real-life 'Franken plants?'"

Ray stopped for a minute and considered her question. "Yes, I guess you could say they were some sort of lab-created plants—'Franken plants,' for lack of a better phrase. They have changed subtly, but changed nonetheless."

"What about the other container?"

"Those plants and water had been exposed to SCAB already. I don't know how much or how long ago, but I wanted to see what we can expect in the near term."

Ray showed her a graph that appeared as a mirror image of the first, except this line was charting steeply downward. "It seems once exposed, over time, the plant cannot keep its new 'normal' lifecycle and rapidly deteriorates. That would explain the foul stench in the air I noticed when collecting these samples—an indication of widespread decay."

"What does all this mean?" Sollie asked, trying to put the pieces together.

"It means SCAB could be harming the very plants it's being used to help. It could also mean it may have a disastrous effect on the surrounding vegetation. Of course, this is preliminary. We won't have results for a while, but I can tell you SCAB has affected the water in our sample too. The water turned bright green, indicating rapid algae growth. SCAB has thrown the whole water chemistry off."

"I know Glynn will want these SCAB results right away," Ray mentioned absentmindedly as he gave the computer screen his full attention. "It appears she was right—initially the product is harmless and does cause the desired result. But—and there's a big BUT—after prolonged exposure, the plant's basic chemistry becomes altered. That's when things start to transform for the worst."

"How soon will the report be ready?" Sollie asked. "I'll be seeing her later, and I can give it to her then."

"It'll take another hour or two."

"No problem. Why don't I hang around and practice on more of your samples and then I'll take it with me when you're done?"

Chapter 74

Glynn was waiting at the front of the courthouse when Penna and Iris arrived. The place was swarming with cops and reporters. Everyone wanted a front-row seat to the legal proceedings. It would be the world's first look at McCleary since his arrest. Luckily, Glynn and her friends didn't have to worry about fighting the crowd upon entering. They had reserved seats right behind the defense table, courtesy of Gil. Thankfully, Glynn went unnoticed, as the press was looking for real newsmakers to interview.

The crowd parted as a limo pulled up, and the rear door opened to reveal a dapper Marshall Matlock. There was a crush of cameras and microphones as the press jostled each other to gain access. "Is he going to plead guilty?" one asked.

"Do you think he's crazy?" shouted another.

"We've heard conspiracy theories—what can you tell us about that?" bellowed a third.

"No comment," was Marshall's reply, cool as a cucumber in the July heat. He was so busy trying not to ham for the cameras he missed seeing Glynn standing off to the side.

No matter, she thought to herself. We'll run into each other eventually, and it might as well happen while I'm sitting in court as the supportive wife. In any case, she was glad to have Penna and Iris with her. They turned to go into the courthouse behind the media throng surrounding Marshall.

Once inside, Gil waved her over to the seats he had saved. Marshall had already taken his seat at the defense table next to Gil. On the other side of the room, Arnie Holtzmann stood behind the prosecutor's table, looking plenty unhappy. He and Marshall nodded cordially to each other but remained in their respective camps. Glynn watched Stan Piper and Ted Landis walk in and take seats near A Holtz. They didn't look too cheerful either. Stan was whispering emphatically to Ted, who appeared crestfallen and confused.

"I'd say Ted misplaced something," Penna offered with a slight smile.

"You don't say," Iris responded knowingly. "Wonder what it could be?"

"Uncle Stan looks to be spitting mad. I wouldn't want to be in Ted's shoes," Penna commented on the scene unfolding across the room.

Ted Landis turned a bright shade of red and could barely raise his head to meet his uncle's eyes. Stan's intense anger vibe couldn't be mistaken and was in sharp contrast with his typical detached demeanor. Ted's abject misery was saved by the appearance of the bailiff.

"All rise for Judge Gorman," the bailiff said and continued with his customary courtroom speech.

There were other cases on the docket that morning, but none as high-profile as the McCleary hearing. Gil turned to glance at his wife. Glynn gave him two thumbs-up—she thought he looked confident and ready. She would have been happier if Gil didn't have to share the spotlight with Marshall, who sat in the next chair.

After some minor business, the court officer called the McCleary case, and the defendant shuffled into the courtroom, hands cuffed in front and legs shackled. Seeing the once-prominent McCleary in the jailhouse jumpsuit lumbering to take his seat was a reminder to all that even the mighty can be called to justice. McCleary grabbed the empty chair next to Gil and immediately proceeded to survey the courtroom.

His gaze momentarily fixed on A Holtz, Stan, and Ted before he turned to the front, where he stared straight at the judge.

What followed next was a prescribed set of procedures and legal parries between Gil and the prosecutor. Gil asked for bail, which the prosecutor argued against. Gil presented the results of the medical and psychological tests, all demonstrating current mental and physical fitness, but which also documented a change from when McCleary was first brought in.

Finally, the prosecutor petitioned the court to have the LICE safe opened.

"Your Honor, the people have a right to the contents of that safe. The director of LICE needs access. It is not the private property of Bill McCleary—he no longer has that position. The current director is not without rights in this matter," the prosecutor argued.

"Well, Mr. Patrick, have Mr. McCleary provide access to the safe," the judge stated.

Now Penna leaned in as close as she could toward the defense table, staring intently at the back of Bill McCleary's head.

"For the safe to be opened, you need an eight-digit code and a key, Your Honor. My client can supply the code, but the key was stolen from his home on the night of the LIMBO party," Gil related. "We cannot open the safe without the key."

"Are you saying the key was taken as part of a robbery?" asked the judge.

"Yes, Your Honor. The police are investigating, but so far, they have not arrested anyone in conjunction with this crime or, to my knowledge, have any prime suspects."

"I want to see the police report on this," the judge demanded from the prosecutor. "You have 24 hours to report back. I will rule on the opening of the safe at that time."

Penna opened her pocketbook and scribbled something on a piece of paper. Nudging Glynn to look inside her purse, Penna's downcast expression spoke volumes.

"I only got seven numbers," Penna whispered, fearing their plan would be over before it began.

Unable to hide her disappointment, Glynn tried to reassure her friend it was okay even as failure registered on her face.

Once the judge made his ruling and the gavel hit the table, Glynn, Iris, and Penna stood to leave. Gil waved at his wife, clearly happy she had witnessed his big day in court and nodded to his client as the guard led McCleary back into lockup.

"Marshall, can I have a word?" Arnie called as he shoved his way through the crowded courtroom.

Walking to the door, Marshall didn't care if he spoke with Arnie or not.

"Look, forget about pressuring that associate of yours for the code," Arnie said, obviously happy with the judge's ruling. "Now we have the judge on our side, it's obvious we'll get access." Marshall didn't need to know the anticipated ruling effectively voided Arnie's Plan B—having Ted Landis threaten to pull Crystal Clam's legal business from Shylock.

"That's a load off my mind," Marshall replied sarcastically, "providing the judge agrees with your argument." All Marshall could do was shake his head, having already decided he had enough of the whole safe thing.

"Is there anything else?" Marshall asked, walking away, not caring to continue this conversation. Like a balloon leaking air, he had lost his appetite for the ChemoCo business. It somehow didn't seem worth all the effort.

Meanwhile, once the judge's gavel banged, Stan almost jumped out of his seat. He couldn't leave the courthouse fast enough. He needed to update the ChemoCo CEO with the good news and was on his cell phone before reaching the door.

"As it stands, we'll likely have access to the safe's contents in a little more than 24 hours," Stan told Bennett. Thankfully, there had been no need to tell Bennett about the whole key fiasco. There's no sense in mentioning it at this stage.

"Judge Gorman, huh?" Bennett remarked. "Let's make sure we take care of him, okay? That was smart to bring him in," Bennett remarked. "Otherwise things could have been a real mess."

"You're so right," Stan replied, glad Bennett didn't know the half of it. Stan ended the call quickly—no need to have all the nosey reporters eavesdrop on their conversation. Then he turned to address his nephew, still not satisfied with Ted's explanation of the lost key.

"Tell me again what happened," Stan asked.

"I went to bed with it around my neck, and when I woke this morning, it was gone," Ted confessed.

"Well, where were you yesterday? Who did you see?"

"No one. I spent the day doing paperwork in my office, got a headache, and went to bed. That's it. I was obviously robbed. Someone must have broken into my home and removed it while I slept. What other explanation could there be?"

"Robbed, just like McCleary was robbed," Stan spat back contemptuously, not believing his nephew's story for one minute. But he didn't have an alternative to offer either.

Outside of the courthouse, Glynn, Penna, and Iris huddled off to the side and away from the press.

"I'm sorry," Penna repeated. "I think it was all the excitement in the courtroom and the people near McCleary—I lost concentration."

"Don't worry, you did your best. We'll have to figure out another way to get into the safe before the judge orders it opened," Glynn responded, not sounding too confident that would even be possible.

"I have an idea," Iris began. "I seem to be good at guessing what will happen with stocks. It's all about the numbers—will the number be higher, lower, or stay the same? I'm able to know how the stock price will go, but only at the moment of decision. I believe I'll be able to divine the last number, but only when we're standing in front of the safe and the other seven numbers are entered. I feel good about this! I believe I'll be able to plug in the last digit at the final moment," Iris proposed.

"That's a big gamble," Glynn replied, not as convinced as Iris seemed.

"I think it's worth a try. We've come this far already . . . What's the harm?" Iris countered, knowing a multitude of things could go wrong even in the best of circumstances.

Glynn glanced over at Penna, who nodded her approval.

"Okay," Glynn announced with a sigh, "we're still a go," hoping this wasn't going to be another mistake she'd regret.

Chapter 75

"We had a good turnout," Gil said as he joined McCleary in one of the jailhouse rooms. "Did you see Stan and Arnie? They did not look happy. Wish I could have gotten you out on bail, but we knew that was going to be a long shot," Gil was recapping the courtroom events. Like a stream of consciousness, he spoke off the top of his head, mentioning various things that had happened as they occurred to him. "Gorman's tough, but he has a reputation for being fair. Let's see what he says tomorrow when the prosecutor presents a police report that shows nothing has been done to locate that key."

McCleary nodded. He had other things on his mind.

"I think it'll be interesting tomorrow," Gil repeated, wondering what could be occupying his client's attention.

"Who was the guy standing next to Stan Piper?" McCleary asked.

"That's Ted Landis, owner of Crystal Clam Winery and Stan's nephew. Why?"

"Seeing them both in court today jogged something in my memory. I don't know Ted—don't even think we've ever met—but seeing the two of them together, it felt damned familiar. It was something about Ted's expression, about his posture," McCleary stated as he looked Gil straight in the eye.

"Are you telling me you think Stan Piper and Ted Landis were the ones that did this to you? They both would have motives, but it's a stretch to think a man of Stan Piper's background and social position would be involved in this type of criminal activity. It would be the scandal of the decade," Gil remarked, unable to truly comprehend the old gentleman being involved in such a scheme.

McCleary stared back in response.

"It would make perfect sense. Who would have the most to gain or lose in all of this, aside from the wineries on the North Fork? ChemoCo," Gil explained as he was working out all the angles. "And we know Stan is in tight with Bennett Kingsley.

"But after tomorrow, the key will be useless. I'd take bets Judge Gorman will order the safe opened, key or no key, regardless of what the police report says. It won't matter," Gil stated, pausing for a moment before he asked the $64,000 question. "So do you want to tell me now what's in that safe?"

But McCleary shook his head. "You'll see tomorrow," was all he said.

Part 11

Culmination

Chapter 76

Dinner was over. The check had arrived, but before Glynn could make the individual calculations, Iris picked it up.

"It's my treat," Iris announced. "Well, not technically mine . . . It's ours."

Everyone gave her their full attention. "You know I've been pretty successful picking stocks lately. Well, very successful," she admitted with a smile. "I want you to know I've set up a foundation with some of that money, and each of you has an equal stake. It's called LIQuID 5, after our common experience. I brought the papers today—they're already filled out and ready for your signatures."

"This is unbelievable," Sollie exclaimed, the first to speak. "We're part of a foundation? I don't understand."

"A foundation is simply an organization, it's formed like a corporation, but with different tax implications," Glynn explained.

"Don't worry about managing the funds, I'll take care of that, I'll also see to our investments and make sure we won't lose our initial assets," Iris continued.

"Our initial assets, what are they? We didn't give you any money," Onawhim asked, not understanding how they could have an account without providing money.

"The LIQuID 5 Foundation was opened with an initial investment of $5 million. That breaks down nicely to $1 million each."

The women were too stunned to speak.

"You mean we each have $1 million dollars?" Penna asked. "How did you get this money? What are we to do with it?"

"As you know, I've been fortunate lately. My investments have paid off beyond my wildest expectations. I started with a small sum and began buying ChemoCo shares. But as things have grown and my ability improved, I didn't feel right being the only one profiting. This $5 million is a start—I'm sure it will grow. In fact, I intend to make a trade tomorrow morning that could potentially triple this amount.

"As for who owns the money, it's yours, or I should say, ours. We can use it as we see fit, whether for expenses, like this dinner, or trips, or whatever we decide. Ray might need some additional funding to continue researching our condition. Or we may want to make an investment or underwrite some needy project. I don't know exactly what our future needs might be, but I believe it will come in handy."

The table erupted in a round of spontaneous clapping. Everyone agreed it was a good omen for their evening's plans. Iris passed around the papers for signature.

"I guess this means we can buy the books we read instead of getting them from the library?" Sollie kidded, recalling the original reason for their get-togethers.

After completing the paperwork, the LIQuID 5 members spilled into the parking lot, the same lot where they stood months ago, watching a strange cloud envelope them, changing their lives forever. The girls huddled around Glynn for a final recap before piling into the nondescript minivan Onawhim had rented for the evening.

Glynn drove across town to the Professional Quadrangle, a campus of office buildings home to many of the area's corporations and government agencies. They parked across the street and walked slowly toward Building 1. The place was deserted—not much happened after 8 p.m. midweek in July. Iris was the first to pick out the cameras as they walked up to the lobby door.

"It's locked," Glynn confirmed, as she expected.

"Stand back," Sollie commanded, motioning her companions to stand behind her. A moment later, she pulled open the door. A quizzical look from Penna prompted Sollie to explain. "I moved the door back in time, to a time earlier today when it was unlocked."

"Cool," Penna remarked.

The women entered the elevator and ascended to the 5th floor. The entrance to the LICE offices was directly in front of them. Again, Sollie motioned them to stand behind her as she pulled time backward. All it took was a quick second for the lock to open.

Penna sensed the place was deserted. Once past the reception desk, they entered what felt like a maze of cubicles in the dark. Holding a pocket flashlight, Glynn led the way to the executive offices. For the third time that evening, Sollie pulled back time, opening the lock and allowing access to the director's office suite. As Glynn walked into McCleary's old office, she located the aerial photo of Long Island and quickly touched the proper points on the picture. Five pairs of eyes watched it slide aside, revealing a safe, the inanimate object that has been the focal point of so much scheming. Glynn stepped back, allowing Onawhim and Penna to move closer. Without fanfare, Onawhim took the key from around her neck and inserted it in the safe. A sharp turn to the left resulted in a distinctive click as the digital keypad automatically became illuminated. Next, Penna stepped to the keypad and typed the first seven numbers of the code, the red LED numbers shining brightly in the dark room. The cursor blinked repeatedly, waiting for the final entry. Now, it was Iris's turn.

The stockbroker closed her eyes. It's a leap of faith, she said to the team over dinner, explaining that her ability to predict numbers worked only at the very moment she needed. Stepping forward, Iris opened her eyes and saw exactly what the last number should be and tapped it in. A subtle whirring sound could be heard as the rods and pins gently released their grip, allowing the perfectly balanced door to swing open.

Glynn directed the narrow beam from her flashlight to illuminate the inside of the safe. As expected, it was packed with envelopes and papers. One by one, Glynn emptied its contents. She opened each item, quickly reviewed the contents, and passed them along to the waiting hands of the others. Glynn came across interdepartmental memos and handwritten notes revealing information on various environmental projects and public officials, not the least of which was Arnie Holtzmann. In fact, there was a whole folder devoted just to him.

"Look at this," exclaimed Sollie in a hushed voice, shocked at some of the details going back years. "He knows where all the bones are buried. If this stuff gets out, they'll have to convene a task force. McCleary's current legal problems will look like a walk in the park compared to what some of these other politicians would have to face."

It was astonishing even to Penna, who thought she had heard it all.

Glynn found other LICE reports concerning past environment issues—some completed, while others were still in various stages of testing. The safe was a treasure trove of suggestive and incriminating documents: 30 years' worth of influence and impact.

"Here it is," Glynn whispered, extracting a large envelope.

"I thought it would be thicker," Iris commented, wondering aloud how something this flimsy could contain all LICE's testing results and chemical analysis.

But the answer came sliding out into Glynn's hand.

"Of course, they put it all on this flash drive," said Onawhim.

"Look, we don't have time to view its contents now. I say we stick to the original plan and place our report inside with all these other documents," Glynn suggested.

"Wait a minute. You think we should replace these incriminating and salacious items? Put them back in the safe?" Sollie asked. "Let's rethink this."

"The only person who will know the contents of the safe were tampered with is McCleary, and he's in no position to object to anything," Onawhim pointed out. "Maybe we should take these other documents, you know, protect them from prying eyes. Once the judge orders the safe opened, all these papers would most likely leak to the press. I say we keep them. Maybe some good can come from all this nastiness."

"I've been skimming through some of the items, and they're incredible: kickbacks, improper payments—some may be illegal, others improper. Having these documents released would be damaging, it would open a whole can of worms. I think Onawhim's right," Iris agreed. "Let's hold on to them for safekeeping until we figure out the best way to deal with all this information."

Glynn glanced over at Penna, who nodded in agreement. She had been around plenty of shady characters and didn't need to hear any more to conclude the stuff McCleary was sitting on was dynamite. "Okay, we take everything and leave only our SCAB report," Glynn summarized, noting they were in full agreement.

Sollie handed Glynn the SCAB findings compiled by Ray and his colleagues in Lab 8. "Regardless of what the LICE researchers found, we know it'll be difficult for ChemoCo to get approval for SCAB once this report is made public," Sollie said, feeling confident Ray and his team knew what they were doing.

"Well, after tomorrow, things will be set straight," Glynn summarized. She placed Ray's SCAB report in the safe and closed the door. The locks clicked into place, echoing softly in the dark stillness of the office, a perfect audible conclusion to their mission. Glynn removed the key, repositioned the aerial photograph of Long Island, and looked around to make sure the room appeared exactly as they found it. "I hope Ray is prepared for what will be a media storm at his lab tomorrow."

"They are," Sollie confirmed.

One by one, the LIQuID 5 women filed out of the LICE office and reentered the elevator for the ride to the lobby. Sollie made sure to have all the doors returned to the present time—she even "reset" a couple of security cameras back to the moment before they arrived. Their visit was erased.

"I don't get why McCleary would leave all that damning material in the safe," Onawhim said. "He was already cleaning out his office. Why leave that stuff to the end? I'd have taken all that out as soon as I learned I was exiting."

"Maybe he was going to take it out but got waylaid after lunch," Penna suggested, reminding them McCleary was drugged by Pauly at Tully's Tavern.

"Or maybe he wanted A Holtz to find it. Maybe he thought A Holtz was enough of an asshole to actually use that stuff and ultimately incriminate himself," Iris mused.

"My guess is he didn't expect the lengths Stan and Ted would go to," Penna added.

"Aside from McCleary, we're the only ones that know the true irony of his situation," Glynn summarized. "Here he spends years collecting dirt on key power players, quietly positioning himself to be the one to contain and control this information, only to find himself out of a job, being drugged and framed for shooting up a party and endangering hundreds of people. He was victimized by the very people he was looking to protect. My guess is he never considered the lengths his opposition would go."

Chapter 77

"Lee, it's Stan. How are you this evening? I wanted to see if you gave any thought to running for the board. Yes, you're right, I haven't given you much time. Sometimes the board likes to see how a man reacts under pressure," Stan gave a little half-joking, half-serious chuckle into the phone.

"So you'll do it, excellent. I'll let the board members know tomorrow. We'll have you come to the next meeting. But more about that another time.

"One more thing. A friend and I were having a discussion about the McCleary case, and we were confused about the issue of ownership. Let's say you open the safe, and inside are papers and such. What happens to them? I mean, who do they belong to? Do you just hand them over to McCleary?

"I see. Well, thanks for clearing that up."

Chapter 78

Once again, Glynn found herself seated behind her husband in Judge Gorman's courtroom. She looked around as everyone waited for McCleary to be escorted over to the defense table. You couldn't miss Arnie Holtzmann—he seemed to be in perpetual motion, standing behind the prosecutor's desk, rubbing his hands together in an unsuccessful effort to contain his nervous energy. Behind him sat Ted Landis, chatting it up with Carl Hammerling. The two of them looked downright chummy. Stan Piper was standing in the back, talking to Bennett Kingsley. The ChemoCo CEO had flown in for the day, obviously wanting to see the contents of the safe for himself and not read about it in the news. Glynn noticed Marshall was content to discuss the day's proceeding with Gil, effectively ignoring everything else, even the opportunity to suck up to Bennett Kingsley. Sollie and Penna entered the courtroom together moments before McCleary.

"I checked in with Iris before entering the courthouse," Sollie whispered to Glynn. "She's slowly liquidating our holdings of ChemoCo stock. Once the safe is opened and the SCAB report becomes public, it's likely the stock will plummet."

"What about Onawhim?" Glynn asked.

"Onawhim is spending the morning with Ray and his team. She's helping them rehearse for the inevitable media firestorm that will descend after the SCAB report is released. She wanted to be by his side in case he needs her unique assistance," reported Penna with a knowing smile.

Judge Gorman entered and called the courtroom to order.

"Well, do you have the police report on the robbery at William McCleary's residence?" the judge asked.

"We do, Your Honor. The police report is ready," the prosecutor announced as he stood and walked it over to the bench. Everyone knew the report had no new information about the whereabouts of the key or the identity of the perpetrators. The whole courtroom procedure was merely a formality.

The judge took a minute to peruse the pages, not wanting to overlook anything, appear hasty, or open himself up for an appeal. He asked the police chief some pointed questions about their investigation techniques and the apparent decision to all but walk away from the case.

"It seems we can expect little or no chance of having the key retrieved in the near future. As such, I order the safe to be opened. We will reconvene at the LICE director's office in two hours." The sound of the gavel signaled the mad rush for the doors. Opening the safe was going to be the biggest news event of the day, and every red-blooded reporter wanted a front-row seat.

"A word, please," Stan asked, appearing at Arnie's side before the new LICE director could even exit his seat.

"We believe you will be given the contents of the safe," Stan stated, slowly getting around to his point. "We expect to be included when you review the report. There's a lot at stake here, I'm sure you already know that. Just keep in mind, Bennett does not take kindly to being blindsided, if you know what I mean."

Arnie stared back, not trusting himself to speak civilly. He was getting sick and tired of Stan Piper's requests, to say nothing of his elaborate social customs and long-winded speeches. "I hope it's a report we can all be proud of," Arnie replied, rising so quickly from his seat that he almost knocked Stan over.

Gil had already planned to spend the next couple of hours with his client, hoping to learn in advance what would be revealed to all in a couple of hours. But McCleary remained persistently closemouthed. Gil could only hope the contents would provide proof McCleary was a man acting in the best interests of the community. Whether they'd be able to find the people who drugged him was another matter. Gil had a theory, but cases weren't won on suppositions. You needed facts, and that was something in short supply.

Chapter 79

Handcuffed and shackled, McCleary was escorted out of the jail into the secure prisoner transport. Gil and Marshall followed behind—they would be allowed into the LICE director's office prior to the media. It was a quiet ride; neither had much to say. Gil was still puzzled by his client's refusal to reveal the contents of the safe. That was one of a number of confusing elements to this case. Things he couldn't put his finger on . . .

Conversely, McCleary's case was the last thing on Marshall's mind. He had been sick and tired of Arnie using him and his firm to advance someone else's agenda. At one time, supporting LIMBO and getting SCAB approved looked like the right thing for the economy and for his client, Crystal Clam Winery. But now, all that seemed in question. Today, he felt the only thing that mattered was to see and be seen. *Being part of this high-profile case is as good a fallback position as any,* Marshall thought.

The ride to the Professional Quadrangle took a quick 15 minutes. Gil and Marshall followed the police into Building One and up the elevator to McCleary's old office. The employees had been cleared out. The last thing the cops needed was someone reaching out to their old boss in an effort to help. They didn't want to take any chances and set about securing the building against potential threats inside and out.

It was a bit eerie walking through the empty cubicles during the middle of a workday. Papers were left on desks, and phones were ringing . . . the place felt like it was haunted by invisible workers. Police officers were posted in the lobby and outside the director's office, with six providing guard duty inside. They were joined by the police department's safe unit, a small but especially skilled group charged with opening the locked safe by any means necessary.

"Let's see where the safe is," Officer Hanrahan, the department's chief "safe cracker," requested.

McCleary shuffled over to the aerial photograph of Long Island and indicated where to touch at the two corners, which would allow the picture to slide up.

"Wish we had the key," Hanrahan said, "but you'll be able to supply the code, right?" he asked, looking at McCleary for affirmation. Hanrahan was hoping they could use one of the dummy blanks on the lock. If that didn't work, they'd have to do some drilling. A last resort would be the C4. Easy or hard, it didn't much matter to him.

"We might as well get comfortable," Hanrahan remarked. "Nothing's happening until the judge arrives."

McCleary looked around the room he occupied as Director of LICE for almost 30 years. While it was the same physical space, to him, the office seemed to have changed dramatically. It wasn't HIS anymore. It even smelled different. Arnie had rearranged some of the furniture and added his own photos and personal effects. Anyway, McCleary was glad to be out and done with LICE. *I should have left years ago.* Things had gone stale for him—the daily routine was old, boring, mundane. While he had visions of leaving the job, he never expected to be back as a crime suspect, sitting in his office dressed in a prison jumpsuit with his legs in irons, contemplating the irony of his situation.

Arnie Holtzmann was the first to be allowed in. It was his office, after all.

He set about moving chairs to accommodate those allowed to witness the safe opening.

McCleary glared at A Holtz, watching as the new director took charge. Arnie's cheery behavior stood out like a comedian at a funeral.

"Now's your chance to come clean and prevent us from blowing a hole in the wall," Arnie said, needling McCleary, unable to keep his thoughts to himself. But the prisoner stared back, offering no change of expression or insight to his feelings.

The ringing of Arnie's cell phone broke the awkward moment.

"Yeah. Okay, I'll be right down," and A Holtz turned to leave.

408

Chapter 80

People were mulling about outside the entrance of Building 1 in the Professional Quadrangle. The police had set up a checkpoint inside the lobby and would start checking IDs and inspecting pocketbooks and briefcases after the judge arrived. They even brought a handheld metal detector. It was sure to be a time-consuming process, as no one was exempt.

On the way to the Professional Quadrangle, Glynn, Penna, and Sollie had stopped for coffee. The plan was for them to arrive at Building One early. Glynn figured they had one opportunity, and timing would be everything. This was the last, and possibly trickiest, maneuver of all.

The press had gathered early, forming what would soon be a line of spectators seeking entrance. Other interested parties were arriving and clustered in small groups. Glynn, Sollie, and Penna stood off to the side, they were not planning on going in. Their visit last night had been more than enough.

"Here they come now," Glynn whispered, watching Ted, Stan, Carl, and Bennett exit the limo.

"Hi, Ted," Glynn said, intercepting the foursome. "How are things at Crystal Clam?" It was a sure way to get the vintner to pause for a chat.

"Nice to see you, Glynn," Ted said after shaking her hand. "Where's Marshall? Does he plan on coming?"

"Oh, I'm sure he'll be here shortly," Glynn didn't want to say anything about Marshall working with Gil. Her husband was persona non grata now that he was representing The Enemy.

Meanwhile, Sollie walked over to greet her customer. "We're ready to schedule the closing. Let me know what day works for you," Sollie said, smiling at Carl, who mumbled that he'd give her a call later in the day.

"Hi, I'm Sollie Gold. Carl's real-estate agent," she said, extending her hand first to Bennett, then to Stan, and last to Ted. "This is Penna," Sollie announced, making a brief introduction to bring Penna into the group.

Sollie stepped back to allow Penna a chance to converse with each of the men in turn. They were captivated by her charm, none more than Stan, who loved being in the presence of women with refined social graces. Even Carl and Bennett seemed enchanted, concentrating on her while momentarily forgetting their agenda.

Glynn and Sollie directed their attention to Ted and moved to subtly isolate him from the group. Glynn continued to ask about Crystal Clam's winemaking as Sollie stepped in closer. Then, time stood still for a brief second. A quick nod from Sollie indicated success, and their final task was done.

"Well, it was nice meeting you," Penna said as she disengaged from the men. "I see the police are allowing people into the building now."

Sollie gathered with her friends off to the side as they watched the four men walk toward the entrance.

"Did you do it?" Glynn asked, not quite sure.

"Well, you were standing right there looking at us," Sollie replied, chiding her. "Yes, it's done. He never knew what happened."

The three women melted away, their plan complete.

Chapter 81

Two by two, Bennett and Stan, followed by Carl and Ted, walked to the queue forming in front of the lobby doors.

"I'm at the front door now," Stan announced into his cell phone, alerting Arnie of their arrival.

"We're on the list," Stan proclaimed as he walked right to the front of the line, causing plenty of annoyed looks and grumblings.

"All right," the officer said, gesturing them to move to a place off to the side. "What are the names?"

Stan gave their names, which were quickly found and checked off.

"Please step over here for the metal scan. If you have anything in your pockets, take it out now." The second officer gestured to a plastic box on a table. One by one, Stan, Bennett, Carl, and Ted fished out their keys, wallets, and cell phones from their jackets and pants pockets. The officer wielding the metal detector did a thorough job of scanning each person. It beeped on Carl's chest as he forgot to remove his pen. First, Bennett, then Stan and Carl were waved through the security checkpoint.

"Stan, Bennett over here," called Arnie, arriving in the lobby in time to escort the four men up to his office.

"Hold on," the officer said as he was finishing with Ted. The detector beeped and flashed a red light when he moved it over Ted's right jacket pocket. "Please empty your pocket," the officer asked.

"Is that necessary?" Arnie asked, interjecting himself into the policeman's business. "These men are with me. They're my guests, and I'm authorizing the okay." Giving orders and expecting them to be followed came naturally to Arnie.

"Yes, thank you. Please step back. We have a job to do and you're holding things up," came the policeman's reply, giving Arnie a hard, no-nonsense look.

Ted glanced at Uncle Stan and then at Arnie. Both were standing impotently off the side.

"Your detector must be malfunctioning. I don't remember putting anything in this pocket," Ted announced as he slowly fished around inside.

"What do we have here?" the officer asked, retrieving an odd-shaped key dangling from Ted's outstretched hand, holding it up to the light, examining it like a precious artifact.

"I don't know where that came from," Ted blurted out, clearly surprised to see the key in the officer's hand.

Stan's face went white. Arnie, who had been chatting with Bennett, turned to see what Ted was referring to.

"It looks like a key," the officer stated, turning it over in his hand. Nothing threatening. He was getting ready to give it back.

"Hey, let me see that," demanded Arnie, stepping into the officer's scanning area.

"Sir, please stand back," the officer instructed in his most authoritarian voice, alerted by the way Arnie was acting.

Ted stood like a statue, pale and lifeless. Even breathing was difficult. "Hey, give that back," he croaked with his arm extended.

Arnie grabbed at the key. "This looks like it could open the safe in my office," he announced. He had stared at the safe long enough to visualize what the key might look like in case he'd run across it.

Stan's insides turned to jelly. He was visibly shocked. "This is where you lost the key?" he hissed to his idiot nephew.

"I need to take this upstairs right away. The judge will want to see this," Arnie proclaimed with the key tightly clenched in his fist as he pivoted toward the elevators.

"Freeze!" the officer yelled, one hand on his gun and the other on the club he smoothly released from his belt.

A hushed silence descended on the lobby as everyone paused.

"I'm sorry, sir, but you'll have to give me that key now," the officer commanded.

"It's the key for my safe," A Holtz countered, raising his voice as if talking to a wayward child.

"Wait a minute, Officer. This is simply a key, not a gun or knife. I'm sure you don't think it represents a threat, do you? Why not give it back to Ted here?" Stan suggested, struggling to find a way to shut Arnie up.

"Really, Stan, if it's the key to my safe, then shouldn't I have it?" Arnie countered matter-of-factly.

"Yes, of course . . . if it even IS that key. Who can say? Officer, please hand it over and we'll be on our way," Stan suggested, trying with all his might to appear calm and civilized next to A Holtz's ranting.

"I'm sure the judge would like to see this key for himself," the officer stated, calling upstairs.

"Release him, I insist," Arnie demanded. "We need to go to the office now before the judge arrives." Arnie continued walking toward Ted as if turbocharged for confrontation.

"We're all going upstairs," the officer declared as he hung up the phone. "Let's go," he said, staring at Arnie while pointing to Bennett, Carl, and Stan as he grabbed Ted by the arm to lead him to the elevator.

Holding Arnie back a couple of steps, Stan wanted a private word.

"Look, Arnie, I'm not sure how Ted came upon that key. You saw how surprised he was to find it in his pocket. Someone must have put it there. Framed him. Who knows?" Stan offered, trying to sound reasonable as his calm veneer was quickly rubbing away.

"By the way, how did he happen to get that key?" Arnie asked, staring with a new set of eyes at Stan.

"Not now," hissed Stan, unable to believe what an asshole he was.

Arnie, Stan, Bennett, and Carl filed into the elevator behind a pale and shaking Ted. Stan didn't look too well himself, as his elaborate plot was unraveling. Glancing over at Bennett, Stan could tell by the shake of his head that Bennett was getting ready to cut ties.

"The ChemoCo board is going to want a full report," Bennett said as he looked over at a freaked-out Ted. His raised eyebrow spoke volumes.

Chapter 82

Bang went the gavel on McCleary's former desk as Judge Gorman called the crowded room to order. Conversations abruptly stopped as everyone waited for the judge's orders.

"Let me see that key," Judge Gorman requested. The officer walked over and placed it on the desk. "Will this key open the safe?"

"Yes, Your Honor," Hanrahan, the police safe expert, replied.

"Where did the key come from? The police testified it was stolen and unrecovered." The judge gave the lead investigator a cold look, clearly not happy.

"The key was recovered from the pocket of this man," the police officer explained, pointing to Ted Landis. "He was entering the building and it set off the metal detector. He claims no knowledge of the key or how it came to be in his possession."

"According to your report, the people who broke into Mr. McCleary's house stole the key. It's been alleged by the defendant that it was those people who were responsible for drugging him. Step forward," the judge ordered Ted. "Officer, have you read this man his rights?"

"Excuse me, Your Honor," interrupted Stan, using his relationship with the judge. "Ted is my nephew. Would it be all right if his attorney spoke on his behalf?"

"Who here is this man's counsel?" The judge asked.

"Marshall Matlock," Ted announced.

"Mr. Matlock, please step forward," requested the judge.

"I'm assisting Mr. Patrick in Bill McCleary's defense," explained Marshall, gesturing toward Gil.

"Is that correct, Mr. Patrick?" the judge inquired, clearly losing patience. "What shall we do?" asked the judge sarcastically.

"Technically, I am the sole counsel for Mr. McCleary," responded Gil. "Mr. Matlock, as head of our firm, has been providing assistance."

"Well, this is an interesting state of affairs," the judge remarked. "I don't believe I've come across a case where both defendants connected to the same criminal case are represented by the same people at one law firm. Step forward, Mr. Matlock," the judge ordered. "Are you prepared to represent your client in this matter?"

Blindsided by this new state of affairs, Marshall left McCleary's side and walked over to Ted Landis, now standing between two police officers.

"Yes, Your Honor. I am his attorney and I request a chance to meet with him alone."

"Yes, fine. After we use that key to open the safe," Judge Gorman decided, handing the key to Hanrahan. "Let's proceed."

"We need the code," Hanrahan said as he looked over at McCleary.

Bill McCleary had a queer look in his eye—part fear, part defiance. Gil stood off to the side, waiting for his client to respond.

"I'm not sure you will be happy with what you find," McCleary replied.

"I'll be the judge of that. The code now, if you please," the judge commanded.

"4, 4, 2, 8, 6, 3, 5, 7,"

The room fell silent as Hanrahan inserted the key and plugged in the eight numbers.

"The contents of the safe belong to me," McCleary announced as the door swung open. He turned to Gil to make sure there was no misunderstanding. "Get me those papers," he breathed to Gil.

"Your Honor, we remind the court that all papers found inside the safe belong to my client. They should be turned over to him immediately," Gil announced, wondering, like everyone else, what was inside.

"Hand the contents to me," demanded the judge.

"Here you go, You Honor," Hanrahan replied, handing the envelope over to Judge Gorman. "Is this it? Is this the only thing inside?" the judge asked, wanting to make sure the record reflected one envelope.

Gil watched his client's face register disbelief as the envelope was given to the judge.

"That's not possible," McCleary pronounced. "I was the last person who opened that safe. Only I knew the code and had the key until it was stolen. No one could have opened the safe until now. It's not possible," he repeated, shocked that all his papers and notes were missing.

"Obviously, you're mistaken, Mr. McCleary. Maybe those drugs you claim to have ingested have confused things, or you simply do not want to remember. Regardless, determining those facts will be left for another time." Judge Gorman picked up the envelope. "It says *SCAB Evaluation: An Environmental Analysis, June 28, LIQuID, Lab 8*." He read out loud.

The room erupted as every newsperson reached for their cell phone and called their assignment editors.

McCleary turned to Gil. "The safe was filled with all sorts of papers. I'm telling you, someone must have emptied it."

"What do you mean?" Gil asked, not able to follow. "How could anyone other than you get in?"

"It's a plant," McCleary replied. "Someone took out all my papers and left that envelope—I never saw it before."

Dumbfounded, Gil looked at his client as if seeing him for the first time.

"We will have copies made for counsel," Judge Gorman announced. "We are adjourned until 10 a.m. Monday morning." At the bang of the gavel, every news reporter cleared the room, rushing to track down Lab 8 and file their story.

Ted was read his rights, handcuffed, and led away with Marshall Matlock in tow. The police finally had their first suspect in the McCleary case. Stan Piper followed discreetly behind, wondering what he'd need to do to contain the situation. The fact that he may be implicated in the theft and ransacking of McCleary's residence, or even included in the whole setup, didn't even occur to Stan. Those were things that happened to other people.

Bennett and Carl remained motionless in the corner. "Tough about Ted," Arnie remarked as he joined them. "He's going to have one hell of a time trying to explain how he came to be in possession of that key. And as for the report—there's nothing I should worry about, is there?" Arnie asked, realizing his new job as head of LICE might be compromised. "Perhaps it would have been nice to know weeks ago before I leaked that bogus SCAB report to the press stamped with LICE's approval.

"No matter," A Holtz continued, mentally stepping into his old LIMBO role. "ChemoCo has a bright future on Long Island regardless of what that report says. We'll figure this out. By the way, I've come across a piece of property that would be perfect for your new ChemoCo complex. Yes, I see a bright future for you here," Arnie concluded.

Three Months Later

Tonight's the night, Glynn repeated to herself. Finally, she could see the light at the end of the tunnel. It had been a while since they got together after work. Between defending Bill McCleary, Ted Landis' court case, ChemoCo postponing the release of SCAB throwing the GRowLers into a panic, LIMBO and LICE tossed into confusion, plus her LIQuID research meetings, Glynn was ready for things to return to normal, whatever that would be.

She thought back to before becoming a guinea pig. It felt like a lifetime ago. Being the smartest person in the room still took some getting used to. But after eating a large portion of humble pie, at least now she didn't take herself too seriously.

Her book club friends—aka LIQuID 5—were adjusting to their changes, too. Penna ended up spooking most of her uncle's associates. Pauly was apprehended and awaiting trial for his part in what's become known as the *LIMBO at Sunset* fiasco. Onawhim started dating Ray. They were taking it slow. Sollie had become a one-woman real-estate powerhouse, racking up sales. Iris signed a couple of clients to her new Investor Relations business in addition to managing their LIQuID 5 portfolio.

Glynn's LIQuID friends had decided to keep their changes to themselves. They had no desire to reveal their new abilities to family or friends. But Glynn didn't feel that way. She needed to tell Gil. Thankfully, they understood and didn't stand in her way. She assured them their secret would be safe. But that wasn't what was troubling her. *What if he doesn't like the new me?* She thought, exhaling a sigh.

Gil strolled into the Wine on Vine, looking more relaxed than he had in a while. He bent to give his wife a kiss and took the seat across from her. Glynn steeled herself. She had been looking forward to this moment yet dreading it at the same time. *No going back now.*

"I talked with McCleary today," Gil announced after giving his order to the waitress. "He's relocating out West and leaving next week. As a free man, he can go where he pleases now. Not exactly what everyone thought would happen, if you recall. The whole world had him convicted and locked up. It just goes to show you can't always believe everything you see," Gil related with a well-deserved sense of satisfaction.

Glynn nodded in agreement. She was glad he'd untangled that convoluted mess and was able to clear McCleary's name and legacy.

"I'm still puzzled by a couple of things," he continued. "McCleary insists the safe was full of reports, with some documents going back almost 30 years. And we're both dumbfounded as to how LIQuID's Lab 8 could have gotten the SCAB formula to analyze and then have their report miraculously appear in the safe."

"If you remember, McCleary thought you gave the safe's code to Marshall, who relayed it to Arnie, then passed it on to Stan Piper, who shared it with Ted Landis," Glynn added. "After all, Ted had the key. It's only logical he'd be the one who opened the safe and took those documents." She knew this was what everyone thought—everyone except the LIQuID 5 team!

"Yes, but how did Ted Landis get hold of Lab 8's report? We're certain Ted didn't know any of the Lab 8 researchers. And what happened to all those missing documents?" Gil asked.

"I thought Arnie was going to have a stroke when they uncovered the real effects of SCAB," Glynn mentioned, redirecting the conversation.

"He was looking forward to being head of LICE, itching to get in there, so to speak," Gil said with a smile. "The big reveal of the SCAB report certainly squashed things for A Holtz. At least he had LIMBO to fall back on.

"These last months have been toughest on Marshall. He lost his bid to keep Ted Landis out of jail and had to call in favors to save Stan Piper's ass. Then there was the constant handholding to mollify the GRowLers, who were quite pissed after being denied access to SCAB."

"What I find amazing is that Ted Landis turned out to be the perp. I would never have figured he'd be the guy who drugged McCleary and stole the key," Glynn said.

"What's really amazing was Marshall keeping Stan Piper out of jail. What is the chance Stan didn't know what Ted was up to? I hope I live long enough to learn the answer to these mysteries! The takeaway lesson is that people are not always who you think they are. Certainly not based on your initial impression," Gil admitted.

Glynn cringed at the thought. *It's now or never!*

"I have a confession to make," she began, staring deep into his eyes. "Remember the report Marshall leaked, the one I wrote about SCAB? I was able to come to those conclusions because I taught myself chemistry in two days. Pretty astonishing, huh? Of course, being an inexperienced chemist, I didn't realize the formula was incomplete. A rookie mistake," Glynn admitted sheepishly.

"It turns out I can do a lot of remarkable things. Not only is my memory photographic, but I can also recall things I don't consciously know. All sorts of facts and information simply appear. And I can draw inferences, make connections, and cite little-known references. It's like I'm a walking computer.

"I've been changed," Glynn concluded, watching Gil's expression grow more puzzled as she spoke. "There's no easy way to say this—I've been affected by powerful mind-altering chemicals which have enhanced my brain function beyond what it was . . . Way beyond what is normal." This was the moment of truth. Will she be another casualty of Gil's failed first impressions?

"Have you been doing drugs?" Gil asked, not quite believing what he was hearing.

"Not in the way you think. About four months ago when leaving a restaurant near the LIQuID facility after my book club meeting, I breathed in chemicals from an experiment gone wrong. Lab 8 was conducting experiments on brain function and memory. One of their processes got out of control and the failed result was vented outside. I was near the LIQuID building at just the right—or wrong—time and inadvertently breathed in those compounds."

"Are those the same guys in Lab 8 who wrote the SCAB report?" asked Gil, whose mildly interested expression changed to one of increasing curiosity.

"Yes, the same. I've come to know Ray, the lead researcher. He helped uncover the true nature of SCAB. He's been monitoring my condition this whole time."

"Are you all right? Are there any side effects? Did this affect the other book club members, too? Why haven't you said anything earlier?"

His care and concern were touching. It broke Glynn's heart to see him so worried. "I'm fine, really. There's nothing wrong with me or the others. I was handed an amazing gift—one I've been learning to live with."

"You should have said something," he said quietly.

Glynn shuddered. He was right. She should have.

"The effects came on gradually. By the time I realized what happened, we were in the thick of the *LIMBO at Sunset* fiasco. It never seemed like the right time. I hope this doesn't change the way you think of me," Glynn said with a touch of worry in her voice.

Gil grabbed both her hands and leaned across the table to plant a kiss. "You think some chemical changes would alter how I feel? So, were you the one who gave the SCAB formula to Lab 8 to test?" Glynn nodded. She could see the wheels turning. "Then how did they get their report into the safe?"

Glynn smiled and let go of the breath she was holding. There was love in his eyes, and she knew his feelings hadn't changed.

"Is there anything else you want to reveal?" he asked, amazed Glynn might be able to supply some of the missing information he sought.

"Well, yes," she replied, watching his anticipation. "I'm pregnant!"

426

Liquid 5 Glossary

ChemoCo: Large chemical manufacturing company traded on the NY Stock Exchange (CHEM); Bennett Kingsley, CEO; Carl Hammerling, Head Researcher

GCGC: Gold Coast Golf Club; Stan Piper, founding member

GRowLers: The Wine Growers League; East End Wine Growers Association

Ted Landis: President of Wine Growers League and owner of Crystal Clam Winery

LIAR: Long Island Agricultural Resources; local agricultural organization

LICE: Long Island Conservation and Environment; Bill McCleary, Director

LIMBO: Long Island Metro Business Organization; Arnie Holtzmann (A Holtz), Executive Director.

LIQuID: Long Island Quality Intellectual Development; home to Ray and his team at Lab 8.

LISP: Long Island Superior Property; real-estate office of Sollie Gold

SCAB: Selective Chemical Agricultural Bioproducts; ChemoCo's new fertilizer/weed suppressant.

SHYLOCK: Shuster, Yleskin, and Matlock; law firm where Glynn and Gil Patrick work; Marshall Matlock, Senior Partner; Rose Mantle, Office Manager and Administrative Assistant to Marshall Matlock.